THE
TRUE ADVENTURES
OF A CABIN-BOY

by

MJ Gutteridge

Grosvenor House
Publishing Limited

This book is published by
Grosvenor House Publishing Ltd
28-30 High Street, Guildford, Surrey, GU1 3HY.
www.grosvenorhousepublishing.co.uk

A CIP record for this book
is available from the British Library

ISBN 978-1-908105-61-5

"Since every man whose soul is not a clod
Hath visions, and would speak, if he had lov'd
And been well nurtured in his mother tongue."

Keats.

To Aya

CHAPTER ONE

I am suddenly awake, my heart pounding, sweat running down my face, staring into the pitch-black darkness; not the passive, familiar darkness of my bedroom but a forceful, active darkness that shoves my head brutally into the wall behind me and then with equal ruthlessness drags me back down; slowly deliberately, maliciously racking my desperately tired body; a darkness that vibrates, hammers and shudders whose breath is warm .. rancid. . .acrid . foul..

Where was I? How? Why? Why? I jerk up upright my head scraping the ceiling and fall back onto the thin, unyielding mattress, my mind groping feebly through a chaos of images..

Lit by the weird orange glow of the street-lights I am walking down the path to a front door; but who is beside me? So close and yet so utterly distant? Yes .. yes.. of course.. I am escorting her home after the Class of '62 Graduation Dance in the school gym; a solid, plumpish girl her babyish face a bright pink, my absurdly expensive gardenia corsage bobbing up and down on the rigid bodice of the shiny yellow dress as we danced ..now is the moment, blindly I offer my lips into the shadows of the porch. . .. the screen-door crashing shut in my face..

Lying stiffly in the sour, oil-tainted darkness my body flames hot; shame. . humiliation. . anger. Yes, anger that clenches my fist. And so that was why, was it? No.. no.. the idea just came of itself out of thin air; my destiny, no less revealing itself..

But it hadn't been so simple... had it?

Out of the heaving, sour-smelling darkness my mother's face appears: pale blue eyes, and greying hair her face, gently lined with her forty two anxious years.

'Probably its for the best Pip, in years to come, you'll be glad it didn't work out. A good education is so important

1

these days.. Remember you're only seventeen..' Her voice rings again in my memory, plangent with relief...

And then my father, his calm face, broad forehead, eyes tired, in a rumpled suit, tie askew, just home, from a day in the office, handing me the business pages of the *Vancouver Post* for yet another pointless perusal of the Shipping List. How those brief, plain words inflamed my imagination; the ship's names, at times so fanciful and evocative ..*M/V Seasprite* or *M/S Ocean Commander* and even the mundane lists of cargoes: lumber.. hides .. machinery ..iron-ore.. wheat.. took on an almost poetic ring to my ears while the ports of origin: Yokohama.. Sydney.. Lagos.. .. Manila.. ..were so many siren calls.. vibrant echoes of other lands across the seas.. calling me out of the uneventful existence of a suburban home life.. speaking to me of adventure and excitement ... daring me.. .

I hear again my father's voice; kindly, world-weary. 'Sometimes Phil know, you have to accept the inevitable. Necessity is a hard master but when you come down to it the key to a successful life is application..'

And remember my silent, defiant, no.. no ..never would I give up...

And yet what had been the result of my defiant resolve? Futile trips to the towering office blocks, where after carefully studying the brass plates in the lobby, I allowed myself to be lifted to top floors to tip-toe down thickly carpeted corridors to enter with fast-beating heart one of the row of frosted glass doors.. only to be summarily dismissed by a bored receptionist. Or even worse be told to wait.. wait .. my life slipping away. second by second.. mindlessly skimming through old shipping magazines until my eyes ached and then only finally to be sent away by some smartly-suited executive irritated at being summoned for the purpose. Or even more hopeless, following an address from the telephone directory to find myself in shabby offices down dingy side-streets only to be repulsed by disbelieving, impatient head shakings of bored officials.

And yet still undaunted, I had begun to make solitary bus journeys from the family home down to the harbour where I would stride with pretended nonchalance down the long, tarred wooden piers sticking out into the dark green waters of the Burrard Inlet, opposite the steep slopes of the North Shore Mountains, the crests, even though it was already June, streaked white. Now it was, that the newspaper Shipping List became palpable: *M/V Orion* revealing itself as a rusty old freighter.

After ten minutes contemplating the inscription *PIRAIVS* on its stern I had gathered up enough courage to mount the gangway, to be met by a pot-bellied old man with big moustaches, smelling strongly of garlic, in a dishevelled, dirty white uniform who had contemptuously waved me away. 'You only leetle boy..only babby…Go away pleese…No use on ship.'

So I had turned away in bitter chagrin. But wasn't it true? I accused myself, as I had wandered despondently off down the dock. What did I know about ships or seamanship? When it came to it, what did I know about anything? English. Maths. History. A smattering of French. Physics and Chemistry… Book knowledge.. school-learning… .. nothing to do with the real world…

Yet still I had persisted, perhaps if only to prove to myself how impossible it all was and next time much to my surprise I had unchallenged crossed over the gangway of the ship, registered *Bremen* and before I knew it found myself below decks; turning this way and that down narrow, bright lit passageways, to be suddenly confronted by a tall, smiling, smartly-dressed officer with crisp blond hair, his clipped precise English even now ringing in my ears: 'My dear young man, a very stupid idea, sheer romantic nonsense believe me.'

Surely now I would give it all up? I had thought, standing shame-faced, under one of the giant spider-like cranes that bestrode the jetty, staring moodily down at the flotsam jostling in the oily scum of the green harbour waters, bright in the sunlight; a tarry smell rising from the pier timbers. Admit it.. he is right, just a stupid, romantic day-dream, so I had taunted myself, before beginning another bitter retreat home.

Only stopping further down the pier to watch two seamen sitting side by side, on a couple of planks, suspended by ropes down the ship's sides. I listened as they stabbed at the hull with brushes tied to short poles, dipping their brushes into little metal buckets suspended on long cords.

'A 'ard life us seamen, eh matey 'ardly a day off even in port. Who'd go to sea I asks yer. We must be f---- n' nuts.' The younger with a thin sallow face one had sniggered in a whining English accent, waving his stubby paint brush carelessly about, so long dribbles of dark red paint had plopped into the oily green harbour waters below.

'Yer speak the Bible truth me old cock, n' the 1st Mates..a f----' sadist..n' no mistake.; His grizzled companion had commented gloomily, continuing to jab sporadically at the orange blotches on the hull.

I had walked away, the mocking, sardonic exchanges of the two sailors ringing in my mind; wasn't that what I was seeking after all? Life raw ..without pretence .. unvarnished .. crude .. yet above all vital.. real....

And all around me were the long piers, reaching out into the dark green waters, lined with the ships, their square tops and funnels reaching up into the blue sky. Surely, surely, out of so many, there was one that would have me?

Or was it my fate to always fail in what I most wanted from life?

And so I had given up going to the docks and Shipping Offices; keeping instead to my bedroom or taking solitary walks along the winding paths through the dense second-cut woodlands near the family home; the summer more or less dribbling away; the start of the university term, an ominous cloud on the horizon of my mind...

Hopeless, completely hopeless I had concluded grinding my teeth in frustration and self-contempt and yet even then beneath the despair lay a calm.. a conviction ... how strange.. baffling that was .. as if my all my striving and anguish was of no account .. and all I had to do was wait .. just wait and all that I frantically sought would come to me of itself...

Or was that just the self-indulgent conceit of a diseased mind?

But what more could I do? And so I had waited either shut up in my bedroom or in the back-garden lying on the grass in sun, desultorily reading.. usually poetry from my High School Anthology.. the Anglo Saxon Seafarer.. Blake Keats.. Shelley .. Wordsworth.. Pound and Eliot . And daydreaming... endlessly daydreaming; single-handedly I fight my way up to the upper decks..; dive fearlessly into the shark-infested seas.. out-face a mutinous rabble; steer through violent storms, survive bullets, knife thrusts.... and always at the end, to take the soft hand, pulling me irresistibly towards her smiling, full lips, bright laughing eyes....

How the hard sun-browned lawn had throbbed beneath my prone body, the musty scent of the dry grass filling my nostrils; a vast longing swelling irresistibly through me...

From far, far away I heard the telephone ringing only barely audible and yet somehow of immense significance in the silence of the hot afternoon, cutting through the incessant drone of a lawnmower two gardens away; rinnnngggg rinnnnggg... rinnnnggg.. rinnnnnggg; on and on.. insistent.. unrelenting... ..inexorable.. ceasing with dramatic abruptness.

'Its for you, Pip. The Harbour Master's Office...' So my mother had called out from the back door; a slight catch in her voice.

Blinded and dazed from the sun, I had pressed the telephone receiver against my ear; the strange voice coming to me distinctly and yet as if from some other world.

'Um.....well yes, this is er Phillip er ..Wight....'' I had stammered stupidly seemingly not quite sure who I was. 'Yes..sure.. Tomorrow.. 10am... '

Thus it was that I had found myself in large, gloomy room in a square old-fashioned brick building with classical pretensions not that far from the harbour, staring around at the dark paneled walls, wondering how it was I had got myself to this position, fascinated by the fly buzzing feebly in one of the tall windows, the bottom half painted a dark green; suddenly struck by the irony that it had been mother who had suggested I leave my name with the Harbour Master. Yes so ironic... Or was it? Finally I had been beckoned forward by the scrawny old clerk with a green visor and metallic arm-bands who lifting a flap in the gleaming mahogany counter allowed me to duck past; my heart beating dully..

The Harbour Master a bluff hearty figure with a full beard and moustache wearing a navy blue uniform with gold braid on his cuffs had waved at the man at the side of the large desk.

"Captain Purser, *M/V Grimethorpe* needs a Cabin Boy..hrrrumph .."

I had nodded absently; the deep voice echoing fuzzily in my ears, my eyes fixed on the prints of sailing ships on the wall; was this really *me* . .. sitting passively.. .being assessed .. judged.. as a *seaman* ?

Out of the corner of my eye I saw Captain Purser balding, smooth-shaven with a pointed chin, skin greyish, more like a bank manager than a ship's captain staring at me suspiciously

'British eh.' He had finally commented peevishly, flicking at my passport. So what er.. you doing here er.. in Vancouver?'

'My family...emigrated here from England...Five years ago.' I had muttered as if confessing to some heinous conspiracy.

Lines had formed on Captain Purser's forehead and he had given a doubtful sideways look at the Harbour Master.

'You do know what you're doing, what?' The square-shouldered Harbour Master had demanded gruffly. 'Pretty rough some of these ship's crews, eh Captain? Going to sea's no picnic, son...'

I had flushed, gulping down my sudden fears. 'Yes ..sir.' I had replied with impulsive boldness, my voice echoing loudly around the dark wood- panelled office. 'My grandfather was in the Royal Navy... '

There was a deep silence and I became aware of the fateful ticking of the old-fashioned wall-clock.

'Er.. right then...' Captain Purser had snapped testily. 'You'll need er.. a Medical. Come back here and sign ..er.. Ship's Articles. Er Board of Trade.. British Merchant Marine.. er. We sail 1600 hours tomorrow. Don't be late. My ship sails.. with or without er you..'

But I had hardly heard him. 'I'm going to sea...Going to sea.. Going to sea' had trumpeted exultantly in my head .. everything else becoming vague.. obscure.. meaningless..

Out of the acrid, throbbing blackness my memory throws up the starkly modern office glass and concrete building on West Broadway far from the harbour and there I am standing on the wide steps looking blankly down between the tall office blocks thoroughfare down which he four lanes of traffic passes endlessly.. But of course .. the Medical.. and how smoothly, effortlessly the lift takes me to 3rd floor and just beside the lift is a frosted glass with No. 303 on it. Inside the large modern room smelling of antiseptic I find myself studying the triangular name-plate on the large desk; the gold lettering reads: *DR. D. Sticherly* 'D for what ..? David or Donald or even Daniel perhaps? I wonder ; looking for a clue at the thin, lined face glancing occasionally at me through thick lens of his tortoiseshell spectacles; the red tie just visible between the suit lapels and white coat has a small crest on it, I notice.

'Phillip Wight is it ? 'Dr Sticherly asks glancing down at the form before him.

I nod; yes it's me .. having a medical ..going to sea.. How impossible that seems...

'Now.. Family History: TB, Mental Illness? Diabetes? Alcoholism? ...' The voice is slightly bored; utterly professional ..indifferent to my fate...

I methodically shake my head the small hand jerking precisely down the long form spread out on the desk then letting my eyes roam about the room, surveying the different cabinets the shelves crowded with array of jars, boxes and little bottles; what did this have to do with me.. and my adventuring to lands far across the ocean?

'Childhood Illnesses: Measles ? Mumps.? Whooping Cough?'

Hesitantly I nod in turn.

'Shirt up'

Childishly I flinch at the stethoscope's icy touch on my bared chest; his hands though are pleasurably warm as he gently yet firmly presses and taps on my back.

'Cough .. Again ..'

From the top pocket of his white coat he produces a tiny torch.

'Mouth open..'

His fingers are soft as he turns my head and peers into each ear by turn; surely this isn't necessary I think, suppressing my irritation; it's obvious I'm healthy. .. .

Conjuror-like he flourishes a white card with a circle, divided into red and green segments, pointing at each in turn with the silver pen.

'Red.. green...red...' I respond frowning impatiently.

'Testing for colour blindness; very important at sea.' Dr. Sticherly comments mildly.

'I see…Yes of course..' I murmur abashed; yes, everything has a meaning.. a purpose.. if you know enough.. I tell myself.

'You'll feel pretty unwell by tomorrow.. .. faint.. dizzy...nauseous.. that sort of thing…. 'The muffled voice is casually ruthless, the white coat turned towards the small fridge.

I watch suddenly fearful as the slim fingers, one with a gold ring, puts a large shiny syringe and packs of disposable needles on a metal tray with some vials.

'All the common tropical diseases; Cholera.. Yellow Fever.. etc etc ..

I had nodded not daring to look, as one after another, the needles with a pricking sensation entering my bared upper arm.. A traditional ritual I muse ..the tribal shaman, endowing the novice voyager with strength and courage.

'Stand up..'

I stare fixedly at the large syringe.. held upright.. poised ..before me, the long needle oozing drops of liquid.. I swallow and try not to wince as it pierces my right buttock deeper.. deeper ; a test of your bravery, like the Blackfoot Braves Sun-Dance, I rationalize ;the alcohol swab stings slightly and a relief sweeps me; not such a coward then..

'Underpants..' Dr Sticherly insists quite as if I was a scientific specimen under examination, I think becoming embarrassed.

I stand stiffly feeling absurdly helpless; trousers and underpants draped around my ankles; staring blankly at the far wall; just pretend this isn't happening to you, I tell myself the gentle touch on my scrotum, a casual push at my penis, producing a strange burning sensation that runs down my legs...

Seated in front of the desk again I frown fiercely, absently watching the silver pen flicking it's way down the form; my face hot.

'Examining for S.T.D.... Sexually transmitted disease' Dr. Sticherly observes. 'What the sailors sometimes call "The Clap". Very serious unless treated promptly. You understand..?

I study the eye-chart on the far wall; my entire body flushing with humiliation and shame.

'After sexual intercourse of course.. ..' Dr Sticherly adds.

I nod curtly, a cold sweat leaking from my armpits; was it so obvious that I had never been with a woman?

'I suppose your parents know all about you going to sea? The question comes from nowhere.. hangs before me.. gently threatening..

From the corner of my eye I can see the face crinkling softly, the glasses dragged aside.

'Yes.. ..' I reply defiantly, resolutely keeping my eyes down.

'Right.. just thought I'd ask' comes the resigned response and eyes follow his glance to the large glossy calendar on the wall; July has a panoramic view of a mountain range ;

the silver pen dashes off a signature on the bottom of the form; the arcane ritual now complete..

Clutching the manila envelope to my chest I retrace my steps, in the empty lift the final remark echoes solemnly in my head: 'You've been passed fit for normal duties at sea..' But why that curious look as he handed me the sealed envelope..? I pass through the marble and glass foyer, and pause at the top of the wide steps; the traffic moving in both directions in endless procession ; just below me the throngs of pedestrians, pass and re-pass in the late afternoon brightness. Who would have thought the world held so many? Like bloodless ghosts.. I scorn .. dead forms.. moving blindly along.. without real life or purpose .. But wasn't I one with them?

No!.. No!' comes the exulting inward cry; with a leap I clear the steps, brandishing the buff envelope, the close-packed bodies shrinking away at my wild onward rush..

Was it true? Was I really going to sea? Or was it all just an absurdly complicated dream? I am back in my bedroom, the familiar dim shapes all around me; a pale orange glow from the street-lights showing around the curtains; from the main road a few blocks away a car hums itself into oblivion; the bed-side alarm clock ticks on.

A shaft of light breaks the darkness, through half-closed eyes, a shadowy form silently standing over me.

'You don't have to go, you know, Pip dear...Its not too late...There's nothing wrong with changing your mind. It's a sign of maturity..' mother's voice is soft, gentle yet there's a latent sharpness too.

I wait in stubborn silence listening intently for the departing rustle of her dress but once again the gentle voice fills the faintly ticking silence of the bedroom.

'You see, you don't really understand what you're doing...After all what's wrong with University? Really you should be grateful of the opportunity... So many are denied the chance to better themselves..'

I press my lips tightly together; how to explain? Into my

mind comes the memory of the ranked seats of the classroom; the teacher's voice droning on as I stare through the window touched by the horror of my life passing ..to no purpose..

'But what about grandfather he ran away from home when he was 15, to become a stoker on Royal Navy battleship?' I offer a feeble tribute to the insistently demanding silence.

'But that's completely different...He had no choice, you do.. Oh, really Phillip dear.....'

I glimpse the pale oval of her face, her hands pressed to her breast.

'There's so much you don't know.... 'There's a pause that stretches painfully on. on.. to be finally broken again.

'Women.. and.. well that sort of.. thing... You have no idea.. You're still a boy..' The words echo faintly around the room and then all is silent again.

A faint touch grazes my forehead, brushing ever so lightly through my hair.

"Please.. Phillip.. for my sake.." The passionate whisper roars in my ears.

But my lips are sealed, my whole being stiffly resistant cased in an impenetrable armour, forged in long, lonely vigils; proof against all womanly pleadings.

From out in the landing comes my father's sleepy voice. 'Come on dear...its no use. He's made up his mind.'

The light vanishes; the faint sobbing fades away into the deep silence of the night across my sleep-dazed mind floats softly yielding images giving rise to urgent sensations.. shameful.. wonderful.. ... .

Chapter Two

'Help.. Help' I gasp out, an obscure shadowy mass is slowly deliberately crushing me and then just as deliberately, malevolently ripping me apart.. ..I struggle hopelessly... my legs and arms paralyzed, refusing to respond to my wishes.. But who is that that looking at me? Floating along beside me.. an ironically gentle smile on her lips.. Yes of course.. Marta.. But surely it must be a dream.. Yes a dream.. nothing but an absurd, meaningless dream.. Only where am I? I blink dazedly into the tainted, throbbing darkness, conscious of my body being slowly ruthlessly dragged apart. 'Of course.. I am at sea ..' I tell myself still not entirely certain, slowly making out the dim outlines of the cabin; from below come unmistakable sounds of snoring. I smile to myself. It is my new cabin-mate, Billy, about my age, perhaps a year older.. a head taller.. He's been at sea for years.. I remind myself. At once an anxiety creeps into my mind. Does he consider me as a proper seaman or just someone playing at it? A shudder passes through me. So it's true.. It really has happened .. I'm at sea.. But who would have thought it would all happen so quickly? Just like a speeded-up film.. scene flashing after scene....almost impossible to follow..

Yes.. there I am in the back-seat of the family saloon, clutching tightly the bulging old canvas kit-bag I'd triumphantly discovered hidden away at the back of a second-hand shop. How unreal it all seems though.. How often did I ask myself, can this really be me? Hardly ever been away from home overnight and now.... and now.. committed to spend weeks at least in a strange bed.. amongst total strangers.. I have to continually swallow against a rising nausea, even though my stomach is empty, despite my mother's repeated urgings I was much too excited to eat; shivering violently alternate hot and cold waves sweep over my body ; the promised side-effects of the injections, I conclude wretchedly.

As if from maternal instinct my mother had turned from the front seat to look at me, her face shadowed by a headscarf, looking older than I had remembered, her eyes red and tired.

'O.K.? She asks pretending a casual enquiry.

"Sure .." I lie looking away; block after block of suburban houses flicking past, shrubs and lawns, sprinklers jetting glittering sprays into the air.. Like a stage-set or advertising hoarding .. empty.......lifeless .. I think as it all swam slowly about.. became fuzzy .. blurred. I'm going to faint.. I think, my bones aching painfully.

'OK you're right its not worth it, lets go back home.' But the words fail to come; my will somehow rendered impotent; it *must* be my destiny, I marvel distantly.

And soon...very soon I muse these busy streets and houses and gardens.. the very city itself .. .will be as nothing to me. And yet even so I fret at every intersection with the interminable queues of traffic; forced to sit patiently clasping the kit-bag, lumpy from a few books and my shoes, as if for reassurance.

And still houses and more houses are rushing past closer together, smaller with small bare, front gardens as we reach the East side of the city; the car slowly cresting a long slope and through the windscreen the peaks of the North Shore Mountains pierce the blue sky, faintly smirched with brown smog.

A slow descent through deserted streets and finally a cul-de-sac between blank warehouse walls and then ever more slowly through an open chain-link gate before us a wide expanse of concrete, empty, deserted; the harbour waters glisten darkly in the sunlight; behind massive fluted concrete silos shut out the sky.

'Are you sure this is it?' my mother says daring to hope.

'Pier 24.' My father says in his usual confident manner.

I had pressed my face against the car window glass seeing a succession of rusty oil drums, broken crates, heaps of coiled wire strewn over the cracked concrete. Was my mother right? Was it all a mistake? Was this like everything

1 3

I attempted in life doomed to failure? Had the ship sailed without me?

'Stop!...Stop!..' I hear myself cry; flinging open the door and jumping out, to stand in nervous wonderment before the dark green and white angular steel mass topped by a large black funnel and on the bluntly, rounded bows, embossed in white letters: *M/V Grimethorpe*.

'Bulk-carrier. Registered, Hartlepool. Cargo: Wheat for China.' I had silently recited the two small lines from the Shipping List engraved forever in my memory, my eyes moving along the vast hull, front and end held securely by numerous thick ropes to the dockside. How big it is; almost a city-block long.. and this is ship I am to sail in... *my* ship; a dizziness comes over me and the ship and all around wavers and blurs.

My father's voice comes faintly to me.

'Do you want us to go aboard with you?'

I violently shake my head, dragging my kit-bag out from the back seat.

'Here Pip.. take this.....please..' I jerk back hearing a sob in the voice, her hand holding a small black book out of the car window. Rudely I snatch it noticing the gold lettering: *New Testament And Psalms,* impatiently untying the kitbag and thrusting it inside before throwing it onto my shoulder.

A backward wave and I am marching determinedly across the dockside; noticing as I get closer that the ship's hull is spotted and dribbled with orange-brown rust.

A toot from the car had abruptly forced me to turn, my mother her head out of the window is saying something, her face flushed, almost girlish-looking, her lips carefully forming the words. I glare irritably back. What now? 'Don't forget to write..' the words finally reach me and I had nodded curtly before carrying on.

The gangway sways alarmingly beneath me, as if to frighten me off and to my surprise there is no one there to welcome me aboard. I think to glance back; the dock-side.. deserted ..

'You've well and truly done it this time...Pip me old cock as granddad used to say 'I grin with a odd tremor, passing along past a row of blankly staring portholes and a dark, open doorway. What shall I do, I wonder moving slowly down the dec the kit-bag already becoming heavy on my shoulder; somehow wary of entering the ship, uninvited or even climbing the metal stairs to the deck above, dominated by a huge squat black funnel. Looking down I grimace, seeing my carefully polished shoes are already covered with a whitish dust.

A clanging of boots makes me look around; a gang of men scuff loudly across the deck toward me; now I'll be told where to go, I think smiling engagingly become doubtful as the motley group their faces and clothes coated with dust, close in on me; their harsh, thick-vowelled speech not like usual English to my ears. I stare back unable to speak under their hard, unflinching gaze.

'Well...well f----n' look whaat t' f-----n' caats druuged in will tha."

One of them booms out. I flush at the obscene language, glancing at the heavily-built man with bushy eye-brows and blunt features, his ham-like upper arms thrust out of a dirty vest. He had looks fixedly at me, a look that makes me makes me flush.

'Looks loike ter cat's swallowed the f----g cream.." Another of them had bellowed to roars laughter.

'Must be a f-----g cream-puff! '

I had stood stiffly indignant under the retreating crash of boots and guffawing laughter.

Why am I doing this to myself? I had wondered sickened and faint feeling; turning to look across the harbour the North Shore rising steeply to the forest-line bristling darkly beneath the snow-streaked peaks; on the lower slope the windows on tall apartment blocks reflect the sunlight and on the waterside, symmetrical heaps of coal and fluorescent-yellow sulphur. How well I knew this view; surely this was where I really belonged? So why not admit it was all a silly mistake? How easy it would be; back down the gangway.. across the dock…a bus ride to down-town and then the No. 19 trolley-bus journey down Granville St. across False Creek finally the lumbering ascent up Dunbar St. lined by small wooden houses to the terminus itself and then the tediously familiar walk past the trees and neatly clipped and edged gardens.. and so down the straight concrete path to the front door and my mother's disbelieving joy, my father's quizzical, welcoming smile.

Empty and dizzy feeling, I wander hopelessly on down the deck, scattered with coils of wire and boxes all covered with a floury dust. Surely the ship couldn't go to sea like this? I think going over to the waist-high steel wall running down the middle of the deck and peering down into the gloom of the interior making out softly rounded heaps of pale golden grain; dust-motes dancing in the shafts of sunlight.

'Wheat.. from the Canadian Prairies..' I had murmured recalling the evening TV news, with their pictures of mile-long lines of box-cars from the Prairies hauled at walking pace with double locomotives through the Rocky Mountains and so down to the Pacific Coast… And now, here it was, reaching almost to the top of the ship's hold, to be taken all the way across the Pacific to feed the famine-stricken Chinese people.

What a great feat of organization and endeavour, I consider soberly, walking back down the deck. Yes, of course a bonanza for the hard-pressed farmers and huge profits for grain dealers, agents and shipping companies but somehow all that self-interest transmuted to help save the lives of fellow-humans. Really I shouldn't let my feelings stop me from taking part in such a great enterprise … a significant event in modern history ….

I come to the open doorway and was just about to step into the shadowy interior when I came face to face with a boyish looking man in a navy blue uniform who I take to be an officer. At once he glowers furiously at me, pushing his peaked cap back over thick curly fair hair contemptuously waving off my stuttering explanation that

I was a new cabin-boy, ordered me off the ship before pushing past and swinging lithely up the stairs to an upper deck muttering something about the ship going to the dogs..

'Admit it, you're not wanted, go back home' I concluded bitterly gazing away to the Second Narrows Suspension Bridge high above far above; the windscreens of the steady commuter traffic reflecting the sun in heliograph-like flashes. But do you want to be one of them? I ask myself; to be trapped forever in a monotonous repetitive existence like them; surely anything was better than that..?

At that moment a sudden roaring fills the air, making me start; rust and dust particles leap about as a violent vibration tears at the metal plates, passing through the soles of my feet up into my legs and body. The ship, no longer an inert, static mass of steel resonating fiercely with uncompromising purpose and through the nausea and misery comes the astonishing conclusion that it was despite everything.. my destiny . ..to go to sea....

And was then as if on cue, Billy, now peacefully snoring below me, emerges from the shadowy passageway and at once laughs scornfully at my grey flannels and Harris Tweed jacket, my foolish attempt to look authentically British. He was dressed in old jeans and a smutched T-shirt... for all his disdain I couldn't help but admire his saturnine, good looks.. a bit like Errol Flynn I thought as he flicked back the long quiff falling from his glossy black hair. Even so I consider it was very callous of him to chuckle so gleefully when I had tripped on the brass-edged sill as I followed him inside.

Even now lying in the darkness I can reach down and find the rough scab on my shin-bone smart at the touch of my finger and remember Billy's callous jeer: 'That'll f----'n learn ya..'

He had told me in a superior way that I should have asked to see "The Sec." when I first came aboard. But when I ask him who is "The Sec.", he only smirks and says I'll find out soon enough and when I told him that some officer had ordered me off the ship, he had looked at me pityingly

1 7

and told me in his slightly nasal accent. "'e aint nuttin' but a f-----n' jumped-up Third.." Even now I'm not sure what a "Third" is…

How sharply it is all etched in my memory, every detail minutely recorded as I had followed Billy along the narrow passageway between the walls of cream-painted steel, lit at intervals by dim-burning lights obscured by thick glass, smelling with instant revulsion the pervasive smell.. What can it be from? .. the same smell that fills my lungs lying in the darkness.. though strangely less potent already.. a mingling of smells ..diesel-oil.. overcooked cabbage.. sweat.. and stagnant pond-water..

Billy had explained that I was to share a cabin with him, opening the second door in a row of doors along what he called the "Companionway.2 More like a long cupboard than a room I had thought, looking into the narrow space with barely room to stand between the bunk-beds and with wood-effect paneled wall; a wash-basin between the bunk and the end wall set with single porthole shedding a faint light.

It was then that Billy had told me that it was pure chance that they needed a cabin-boy as it was only because the previous cabin-boy had without warning left the ship in Seattle. But when I asked why? Billy had merely shrugged and shaken his head as if I shouldn't ask. Now lying awake being pressed and squeezed in the darkness I can't help but wonder why.. ..surely there must be some simple explanation.. and yet somehow there was something mysterious about it.. and yet without his action I wouldn't be here.. wouldn't be one of the crew ..

But was I .. really ..? Billy had taken me back out on deck to join four others lounging along the ship's side two of them in grubby whites, lounging along the ship's side looking down at the dockside. Three of them had ignored me completely the fourth with round pink fat face his barrel-chest bursting out of a too-tight waiter's jacket, had turned and told me in a Canadian drawl that he was Pete, an Assistant Steward and was sure we'd get on just fine and then grabbing my hand had crushed it in a massive fist. I had smiled politely gagging at his overpowering body smell, sickly sweet rather like over-ripe oranges .. I had thought. Only then was it that I had realized that Billy had vanished; abandoning me to the little group determined it seemed to deny my very existence only once, one of them, a small bandy-legged man with a craggy face, wispy ginger hair circling a bright red bald patch, had given me a not unfriendly nod but as the afternoon wore away the steel beneath my feet trembling impotently; .. excluded by the incomprehensible murmuring voices.. not daring to speak hungry .. faintly nauseous, feverish and aching.. longing for an encouraging word or look.. I had again endlessly questioned my decision to come to sea.. and yet without the will or energy to do anything .. stuck against the ship's spasmodically vibrating iron sides .. forced to suffer forever..

Now and again I had indifferently observed several men in dungarees on so far deserted quayside, trailing long shadows they had ambled back and forth without any discernible purpose. So when on an vague impulse I had peered over the ship's side I had been shocked to see a dark abyss had opened up between the ship's hull and the dockside. Even then I didn't quite understand even as the steel around me was seized by spasmodic, frenzied vibrations; from nowhere there was a deafening roar; on the dockside the last remaining figure un-loops a rope from the bollard and with supreme indifference tosses it over the dock-side, to splash gently onto the harbour waters...

Then.. only then ..my fingers pressed into the rusted iron of the ship's side, as if to fix the significance of the moment into my very flesh, had I understood; whispering to myself .. it's really happening... to you... yes... to *you*... now.. at this very moment . all my doubts and fears and unhappiness subsumed in this most momentous event of my life since my birth..

And so I had stayed in trance-like awe watching in dignified procession the office blocks of the down-town Vancouver, bathed in a golden light of the declining sun, pass me by; the myriad windows glaring brazenly, topped by the copper-green copula of the Hotel Vancouver..

Pass inevitably pass and then before my still dazed awed gaze we are sliding through the flat dark waters of Coal Harbour, the garish colours of the neon signs of the Oil Companies on fuel-barges bobbing energetically in response to our passing; the coloured reflections breaking and reforming and breaking.. but then they too are passed.. . my eyes catch eagerly to the pricking masts of the yacht club, the tops of the fountain jets in Lost Lagoon just visible but then .. they too had passed ..

Next the massed varied greens of Stanley Park had come before me ..the groves of massive trees and grassy clearings with wooden picnic tables.. scene of numerous family outings, a vaguely remembered past slipping inevitably, inexorably past yes.. .forever..

Dimly I had heard Pete, the barrel-chested steward drawl out how the leafy, grassy park that appeared was the background for fornication and other vices that if generally known would bring scandal to the best families of Vancouver.

I had stared ever harder at the massed evergreens, some of them thousands of years old, their tops reaching into the sky and shadowing the ferny paths and hidden glades. Could that be true, I had wondered, quite shocked at the suggestion; thinking that I was finally beginning to know ways of the world.. the grim truths lying beneath life's glossy surfaces.

With unswerving intention the ship had approached the Lion's Gate Bridge; the swooping steel wires holding up an inflexible line between the ever-narrowing shorelines; absolutely preventing it seemed to me, our onward passage.

Even as Pete continued to gasp and wheeze more comments; identifying the channel as the Burrard Inlet after a British Naval officer, all my attention was on the bridge, the ship pressing ever closer. Surely a collision between bridge and ship was inevitable and yet at the same time I knew it wouldn't .. and even as I had watched in certain-uncertainty the stationary lines of shiny cars, the railings and towers and cables had magically risen into the sky and the ship was safely passing beneath the steel deck and I had grinned to myself, secretly relieved..

Pete had by this time overcome a violent bout of coughing which had turned his pink face purple and now pompously declared the bridge was called Lion's Gate because of the stone lions on both ends had been built by the famous Guinness family in the midst of the Depression at that time was considered a most foolish investment but since the growth of the fashionable suburb of West Vancouver, the tolls it levied had given the company vast profits.

I had noticed the others exchanging contemptuous glances but then another bout of racking coughs, had gripped the huge man his eyes bulging from his fat face, finally stabbing a handkerchief over his mouth he had shuffled away, even then muffled, desperate coughs had echoed around the steel sides.

'Teach im to shoot 'is f-----g mouth off ..' One of the other men, a pudgy little man with a blotchy face and small, blood-shot eyes had jeered savagely and then fixed me with a fierce stare as if I was thinking of disputing the point. At once I had looked away my heart racing, as if to show my total absorption in the passing shoreline.

Already we were level with English Bay backed by an irregular palisade of apartment blocks, the windows blazing and below the broad swathe of white sand, a scattering of tiny dark figures, the very last of the sun-bathers... ..soon to happily roll up their mats and beds and return home, I had considered musingly.

But already the ship was further out and only by straining my eyes could I make out Kitsilano, the beach and outside pool and tennis courts where I had once played with father and sister backed by rows of wooden houses and squat apartment blocks and as the ship pressed on I could just make out Jericho Beach, the sails of the few dinghies mere white specks on the gilded waters and the yacht club itself with the compound of bristling masts and then the long beach so familiar from family picnics; bringing to mind a time how with my back against one of the bleached driftwood tree-trunksI had gazed out over the shiny harbour waters, watching the sea-going freighters pass against the mountain peaks of the North Shore, then an idle spectator, day-dreaming of how it might be if... always if.. .... but . now ..now . I had shaken my head in awed wonder, turning, my eyes following the broad swathe running up the blackly forested slope marking the path of the cable-car up Grouse Mountain to the glint of reflected light from the panoramic windows of the restaurant on the summit; remembering a family meal to celebrate my father's fortieth birthday; my gaze following along the long mountain ridge called the Sleeping Princess, and the back to the city's cluster of office blocks now become fabulous towers of glistening gold in the evening light....

'And so farewell' I had murmured swallowing hard, looking resolutely ahead to where the darkening whale-like hump of Point Grey, shoulders the ship into a fiery path blazed by the setting sun... to the world beyond the horizon and my new life at sea..

But where was everybody? Suddenly I had realized that I was all alone. Twice small groups of men had slowly clumped past, talking in low voices ignoring me entirely. Was this what my new life at sea was to be then .. to be entirely forgotten.. ignored ..?

Absently I had noticed how broad streaks of milky brown laced the shining green sea water .. so already we were passing the Fraser River delta, I had concluded; moved to think how the river risen in the distant Rocky Mountains until swollen with silt it had been a frequent sight on my lonely ramblings and now was vanishing in vastness of the Pacific Ocean.

Then straining my eyes I had made out glaciered peak of Mount Baker, a dull red beacon for the vanishing North

American mainland.. ..the last sight of the land that held all that was familiar and dear... .. What had I done.... ?

Go to sleep .. it's all past.. I urge myself shutting my eyes pressing my face into the hard thin mattress. It's part of life to be ignored.. forgotten.. and hadn't I finally overcome my nausea and faintness? Yes.. returning to the cabin I had found the biscuits that I remembered my mother over my objections had put in my kit-bag and going back out on deck had gratefully eaten them watching the ship's slow yet deliberate passage through the Gulf Islands with renewed energy; the setting sun piercing the tall cedars striping the flat water with brazen bars, scent of pine and earth heavy on the warm air stirring dim emotions; amazed too that the ship's vast steel mass could pass so close to the jagged rocky shore rising abruptly from the dark waters, sometimes so close that I had been able to see the strips of red bark peeling from the soft-limbed Arbutus, its dark green leaves trailing in the surging, frothing current. Recalling with a faint pang that it was my father who had told me with his usual seriousness while on a family trip on a ferry to Vancouver Island that the narrow yet deep water channel was named after *HMS Active* a 18th Century British Frigate exploring the then uncharted Pacific West Coast; like the Spanish, Russian and American explorers the places bearing their names now the only testimony to their presence here long ago. But what I had mused distantly, brought them here, so far from home was it a dissatisfaction with the known and familiar.. the thrill of going where none had gone before or perhaps the lure of riches. But why some men and not others.. was it chance .. or ineluctable destiny?

My eyes had been drawn to an ancient lighting-struck cedar, it's ghostly-white limbs projecting over the darkening water, just visible in the fading dusk, a solitary Bald Eagle perched on the topmost branch and I had reminded myself how the eagle was one of the totems of the West Coast tribes and how these islands were their ancestral home; seeing in my imagination, the ragged column of smoke rising out of the dark forest and in a clearing the cedar lodges overshadowed by weathered totem-poles; the guardians of a deeply ceremonial, hieratic, communal life.. beyond individual consciousness ..and now irretrievably broken into chaotic fragments.

It was then that I had been startled to see another ship sailing close by, passing us the other way towards Vancouver. Had I thought the ship I was standing on was the only ship sailing the world's oceans? Somehow it seemed so and yet here was a most material contradiction, hull and superstructure and funnel a most solid grey even in the fading light and at the ship's stern, a flag fluttering in the light breeze, showing a crossed hammer and sickle on a dark red background. 'A Soviet..' I had thought with a frisson of excitement but even as I had watched the square outline had vanished into the closing darkness, the last rays of the setting sun vanishing into a darkly clouded sky.

I open my eyes instantly awake, listening intently, even the faint snoring from below has stopped; the thin mattress lies flat and unmoving beneath me. Why have we stopped? What can be happening? I reach out a hand and touch the cold, damp steel of the wall by my head, a faint vibration passing down my arm. A sudden thought makes me jerk upright; what if my mother had got the coastguard to intercept the ship? Impossible.. and yet.. what was that? Hurried footsteps...... faint clangings Any minute would come an authoritative knock on the cabin door, I think my heart pounding, even as I dismiss the suggestion as utterly absurd...Minutes pass... from far away I heard muffled thuds.. a sudden clang.. then the same faintly vibrating silence..

Impulsively I slip down from the upper bunk-bed giving a glance at the long mound in the bottom bunk, the lino cold to my bare feet, opening the cabin door as quietly at I could. I move feeling strangely disembodied, quickly along the shadowy passageway dim-lit corridor and on through the open doorway, my toes curling at the cold rough steel of the deck I pass down the ship's side and press against the trembling ship's side looking up into a vast cloudy darkness. Almost frighteningly dark, I muse remembering the invariable sickly glow that lights up the Vancouver night sky..

A muffled banging attracts me and I move towards a glaring light shining through a doorway further down the ship.

At first dazzled by the mast high floodlights I blink at the shadowy forms emerging from the darkness beyond, puzzled by a sudden clattering noise that as almost instantly ceases. What could it signify? I watch as two shapes separate out of the shadows and then as in a monstrous puppet-show, approach each other and solemnly shake hands, sensing an awful finality in the brief gestures.

"Ready...sir." A deep voice growls portentously from out of the dark. One of the shadowy forms rises above the ship's side turns and instantly vanishes... How fantastical... just like a dream but I shiver from the chilly air and know with certainty I am fully awake.

I turn and look over the ship's side; in a pool of light rocking gently on the mirror-like dark waters, is a slim motor launch, chrome work glinting, making a throaty burbling noise.

Motionless two figures stand on the narrow deck, long poles pressed against the ship's side rising like an iron wall beside them; a bulky shadow slowly clambers down a swaying rope-ladder to land with a dull thud on the launch's deck and disappears below without a word. At once the gasping throb of the launch changes to a harsh roar, the sound spreading out into night; a dash of white gleams out of the darkness; tiny green and red eyes wink back at me, then suddenly are gone leaving the ship marooned in a vast, cloudy blackness..

Through the doorway comes a hoarse laughter; reckless .. defiant, I think as a violent tremor tears through the faintly vibrating steel; the deck lifting under my feet. I move slowly back to the cabin pausing to look out into dark; far away a tiny point of light gleams and then fades and then gleams again; with a convulsive shudder I realize that it must be Esquimault light-house the furthest westerly point on the North Pacific Coast..

A vast yawn tears at me and I turn and shuffle hurriedly back to the cabin and haul myself into the steadily see-sawing upper berth. 'So you've done it, Pip me old cock you're at sea ..' I murmur in awed contentment slipping back to sleep.

CHAPTER THREE

'Fool.. fool. Go on say it F-----g, f-----g fool.'

I was kneeling on a red vinyl settle, rising and falling with the movement of the ship, staring through one of the square portholes in the Officer's Smoking Room on the second deck; a dense, writhing fog blanked out ship, sea and sky; a faint sea-sickness gnawing at my insides. I was meant to be polishing the brass catches and frames of the portholes; pitted and green with corrosion, it seemed an impossible task; the rag dropped from my hand and the Brasso began to sting in a scrape on my knuckles. How unhappy I am, I thought and tears filled my eyes....

And yet it was all my own fault.. all my own doing; I had no one to blame but myself; how bitter a thought that is remembering with what fervour my dear mother had tried to dissuade me. And how I had rejoiced in my stubborn pride. And not only her... First there had been the fat Greek ship's officer who reeked of garlic; then the correct German officer but also the expressions on the face of the Harbour Master and the doctor who had examined me for the medical. "Fit for sea.." How ironic! Yes, how well I understood now what they were thinking.... pitying me .. for my innocence.. ignorance.. stupidity .. Yes. .. f-----g fool.. How pathetic all I had learned was to use obscenities..

And now too came flooding into my mind a scene in the back-garden, two weeks or so, before that fateful telephone call from the Harbour Master's Office..

Two school friends had rather unexpectedly come to see me; Marta a small, vivacious girl who secretly fascinated me; a Hungarian refugee she wanted to be a civil engineer. With her had been Ralph, an old school-friend of mine, now her boyfriend, like me still undecided what to study. Subduing my envy I had listened in silence to their account of the party they had gone to after the Graduation Dance and how afterwards they had all gone down to the beach in cars to watch the sun rise. But when they had begun to discuss the different University courses, I had been gripped by a mounting anguish. How could they voluntarily commit themselves to years and years of such soul-destroying tedium? To sit hour after hour, passively listening to a bored lecturer fill up the allotted time, regurgitating material from a text-book?

Without thinking I had jumped to my feet. "I'm not going to University.." I had declared loudly my voice no doubt carrying around the neighbouring gardens.

"But Phillip. What do you do then..?" Marta asked in her attractive foreign accented English, tiny frowns creasing the forehead of her small pixie-face.

"I'll go to sea.." I had announced without the least thought and yet somehow at that very moment I had decided as if some unseen power had taken hold of me.

"You're nuts Phil. You don't do that kinda thing nowadays.." Ralph had interjected with a sober shake of his head..

"But Phillip.. dear.." Marta had murmured sweetly, her head on one side.

"Will it make you really happy? I don't think so, I sure.."

How right she was, I thought sadly remembering the look of sympathy in her eyes; perhaps I should write to her, confess everything; a letter forming in my mind.

'Dear Marta..

I am so looking forward to seeing you when this stupid trip is finally over. I dreamt about you the other night. I was being dreaming I was being crushed to death, probably that's because the bunk-bed I sleep on moves up and down with the ship, so first up so your head is pressed against the wall then your legs are dragged down. It stops me sleeping properly and I wake up all stiff and dazed feeling. Anyway you suddenly appeared out of nowhere and smiled kindly at me.. But really I am regretting the whole thing..

Already two days have passed in the middle of a thick fog and if it wasn't for the constant vibrating and noise of the engines you wouldn't know we were moving and I thought the Pacific meant blue seas and coral lagoons .. What a dope eh? Actually Marta, I have to confess you were right when you said I wouldn't be happy. It's just awful.. the food is really terrible. The cooks aren't real cooks at all but went to some Merchant Marine Cookery school for a couple of weeks so they could learn about the Board of Trade regulations how many pounds and ounces of the ingredients per man.. rules but not real cooking at all. So I can hardly eat anything...

Everything is against me. I keep tripping over the door-sills, they're really high I suppose to keep out water when it's rough weather and they have brass edges and so my shins are cut almost to the bone.. Billy the other cabin-boy, thinks it's terribly funny though I think he quite likes me but quite enjoys teasing me because I don't know anything about ships. For example you call the corridors, "Companionways." They're gloomy and really smelly I share a cabin with Billy in the middle of the ship which you call the "Amidships".. and if you go to the front of the ship it's called the "fo'rard" through the "foredeck" above the ship's bows and if you go to the stern you go "Aft" to the "Afterdeck." And the toilet which is next to our cabin is called the "Head" though Billy say's 'ead.. he misses out all the "h's" .. usually it's the "f----n' 'ead.." All of the crew use that word.. I don't even think they know they're saying it.

The showers are hopeless too... cold and weak. I have to get up every morning at 6am.. it's pitch dark and the Sec. that's what we call the Second Steward, bangs on our cabin door and shouts at us to get up and switches on the light. Billy really loathes him, he's a Karate expert spends hours toughing the edge of his hand by banging it against things... He's quite strict though he's doesn't smoke or swear but he gives me such stupid jobs .. like polishing brass on the portholes .. I don't think they've been cleaned for years.. all pitted but I don't dare complain. Being on a ship at sea, is completely different than on land.. At sea you have no rights. There's a document framed on the wall of the Crew-Mess which is the crew dining room.. Called Articles of Sea or something.. one of them is that if two of you refuse to obey an order it's considered Mutiny... and you could be shot.. Billy says they there's a case with guns in the Captains cabin.. or you could be shut up in the "Brig" ..the name for a ship's prison though I'm not sure exactly where it is. Billy also told me the Cabin-Boy I replaced "jumped" ship.. not sure exactly why.. couldn't take it any longer I guess....

My main job is in the Pantry next to the Officer's Dining Room bringing the meals from the Galley the name for the kitchen across the companionway. There's two (so-called) cooks Ronnie he's the 1st cook Ronnie a Cockney always sneering at the 2nd Cook a Scotsman a real character he goes around with his chest stuck out chanting "I'm Willie McCluchy frae Autchermuchty" ..not sure how you spell it.. I guess some place in Scotland, everyone calls him Jock anyway. There's two Assistant Stewards, a Canadian, called Pete, a real lard-barrel he's very friendly, too friendly really, when he comes close to you he smells so strongly you almost faint. Billy and I call him "Old Smelly".. The other Assistant Steward is called Mitch .. he's a Scouser ... which means he comes from Liverpool. Billy told me he was sent to prison for stabbing his brother in law at the wedding, with the knife they were cutting the wedding cake with! I don't think he likes me. Somehow he guessed I was feeling sea-sick. The Sec. said I could go back to the cabin but I refused, anyway this Mitch put a plate of fatty bacon in front of me and asked me if I'd like it. I was almost sick on the spot....the others all thought it very funny. His arms are covered with a mass of tattoos.. but it's his eyes that scare me, tiny blood-shot eyes. Billy says he's pure evil. I think he despises me for not being a proper seaman.. Maybe they all do ...

There's a Chief Steward too, but I haven't met him. Billy says he's an alcoholic and stays in his cabin drinking all day. He and Mitch are thick as thieves ..

Then there's the Deck Boys. I rather envy them working out on deck and not like us Cabin-Boys shut up inside washing dishes in cold water etc. What an odd couple they are though. Tad, a Pole.. thin and bony looks like his half-starved always jerking and twitching .. always shrieking and squealing in this broken half-Italian English. 'a real nutter' is what Billy says and then Norrie from an English fishing village ..the complete opposite to Tad.. fat and solid he looks really dumb with this silly grin on his face and his ears sticking out.. They are our sworn enemies according to Billy though actually we sometime lark about with them.. One time Tad came into our Pantry and began mock sword fighting .. leaping about the counter tops.. really like a madman... another I forget how it started we began playing at cops and robbers ..like kids running about in this thick fog hiding behind parts of the ship and pointing imaginary pistols and going bang! bang!.. at each other. I really don't know why I joined in.. really stupid.. I suppose it helps break the monotony of it all But really I thought is why I came to sea to end up playing silly games with a couple of weirdos.. .. Thank goodness I only have to survive for two more weeks at the most and then I'll be back and can begin a normal life.. ..'

I started, looking around staring around the narrow room as if waking from a sleep. How pointless. I wasn't even sure of Marta's address.. No I was on my own and had better get used to it. Just live for the moment. Here.. now.. in this gloomy room, reeking of stale cigarette and beer smells, just like some shabby back-street bar I thought, surveying critically the wood effect panelled walls and the small round tables with hammered-copper tops and the stools padded with red vinyl and bolted to a stained carpet, spotted with cigarette burn-holes; in front of me was a dart-board, the wall around it pitted with countless holes, as if I thought sarcastically, the Officers preferred hitting the wall rather than scoring points on the dartboard....

I gave a long sigh wondering if it would become easier.. Each day exactly like the other beginning with the sleep-shattering bangs on the cabin door and a shout: "Let's have ya Cabin-Boys".. Half-falling out of the bunk.. struggling into my clothes on the cabin floor then staggering like a drunk along the narrow Companionway, sparsely-lit, acrid smelling and into the harsh glare of the white-tiled "Head". I have to press against the wall to steady myself against the roll and pitch of the ship; the dark yellow stream wavering, unpredictably around the urinal...thinking yes.. yes.. this is my life..

And then down to the Pantry isolated from the vast pre-dawn darkness outside, a cube of cream-painted steel lit by two florescent strip lights reflecting off the stainless-steel counter tops, the floor of corrugated grey tiles; the two portholes showing as shiny black squares; the vast darkness beyond; alien .. hostile.. unforgiving.. watching for the slightest weakness .. so it seemed to me ..

Soon though the rest of the catering crew, as they're called, arrive; coughing, scratching and yawning: uncouth, like two-legged creatures just emerged from their lair, exchanging subdued low growls amongst themselves, ignoring me except for Mitch who sometimes fixes me with a hard stare that makes me tremble.

Billy and I sit ourselves on the dented and scratched stainless steel counter-top, everything vibrating around us, an incessant clinking and rattling of the crockery on the wall-dresser. Feeling this great hole in my stomach I silently bolt down the thick slabs of ship's bread, spread with a synthetic-yellow margarine, smeared with a lurid-green gooey paste, swimming with large seeds, spooned from a large catering tin, labeled *Strawberry Jam*; washing it down with a peaty, tannic tea from poured from a massive kettle kept on a stove in the Galley and sweetened with dollops of Nestles condensed milk; all the time I am conscious of the Sec. who stands frowning slightly in the Pantry doorway, watching everything in silence...

Then with the hasty gulps of tea and lumps of undigested bread swilling around inside me I am struggling up heaving stairwell to the upper decks with a large galvanised-pail sloshing cold water and banging my shins; to begin washing the companionway floors on my hands and knees the double row of cabin-doors stretching away. Sick-feeling, the brown lino floor rising and falling, before my sleep-crusted eyes. Pushing the pail of water before me, I swipe despairingly with the thick knitted floor-cloth and then strain to wring it out, the dirty cold water trickling down my arms. And so wiping and wringing, crouching or crawling I force myself along; trapped in some surreal, farcical existence. Am I really at sea? Or perhaps in a mine-shaft deep below the earth yet a poorly lit tunnel that slides and shudders and trembles convulsively........

'Bang! Bang!' I start convulsively, it is the sound of cabin-doors shutting echoes like gun-shots along the Companionway.

It's the officers getting ready to go down for their breakfast, and soon I will have to endure their gratuitous jeers as they pass me by.

I try to work faster to get away but I just like in some awful dream muscles wont respond; the thought that tomorrow will be exactly the same.. and the day after and almost suffocates me. Can I last another day? Another hour? Another minute? Yet somehow I keep on swipe, drag, wring; swipe, drag, wring; losing myself in the dull monotony of effort... Already I am on the landing, only one more flight of steps and I will be finished.. but too late. Footsteps sound on the steps just above me, I keep my head firmly down; guessing from the loud voices that it's the two Irish radio operators; the Sparkies as everyone calls them.

"Nice fanny, eh boyo?" One of them jeers in a thick Irish accent.

"Howsa about a go, darling?" The other drawls.

I pretend I haven't heard and guffawing and sniggering they clatter noisily on down the stair-well.

Now as I stared through the port-hole into the dull wreathing greyness beyond the misty glass of the port-hole, an impotent rage stirred within me. How humiliating. Billy would have given them as good back again but all I can do is keep a cowardly resentful silence as I hurry back to the bottom deck. Through the Pantry Hatch I can see taking their seats, with their fellow officers. I rather envy them, all of them smart in navy blue uniforms talking and laughing carelessly as they wait at the long tables covered with stained white cloths, napkins and cutlery and tarnished silver cruets. The flowery patterned carpet on the floor and the chintz curtains over the portholes rather reminds me of a pretentious, low-class Hotel Dining Room. Before the last the officers have taken their seats Billy and I are busy ferrying the breakfasts from the Galley and putting them through the Hatch. On the other side Pete and Mitch, the two Assistant Stewards, like over-weight penguins, in white jackets and black bow-ties, are calmly waiting to take them to the tables.

Back in the Galley, it is a completely different world, the two cooks in their grubby whites dashing about in clouds of blue smoke, the tiled walls echoing to the crashing of pots and pans.

"Get yer f-----g finger oot laddie!" Jock yells at me, his face a bright red as he ladles out the porridge, bubbling like volcanic mud, from vast cauldrons fenced in by narrow rails on the top of the huge steel range.

The bowls of half-eaten porridge are barely put back through the Hatch to be piled up in the sink before Mitch and Pete are angrily demanding toast.

"Toast please.." I ask back in the Galley but the cooks but completely ignore me, busying dragging out from the gaping oven, vast aluminium trays of shrivelled rashers, burnt sausages spitting in fat and coagulated sheets of rubbery fried eggs.

"Get yer f----n' finger out!" Ronnie yells pointing at the plates on the warmer the half-burnt contents afloat in pools of watery tinned tomatoes.

I rush back to the Pantry the hot plates burning my fingers even through the tea-towel.

"Slow as a snail ain't ya.." Mitch snarls I push the plates through the hatch. "An where's f-----n' toast yer useless tit?"

"It's not fair.." I moan passing Billy in the doorway with two silver tea-pots in each hand..

"Just get a f---- move on will ya." He growls back at me. Are they all mad? I wonder distractedly, dazed by all the shouting and clashing of dishes and pots; now ordered to the Galley then back to Pantry.

Then as abruptly as it has started, it stops, the Dining Room is suddenly deserted and the dirty dishes are piling up in the Hatch. Billy goes out on deck, for what he calls a "fly" smoke, leaving me to start the washing-up. I stare with dismay at the piles of dirty dishes jiggling and clinking insistently. For one thing the water is only just lukewarm and I have been warned not to let the tap run for too long as there is a limited supply of fresh water. The day before I had watched with amazement as Billy had cut slivers from a long bar of rock-hard yellow soap and put them into a rusty tin gashed with holes, with a piece of wire attached to the top for a handle. Now I drag the tin back and forth in the sink full of tepid water producing a few transitory bubbles.. A despair numbs me as I think of twenty or so porridge bowls, dinner plates and side-plates, as well as cups, saucers milk jugs and cutlery have to be washed in what quickly becomes a sink full of suds-less water floating with a grey scum.

And what depresses me further is that no one seems to understand how impossible it is to do a proper job...

"Just f-----n' get on with it will ya." Billy snaps when he finally returns and I try to explain how difficult it is without hot water and detergent..

More wiped than washed, the dishes are somehow clean enough and safely returned behind bars on the floor to ceiling dresser that takes up the entire wall between the Pantry doorway and Hatch. After wiping down the counter the final task is to empty the "Marie"; such an incongruous name, I had thought, for the battered galvanised bucket used for the left-overs, scrapings and tea-slops.

"Just 'eave her over the side." Billy had told me with a funny grin on my first morning.

I should have guessed there was a trick, but I was so pathetically eager to show my worth, How well I remember my satisfaction as I managed to get over the door-sill, the bucket brim-full, bits of toast floating on the greasy surface and so out into the icy cold morning mist, shivering as I had quickly crossed over the covered deck-space and then with all my strength heaved the bucket up and over the ship's side; a glimpse of swirling white fog, a rush of wind blasting my face and I had staggered backwards half the contents of the bucket blown back on me. For a moment or two I had stood there, to shocked to move, my face and chest dripping stuck with tea-leaves and food-scraps; loud shouts had brought me slowly around; in the doorway was Billy with the two Cooks and Pete and Mitch laughing and smirking and behind them The Sec. a faint smile on his impassive face.

"Next time throw it down wind" He has said as I had pushed angrily past them to get myself cleaned up.

Not one word of sympathy from any of them, I thought, burying my face into the slippery, cold vinyl of the settle. Even Billy who had I thought would be a real pal to me, would without warning punch me in on my upper arm and stood grinning as I ruefully rubbed the hurt.

"F----'n learn ya.." He would laugh callously.

I gave a long sigh, the truth was I had a made a terrible mistake .. I just wasn't up to a life at sea… If only I knew how much longer I had to hold out, but no one seemed to know how many days it would take to get there or even the name of the port in China.. Just like some stupid pointless dream.. I mused gloomily suddenly conscious that I was being watched.

"Just er having a little rest .." I said turning around, flushing guiltily.

The Sec. wearing creased black trousers and a tight-fitting white T-shirt which showed off his muscular torso, stood in the doorway; a slight frown creased his forehead.

"See hurt myself. It's so not fair...." I whimpered holding out my blood-crusted knuckles.

"I don't know why you came to sea, son..." the Sec interrupted in a even monotone, running a hand though his crisp, light-brown hair.

I looked down; yes.. why? why? echoed feebly in the back of my mind.

"Well, it's none of my business. The point is you signed Ship's Articles as a Cabin Boy right?" The Sec. went on insistently, gently banging the edge of his hand against the door-jamb.

I nodded dumbly watching the full biceps flexing with each movement of the arm; Billy had told me a single blow could kill a man, I remembered absently.

"And so when I tell you to do something ... Are you hearing me, Wight." The Sec. demanded impatiently; his arm suspended in mid-air.

"Yes.. sorry Sec." I murmured glancing back at the dingy portholes. "It's just.."

"Just do it .. understand.." The Sec. went on his face stern unrelentingly stern..

Again I nodded biting my lip; how unreasonable he was.

"So don't let me find you skiving again .." The Sec. finished; for a minute or two he stood in the doorway rocking gently back and forth on the balls of his feet, looking at me thoughtfully, then he was gone as silently as he had appeared.

How unfair.. I thought as I picked up the rag and desultorily rubbing at the dirty brass; after all the others are always disappearing for a smoke and he doesn't say anything. Why is he picking on me?

Is it because he knows I can leave the ship once we get back to Vancouver, I wondered remembering Billy had told me that the Sec. had chosen to enlist in Merchant Marine for his National Service rather than in the regular Armed Forces which meant he had to do twice the normal period and then the government decided to abolish Conscription completely but the Sec. had to complete the years he had signed on for and at National Service rates of pay. So he was picking on me out of frustration with his situation .. and because I was new and couldn't answer back.... How unfair.. but everything on the ship was unfair.. absurd.. the awful food .. having to wash floors without mop or squeegee .. no hot water or detergent.. and now this.. With sudden disgust I threw down the Brasso-soaked rag, gagging at it's chemical smell. So let them lock me up in the Brig, I thought impulsively going over to the door the deck and after a struggle flinging it open with a loud crash.

Outside an icy-cold wetness smeared my face; a dull roaring from the ship's engines sounded loudly in the misty air.

'Perhaps I should end it all', flashed through my mind as I crossed the deck slippery with surface water. 'No one would care in the least..' I mused holding onto the dripping wet rail vibrating fiercely beneath my grasp; below lay a swirling fog, like a white blanket and yet every now and then there were sudden gashes revealing foamy patches of greenish black water. Was that what the previous Cabin Boy had felt? I should have asked the Captain why he needed a Cabin-Boy so urgently. But of course I was so eager to go to sea. Why? Why? Why couldn't I be like everyone else? Go to university.. then a job.. a normal life. Did I really believe I had a special destiny..? How vain .. foolish.. absurd.....

I looked up towards the ship's stern, angled shapes drifted in and out of the ghostly grey-whiteness, like a partly submerged tidal wreck.

Only the relentless up and down movement beneath my feet and the insistent vibration of the steel work reminded that I was aboard a ship. But how could I go on? I just couldn't .. everyday the same tedious mind-numbing tasks .. unbearable.. and yet what else was there? I gazed wonderingly at the tiny water droplets hopping madly on the metal rail before streaming off down the stanchion....

After all I couldn't just go and catch a bus and go home, I thought wryly. "Home.. home" I sounded the word several times, mouthing it into the cold misty air as if to give it meaning, force but somehow it remained void of emotion.

Only the present is real, I thought gloomily, the inescapable present: Do this now ..Do that....now... now .. now.. yes unbearable...

From the corner of my eye I caught a sudden flash of white and turned sharply. How amazing! Before my startled gaze a sea-bird, wings outspread, was wheeling freely over the frothy, dark green waves. How? Why? Where from? I marveled smiling, feeling a kinship. "One too like thee.. tameless.. swift and proud...." I breathed ecstatically.

Then abruptly it was gone, swallowed up by the densely, wreathing white greyness; almost as if I had imagined it, I thought but no.. vision-like.. the brilliant white outstretched wings sweeping over the dark waters fixed forever in my mind...

I stepped back into the thick stale-air of Officer's Smoking Room and pulled the heavy deck-door shut with a dull thud, vaguely aware of feeling strangely different. But what was it? Had something happened to me?

I went back to the settle and began to work with renewed energy and soon the brass-work was flashing with a glossy sheen. I smiled back at the he warped reflections of my face, "Yes.. it's Phillip Wight" I murmured "Cabin-Boy, on board the good ship *M/V Grimethorpe* sailing towards the mysterious East on his great adventure."

CHAPTER FOUR

Stripped to our shorts, Billy and I lolled on cast-off dining-room chairs our feet resting on the stern rail, vibrations from the propeller-shaft below tingling through our bodies, the sun blazing down on us; human sacrifices to the sun-god I mused, my bared skin burning hot. 'Bronzing. ..' Billy called it.

And even then still vivid in my mind was that moment out on deck by mere chance when I had witnessed our passage out of the dense white fog into a new world of brilliant blue skies; now everyday the sun rose in a rich pink flush to blaze down on us from a cloudless blue sky until finally sinking into the golden calm of the Pacific in a fiery glow that almost instantly became blackest night spattered with numberless glittering stars... so amazingly bright ..

I stole a sideways glance at Billy beside me, his body tanned a golden brown then glancing critically along my still pale torso and legs. What a relief I considered that now we could now spend our afternoon break out on deck, before the icy foggy air had confined us to our cabin; Billy in the bunk below, reading over ancient dog-eared war comics, I staring at the ceiling just above my face, quite unable to read, pondering on life.. and what might yet be...

How much better it was the minute the lunch dishes were washed dried and stowed away in the dresser and the Pantry floor and counters cleaned, that we could leave the heat and smells of the Amidships to walk freely the length of Afterdeck, the ocean glittering on all sides, past the cargo hatches, tightly covered by green tarpaulin covers, giving off a tarry smell in the hot sun, past the Crew Accommodation Block to a narrow space between poop deck and the stern rail where a blistered, bare flag-staff pointed over the glistening immensity of the Pacific, towards the far-off horizon.

And somewhere far beyond that faint line, I reasoned, was Vancouver; mentally re-tracing a path through the heavily dark green Gulf Islands then Burrard Inlet overlooked by the North Shore Mountains, and through the Lions Gate Bridge, the myriad glinting windows of the down-town buildings.. and a longish bus ride away a grid of wide suburban streets.. neat lawns and severely clipped bushes.. tall leafy trees and a cracked concrete path leading up to the low steps and the front door of a white-painted, clap-board bungalow...

But that was the past, every day seeming to become fainter, ever less real... It was now .. this passing, present moment that pressed so implacably on me; treasuring each one of the precious forty minutes of rest between lunch and the preparations for the evening meal so soon it was time to stagger sun-dazed back to the oven-like confines of the Amidships..

But surely we were almost halfway to China already, I kept thinking; day or two to unload and then the return journey.. and yet that too was so indefinite .. vague; the future like the past not quite believable..

"How far d'you reckon we've come?" I wondered out loud my leg muscles beginning to cramp and sitting up.

"Dunno.. Don't matta much do it?" Billy yawned indifferently, neatly flicking his cigarette butt over the rail.

"No.. I guess not." I murmured abashed, yes .. only the present mattered.. the implacable insistent present of throbbing steel walls .. the acrid smells and cloying heat; from the sudden banging on the cabin door the unchanging routine until at the end of the day I dragged myself to the upper bunk .. my body submitting to the ruthless.. tireless.. push and pull of the ship...

"Bet yer t'inkin' of getting' back 'ome eh?" Billy said reaching out a tanned muscled arm to retrieve his pack of cigarettes from under the chair.

"Not really.." I muttered detecting a jeering note in Billy's voice. Abruptly I got up and went to the stern rail, grasping the trembling steel and looking down at the frothing, bubbling water relentlessly churned up by the ship's propeller; a chaos of frothy whirlpools that streamed away in a seething, bubbly spume becoming a brilliant white band of lace floating calmly away over the glittering flat waters..

Could it be that Billy was envious of me; I wondered remembering some of what he had told me about his life in England; growing up in what sounded like a rough area of London; bringing to my mind, films I had seen, the camera panning over terraced houses, coal-smoke drifting up from the chimneys lining the ranked slate roofs under a grey skies

I guessed from what little he had said that his family life had been unhappy one; his father a Railway Porter, had been unjustly dismissed, or so Billy believed, and nagged by his wife for his laziness he began to drink heavily at the local pub sometimes not coming home for days on end and then finally disappearing altogether, leaving his wife to bring up Billy and an older sister on what she earned as a cleaner..

Billy had contemptuously dismissed school as boring and almost naturally it seemed he had begun to truant; "wagging off" was his name for it; a little gang of them mostly boys would get together under a railway bridge, smoking and play-fighting. ..

"Really great.." Billy had enthused. How different to my life I had thought, envious and yet doubtful.

And then at night.. .Between puffs of cigarette smoke blown into sun's glare, Billy's words had aroused my imagination with images of crowded, noisy dance-halls and pubs, the air thick with cigarette smoke and beer and frying food smells; in the lurid glow of street-lights, gaggles of skimpily dressed heavily-made up teen-age girls tottering about on high-heels, and jostling gangs of youths with slicked-back hair and tight trousers, sometimes seeking each other out in the deep shadows of back lanes or under bridges, to touch and rub each other under their clothes.

I had felt myself go hot, my pulse throbbing at Billy's descriptions.

"I don't know any girls like that.." I had laughed trying not to sound too jealous.

"F-----'n sluts t'lot of 'em. "Billy had jeered, lighting up another cigarette, a bitter tone coming into his voice.

Yes he is a little bitter but perhaps he had reason I considered; thinking how upset I would be if my mother had let different men come to stay. Strangely though Billy didn't seem that upset some of them were alright gave him money.. even took him to football matches or greyhound races; until that was one had taken up permanent residence in the small terraced house.

"Don'tcha t'ink 'arold a f-----n' stupid name..." Billy had demanded flicking his cigarette butt over the rail, in a gesture of disgust.

"Yeah.. .." I had conceded not wanting to admit I had an uncle of that name, though Billy didn't seem that interested in my history; embarrassing me once though by asking if my sister was good-looking and if she would go to bed with him.

"Almost f-----n' killed 'im didn't I.." Billy had boasted telling the story of how one evening after endless rows and shouting matches he had gone for Harold.. knocked him down .. his mother and sister screaming and dragging him off.. Neighbours had called the Police but Billy had got away before they had arrived. He had tracked down his father in his favourite pub and then stayed with him a couple of nights but that wasn't much fun either his father almost continually drunk so when a friend of his father, a steward on a Castle Line ship sailing to Capetown, had suggested he sign-on as a cabin-boy and escape the attentions of the Police he had quickly agreed. After a disagreement with the Chief Steward he had left but after a few weeks ashore he had found another berth.. on a banana boat.. this time and so different ships... different ports.... different bars..and drinks.. and different women. . .....

With an pretended nonchalance, my heart beating heavily I had listened as Billy casually recounted his various experiences with them.. In Hamburg there were certain streets near the docks where women in flimsy underwear sat at open windows pleading with the passers-by for attention. .... .

"Some of 'em not bad looking" Billy had said rather scornfully.

Then there was a woman in Kingston who wanted him to live with her and made a scene when he left to go back to his ship.

"Black as f----n' coal weren't she .. All ya could see at night was t' whites of her eyes" He'd joked blowing smoke into the shimmering air.

I had snorted expressively as if it was something I might well have experienced.

"That sure sounds er great.." I had stammered squinting up into the glare as Billy had recounted his visits to government regulated brothels in Venezuela.

"Doctor check's 'em regular So's yer 'nows t'ey don't 'ave t'clap .." Billy had added authoritatively, describing the landscaped park of trees and flowers where in the doorways of little wooden cabins lazed the waiting prostitutes; almost dizzy my imagination was swept with images of, exquisitely voluptuous Creole women... waiting... inviting..

"Just f----n' tarts though." Billy had sneeringly concluded. "What I fancies is them real classy American High School girls, like yer sees in the films, in tight jumpers.. blonde wit blue eyes.. all sweet and innocent looking but real 'ot once yer get's to 'em.. What yer say Phil"

Billy had winked knowingly at me.

I had smiled feebly; recollections of guiltily nervous perusals of half-naked women in Men's magazines in a second-hand bookshops and the lingerie section of mail-order catalogue flashing through my mind.

"Betcha that's what ya go fer eh Phil?" Billy had said wistfully.

I had shrugged; should I make up something, I wondered, remembering the heavy perfume and stiff rustle of her dress on the night of the Graduation Ball my vain attempt to kiss her in the porch and the sudden crash of the screen-door in the night-time silence.. and my hopeless feelings for Marta...

"Yer not f-----n' fruity are yer?" Billy had grinned. "That's what Mitch is sayin'.. yer a right pansy.

"A pansy.. ?" I had murmured confusedly.

"Yeah.. Yer knows queer... a f-----n faggot.."

I had felt my face glow hot with shame unable to speak, gazing helplessly over the dazzling waters; so that's what the others thought ..Mitch .. the Irish Sparkies.. Was it true perhaps?

Billy had given a low whistle. "I gets it! Yer a Cherry Boy. ..."

I had stayed silent ; acutely conscious of the vibrations from the propeller rising through me . "Cherry Boy...?" I finally said wonderingly.

"Yeah...Yer knows...never f------n' 'ad it. Screwed a woman.." Billy winked.

An indignant protest rose within me and then failed leaving me utterly ashamed ..humiliated.

"Tarts'll f----n' go fer yer Phil. Like f-----n' bees to f-----n' 'oney" Billy had added smirking affably.

"Oh, really .." I had murmured a sudden fierce throbbing in my veins; vague images floating before my half-shut eyes.. soft .. inviting voluptuous.. yielding. ...

"Say Phil, yer wanna try a fag?" Billy had asked suddenly holding out a pack of cigarettes.

"You bet.." I had said, examining the slim white tube; what would my mother think? Billy had scratched a match and I bent towards the tiny flame from the match almost invisible in the sunlight. Yes . this was real life..

I had leant back on the chair, sucking apprehensively then began coughing and choking violently, my eyes watering.

Billy had laughed. "Ya gets usta it after a bit."

"Yeah.." I had laughed still choking, a dull nausea forming in my stomach. Nervously I took another quick gasp and then quickly blew out; a plume of blue grey smoke ballooning in the sunshine.

"Now yer getting'it" Billy grinned approvingly.

I nodded, cautiously inhaling, luxuriantly rolling the smoke around my mouth, imagining the nicotine slowly passing through the walls of my mouth into the blood stream.. flooding the brain.. calming ..soothing. gratifying ..even the faint nausea somehow pleasing me. Was I becoming addicted so easily?

"Say Phil yer 'ave to buy some fer yerself when *Bond* opens next "Billy had commented when a little later when I had asked him for a another cigarette.

"What's the *Bond*?" I had wondered, conscious of pleasure in just having the pencil like white stick between my fingers.

"Don't know nuttin' does ya.." Billy had chuckled, cupping his hands around the small flame as I bent for a light. "Real Cherry Boy ain't ya."

"Yeah.." I had laughed happily.

Billy had gone on to explain that *The Bond*, was a kind of shop where the sailors could buy all the personal items needed on a long sea-voyages; necessities like soap and shaving cream, razors and toothpaste but also biscuits and sweets as well as beer and spirits and cigarettes, all very cheaply too, since once the ship was in International waters, there was no Excise Duty to be levied. But it was the Chief Steward who decided when it would open, at times a rumour that it was going to open that night would sweep the ship and sailors would gather expectantly but then it would turn out to be false which only added to the general discontent.

"'e don't care do 'e.." Billy had snarled. "Spends all day up in his cabin. Lazy fat.. bastard…"

"Hey, I think I might have seen him." I had cried out, recalling how I had been washing down the stairs to the top-deck when a strange gasping noise made me look up; sitting on the top of the steps was a fat little man, the white flesh in rolls; his small eyes peering at suspiciously down at me. Before I could get over my surprise the lump of flabby white flesh, with only underpants on had heaved itself up and with a loud gurgling belch shuffled off down the companionway.

"Yeah.. that's 'im.." Billy had laughed. "Pissed as newt.. all day long.. n' Mitch is 'is pal.. get all the booze n'fags 'e wants."

How unfair, I had thought becoming angry; why shouldn't I be allowed to buy cigarettes if I wanted; such a contempt for others and I had become even more indignant as Billy went on to tell me how as well refusing to open the *Bond*, the Chief Steward was notorious for purchasing poor quality goods from unscrupulous ship's chandlers at discount and then defrauded the Company by charging them full price.

"But why doesn't someone tell the Captain?" I had wondered shaking my head n puzzlement.

Billy had only laughed at me; the Captain was equally dishonest; the reason we had to be careful with the hot water was because he had had one of the fresh-water tanks removed to make space for wheat he bought privately; there was even a danger we might even run out of drinking water.

"What about the Company? Don't they know what's going on." I had asked despairingly. Billy had shrugged. Why should they care, as long as the ship made a profit? The company was owned by a German who had come to Britain a refugee just before the war.. he'd managed to buy a couple of old freighters, then when war was declared and he leased them out to British Government, they were sunk but be was able to claim compensation for more than they were worth and replace them... Now he had fleet of a half a dozen ships all with names ending in *Thorpe*.. like the *MV Scunthorpe* and *MV Cleethorpe* but rather than enjoying his wealth he was a miser, worrying about every expense... sacrificing anything for a greater profit.. the ship's engines were badly needing an overhaul; the life-boats weren't properly stocked and if they were needed they probably wouldn't come off the davits as the running gear was defective; though they hadn't been tried.. the whole ship was badly in need of a re-fit but as long as it floated the company ignored the problems..

I stared out over the unruffled shiny water; how could it be that that some penny-pinching old miser, the other side of the world, was putting the lives of some forty or more seamen in danger.. And how had he got so rich? Was it cleverness or ruthlessness.. or just luck.. ? If his ships hadn't been sunk by enemy action for example… but then didn't they say you made your own luck.. But surely he had a responsibility to do his best by his employees.. but then if he guessed the Captain and Chief Steward were swindling him .. But that wasn't the crew's fault ..moreover they had been promised the ship would be back in Britain last Easter but there was still no certain knowledge of when they would get back.. they had already been away twice as long as they had signed on for.. .

In a low voice tone Billy had added, the crew were so angry there was talk of taking direct action; their grievances exacerbated by the outcome of the recent strike.

Billy had gone on to describe the bitter strike of the previous winter; the Seamen's Union had made a demand for higher wages however the Ship-Owners Association said they couldn't afford it…profits were falling, trade was down and their was cut-throat competition from foreign companies especially those using flags of convenience; they offered half what was asked and not a penny more.

"Aint't we's the ones that makes 'em rich?" Billy had growled becoming more excited as he recalled the struggle between the Seamen's Union and the Ship-Owners Association supported by the Government that had became increasingly bitter. The Officers had their own union and had been bought off by a separate offer but still the seamen refused to give in despite the hardship it was causing their families. Occasionally there were violent scenes at the dock gates, the Police escorting the "scabs" trying to get through the picket lines.

Somewhat shocked I had listened in silence as Billy had told how he had seen a policeman his helmet knocked off by a stone, blood streaming down his face. "Serve 'im f----

-n right didn't it. I chucked a few too... smashed a few bus winders.. Scared 'em f-----g scabs stiff.." Billy had chuckled.

I stared away in silence, a momentary breeze flecking the gleaming surface; confused violent images dancing before my eyes. What would I have done? Would I have been swept up in the excitement of violence?

"You seen Docherty that big Irish A.B. in the Crew Mess. Well 'e mashed one of them f----g' scabs with n'iron bar." Billy had added his eyes fiercely bright.

Out of the glare of sunlight a giant phantom rose before my eyes, with cold horror, I saw the cowering scab, his fearful eyes, hands feebly up-raised, the iron-bar slowly coming down on the unprotected head and body.

"'E never got caught though. No one saw 'im..or too scared to say anyt'ing..." Billy had gloated.

I has smoked in silence as Billy had finished by explaining the newspapers most of them in the pay of the Ship Owners had exaggerated the violence and public opinion turned against them, the majority of seamen, especially those with families felt they had no choice but to accept the ship-owners offer. Some of the crew looked upon those who had agreed to call off the strike as traitors and all of them despised the Officers for not supporting them, especially the Captain who'd even tried to put to sea with a "scab" crew. The 1st Mate was the only officer that had any respect among the crew, even if he was a bully, at least he wasn't a tell-tell like the 2nd Mate..

Billy had even hinted at some plan being hatched by Hobbsie, the leader of the Day Gang a right Commie and Docherty. But he had warned me not so say a word to anyone, especially the Sec; one of his duties was cleaning the Captain's cabin and taking him up his meals as he never came to the Dining Room. 'A right f-----n' snitch...'e is ." Billy had concluded.

"Don't worry I hate his f------g guts.." I had snarled surprised by my vehemence; did I really hate him or was I becoming infected by the undercurrent of frustrated rage that possessed the crew ?

And yet all around us, I mused lay the serene, glittering vastness of the ocean.. I looked upwards seeing great white puffy clouds drifting majestically across the sky, imagining myself lying on the cottony softness looking down, the ship a tiny pointed chip, trailing white threads over the endless blue of the Pacific...

"C'mon Phil stop dreamin'. 'ave to get back ..Sec.'ll do 'is nut if we'se late back." Billy said coming up behind me and giving me a thump on the back.

"Hey!" I protested; once again the unchanging daily routine like some blunt iron-toothed wheel was dragging me helplessly around... and around.. endlessly around..

"C'mon then ..." Billy shouted over his shoulder, moving down the deck.

"Beat yer..." I challenged, dashing past him; my rubber thongs making a sticky thwacking noise as I dashed wildly down the Afterdeck.

Yes.. this is my life, I thought; leaping nimbly over the sill into the gloom of the Amidships Companionway, gasping in the hot, diesel-tainted air.

CHAPTER FIVE

"Pssst..! Phil,. Oi, Phil...! psssst."

What now? I thought irritably; braced against the roll and pitch of the ship my calf muscles ached; on all sides the piles of dirty dishes clattered and clinked; before me the grey, scummy dishwater rhythmically sloshed about the sink. And had I really grumbled about washing dishes at home, I mused remembering, as in some wonderful fantasy, steamy hot water gushing endlessly from the tap into heaps of foaming, gleaming suds.. .

"Psst... come here a mo. son..." Again I pretended I hadn't heard the hoarse whispering from behind me; why was it

Old Smelly, the nickname Billy and I had given Pete only bothered me when Billy wasn't around? I wondered

"Psstt.. just a mo.. gotta tellya oi Phil son.. .."

With a sigh I turned around to face Pete his bulky torso topped by a pink shiny bald head pushed halfway through the Hatch; only half listening to the usual complaint about the *Bond* not being opened even though we had been in international waters for weeks.

"And that ain't all .. by Harry... Engines .. is in a bad way..." Pete gasped his face a dark red colour, sweat coursing down his face and dripping off the rolls of fat under his chin.

"Really.." I murmured what if he got stuck in the Hatch? I thought suddenly; imagining how Billy and the two Cooks and I would have to form a line in the Officer's Dining Room .. all of us tugging with all our might at the enormous body until suddenly popped it out, sending everyone sprawling; just like an episode in silent movie comedy, I thought grinning at the mental image.

"Aint't no. . . laughing matter. .son.." "Pete puffed impatiently, the veins like twisted cords." Plates in hull., by Harry is splittin'.... Yer hear me.. ."

Yes . ? Well Jock always says that the old-fashioned rivets they used in the Clydeside shipyards are far superior to modern welding. "I observed trying to sound interested.

"Don't make no… difference now. .by Harry. * son. Seawater leaking in .. see.. wheat swells . ." Pete's gaped desperately for breath, his eyes starting from his face, now a dark purple colour.

What if he is about to have a heart attack, I thought staring fixedly at Pete's large flat nose, remembering Jock, had told me that when a sailor died at sea, the ship's carpenter had to sew a canvas shroud around him, finally passing the sail-makers needle through the dead manes nose to make absolutely sure that he wasn't still alive.

I grimaced thinking of a big needle going through the fleshy cartilage

"Hull' 11 burst … like a ripe melon…" Pete panted his massive chest heaving

"Yeah?" I murmured still thinking that there would have to be a funeral at sea; picturing the officers and crew, bareheaded at the ship's side.. a solemn voice intoning, 'Let us commit this soul to the deep..'.. then the desperate heave of the massive body over the rail; the large canvas parcel splashing down with a glitter of spray, as it slipped below the waves…

"N'down she goes…. Straight to the bottom.. see.. sudden by Harry… .lifeboats useless.." Pete managed to finally gasp out. "Really?" . I smirked imagining the canvas shroud drifting slowly down through the clear depths of the Pacific….

"No survivors see.. not a bloomin' trace by Harry… Not a trace. ." Pete puffed desperately his eyes bursting from his head.

"You don't say .." I murmured, in my mind's eye seeing the canvas rotting away revealing a white pulpy blob, stirred by the ocean currents, nibbled and sucked at by the grotesque creatures of the ocean floor…

"Kaput! Finito The End… Every man jack of us!" Pete groaned triumphantly and with a supreme effort jerked himself out of the Hatch back into the Dining Room.

Giggling to myself I went back to the sink and stared at the grey greasy dishwater sloshing back and forth in the sink.

Wasn't it in Conrad's *Lord Jim* that a cargo of rice had swelled with seawater during a storm and burst the ship's hull and sunk the ship? But surely it couldn't happen to a modern ship? And yet it was possible.... Old Smelly was exasperating but he did know a lot just the same.. and always there were unexpected disasters.. My poor parents! But how would they find out? A telegram from the Ship-Owners.. presumably.. my father frowning, as he carefully slit open the flimsy yellowish paper.

Ref: MV Grimthorpe registered Hartlepool Stop: *Failed to arrive China.* Stop: *Presumed sunk.* Stop: *All hands believed lost.* Stop.

And my mother.. her face white, staring, as she snatches the fatal telegram, reads it over., a desperate cry as she falls to the floor

I took a deep breath; the dull throb of the engines, the constant rattling of crockery, reasserting themselves.

"No. .no..". I protested angrily. "Not me.. not to me... .it couldn't happen to *me*... this was *my* life.. .nothing so awful could happen to *me*.... *me..*"

Through the port-hole above the sink, I watched the King-Posts sketching slow ellipses against the boundless blue sky. But wasn't that just egoism? Weren't the newspapers daily reporting tragic events.. ; traffic accidents . house fires.. plane crashes.. usually just a few columns of print .. just "news" to the indifferent readership..

And what if this thudding, vibrating mass of steel with a cargo of wheat and men were to suddenly founder? How quickly the frothy wake would quickly dissolve into the gleaming blue waters and the serenely glittering ocean would be as it had been ever since the beginning of the world...

My chest tightened and I gasped for breath; the ship's slow forward pitch vaguely threatening; no.. it couldn't happen... just couldn't.. impossible.. and yet why not?

"Wight. ...You almost finished here?" I started at the Sec.'s voice, wondering how long he had been watching me from the doorway.

"How about a look around the Engine-Room and the Bridge?'~ he proposed sternly, briskly thumping the door--jamb with an open hand.

"Sure.. .yeah.. .Sure.. I agreed without thinking, eager to free myself from morbid feelings clinging to my mind.

With unusual energy I quickly finished washing and drying and putting away the dishes, wondering why the Sec. had suddenly offered to take me on a tour of the ship; vaguely speculating what Billy might say.

A little later the Sec. returned and with a glance back around the Pantry I followed the lithe figure down the companionway; the bulkhead lights shining on the cream--painted metal breathing the hot acrid air feeling strangely remote quite as if I was a visitor being taken on a tour of the ship.. and would soon return home...

"Hurry up .. we haven't got all day.." The Sec. urged standing beside a wide metal door set into the companionway that I had passed everyday but never noticed.

He pulled down on a long handle shiny from use and tugged firmly the door rolled back with a dull rumble and a blast of oven-hot, oil-laden air, nauseating, suffocating swept over me.

The Sec. rammed the door shut.

"Like hell!" I laughed putting my hands to my ears against the hammering roaring noises.

Cautiously I followed the Sec. along the perforated metal catwalk, half-deafened by the noise punctuated by regular incessant pounding, as if somewhere far below a giant was bashing determinedly away with a sledgehammer.

Holding tightly to the guard-rail I gazed down into the subterranean depths, through a bluish oil-haze the glaring arc-lights reflecting off the expanse of machine casings, walkways and gratings in all directions ran bundles of shiny copper tubes and steel pipes leading to highly-polished brass knobs and levers; glimpsing of pallid human forms, with fluffy wads of cotton-waste and long-nosed, oil-cans, moving like sleep--walkers amongst the complex of machinery pausing to peer red-eyed at the various gauges and glass fronted dials..

Really like lost souls I thought both admiring and appalled, condemned forever to this thundering, thudding, oily hot hell... .

I glanced up, far above my head through the glinting skylights, was a vivid blue sky. Can this be the same world? I wondered dazedly following the Sec. along the narrow grating and back into the companionway.

"So what do you think of that?" The Sec. asked abruptly sliding the door shut with a crash.

"Pretty awful." I admitted shaking my head; the noise of the engine-room still ringing in my ears,my throat sore. " "

"You wonder how they can bear it.."

"You can put up with anything, if you have to..." The Sec. replied sternly pausing at the bottom of the stairs to next deck. Just like my father, I thought resentfully, pulling myself up by the handrail.

We reached the top deck without further words; the landing moving slowly up and down we crossed over to a door set in the dark wood-effect panelling on the bulkhead.

"Keep quiet now..." The Sec. warned opening the door to let me through first. "Captain doesn't tolerate noise on his Bridge." Immediately I was conscious of a hushed solemnity, several figures in white uniforms standing, legs apart.. motionless... silent.. gazing intently outwards through the wide windows running the length of the bridge. I stepped forward and gazed through the shining glass into an endless expanse of sparkling, dazzling ocean; the ship's gleaming white bow waves gently creasing the unruffled surface.... A tremor passed through me; ; such immensity of sea and sky.. a boundless.. unbearable empty vastness.....

I looked aside for relief taking in the tall figure of the Helmsman on a raised grated wooden platform, long legs spread wide, hands grasping the brass--tipped spokes of highly--polished, chest-high wheel, his eyes intent on the glassy dial shadowed by a hood of gleaming brass in front of him.

'Why it's Hank ~. the Yank'.. I murmured to my self, recognising the long, mournful face with a white scar on one cheek and a droopy moustache from the evenings in the Crew Mess; remembering how it was said he was on the run from the death-row of an American penitentiary.

As if sensing my look he gave a glance towards me and to my surprise winked at me. I smiled back.

At once a low warning voice broke the hush.

"Aye aye.. Sir.." Hank drawled obediently or was it disdainfully? I glanced towards at the speaker; his dark curly hair and ruddy face set off by the crisp white shirt, instantly recognising him as the Officer who had ordered me off the ship when I had first come aboard; conscious of an instinctive dislike and yet didn't I rather envy him.. up here on the Bridge.. giving orders.. smartly dressed in sharply creased white uniform, gold bands on his shoulder flashes.

No doubt he felt utterly superior to me.. a mere Cabin-Boy in ragged cut-off jeans and dirty T-shirt.

Now he glanced knowingly towards the clock-face control on a brass stalk beside the wheel, the shiny handle pulled down, the pointer on the white face indicating *FULL AHEAD*.

How amazing I thought that this silent, still place was intimately connected with the Engine Room and it's roar and stifling heat and oil--stench and yet they depended absolutely on the other; but then I considered neither of them could do their job without their daily meals; by necessity all of us were dependant on each other.

A gruff laugh made me look aside through the open doorway to an open-air extension of the Bridge where the Sec. was talking to a heavily built man in a short--sleeved white shirt with shoulder flashes. I felt myself go hot, as he fixing a keen gaze on me from under bushy eyebrows; the frowning severe look emphasized by black moustache and full beard. At once I guessed that he was the chief mate I had heard so much about; the one officer the crew, grudgingly respected or feared...

Were they talking about me, I wondered, daring a quick look back, the Chief Mate was still steadily watching me, one hand stroking the black wiry beard. Was he agreeing with the Sec. that the Captain had made a mistake in taking me ? I wondered my heart thumping under the stern look.

The Sec. came back to me, leaving the heavy--set, powerful figure his legs apart in an easy open stance, arms clasped behind the back, fearlessly gazing into the glittering vastness of the Pacific; surely nothing can go wrong with the ship if he is in command? I thought admiringly.

"This is the Chart Room." The Sec. said nodding towards an open door behind the Helmsman.

I peered inside, in a glance taking in a large sloping desk with an angle--lamp; above it rows of pigeon-holes filled with paper rolls;

"This is where the Navigation Officer plots our course.." The Sec. explained. "In bad weather the Deck officer can sleep on the bridge..."

I nodded, noticing at the far end of the room a single bunk-bed with tied-back curtains.

On the desk was pinned a large square of paper, a single fine line drawn straight through widely spaced concentric bands; just empty ocean, I thought with shudder.

"Door to skipper's cabin.".." The Sec. continued indicating a closed door at the back of the Chart Room.

"Captain Purser.." I murmured ; since I had been aboard I hadn't seen him and so had come to regard him something of theoretical entity; an ultimate authority that everyone referred to yet perhaps didn't actually exist..

"Wireless Room..." The Sec. waved towards a room near the door, partly hidden by a curtain draped over the entrance.

Inside could see a swivel chair in front of a narrow desk facing stacked grey-metal boxes faced with an array of knobs, dials and switches; there was a low hum underlined by a faint hissing with intermittent clicks.

"If it wasn't that the radio waves bounce off the ionosphere we wouldn't be able to receive radio waves so far from land" I remarked; was I trying to impress the Sec., I wondered at once feeling a little foolish.

"Perhaps you'd like to be a ship's Wireless Officer." The Sec. remarked thoughtfully as we moved to the Bridge door.

"Not really.." I said petulantly; really I shouldn't have agreed to come..

"Who do we have here?

An Officer, with a freckled, babyish face and pale ginger hair stood smiling at us as we came out onto the top-deck landing,

"New Cabin--Boy., signed on Vancouver.." The Sec. answered for me. "Wight this is the 2nd Mate.."

I nodded curtly, rather abashed by the softly spoken, smiling Officer.

"Seems a likely sort.." "The 2nd Officer commented, twitching his eyebrows, bleached by the sun.

"He does.." The Sec. said dryly. "Come on Wight, time you were back to your duties below."

What is he thinking, I wondered as side by side the Sec. and I went down the stairs together; conscious of a faint tension.

With each flight passed, the thudding of the engines and reverberations of the steel walls became stronger and the all- pervasive cooking and diesel smells; yes… down below decks is where I belong, I thought grimly.

"Finding it tough going are you, Wight?" The Sec. asked abruptly, as we neared the bottom deck; his voice less stern than usual.

"No.. not really.." "I muttered conscious of a choke in my voice.

There was a long silence; really I shouldn't of come I thought remembering Billy's warning..

"You and Billy getting on O.K?" The Sec. wondered casually.

"Sure.. we're best mates." ." I responded sullenly.

The Sec. regarded with a faint frown. "A word to the wise don't let him influence you too much." He remarked stiffly, adding "Better get back to work now…"

I looked after the trim, muscular figure in black trousers and white T--shirt passing down the companionway. So he he must think that I was too much under Billy's influence? Was it true? I wondered self-critically.. was I losing my own identity..? *

Turning quickly I almost bumped into Mitch coming the other way "Watch it ya mincing pansy!" He snarled glaring fiercely at me. "One of these days….."

"Sorry Mitch." I whimpered my heart jumping, ashamed of my fearfulness; perhaps he was right to despise me I thought, sighing, more than ever conscious of my isolation .. .

"Right brown nosin' sneak ain'tcha…" Billy sneered already he had heard about me going to see the Engine Room and Bridge with the Sec.; there was very little of what went on that wasn't known by the entire crew within a few minutes of it happening I had learnt.

"No.. no." "I protested yet somehow without conviction; unable to remember how it had come about; as if it had happened without my consciously wanting it.. as if I had no will at all.

"Betcha 'opes 'el1 give yer an easy time of it.." Billy grumbled his face a cruel mask behind the cigarette smoke.

I shook my head; how unfair, I thought yet really I deserve it..

"Ya.. listenzee .. ze *Bond* . .zee *Bond* she.. open!"

It was Tad, one of the two Deck Boys, at the Crew Mess doorway his gangly body jerking and twitching convulsively.

Ya.. it true.." He screeched his pinched, pitted face contorted with grimaces but still no one in the Crew Mess moved, perhaps not quite believing the news after so many false alarms I thought and then Tad with his screeching voice and bulging, staring eyes could hardly be considered a reliable witness.

"Ain't no lie.. *Bond* be . .open mateys!"

This time it was Norrie, the other Deck Boy who had pushed past Tad to make the announcement in a languorous drawl; his round face beaming contentedly.

Still no one moved and then as one or two got hesitantly to their feet glancing doubtfully at each other then there was a scuffing of boots as everybody except old Paddy, rushed to the door, eager to be as close to the top of the queue as possible.

Billy had already warned me that the Chief Steward sometimes shut the *Bond* without warning even though everyone had been served.

As if by some instinct seamen were arriving from all over the ship and the companionway was soon full along it's entire length; a solid mass of men jostling and laughing excitedly.

Like a crowd before a football match, I thought managing to squeeze myself in between Billy and the two Deck Boys. Beside me were a couple of Greasers, bare to the waist, the gaunt bodies were pallid, faces smirched with oil, teeth gleaming white between bright red lips as they chatted cheerfully in a soft lilting accents; the colourful bandanas around their necks giving them the appearance of gypsies or tramps.

How much longer do you think.." I asked Billy after awhile beginning to feel faint in the muggy air, heavy with diesel and sweat smells; caught in the see--sawing movement of the close pressed bodies.

-"Look out!. Let the youngster pass"

"Needs room.. give 'im more room loike.."

Cheery voices bellowed around me and I felt myself propelled forward by rough hands to find myself standing in front of the Chief Steward ensconced behind a flap across the doorway of a large cupboard next to the Galley. Beside him was Mitch, leering sarcastically, a cigarette hanging from his lips.

Behind them in shadowy recess lit by a bare light bulb swinging slowly on long flex, I could see long shelves with a scattering of cardboard boxes; biscuits.. chocolate-bars.. cartons of cigarettes..

So this was the *Bond,* I thought wryly, after all the speculation excitement and anticipation just a large cupboard with half-empty shelves; even so I felt a joyousness; noticing the familiar red wrapper of McVities Digestive biscuits; my mother's favourite with her cup of tea..

"Come on.. then .. What' it be. What it be!" The Chief Steward demanded peevishly, glaring at me over half-moon glasses

"Cat got yer f----n' tongue." Mitch snapped thrusting his face close to mine.

I stammered out a request for biscuits and cigarettes and noticing aerogramme letters and asked for a packet.

"Writin' to Mummy are we... .' Mitch sneered putting down the pad along with my other requests.

I flushed hotly. "And some razor blades, please." I added remembering I'd forgotten to bring any and absently touching the fluffy down on my chin.

"Shavin' yer armpits again are we darlin'" Mitch drawled in a falsetto; the companionway rang with shouts and hoots of laughter "Enough of that!" The Chief Steward ordered shrilly, raising his head, his small eyes peering coldly at me.

"This will be deducted from your wages of course." He squeaked pompously, handing me a pen and a fat pink finger pointing to line in the large ruled ledger open on the wooden flap.

I signed my name without even looking, desperate to get away; clutching my purchases I went past the darkened Pantry and out on deck, taking a deep breath; how humiliating .. to jeered and laughed at .. Behind me I could hear one of the seamen arguing about the cost of some item.

"Thaat be five toimes whaat it be baak home" He was shouting. "Bloody highway robbery I caalls it. Whaat yer say Maateys?"

An low rumble came from the men packed in the companionway. Was this the spark that would ignite a mutiny I wondered; wasn't it always some tiny incident that brought about violent upheavals?

"Stop this noise this instant or I'll close the *Bond.*" "The Chief Steward ordered a steely note in his squeaky voice and at once there was almost complete silence.

What a brute he is; to swindle them when they have to work so hard and yet they can't help but obey him I thought moving along around the outside of the Amidships, finding a relief in the dully throbbing, shadowy darkness on deck.

The queue had shrunk by the time I reached the door from afterdeck and I was able to slip down the companionway and get into the cabin unnoticed. Like Christmas, I grinned putting my purchases on the bunk-bed.. and pulling myself up onto my bunk-bed; carefully opening the packet of biscuits and slipping one out ; relishing the moment; my mouth watering ..

"Uggh! ... stale.. and horribly rancid." I exclaimed in disgust; probably years old; what a shameless cheat the Chief Steward was.. selling off old goods at inflated prices...

No wonder almost all the seamen smoked, I considered now tearing open the carton of *Camel* cigarettes.. our one consolation..

I lit one up thinking how I was defying the Sec. who had forbidden smoking in the cabin. Did he really think I was being corrupted by Billy? I wondered. But what business was it of his anyway? I grumbled to myself watching the smoke from my cigarette tip curl away and fan into a thin wisps. It was true I was already addicted to cigarettes but perhaps I wanted to be corrupted; wasn't that,in a way, why I had come to sea? After all wasn't it essential for a man. . .to know the bad in this world as well as the good.. ?

But where was Billy? I jumped down taking the packet of stale biscuits and went back out into the companionway; already it was deserted with no sign of Billy or the two Deck Boys. I went out on deck and flung the biscuits into the darkness, the packet vanishing without sound. Let's hope the fishes aren't so fussy I grinned, going along the amidships until I came up against the heavy steel door that led to the foredeck.

Never before had I passed through it, somehow considering it off bounds to all but the Deck Crew, now seeing the large clasps were hanging disengaged, on an impulse I pulled it wide enough to slip through; pulling it quickly shut behind me.

For a minute I stood still, the hollow clang fading away in an eerily silent world, the dull insistent throbbing of the ship's engines abruptly cut off.

Furtively I moved out along down on the darkened foredeck, my eyes straining at the vague outlines; king posts.. stanchions, hatches and booms dimly emerging out of the shadowy blackness.

I kept on, the deck rising to meet me, shuddering slightly, before falling away, only to lift again in a slow, irresistible rhythm; my rubber thongs making a soft squishy noise, all about a vast impenetrable darkness and above a dense web of brilliant glittering stars ..so intensely bright and so many.. .. so many.. beyond numbering.. I marvelled with a sharp ache.

I walked slowly on feeling myself drawn forward, hearing my heart beating, almost as if I was sleep--walking, straight on, not daring to look around for some reason.

I came to a short flight of metal stairs that had appeared out of the shadows, without hesitation I quickly pulled myself up by the handrail; pausing at the top, making out shadowy humps scattered over the fo'c'lse deck.

I listened intently, catching at a faint hoarse shushing sound.. like the wind in the trees.... enticing . .persuasive... I turned aside pressing my chest against ship's side then with a quick scramble I had pulled myself onto the bulwark, leaning over edge, a draught of salty air rushing over my face, far below a faint white band glimmered out of darkness.

'To cease upon the midnight with no pain.. Half in love with easeful death..' passed through my mind, imagining myself slipping downward, plunging irrevocably toward the whispering pale shimmer below..

"Harrahcccch!"

I dropped back onto the deck, my heart thumping.

"Harrahcccch!"

And then the sound of a noisy expectoration, I smiled to myself, it must be the Look-Out thinking himself alone vigorously clearing his throat and spitting.

I stretched myself out, the deck rising and falling beneath me; the black outline of ship's bows sawing vainly at the starry night-sky; hearing a faint rasping hiss; the ship pushing endlessly through the infinite darkness; a sad hopelessness taking hold of me.. to what end. - to what end..?

Slowly I became aware of a faint warbling, a weak, tremulous piping... the Look-Out, singing to cheer himself on his solitary watch; and I smiled to myself somehow reassured, the weak tuneless, quavering, mediating the infinite immensity of the night.

Abruptly it ceased to be followed by repeated scratching noises; like some tiny animal or insect I thought; then the unmistakable smell of cigarette smoke wafted to me through the warm air and I understood the Look--Out who ever he was, must be risking a 'fly' smoke without being seen from the Bridge; remembering that Tad had been severely reprimanded for disobeying the prohibition on showing even the tiniest light while on look-out duty.

Better get back, I thought suddenly heavy with fatigue; sleepily I made way back down the steps and started along the foredeck.

Looking aside I saw with a start of wonder, that the moon had risen, perfectly round, laying flickering silvery pathway across the black waters;.

How lovely, I thought, starting on down the deck; dogged by a small shadow awash with moonlight; the king-posts and stanchions pointing black accusing fingers out over the silvered water;

Before me the amidships rose up like some enchanted silver-walled castle studded with square shot-holes, the Bridge showing a faint greenish glow.

My legs seeming to be moving of their own will, down the sloping deck; the gleaming luminosity dispensing a deep serenity over all around me. .

Was this really me, Phillip Wight, I questioned absently .. . here.. now...in this moment of pure silver radiance fallen out of endless time.. ..

A ghostly, moon-lit figure appeared above me, I must have been spotted by the Officer of the Watch, I thought calmly ignoring the single shout into the silent night, only intent on gaining the upper berth.

With a muted squeal the door to the Amidships swung open at the first push and I stepped through pulling the door shut; the sonorous clank instantly absorbed by the dull thudding of the engines.

Was it all an illusion, I wondered sleepily stumbling down the dim-lit companionway, breathing the familiar sickly, stifling air; thinking of the mutinous anger smouldering amongst the crew.. yes it was all here.. waiting for me.. unchanging . . .inevitable.. to be accepted .. endured.. Were my father and the Sec. right then? You can endure anything if you have to..?

CHAPTER SIX

A cigarette smoking between my fingers, I let my eyes wander around the cream-painted steel walls of the crew-mess, starkly bright under the bare fluorescent light tubes; like a factory canteen I mused, examining the eight greyish patterned formica-topped tables with black tubular legs bolted to the heavily scuffed brown lino floor and the attendant black metal chairs with red vinyl seats and backs. But then I considered, sending a plume of smoke towards the nicotine brown ceiling, the incessant dull thudding of the ship's engines and the unique odour of diesel, male sweat and cooking smells made it very different. .. and of course the four oblong portholes along one wall.. ... black and shiny.. reminders of the vastness of the Pacific Ocean the other side of the steel bulkhead.

I took another deep draw on my cigarette; imagining the nicotine entering my blood stream, obliterating the greasy rancid aftertaste of the dinner; smoothing away my anxiety and discontent... .. yes cigarettes were a wonderful thing.. a necessity. ..

I was waiting for Billy to come back to start our next round of cribbage .. now a part of our regular routine. As usual at this time a crowd of seamen entered the crew-mess their voices ringing around the metal walls their boots scuffing noisily before choosing different tables and settling to card-games.

Casually I studied them stripped to the waist, showing gaunt bodies their, toil-worn faces made leathery by wind and sun, now silent except for the occasional low growl. My eyes moved on to a few solitary individuals, their grizzled heads bent almost to their knees, smoking or silently staring into space

What are they thinking? I wondered, the intently staring eyes, telling of long hours at the wheel or lonely vigils on Look-Out... gazing unwearyingly into the vast empty glare of the open sea by day or the infinity of the starry sky at night..

And am I becoming like them? I wondered; living beside them in the same vibrating throbbing metal walls.. getting up in the dark .. ..breathing the same close oven-hot air.. eating the same sodden, soggy tasteless meals.. and smoking ..

Absently I watched the smoke from the tip of my cigarette curling and wreathing upwards, merging into the blue-grey haze from the numerous cigarettes clinging to the low ceiling; looking away, my eyes went to the Hatch at the far end of the room closed of from the Galley by a grey metal shutter; on the counter below, for the Watch still on duty were set out four covered dishes containing as I knew from my own evening meal a congealed stew of gristly meat with watery potatoes and luridly -orange tasteless carrots.. and beside the plates, four bowls with an almost inedible rubbery steamed pudding and thin, sugarless custard..

Just the thought of it made me feel faintly nauseous gorge rise.... and yet no matter how much the crew grumbled about the bad cooking, I noticed they always ate it greedily and often competed for second helpings; not to be hungry was quite sufficient . .

Perhaps in time I might be like that too.. I mused gratefully inhaling the soothing cigarette smoke; yet always at the back of my mind was the knowledge that for another few weeks and I would be gone .. for them it was their life.. in the thundering and stifling oily heat of engine room or out on deck in all weathers .. the burning sun and icy spray-laden wind.. enduring hardship and discomfort with a stoical acceptance that I could only marvel at...

"Dreamin' of tarts betcha.." Billy laughed coming up to the table.

I flushed hotly, shaking my head; Billy enjoyed teasing me of my ignorance of women.

"Actually I was wondering about the old seamen sitting staring.. What d'y reckon there thinking about? Maybe of their life at home ..or the ships they sailed on or old ship-mates.. maybe drowned at sea."

"Bad luck to say that . "Billy frowned putting the cribbage board and deck of cards on the table.

"Some of 'em 'ardly ever goes ashore.. never get pissed or go with tarts.. like we'se gonna, eh matey.." He added sitting down opposite me.

"Sure thing. "I grinned again flushing hotly.

Billy began breaking up match sticks to use as markers; the cribbage board was too, was make-do, a length of old wood with holes burnt in it but for Billy and me it was a cherished object, kept safely in a clothes drawer in the cabin until fetched to the crew-mess for our ritual evening game.

Billy began to deal out the cards and then leant towards me speaking in a low voice.

"See Old Paddy.. Seventy if 'es a day.. Never goes ashore when we're in Port.. volunteers to be Watchman. a real money-grubber.. Jus' look at 'im. Should be in a f----'n nursing 'ome."

I twisted around to look at the old Irish greaser, who always sat in the same place in one corner of the crew-mess; wearing a string-vest, the loose skin and scrawny neck made me think of a plucked chicken.

His head of sparse white hair was bent over a Bible, a single gnarled finger moving slowly across the page, his thin lips moving slightly as he mouthed the words.

Billy's right I thought contemptuously, he's much too old and feeble to be at sea.. you need to be young and active..

I picked up my cards and began to examine them, somehow the familiar dog-eared greasy playing cards drew me into another state of existence; timeless, ordered, purely symbolic and yet rousing the fiercest emotions; bitter disappointment at a low card; unbounded joy at a face-card, Jack, King, Queen; stiff, sternly staring, formal, unchanging yet utterly faithless, shamelessly ready to serve either player; bringing joy, grief, resignation, hope; all at the turn of a card...

"And twenty one and out!" I cried, pegging the match-stick to the last hole.

"Yer jammy Bastard." Billy grinned.

I tapped the ash off the tip of my cigarette into the flimsy metal ashtray, gazing complacently around at the worn gaunt faces obscured by the wreathing bluish-grey smoke; flushed with triumph.. just as if it was real life, I thought absently.

"Hobbsie's 'aving a go at Paddy." Billy said with a jerk of his head, pausing as he shuffled the cards.

I glanced around. Standing over the old greaser was a powerfully built man, stripped to the waist, a pelted stomach bulging over his trouser belt, his dark mahogany coloured skin gleaming under fluorescent light. I remembered him very clearly as the seaman who had stared fiercely at me when I had come aboard in Vancouver.

Now I knew him to be Hobbsie, something of a power amongst the crew, feared and admired and like Murdoch, a stalwart of the Seaman's Union. He was the leader of the Day-Gang, a much-envied elite who only worked 9am to 5pm each day and had Sundays off; he was renowned his undisguised contempt for the Officers generally and the Bo'sun in particular.

This was the first time I had seen him in the crew-mess; usually preferred to keep to his own cabin with a few favoured mates rather than mix with the rest of the crew.

"Caom on Paddy," He boomed out in a thick Geordie, as I had learnt to recognise it, accent intent on attracting the attention of the others in the crew-mess. "Tell us ignorant heathens.. whoat's so f----n' interestin' abaat t'Bible, heh?"

"What ever you say, Mr Hobbs sorr" Paddy piped in a soft Irish accent, nervously running a hand through his thin white hair.

"No, What ever *tha* say.. ." Hobbsie insisted turning to wink at the other seamen all eyes on him.

Paddy's pale blue rheumy eyes looked sadly back, a deprecating smile twitched over his thin lips.

"Coame on yer oald boag-trotter.." Hobbsie drawled irritated by old greasers passivity. "Leats haave soame o'yer Irish f-----g blarney eh lads?"

"Betta no let Murdoch hear you slagging of t'Irish loike…" One of the seamen looked up from his cards to call out and the crew-mess rang with raucous laughter.

Hobbsie shrugged his broad shoulders, glistening with sweat.

"'E knouws Murdoch's got put t' lookout-duty fer calling t'Bo'sun a buuggering uld goaat.." Someone else shouted out.

With a nimbleness surprising for a such a heavily-built man

Hobbsie turned about and scooped up the Bible, holding it over the astonished old greaser in large paw-like hand.

A low gasp echoed around the room

"So whoat ye going doa noaw? Turn t'other f-----g' cheek wouald tha?" Hobbsie roared out, holding the black bound Bible aloft; turning triumphantly towards the others.." Doan't look loike the meek will inherit t'earth do it."

"What a laugh! Look at Old Paddy…f-----n' shittin' 'imself"

Billy grinned from behind a veil of cigarette smoke.

"Yeah.." I sniggered; somehow the flabby white skin of the old greaser disgusted me and why did he have spend every evening, mouthing away to himself oblivious of all else?

"C'mon Paddy…." Hobbsie jeered, his arm of bulging muscle and taut sinew holding the Bible over Paddy, his eyes upraised beseechingly.

"Tha' knoaws it be a lot o' f----g claap-traap… T'Virgin Birth.. Changing water t' wine.. Hung on a cross n'risen from the deaad in three days…Tha doan't reaaly believe tha' does tha.."

Still Old Paddy kept a pathetically passive silence; his Adam's apple bobbling convulsively.

"Coom, Paddy saay it's all nowt but fairy stories, n' I'll giv'it tha back." Hobbsie teased lowering the Bible in front of the old greaser's eyes.

The crew-mess had fallen silent; the engines pounding dully through the metal-walls.

"So whaot yer say if I goes n' chuucks yer Holy Bible, f-----g overboard.." Hobbsie demanded making to step away from the table.

A low growl filled the crew-mess.

"Bad luck thaat Hobbsie.." A voice said gravely.

Hobbsie shrugged and contemptuously dropped the Bible with a bang onto the table. Paddy started and then reached a trembling hand towards it .

"Thankee Mr Hobbs surr, thankee greatly." He crooned, a thin line of spittle running from the corner of his mouth

"Just right fer a fool in his dotaage…" Hobbsie growled in deep voice moving heavily away, his cropped head ranging from side to side, making me think of a glossy-coated bear reared up on it's hind-legs scenting the air ..

I quickly began dealing out the cards, keeping my head down, my heart beating, thinking that I could be the next victim. 'Please God .. not me,.. not me' I silently pleaded, blaming myself for being so heartless towards Paddy.

I stole quick sideways glance, feeling a momentary relief at seeing Hobbsie in close conversation with a skinny thin-faced man, his bald head fringed with grey hair, bobbing up in down as he expressed his utter agreement; a real toady, I thought my eyes drawn to the fleshily muscular, supremely confident, leader of the Day Gang. Instinctively he turned and our eyes met; with dismay I saw him shambling purposefully towards me, a broad, sardonic grin on his fleshy face.

"Now yer saw me taalking Tommy didn't tha?" He boomed genially, deliberately planting two large hands on the table before me.

I nodded staring at the large paunch pressed into the table-edge, the sausage-like fingers splayed out, supporting his trunk-like arms; suffusing me with powerful feral-like body odours.. yet somehow familiar.

"I was tellin' him see that new Cabin boy over there just t'chaap to help us." Hobbsie carried on affably and yet I sensed a faint menace too. "College boy n'all"

"Er not really.." I laughed noticing the cigarette between my fingers trembling. "I should have.. er started this September you see.. but well I came to sea.. instead...." I gave an appealing glance.

"Is thaat so. Well.. Well.. Coom to sea did tha raather than College.. Well that's a good un' ain't it laads?" Hobbsie guffawed his mouth gaping. A hoarse murmur ran around the crew-mess.

"But tha's clever chap, any road...intelleegent loike eh...." Hobbsie flung out an arm and caught up a chair and dragged it scraping noisily over to table.

I glanced over at Billy his chair tipped back watching his carefully formed smoke-rings disintegrate into wispy fragments.

"Tha' knoaws we'se be crossing t' International Date-Line..." Hobbsie he drawled enticingly.

"International Date Line... sure, sure..." I chirped nervously visualizing the brightly-coloured map of the world hanging on the classroom wall and vaguely remembering a line dissecting the bright blue space identified in large letters: *Pacific Ocean*. And now I'm crossing it; I thought dizzily.

"So what we ignorant sailors want to knoaw is.." Hobbsie paused for dramatic effect, revelling in the attention he was getting from the others.

"Does we gain .. a day or lose a day...?"

"Well..er ..it depends what you ..er mean by lose... or by gaining.." I stammered conscious of all eyes on me; my head whirling; a sickening feeling in my stomach.

"Tha doan't knoaw does tha?.." Hobbsie roared delightedly.

"Actually from East to West you gain a day." I blurted out; my heart thumping.

There were grunts of approbation and nods of agreement and I grinned with relief; I must have guessed correctly.

"So tell us this.." Hobbsie demanded his elbows closer to me; his stale breath hot on my face.

"Tha not loike old Paddy art tha? Tha' doant believe in that superstitious claptrap.. God.. n' goin' to Church.. ?"

"Not really .." I said weakly; struck by sudden flashes of memory; a little boy, bored and yawning being fiercely nudged by my sister in a pew at Sunday service and the dinner time when mother had left the table in tears, when in an argument with my brother I had denied the existence of God.

"Not really?" "Hobbsie snorted contemptuously, his teeth gleaming white in his darkly tanned face." I thought tha were a clever laad..

I looked down at the table, my heart beating heavily; surely I could admit I didn't believe in God. . .

Around me came a murmur of voices.

"Doan't be too haard on him Hobbsie."

"He's just a laad.."

"Easy does it Hobbsie.."

"Aye.. aye.." Hobbsie guffawed genially reaching out an arm.

I tensed stiffly, as his roughly calloused finger chucked me on my chin.

"A right good laad.. ain't he mateys? Bet his mummy warn'd him abaout us heathen mariners loike..."

"C'mon let's play cribbage.." Billy interjected irritably; laying down a card.

Hobbsie slowly pushed himself upright.

"What I was thinking' you being almost almost a college laad loike if you'd help sum of us, write letter's home.."

I nodded slowly, flushing warmly; was this my chance to become accepted?

"Seein us ignorant mariners.. never haad no schoolin' how to write and spell proper.. What'dy say laad..?" Hobbsie added with a slyly kindly smile.

"Yes.. I be only to pleased.. delighted to help...." I heard my voice ring out, glancing over at Billy behind wisps of cigarette smoke, a disdainful curl on his lips.

"What a right decent chaap! Ain't he mateys?" Hobbsie bellowed heartily.

"If yer say so Hobbsie!" One of them looked up from his cards to call out to a sudden ripple of laughter.

For a minute or so, Hobbsie stood his arms crossed over his broad, chest surveying the crew-mess with a complacent lordly mien before giving me a broad, conspiratorial wink he turned and left the room sliding the door shut with a loud thump..

The seamen's voices became a distant hum with the inescapable thudding of the engines; as if I had entered into a trance I played on; my hand mechanically moving the broken match-sticks in quick stabs up and down the home-made cribbage board; taking my turn with Billy to shuffle and deal.. both of us silent except for the odd grunt or groan.

All the while my mind was flooded with glowing visions.. seated figures, their grizzle work worn heads noses almost touching the crew-mess tables, work-hardened, clumsy fingers laboriously tracing out letters, absently biting the pencil tops while…. I fulfilling my destiny, even I.. walked slowly past gently correcting and complimenting, dispensing with supreme generosity my hard-won, school-learning …

A gentle hissing made us both look around. Near to the door a lanky figure was bent over a small square wireless-set fixed to a small shelf at once I recognised Hank,the American seaman who I had seen as Helmsman. His eyes staring away into some distant place, his droopy moustache almost touching the cloth-covered speaker, his long fingers on one of the small black bakelite knobs.

All around the room heads looked up; watching ..frowning critically… The hissing grew louder, fiercer followed by a faint high-pitched squealing.

Voices came from all around the room.

"He never give's up does he?"

"At it again is he?"

Yer a blasted maniac, Yank…"

Oblivious to the comments, Hank stayed stooped over the little wooden-box one hand resting lightly on the top, his head cocked, listening intently to the hissing and cracklings, his eyes growing bright as a gabble of voices emerged from the chaos of static. A smile of deep contentment creased Hank's long lined face and he turned up the volume. "*In the interests of world peace, universal harmony and understanding, the United Soviet Socialist Republics….* "The anonymous announcer declared in a formal yet accented voice, all around the crew-mess heads turned to listen but almost at once the voice became fainter, drifting off into an incoherent warbling and squeals before vanishing altogether in an infinity of shrill ear-piercing hisses … .

Ya! Put f-----n' sock in it will ya!" One of the seamen shouted angrily.

Hank gave a deprecating smile, shrugged his bony shoulders and reluctantly turned off the set with a decisive click, before ambling to the back of the crew-mess.

What is going through his mind? I wondered watching the lanky figure drop into an empty chair and place his head between his hands to look sadly at the floor. Was it true he had killed his wife. .? Perhaps he was reliving that moment of blind jealous rage when his fingers pressed her soft, pulsing neck, the bulging eyes staring up at him in mute, helpless appeal, then the kind of relief, even ecstasy, as the body went limp.. and then…. the horror of realization.. Or had the memory faded become indistinct … dream-like blurred; almost as if it happened to another person.

"C'mon your turn." Billy said sharply. "Yer gotta concentrate on what yer f----n' doin' Or yer keep losin'"

"Sure .. I was just wondering about Hank." I said picking up my cards. "Practically every night here on a ship out in the middle of the ocean he twiddles away at that ancient wireless and almost all he ever gets is this awful static.."

"A f-----n' nutter ain't 'e. "Billy said smoke drifting over his face from a cigarette in the corner of his mouth.

"It's like he's obsessed with searching for something ..that maybe doesn't even exist…" I said staring hard at my cards; how to know what went on in someone else's mind..

"Hurry up will ya.. .." Billy grouched tapping ash from his cigarette.

"Sure .. sure.." I said picking a card almost a random from the corner of my eyes seeing the flimsy metal ashtray meandering over the table-top and then the cigarette packets match-box and cribbage board began to slide too.. like some weird dream I thought absently.

From across the room came a loud crash as an empty chair flung itself across the room; vaguely I was conscious of my own chair trying to escape from under me at the same time as an invisible force pressed me into the table edge.

I glanced around, clutching the table to keep my balance noticing the room had assumed an acute angle.

From all sides came muttered oaths and laughter along with scuffing of boots and scraping of chairs.

"She musta come into a helluva swell.." One of the seaman chuckled.

Just as it seemed the room was stuck indefinitely at the steep angle it sank slowly back down but then only to rise in the opposite direction; the cards and ashtrays and other items that had piled up against the bulkhead, now slipping and tumbling crazily back again.

"Bit of fun eh!" Billy grinned, smoking nonchalantly, one leg braced against a table leg.

"Yeah..." I muttered hanging onto the table, my stomach heaving uncomfortably.

Perceptibly the heaving and plunging became less pronounced and I found I could release my hold on the table, the floor settling down to it's usual regular movement.

Giggling and laughing Billy and I scrambled about the floor, picking up the ash-tray, cribbage-board and scattered playing cards and putting them back on the table.

"That was fun.." I joked as we resumed our game; catching a faint note of relief in my voice; had I really been frightened?

Billy nodded and began dealing out the cards.

I glanced around the crew-mess seeing once again a narrow cream-painted steel box, the harsh glare of the fluorescent light shining through the columns of wreathing blue cigarette smoke; the seated figures studying their cards with the occasional low growl or laugh and the others sitting alone staring away in silent contemplation and Old Paddy once mouthing over the words marked by his slowly moving finger.

As if nothing had happened I mused.

"Ya shouldn'ta let Hobbsie 'ave yer on Phil."

Billy's voice came to me from below out of the thudding darkness of the cabin.

I stiffened; had I made such a fool of myself?

"All that writin' letters 'ome .." Billy sneered yawning.

"Yeah .. sure .." I murmured contritely, in my sleep-dazed brain I had been carefully chalking large letters on a make-do blackboard watched by admiring, grateful old seamen.

But perhaps Billy was wrong, I thought, as I began to fall asleep; perhaps Hobbsie and the others genuinely wanted my help... .. perhaps Billy envied me .. . perhaps..

Then I was awake, the bunk-bed rising steeply steadily beneath my stiffened body.. Another swell. I concluded calmly, gripping the mattress tightly .. thinking of gleaming night-black ocean, flat calm beneath the glittering stars .. and then from out of the darkness, rolling irresistibly forward. .. enormous ridges of water.. colossal humped monsters. . .faceless .. formless ..nameless.. travelling across the watery surfaces of the planet.. from what distant place had they come? What power had shaped them? For what purpose.. ? And where were they bound? But already sleep was claiming my exhausted mind ..

CHAPTER SEVEN

"Ye'll be looking for land, sonny."

"Sort of .." I said, turning from the rail. "Can you see anything Chips.. ..?"

The old ship's carpenter put down the faded green canvas hold-all at his feet and gazed keenly, out to sea then slowly raised a sinewy brown arm to point out over the glittering water.

I turned back holding the vibrating rail, staring vainly into the mid-morning brightness.

"Nothing .." I laughed glancing aside at the old Virgin Islander; his silvery hair swept back like a bird's wing, his fine boned face in profile, like sharp-eyed hawk I thought his leathery brown face crazed with fine lines. Billy said he was a bit mad, I remembered.

"Aye... land sure enough.." Chips intoned his sharp head like a carved canoe-prow thrust outward.

I sighed and shook my head, discouraged.

A smile creased the old seaman's face. "Don't force it... best to let it come of itself.. like all things in this world.."

Half closing my eyes I let them pass along the line of the horizon; seeing a long, thin cloud ... yet darker, unvarying...fixed...strangely un-cloud like..

"Yes! land !. . land.. yes ..land.." I chanted excitedly; thinking how wonderfully the word sounded and the idea too ..so solid and unmoving; grass and trees and roads and traffic people.. passers-by ..strangers.

"Aye and we'll be walking on it soon enough.." Chips said in a resigned voice.

"Don't you want us to dock?" I asked, surprised. "All the ship has been talking about nothing else for days."

"Aye.. aye" Chips chuckled good-naturedly. "They might well do but there's nothing but confusion and complication in the end.."

"But we can't stay at sea all the time and anyway I thought the ship badly needed some repair work.." I said gazing longingly a softly-crayoned line rising indelibly out of the shimmering vastness, my heart beating faster.

"Aye.. It's necessary times ... But all those people squabbling over for they don't know what.. ." Chips shook his head dolefully.

"Still it will be good to feel solid land under our feet again.." I insisted glancing back at the old seaman's weather-worn face; was he a little bit cracked perhaps?

"Thy might think so.. but it's only out here.." Chips made a wide sweeping gesture the rolled-up sleeve of his shirt, slipping down to show a lilywhite bicep.

"The sea and sky.. thee can come close to God."

"But it's definitely Japan is it?" I insisted, strangely shocked at the sight of the unblemished white skin ; as if I had seen deep into his soul.

"Aye.. never thee fret.. sonnie" Chips said a smile on his darkly aquiline face . "And here be some to lead us in.." He added with movement of his silvery grey head.

I frowned not understanding but then looking back I was amazed to see, as if created out of air, wheeling effortlessly above the ship's stern birds; their outstretched wings a brilliant white against the clear blue sky.

"Seagulls.." I exclaimed delightedly.

"Messengers . . to bring us to port .." Chips said solemnly and then with a nod at me he shouldered his tool-bag in a single movement and moved off down the deck in a springy rolling gait.

I gave a last lingering look at the dark shadow clinging persistently to the horizon, before turning back with a frown. Surely Chips couldn't be right .. ? I thought stepping over the sill into Officer's Smoking Room; breathing the hot stale air; the walls vibrating with the incessant thud of the engines. Really life at sea was unbearable.. . At the thought of land I felt almost sick with longing .. Probably Chips has been too long at sea.. I decided, picking up the cloth I had thrown down and kneeling on the vinyl settle began to shine brass-work on the port-holes.

"Japan... Japan.. the East .. the mysterious orient.." I whispered exultingly to myself; my heart beating fiercely, almost dizzy with flickering images; vague and shadowy .. small soft hands ..bright smiling eyes.. Ronnie kept boasting how wonderful the Japanese women were .to give men pleasure . How lucky we were that the ship needed urgent repairs.. Or was it more than luck. I took a deep breath.. Fate.. Destiny..

"Have a look out here Wight.."

I started and looked around to see the Sec. in the doorway to the deck; a thoughtfully stern look on his face.

Out on deck I was stopped short, astonished to find we were passing another ship and only a short distance away; rusty orange hull, green superstructure, a single squat red funnel with two yellow bands, dragging a plume of black smoke through the shining blue sky; every detail. .every angle of metal and streak of rust glaringly visible..

"How did it get here ?" I stammered accusingly stepping forward to the rail; after so long alone in the empty vastness the other ship appeared as blatant intrusion. I noticed two figures at the rail and without thinking raised my arm and gave a wave, for a few seconds there was no response and then one of the figures gave a hesitant wave back. Fellow mariners, I thought suddenly possessed by a sense of kinship; the ship forging ahead white foam curling from the bows .. into the vastness of the Pacific..

"Japanese .." The Sec. commented pointing to a white and red flag limply from the stern trailing a frothy wake over the shining water..

"All Japanese ships have *maru* as the last part of their name.."

"Is that so? A bit of a surprise to see another ship.." I remarked, distantly wondering why the Sec. had called me out on deck sensing something in his manner.

We're in a shipping lane now..." The Sec. said curtly." So there'll be other ship's passing us regularly now."

I nodded feeling uneasy; looking back at the other ship, now a dark silhouette on the glittering waters, a thin grey column of smoke rising high into bright blue sky. Was it going to Vancouver perhaps? Strangely I felt no responsive stir of emotion.

"We'll be picking up a Pilot some time early tomorrow.." The Sec. went on. "A repair yard near Kobe.."

"Kobe.." I marvelled trying to suppress my excitement.

"I expect Billy has filled your head with all sorts of stories.." The Sec. said dryly. "But you don't have to blindly follow him.."

I stared blankly away into the distance, feeling a pressure in my chest.

"I'll take you sight-seeing if you want. There's lots of famous temples and gardens.. Shinto shrines.. some of the oldest buildings in the world.. . ."

I sensed the Sec. watching me his words seeming to hang in the air, enticing and threatening....

I tried to answer, my lips dry; what did I want? I felt the rail trembling under my hand; my skin burning hot from the sun's rays, the lift of the deck lifting beneath my feet; my veins throbbing .. life .. I wanted life ... not old buildings..

"Er no thanks.." I stuttered out defiantly.

"Suit yourself.." The Sec. said coolly. "I'll get you some French Letters...."

I bent over the rail, seeing the foamy water swirl past the hull far below; not sure what the Sec. meant and yet for some reason embarrassed and ashamed ..

"No...no thanks..." I managed to mumble.

"Better get back to your duties..." The Sec. said after a long pause, a resigned tone to his voice.

"Sure.." I responded eager to get away from his presence.

"Oh yes.." The Sec. turned sharply confronting me; a faintly ironic smile on his face. "You'll be able to send a letter home, I expect you'll want to do that.. Let your folks know how you're getting on.. ."

"Yes.. Thanks.. of course.." I said flushing as if I'd been caught out.

Back in the Officer's Smoking Room I resumed the polishing the portholes. Why was the Sec. so protective, I wondered distantly; out of the dull thud of the engines I thought I heard a distant voice. I stopped polishing.. listening intently. 'Pip.. don't forget to write..' A shudder went through me, my mother's words echoing in my memory.

And at once a rush of words swept my mind…

' Dear Mother and Father, I hope you are well.. I am fine.. yes, it's tougher than I expected .. a lot tougher..'

Then I shook my head ..really it was hopeless .. impossible to express the reality .. the smells and noise and discomfort.. but more than that.. the vague ache of longing and fear.. that possessed me day and night.. the swelling sensations in my body…. the strange feelings ..

Once again I threw down the polishing cloth and went out on deck. Just live for the moment, I thought going over the rail.. now .. the present .. closer now the dark ragged coastline edging the sparkling sea..

"Japan…Japan…Japan .." I repeated softly to myself; my mind full of childhood memories.. brightly-painted pagodas with swooping roofs.. cherry blossom.. and bare formal gardens .. and women like painted wooden dolls who slept on wooden pillows so as not to disturb their elaborate hairdos .. Geishas that's what they were called.. I shut my eyes losing myself in a dizzying fantasy; alone in a garden, the innocent Cherry Boy surrounded by smiling lovely faces.. dark eyes admiring me through black tresses with bashful, forwardness..

"Hee hee.. young chap. Bloody dreaming of all them lovely Jap ladies I bet .. How d'do. .We ain't acquainted I'm Bo'sun.. Phillip ain't it? Cabin Boy.. signed on Vancouver… am I right?"

I nodded taken aback by the foxy-faced little man with sharp blue eyes his head a mass of fine curly hair who sidled over to me.

"Glad to be acquaint with you Phillip.." The Bo'sun chuckled putting out his hand.

"Nice to meet you. "I muttered releasing the calloused yet clammy handshake as quickly as I could

"Anything I can do fer ya .. don't hesitate. "The Bo'sun sniggered. "Well.. well better be off .. getting ready for the bloody Pilot yer understan' all that being a proper sailor now…"

So that's the Bo'sun I thought with an immediate dislike watching the bandy-legged seaman move away with a hobbling motion.

But what had he said about Japanese women, I turned around to gaze across the shining water; what secrets… ..mysteries.. lay hidden in the shaded grey outline I mused, my head throbbing. Soon soon.. I told myself going back inside.

At night for all my exhaustion, I couldn't sleep; finally sleep-dazed and barefoot I dropped quietly from my bunk and slipped out the cabin and down the companionway. Beyond the open amidships doorway the close night air throbbing with the dull engine roar fastened on me; the vibrating deck holding me as if I was a fixed part of the shadowy mass pushing deliberately forward; above, a dark vaporous ribbon streamed out of the ship's funnel into the brightly speckled night-sky. I crossed to the ship's side holding to the iron edge, looking blindly out into the darkness seeing a sickly violet-yellow aureole radiating into the night sky. Shivering in the cool air I stared into the baleful flouresence smeared across the darkness, obliterating the stars; if signifying some inescapable universal catastrophe I thought as a numbing weariness forced me back to the cabin.

"What will be, will be.." I murmured doubtfully immediately falling asleep .. .

"How many more days do you think?" I wondered unable to settle and getting off my chair and going to the rail.

"Dunno Just 'ave to wait.." Billy growled lighting up a cigarette.

"Yeah. I guess... "I laughed a strange hoarse laugh; somehow the afternoon break instead of being as before a welcome respite from the daily toil only intensified my excitement.

For a long time I stood staring at the dark line fringed with white clinging so lastingly to the edge of the Pacific Ocean, defying the surge and smash of waves, rolling unbroken for thousands of miles..

"Hello whaat we got here? Hiding away are tha?" The unmistakable voice of Hobbsie boomed out. I turned smiling nervously as he come around the corner of the Crew Accommodation block.

"It's a free world ain't it .." Billy growled turning in his chair quite undaunted by Hobbsie's overbearing manner.

"Sorry to disturbe loike.." Hobbsie jeered moving purposefully to the stern rail; his broad shoulders and chest shiny with sweat in the sun, like some rough-cast bronze statute.

Close behind him was another member of the Day Gang, a thin wizened seaman, a grey fringe around his bald head with gaps in his front teeth; like a child born old, I thought.

"What's up Chappy?" Billy asked getting out of the way.

Chappy showed a rolled up bundle he was carrying and pointed to the blistered, peeling flag-staff.

"Run out the t' Red Duster; let the world know we're British." He said in rasping voice; untying the rolled-up flag.

"Juust a coloured bit o' cloath..that's all "Hobbsie blustered contemptuously his large fingers fumbling to tie the strings to the rope on the flagstaff.

"Aye says tha but manys the mariners has been drowned and burned for it. "Chappy responded winking at me.

N' f----g good luck to 'em..." Hobbsie growled running out the flag. "Yer won't catch Archibald S. Hobbs dying a hero fer it..."

"I doan't doubt it..." Chappy smirked standing back to a sketch a salute at the badly-frayed faded square of cloth hanging limply at the end of the flag-staff and shook his

8 4

head. "Me mother's brother being one, lost on an oil-tanker torpedoed in the Med. in the War."

"Really ?" I exclaimed. "Bringing aviation fuel to Malta I bet, I've read about it, the men got extra pay it was so dangerous....they didn't even go in Convoy... "In my imagination I saw the submarine periscope rising out of the shining blue sea, the shimmering passage of the torpedo through the clear water.. the violent shudder to the ship.. the blast of fiery heat.. the moment of awful realization this was the end..

"That't be it.. nowt to do with patriotism .. just fer the extra pay. "Hobbsie crowed. "But whaat about tha..college boy "He demanded suddenly turning on me. "Would tha give tha life fer that worn-out bit of bunting?"

"Well..it's er.. just a symbol..." I stuttered evasively.

"Answer t'f----g question.." Hobbsie bellowed with a fierce look.

I stared fixedly at the drooping dark red cloth, the folds stirring ever so slightly. Would I? Would I? Would I willingly give up my life.. this present moment...this sun shining on the limpid water and the waiting shore...for some abstract ideal..?

"Who knows? Perhaps...." I answered flushing. "What about you Billy?"

The loud laughter echoed in my ears as the two men clumped off down the deck.

"Ya shouldn't let Hobbsie get t' ya.." Billy observed after we had settled back into our chairs, our cigarette smoke drifting up into the bright air.

I nodded, shamed to silence; what a coward I am, I thought; squinting at the seagulls circling slowly above the frothy wake trailing away over the glinting waters. What had Chips called them.. messengers wasn't it....messengers of what though?

Perhaps it was all a dream.. and we were still far from land in the midst of the Pacific, I thought rubbing my eyes stepping out on deck instead of going into the Pantry, crossing to the ship's side to stare wonderingly out across the darkly swelling glossy waters.

Out of the pale pre-dawn greyness a white band gleamed below a ragged blackness. Yes.. land.. Japan.. waiting for me.. I thought yawning widely moving back inside.

"Engines almost finished goin'g less than 'alf speed..." Mitch growled casting a suspicious look at me in the doorway blinking at the harsh glare.

"Tarts in Nagasaki better than Kobe.." Ronnie sniggered.

"Nagasaki..! "I exclaimed.

"Can't wait eh laddie?" Jock said a wry smile on his craggy face.

"No.. it's just .." I flushed and shook my head confusedly; the harsh jeering laughter stopping me from further words.

Let them think what they want, I thought bitterly struggling up the stairs with my pail of water to begin washing the Companionway floor on the second deck. But the thought of land so close soon led me to abandon the pail and go out on deck again to stand at the ship's rail.

Across the darkly rippling water, the newly-risen sun reached out long rays to touch the mossy green hills and vales with a golden glow, columns of sun-bright mist filtered upwards into the pale dawn-sky; everything held in exquisite stillness.

As if it were the first day of creation, I thought breathing the damp air tinged with fragrant woody smells; wreathing veils of gleaming mist slowly lifting from the clusters of smoothly rounded hills; the dark clefts freshly anointed by brilliant sunlight; a land of luminous greens burnished by a golden sun.

Green...so wonderfully green, I thought so different to the empty glittering glare of the ocean; yes it was a delight to see massed green foliage in all the variety of shades; even the ship seemed to be affected moving more slowly, a faint burbling of passing water reaching me from below.. the engine roar muted..

I gave a deep sigh and turned back inside, my heart aching; such exquisite natural beauty.. and yet.. Beginning to wash the floor my mind reeled with images of gently pointed green hills and deep valleys flushed with the light of the dawning sun. And yet, I mused somewhat troubled it was so much more than a show of gilded green; a force.. power.. reaching back to a pristine creation.. before man's existence in this world.... rendering the human presence unnecessary.. irrelevant..

Yet how I felt drawn to the an emerald brightness reflecting the morning sunshine at every opportunity going out on deck to gaze wonderingly at slowly at the passing shoreline dense covered with a dense vegetative green, reaching in tumbled mounds to the blue sky, a static glossy verdant land, silent and empty without the least sign of human activity; as if we were the first to venture into this primeval world, a world before time, perfect in itself; the ship's long bow waves, tunnelling out over the flat shining water to gently break the mirrored foliage to pieces only to slowly reform into leafy perfection..

And still though I felt disturbed by the alien remoteness that I detected in the verdant mossy world slipping so slowly by..

During the afternoon break I opened my eyes from a doze to gaze in amazement to find the ship passing a scattering of fantastically-shaped islets rising abruptly from gently lapping clear green water ; gnarled roots of ancient pine trees clutching at the shattered rocky sides, their scaly bark gilded by the afternoon sun...

Like some exquisite brushwork on an antique scroll painting, I thought. And what were those? I wondered noticing some red painted posts with cross-pieces rising out of the limpid foreshore the vivid green rising up behind.. Were they guides perhaps.. or markers? Somehow that didn't seem right. A symbol clearly.... but of what? Somehow not humanly endearing or welcoming .. yet clearly man-made ..not a triumphal arch or anything like that ultimately rather inhuman. .

But surely there must be people living here, I mused on, thinking I could see a wavering line of smoke rising from the darkly fronded hillside; imagining a rustic hut in a clearing, beside a small vegetable patch. . .But who would live in marooned in the smoothly undulating tracts of dense forests? I wondered; perhaps a setting for a folktale, I thought letting my imagination wander...

'There lived in the midst of a remote mountain of Japan a solitary charcoal burner .. now one day while out gathering mushrooms he heard from a afar sad singing and following the sound came to a small lake in a clearing. Peering through the branches saw a beautiful woman singing as she washed her lovely naked body in the clear waters of the lake; just then he stepped on twig and at the sound the woman turned sharply and to his amazement the charcoal burner met the bright black eyes of a shiny-coated fox; now later that night....'

"Time to get back Phil me old mate.." Billy broke into my thoughts getting up from his chair.

"It's like a lost world.." I commented as together we went back down the afterdeck waving a hand at the smoothly swelling greens absorbing and reflecting the dazzling sunlight.

"Never f-----n' mind that. Just t'inh how you'll soon be getting' it.." Billy laughed giving me a friendly slap on the back

"Yeah?" I laughed back stumbling forward ; the deck rising ponderously beneath me; feeling a strange heaviness coming over me.

The sun was a glaring red ball as I came on deck for a last look at the land, now a shadowy outline, the smoke-like clouds burning with orange fires from the setting sun. I breathed in the warm evening air; a faintly acrid pine scent coming to me over the darkly ruffled water feeling the steel deck beneath me trembling with sudden spasms; quite as if it to was full of barely suppressed anticipation, I mused. Soon you'll be in dock being repaired old girl, I murmured patting the rusty bulwark and what about me? What did I hope for myself.. ? What had Billy been telling me about the Bum Boats.. something amazingly wonderful.. and that fearfully wonderful moment when I would experience a woman.. and yet still a heaviness preyed on my mind..

'Nagasaki.. Nagasaki...' the name echoed dully in my mind.. Yes, of course, that was where one of the Atomic Bombs had been dropped. At once the awful swirling, seething grey-white mushroom cloud of television pictures and newsreels filled my mind; how terrible.... death and destruction on an unimaginable scale..

How to understand? I sighed turning back inside; the land now lost in the dark of night and the myriad stars gleaming forth.

Chapter Eight

"Aye yon's Nagasaki laddie.." Jock said with a chuckle from beside me.

I nodded, surveying with satisfaction the wide bay and surrounding hills against a clear blue sky, leaning against the ship's side.

"The Portuguese were here ... hah first... Special permission.. to open a trading post.. A closed country ..death if ya tried to get in.. then the missionaries .. Jesuits.." Pete puffed heaving and gasping for breath.

What a pompous wind-bag, Old Pete is, I thought glancing along the line of figures at the ship's side; the two cooks in the their smirched whites; Jock his nobbly bright red face, strands of gingery hair covering a bald pate; Ronnie pasty faced with a purplish shadow around his chin and then Old Smelly his pink bullet head, bursting out of his grubby stewards jacket; and next to me, Billy both of us in cut-off shorts and stained T-shirts. I glanced at Billy's face, a long quiff falling over his forehead, a scowl on his tanned face. My ship-mate.. I thought proudly. . Only Mitch was absent and now and then I gave a glance back to the Amidships doorway half-expecting, half dreading his appearance..

This was the first time we had stood in a line along the ship's side since the day I had come aboard in Vancouver I mused, watching two sea-gulls wing slowly across the clear blue sky; remembering how nervous and miserable I had felt standing alongside them watching the Vancouver shore-line slip slowly away....

And here I was, having crossed the vastness of the Pacific, leaning ever so casually, on the hot, rust-pitted steel side, entering Nagasaki Harbour. One of the ship's crew…a sailor.. a seaman… one of those who over the centuries had dared to cross the trackless oceans of the world far from home and land.. .

I looked down at the water slipping along the hull leaving a line of frothy bubbles. Yes.. a sea-farer .... yes...me, Phillip Wight...fulfilling my destiny....

And what is waiting for me there, I wondered lifting my eyes to the sloping shores; the wide expanse of silvery greyish roofs swooning in the heat haze. Would I really be attractive to the Japanese women? I wondered feeling my blood throbbing.

"Ready fer them Jap tarts ain'tcha Phil.." Ronnie sniggered from along the line.

"More than ready eh matey!" Billy laughed.

"I suppose.." I answered doubtfully flushing. The others laughed loudly, the sound ringing out over the shining flat waters and I smiled smugly to myself thinking, yes, I am one of the crew of the good ship *MV Grimethorpe*...

"Owners gone, bust by Harry. .. ." I heard Pete boom out and looked up to see that we had come level with a freighter moored with heavy chains draped in ragged streamers of sea-weed; splotches of dark brown rust starkly revealed in the bright afternoon light.

"Crew defrauded of their pay I doot...." Jock commented grimly.

I stared fixedly at the rust-stained freighter; once she had sailed confidently into the harbour.. but now abandoned to the slow wash of the harbour tides.. slowly rusting away, her sides crusted with barnacles and sea-weed. What had happened? Could the same thing happen to this ship? I wondered with a shiver.

But how slowly we seemed to be moving, the dull thud of the engines almost on the point of stopping altogether; across the shining harbour water the low crowded buildings flickered hazily, evasively in the sunlight; again the distant anxiety; what exactly was I meant to do.. how would I learn..?

A blast from the ship's hooter made me jump and then as the echo died away a dull thundering filled the air, the deck trembling violently beneath my feet. I stared wildly around.

"Anchor's awa'.." Jock remarked calmly, smiling at my confusion.

I leant out over the side; puffs of brown dust shot with sparks hung about the ship's bows, the links of the anchor chain tumbled into the clear water staining it yellow and leaving patches of brown froth to float away over the bright rippling water.

How much longer? I wondered as the ponderous clumping went on and on, interspersed by ear-piercing screeches that echoed around the harbour.

"Like the ship's guts are being torn out" I shouted putting my hands over my ears.

"Yer get's used t' it.." Billy grinned.

Then as abruptly as it had begun the dull rumbling and shaking stopped; the silence ringing in my ears; a cloud of dust drifted away over the water, vanishing into the glare.

"She's wanting back out to sea." I laughed seeing the bows slowly swinging swung, pulling the links rapidly out of the harbour depths.

"Aye, you could say it's her nature laddie." Jock chuckled.

We all watched intently as the links tightened and the chain became rigid, fixing the ship to the sea-bed; the ceaseless vibration in the iron-work fading away to an eerie passivity. "Safely anchored, by Harry. "Pete growled and a solemn silence held the small line of men.

"Home is hunter from the hill; the sailor from the sea... "I murmured to myself.

"What f----'g shite is Pansy spouutin' now.."

We all turned. Mitch shuffled unsteadily towards us; his skin grey colour his eyes blood-shot. He had failed to turn up for his duties that morning, I remembered, swallowing hard at the sight of the morose look.

"Late t' bed, late to rise." Jock said faintly sarcastic.

Mitch merely spat down into the water and glared fiercely out across the harbour.

"Here's the Pilot launch.." Pete announced and we all turned to watch the slim pointed launch all gleaming chrome and shiny mahogany, sweep past, foaming at the bows, sending ripples over the still waters of the harbour to eventually slap against the ship's hull below.

My first real Japanese, I thought studying the crew, in white uniforms with dark blue collars and square flaps, standing stiffly at the launch railings; small pale brown faces, unsmiling, impassive, so very neat and smart... How different from the motley gang, lined up along the ship's side, staring uncouthly down.

"See them there, Nips... that's what they calls themselves Nippons.. not Japanese, no sirree..." Pete wheezed out.

"They reckon the Mikado..that's what they call their Emperor is descended from the sun, thousands of years ago....death even to touch him.. though after the World War Two.. he publicly announced he was just a man... heh.. heh.."

"It's the Jap women we're wantin'." Ronnie sniggered.

"Yer best "Nip" is a dram o' Johnny Walker.." Jock chortled.

Pete puffed on irregardless. "Shut themselves off from the rest world for centuries.. didn't they...but the Yanks wouldn't have it.. no siree.. forced 'em to open the country for trade. Now one going on to be one of the top industrial nations in the world....."

"Och aye, n' tell that t'oor lads in the Jap Prisoner of War camps...starved and mistreated 'em ..died like flies... "Jock snapped.

"Can't bear to lose face that's why. Different to us'ns by Harry.." Pete blustered between gasps for breath. "Rather kill themselves than shame of surrender. Hara-kiri.. they calls it.. stick a big knife in their own guts... traditional. .Code of Bushido ..the Samuri.. Expert swordmen.. Best sword-makers in the world too by Harry.. strips of blue steel hammered together..".

"But had tae come tae Clydeside tae learn how to build ships"

Jock interjected triumphantly. "And Whisky tae!"

"Is that all ya can f----g t'ink of Jockie?" Ronnie sniggered

"Aye, aye... Whisky.. Usquabea...Water of Life...." Jock intoned gravely.

"Now yer Japanese have Sake..." Pete gasped irrepressibly. "Brewed from rice.... complicated process... a ritual for them.. like yer tea ceremony. special spring er water...... ."

"So what does Sake taste like?" I asked smiling at Pete's never-failing pomposity.

"Sake? Nae better than watta..." Jock scoffed dismissively. "Jap whisky's nae muckle better aither."

"We'll have to try when we get to Nagasaki, eh Billy." I giggled excitedly.

"The only drink ya needing is froam a baaby bottle. "Mitch jeered savagely turning on me.

There was a roar of laughter from the others and I felt my face go hot. I looked down at the slickly swelling harbour water below; why did Mitch despise me so much? I wondered despairingly. Or did I deserve it? Was I just pretending to be a seaman..

"Bum boats! bum boats!"

"Here they come lads."

"Get tha ready, mateys.. ."

Several of the Deck Crew clumping noisily through the foredeck doorway were calling to us and pointing out across the harbour.

I stared out of the shining waters, a line of slim, shapes appearing out of the glare; as they came closer I made out ten or more craft with high pointed bows and the sterns standing figures, like cardboard cut-outs, moving long sweeps.

"Are they Sampans?" I wondered excitedly.

"Yes sirree, Sampans.." Pete huffed condescendingly. "Some with motors too by Harry. That's what I calls progress.."

Sure enough I saw two or three boats, trailing a white swath pass quickly through the line of sampans making them rock precariously; a racketing engine noise sounding clearly over the water.

"Now fer some fun.." Billy grinned nudging me.

"Yeah.." I laughed excitedly, the harsh clattering of the motor abruptly ceased and blue smoke drifting upwards the smell of burning oil in my nostrils. Soon almost a dozen sampans, the middle section covered with plaited bamboo or cloth awnings, were bobbing against the ship's wall-like rust-stained hull.

I looked down curiously at the pale-brown, upturned faces looking so eagerly up at me, yet aware of a sadness at the back of the bright black eyes. Was it because of their hard life, I wondered, noticing the lean, sinewy legs and arms of the boatmen; or was it something more fundamental?

Gesticulating wildly they began shouting to us in excited, shrill voices:

"Hey jonnee!" "Nicee thing.." . "Cheap.. velly cheap!" You buy yes! Velly cheap!"

Within minutes the slim boats had become transformed into floating bazaars stacked with various-sized cardboard cartons from which brightly wrapped packets were produced and waved excitedly; carpets and other bundles were unrolled held up and then thrown aside; there were baskets of fruits and boxes of strange exotic-looking brightly packaged cartons. What might they be? I wondered feeling an intrinsic superiority looking down at the vociferous clamour.

Lines had been thrown up to ship and soon some of the seamen gathered along the ship's side were pulling up small baskets with fruit and throwing coins into cloths spread out on the boats below.

"I'm going to get some money.." I told Billy suddenly frantic to buy something… anything really.

"Better take this then…" Billy held out a door key. "Gotta lock the cabin door now were in port.

I nodded and took the key; how suddenly everything was changing I thought entering the Amidships; the dingy, stale-smelling Companionway strangely unmoving under my feet.

And strange too it, to need money I thought scraping out some almost-forgotten notes and coins from the bottom of the drawer.

I hurried back, exulting that I would be able to buy something but conscious of a nagging anxiety; was that what money did to one?

"Hey.. hey ." I called down to one of the boat-men, a toothless emaciated old man his loins wrapped in white cloth, bald but for a few hairs on his scalp, balancing expertly on the bobbing stern of the narrow sampan.
I pointed out to a box of what looked like brightly-coloured cakes in a cellophane covered box amongst the other goods and the old man expertly threw up a rope that fell over bulwark beside Mitch.

"Nowt but f-----g rubbish!" Mitch snarled his face livid and before I could move he had snatched up the line and pulled it violently tipping the packet out of the basket.

"Hey!.. I "said shocked and angry. "Look what you've done.." I pointed down at the packet floating away on the iridescent water while the old boatman looked on helplessly.

"What d'y care.. ain't f-----g paid fer it haave ya?" Mitch sneered glaring at me.

"Look! He's going after it!" "Hope he can swim!."

Other members of the crew at the ship's side had noticed the old boatman trying to fish out the floating package with a pole and were shouting down to him.

There was splash and a roar of laughter and I looked down to see the old boatman floundering wildly in the harbour water.

"Poor old chap...." I cried suppressing my laughter.

"A f-----g poncy Wog lover are ya?" Mitch jeered pressing his pudgy body close to me, his open mouth showing broken, black teeth; his stale breath washing over my face. "What d'ya care? None of that f----g lot does. Look at 'em yellin' n' screamin' like a pack of f----g monkeys..."

It was true, the other bum-boatmen, indifferent to the figure struggling were shouting and yelling just as before; perhaps, I thought, even glad at the loss of a competitor.

"Looks like a drowned rat." I said to Mitch as the old man coughing and sputtering finally managed to haul himself back onto the violently swaying sampan.

"Ya have to groaw up a bit ..afore ya learns how to these f----g yeller slit-eyes." Mitch said scornfully complacent fixing me with a cold stare.

"Sure Mitch.." I murmured watching him toddle back across the deck and inside the Amidships; how easily he dominates me, I thought my legs still trembling.

Down below the shrill cries were as loud as ever, the old bumboat man still dripping wet, joining in crying their wares as earnestly as before.

"Desperate fer siller, puir carles. Aye aye.. Capitalism laddie that's what we gave them them... "Jock groaned coming up beside me.

Was that it? I wondered uncertainly, looking up to where beyond the jostling bobbing boats, the water glittered to the shoreline; how to know why anything was the way it was....?

I lay stiffly in the close darkness of the cabin sleepy but unable to sleep, listening to the sound of Billy's breathing below me.. Just like some old sailor I'm so used to the regular rhythmic movement of the ship at sea that the absolute stillness now we're anchored in the harbour prevents me falling asleep I concluded; letting my mind run back over the afternoon; recalling the time at the ship's side with the bum-boats and Mitch's abuse of the old man... And my response wasn't that equally shameful. . .? Quite as if he had some almost hypnotic power over me.. but only because I let him, I argued, as if instinctively, I was in awe of him .. or was it just cowardice? Or even, in some perverse way I admired him. No. no .. I protested hotly.... Wasn't he everything I loathed ..despised.. and yet hadn't I felt the same smug arrogance?

After a while the bum-boat men had been allowed aboard and turned the ship into an impromptu open-air market. Like superior beings Billy and I had swaggered about, laughing and talking in an noisy exaggerated way as we passed amongst the obsequiously bowing, smiling cajoling vendors. With no intention of buying we had casually examined the different packets and tins and boxes decorated with designs of writhing dragons or florid blossoms or birds in a rainbow of clashing colours merely to amuse ourselves.

Most appeared to be some kind of medicine which according to the bizarre English on the boxes were guaranteed to cure conditions like baldness, impotence and premature ejaculation whatever that was... .

Immediately we touched anything one of the small, sallow-skinned men would shout excitedly in a shrill voice.

"Hey Jonny you buy...yeah..Nice thing..Cheap .. velly cheap you buy.."

Condescendingly I had shaken my head, wary almost fearful of the bright black eyes and quick waving brown hands, feeling myself becoming overwhelmed by the heavy smells that filled the Crew mess, the steel bulkheads echoing to the mingled cries of the traders and seamen raucous shouts. Laughing loudly and shouting and pointing at the different wares the crew seemed almost intoxicated, the days of monotonous toil at sea concentrated into an explosion of reckless extravagance. But wasn't there disdain too, in their faces and gestures a kind of disgust with the very act of spending; often buying fruit or some strange foodstuff and then just as casually tossing it away half eaten or untouched with a jeering laugh.

And what about the bumboat-men themselves I wondered? Smiling and bowing politely and gesturing like so many clockwork toys. What were they really thinking? Did they perhaps secretly loathe the clumsy noisy seamen, concealing their real feelings for ultimate gain? But wasn't there that sad despair in their eyes.. as if they too were doing something against their will; forced to play a part in some inexplicable charade...?

To my relief it had all come to an end as suddenly as it had started, like some demi-god the burly, dark bearded

1st Mate had appeared; so impressive in his white uniform with gold-barred cuffs and shoulder brevets, his eyes under the bushy eyebrows glancing commandingly around as he strode about jollying on the slackers. Like a scene from Conrad's *Lord Jim* I had thought, the calmly assertive English officer ordering about the unruly mob of shrill, gesticulating natives, for their own good.

How wonderful to have the ship to ourselves, I had thought going out on deck and shielding my eyes against the light to watch the retreating bum-boats; the slender silhouettes, inky smudges on a flickering bright screen were lost in the darkening shore; like birds returning to their nests.. each going to his own home, to be welcomed and to tell of his day.. I had mused, conscious of a faint nostalgia . when.. oh when would I be going home.. ?

But how pathetic.. surely this was why I had come to sea? Wasn't this all part of my great adventure.. ..?

For a little longer I had stayed at the ship's side, the silence broken by the muffled drumming from the ship's auxiliary motor; before me a net-work of lights had appeared around the bay, above a scattering of stars dimly visible in the velvety blue-black sky....

A shrill whistle made my heart thump, then came the faint screech of steel on steel; a train.. the familiar dull hammering slowly fading away, taking me back to a time when as a small boy I had stood alone in the twilight at the bottom of my grandparent's garden and listening to the metallic rattle of a train across the field and known a vague desire for travel to faraway places.. I had inhaled the smoky, pungent spicy smells coming over the darkly glistening harbour water.. and now here it was .. all around me.. Japan.. .. the mysterious Orient. ..

CHAPTER NINE

'Dear Mother and father,
How are you all? I am fine. We have come to Nagasaki,
Japan because of problems with the engines and a leak in
the hull. Nothing serious! So I will be able to post this letter
to you. Once we get ashore that is! For the last three days
we've been moored in the middle of the harbour ..half a
mile I guess from shore..'

I stopped writing and looked thoughtfully over the
shining harbour water, the cranes and ships lining the
quayside; inhaling the salty seaweed smells; my bare skin
hot from the sun shining from the blue sky; the tattered,
faded flag drooping from the flagstaff. Yes.. this was me..
Phillip Wight on the stern of a freighter in Nagasaki
harbour but how impossible to describe all I was
experiencing..

'In the mornings there is this thick fog cutting us from
the rest of world and yet we can clearly hear traffic noise
and even voices.. quite eerie.. Then in the evening we get
these burning, sort-of barbecue smells coming to us over
the water .. it's very hot and humid even at night, in the
morning I'm soaked in perspiration ...

Again I stopped writing; staring up at the deep blue sky
and a single sea-gull flying high above.... how far it all was
from my life at home in Vancouver. I glanced over at Billy,
his tanned, muscled body slumped out between the chair
and stern rail. He considered writing letters a waste of time.
Perhaps he was right, I mused. And yet I had promised; so
was it a just a sense of duty? I ruefully shook my head;
somehow I had no choice...

'Some of the officers are allowed ashore using what are
called water taxis actually narrow sampans just like you see
in the films.. with outboard motors.. but the crew aren't
allowed which is pretty frustrating for us as you can
imagine. A few of the officers stay away over night but most

return for their meals. We laugh at them for being so miserly! We're getting regular visitors.. Officials.. and Shipping Agents and workmen in blue boiler suits with white dust-masks--a bit scary when they you meet them suddenly in the companionway or you can see is their eyes.. Sometimes we feel that it isn't our ship anymore.. we have to lock the cabin door now ..another change from sea ..As well as the official visitors we have what the sailors call "bum-boats men" .. Traders who sail out in sampans and set up their displays all around the ship. I've bought four shirts, T-shirts, pairs and trousers and new shoes.. .. They all have the most absurd names like Lord Faunteleboy and Sir Galhadad but really cheap, though as the money comes out of my pay I'm not sure how much I've spent. Actually I found it very strange being able to buy things after being away from shops for so long. And the traders are so crazy to sell things to you, all of them shouting and waving madly at you. Secretly I can't help but despise them a bit though I know it's just because they're so poor. With all their yelling and pressure I probably wouldn't have bought anything at all except for Billy insisting I needed to be really smart to go ashore with him. He's the other Cabin-Boy and we share a cabin. As well as clothes there's fruit and some odd-looking confections sort of doughy and sweet I quite like them but Billy thinks they're disgusting.. He's from London and even though he's only a year older than me he been to almost all the ports around the world. We're good friends now. I have to admit it was a quite hard at first.. Some of the crew are bit rough and ready ..there's one of the Assistant Stewards called Mitch, a Scouser which means he's from Liverpool with a lot of tattoos a really sharp, sarcastic type. Probably father would say a diamond in the rough ... I'm adjusted to routine now though I have to admit I'm looking forward to getting home once we've unloaded the wheat in China.. though I'm really keen to see Nagasaki first.. all the seamen have been telling me that what a great place it is ..'.

I glanced over what I had written, thinking how strange that the little black squiggles were possessed of a meaning and yet too how trivial it all was. Perhaps I should I tear it up, I thought but then considered how glad it would make my mother; out of the bright sunlight comes a plangent reminder; 'Don't forget to write. Pip…. Don't forget..'

'My day starts very early, it's still pitch dark outside when the Sec. that's what we call the Second Steward, he's Billy and mine boss, knocks on the cabin door and shouts at us to get up and turns on the light. Quite a shock, believe me! I think I'll be better at getting up when I get back home ! It took me awhile to get used to the bunk bed moving up and down with the ship but now we're in harbour I really miss it! Just shows how easily you get used to things. Billy and I start work in the Pantry, next to the Officer's Dining room… really quite pretentious.. white table linen etc.. but it's all stained and grubby…. Billy and I have to carry all the plates from the Galley (seaman's word for kitchen) across to the Pantry and then put them through a Hatch to the Officers' Dining Room.. it can get very chaotic with dishes being dropped etc though so far the sea has been calm… The two sea-cooks are real characters.. Jock a Scotsman .. very chirpy .. goes around saying "I'm Willie McClucky frae Aucktermuckty..")! Where ever that is! If it exists! The other one is a proper Cockney and the two are always squabbling. As well as working in the Pantry I have to wash the floors.. you would hardly believe it but we have to use those long yellow bars of soap that Granny used for laundry for washing floors and dishes…. .. and with cold water.. really hopeless but I'm getting used to it.. As father is always saying 'necessity is a great master….'

After serving lunch and doing the dishes and cleaning up Billy and I go to a special place on the stern ..to laze for an hour.. I've never enjoyed doing nothing so much in my life! Just watching the ship's wake trail away .. all the way back to Vancouver.. I guess.. and then it's back to prepare for dinner .. though to be honest the meals are pretty awful . .. don't know how they do it.. a genius of bad cooking….. A lot of the meals get thrown overboard. One thing I've learnt is to throw it into the wind or it gets blown back into your face! Billy and I often joke about what the fishes think of the scraps.. there's this awful rubbery rolly-polly which probably gives them terrible indigestion.. .and the bread is heavy like pudding and sinks like stone... In the evening once the Pantry is tidy and clean.. the Sec. is a bit of a stickler at times though he doesn't seem to care about this awful black slime at the back of the counters.. as long as it looks neat.. Billy and I go to the Crew Mess and play cribbage. Most of seamen are there unless they're on Watch, either to play cards or sit around. It's very smoky and smelly too! The whole ship smells of diesel and stagnant water .. thought I've got so used to it I hardly notice it! We go to bed early.. .so that's my day.. a bit of grind. ..but then it won't be too much longer .. and I'll be coming back.. I think I'll be able to settle down OK at home... .. .

Once again my pen came to a stop and I gazed wonderingly over the flat harbour water to the pitched rooftops, shimmering in a heat haze. My heart beat faster as I thought of beautiful women waiting for me beneath the silvery grey tiles.

'It's really amazing watching the sun rise out of the darkness in the morning, but it soon becomes very hot. The ship being metal heats up like an oven. I am hoping for a letter from you when we get to China.. whenever we get there! But I won't be too disappointed if there isn't.. Love, Pip..

P.S. Hello to Carl and Patty..'

I carefully folded the paper; my forehead throbbing, feeling a faintness came over me; was I becoming ill? Billy had told me there was a condition called "shore-fever" when sailors had been out at sea too long ..

"Whacha writin'?" Billy demanded suddenly turning on me.

I stared at the folded blue airmail paper. What *had* I written?

Really what did it amount to all those black marks on blue paper...?

103

"About me is it?" Billy frowned suspiciously.

"No.." I retorted, flushing. "Well.. just that we bunk in the same cabin.. and work in the Pantry.."

Let's see.." Billy said snatching the letter from me.

"What a f----n' gabber ya are." Billy jeered glancing cursorily over the airmail and handing it back.

I shrugged; was I a "gabber"? Yes ..I thought it was true. I should be more like Billy.. just *be*.. just *live*..

"Hey what's that noise?" I asked suddenly conscious a dull clanking.. slow .. painfully deliberate; beneath my feet the deck trembled.

"That's the f-----n' anchor's bein' weighed. We'se gonna in matey.." Billy grinned.

"Really ? Really..?" I jumped to my feet and before I knew I was running heedlessly down the afterdeck my headache and faintness quite forgotten, the roar of the engines almost inaudible beneath the slow, dull clanging reverberating throughout the ship.

Just through the doorway to the foredeck I stopped short and leant out as far as I could; the dark brown chain, shiny wet, slowly break the water surface, clinging to the massive links were rags of sea-weed bright shiny green in the afternoon sunlight; from the bottom of the harbour, I mused, strangely moved; the ponderous clanking continuing with painful, monotonous regularity; the repeated jarring passing from the steel into my body..

Looking around I saw not far away a small boat with blunt bows and rounded stern, painted green and white, a stubby funnel pouring out thick black smoke, white froth bubbling from the stern.

"A tug boat….. ." I murmured, eagerly studying the small figures identical in dark blue boiler suits and white safety helmets, neatly spaced along the narrow deck; like the little toy soldiers I used to play with, I thought smiling.

Suddenly I decided I needed a better view and turned and ran along the amidships and up the stairs to the lifeboat deck; just as I gained the top step the ponderous clanking abruptly ceased. What next? I wondered reaching the rail just in time to see the tug had moved even closer to the ship, a frothy wake churning from it's low, rounded stern. A figure in a dark uniform appeared out of the tiny bridge to shout something through a loud-hailer to the men just below him, his voice lost in the roar of the ships' engines.

From the corner of my eye I caught a glimpse of a tiny, round object arching upwards, a fine black line trailing across the bright blue sky but then abruptly, lost it's impetus, the line wrinkling, the small dark ball, plummeting downwards, and the trailing line catching on the top rail on the tug's bows.

At once it was seized by two of the helmeted tug-boat men, who began, hand over hand to pull it in. Such a thin rope though, I thought puzzled.

But then I understood .. a thick hawser had been lowered from the ship's side and was now being towed across the flat, greenish water, a tiny crest of foam at it's nose like some speeding sea-serpent.

Reaching the tug-boat's side it rose out of the water, dripping wet, reaching half-way up the tug's side, but then as if dazzled by the light slipped back beneath the glassy surface.

I watched in suspense, the small figures of the tug-boat men locked in a desperate struggle to get the water-heavy, hawser onto the tug-boat; half-admiring the rope's stubborn refusal to leave the watery depths.

But the Japanese tug-boat men would not be denied and heave by heave, the hairy serpent was dragged from it's watery lair; in one final act of resistance, it began to slip back but the men redoubled their efforts until several large coils of thick rope were lying on the deck. At once two of the crew ran the looped-end along the length of the tug to place it, over the capstan at the stern and so crown their victory.

'Well done men!' I cried to myself, considering that determined effort will always triumph in the end. . but then looking up into the over-arching bright blue and I felt unsure surely sometimes failure was inevitable too.. no matter how hard one tried....

Already the tug was moving away out into the harbour, the hawser lost in the boiling froth, dark smoke from the funnel staining the cloudless sky; straining my eyes I made out a shadowy line floating just beneath the water surface, slowly rising and sinking.. ..

On an impulse, I turned about and ran around to the other side of the ship, spasmodic shudders passing through the deck almost knocking me off my feet.

Before I reached the rail I could see lines stretching over the flat harbour water between the ship and the dock-side alternately slackening and tightening as the ship closed broadside on the quayside, closer. . . closer.. the ship's steel bulk looming threateningly over the few waiting, watching figures ..

"The tug. ..!" I exclaimed, turning and dashing back to the other side of the ship. Out in the harbour the tiny toy-like tugboat was moving slowly away torrents of foam spreading from the stern; dark black smoke pouring from the funnel; the hawser a feeble shadowy line lying just below the glinting water.

I held tight to the rail; waiting.. waiting.. Nothing moved or changed; the little tug, isolated on the flickering water impotently foaming and fuming. . ..

But then the hawser jerked free of the water, drawing the drooping line between tug and ship that became straighter.., tighter....and tighter; sprinkling diamonds into the bright air as the rope became a stiff, rigid line between the tug and ship.

My calf muscles tensed as if I was part of the Herculean effort of the small tug-boat.. but how hopeless a task I thought ; the momentum of the ship's mass was far too great to be restrained by a single tug.. it was simple physics....

I turned and ran back to the other side of the deck; the ship's towering vast steel bulk was still moving slowly, inexorably against the quayside.

I stared down at; every detail caught in the brilliant afternoon sunshine; the clusters of green-stained wooden piles hooped with rusty bands, hung with old tyres, rising from the dark rippling water, clumps of dirty froth bobbing gently amongst bits of wood and rainbowed oily patches .. and on the dockside itself amongst the crates and boxes, the few waiting figures, their upturned faces innocently, attentive..

My hand made instinctively gesture of warning, knowing now with calm indifference that a fatal collision was now inevitable; conscious of a perverse satisfaction...

A double blast from the hooter momentarily blanked off the engine's steady roaring and I braced myself ready for the ship to smash sideways into the pier .....

A faint, barely perceptible shock rippled through the deck beneath me; series of rubbery squeals and squeaks died away, the engine roar faded to a muted throb, the rail now tingling gently under my intense grip.

I stared down hardly believing; already the gangway had been lowered and the passively waiting figures were moving confidently towards it....

I grinned sheepishly; how silly of me.. after all, how many times had the crew docked the ship; remembering too the calm authority of the Chief Mate.. and had I really wanted a catastrophe..? Was there some part of me that rejoiced in devastation.. destruction.. ?

"I've been looking for you Wight..."

I turned to find the Sec. standing beside me.

"I thought we were going to smash, Sec." I gabbed, then frowned. "I *mean* I knew we weren't, just that it *looked* like it.."

The Sec. gave a faint smile. "Looks can be deceiving. It does happen too. Some bad collisions.. fatalities... ...You'll be getting Shore-Leave tomorrow afternoon."

"Really .." I murmured, swallowing my excitement looking beyond the row of warehouses to the clustered shiny grey rooftops; soon I would be down among them, I thought with a distant ache....

"I don't suppose you're interested in having a look at Glover's old house "The Sec. continued as we started back.

"Glover?" I echoed trying to sound interested.

"Mmmmmm.. quite an interesting character. A Scot... helped start the shipbuilding industry in Japan. Built a house here.. and married a Japanese woman."

"No.. not really.." I murmured my feeling my heart thudding.

"Please yourself.." The Sec. said a resigned tone in his voice. "You'll get your spending money and a Shore Pass tomorrow up in the Officer's Smoking Room.."

"Great.." I responded frowning; why should I care that I was disappointing the Sec. .. it was my life wasn't it?

The moment the lunch dishes were washed and back in their racks Billy and I had raced each other up the stairs and along the companionway to the Officer's Smoking Room. Already a queue of close-packed seamen patiently waiting their turn had formed. There was an air of suppressed excitement, the seamen exchanging nods and grins and winks. Just like the time of the *Bond*, I thought; as if it were some kind of esoteric game.. or ritual...

Finally I was close enough to see the Chief Steward sprawled out on the settle, his large fat face flushed with pompous superiority. He thinks we should be grateful that he even deigns to dole out our hard-earned wages, I thought petulantly; my legs aching from standing so long.

Billy went first and while I waited my turn, I looked over the Chief Steward. Dishevelled and scruffy looking his too tight jacket was wrinkled and stained, as if he had slept in his uniform I thought contrasting him with the prim Japanese official sitting stiffly upright beside him, in an immaculate tight-fitting dark uniform. I wonder what he thinks of this slovenly dressed British officer I wondered, examining the official's small, impassive face, his eyes unsmiling behind the round wire-rimmed spectacles. I bet he thinks he's a barbarian and yet maybe he's a little afraid of him too.

You'd think he was some ugly little idol squatting on a dais, I mused; endowed with some fearful power that kept the tough, sailors in awed submission. But was that authority solely due to his position as Chief Steward or was it part of his personality.... .a native superiority..?

"Wakey ! Wakey ! "The Chief Steward squeaked drolly.

I flushed and stepped forward, averting my gaze to the grey-metal cash-box next to the large, open ruled ledger on the table.

"P. Wight ain't it? Cabin-Boy..hee.hee." The Chief Steward giggled after several loud burps. "Signed on Vancouver after other'un jumped ship in Seattle, hee hee.. No need to say more..hee... hee... hee...." He added, winking at the expressionless Japanese official who was closely examining my passport.

"After money are we, Wight?" the Chief Steward simpered wiggling his eyebrows in an insinuating manner.

"Yes please sir..." I muttered in a panic that he was going to refuse to give me my allowance with relief seeing the plump white hands take a bundle of sombre-coloured banknotes out of the cash-box and start to count them.

I leant forward and signed the ledger; my heart beating as I took up the slim bundle of crisp notes; somehow it was more than just money..

"What d'ya think he wants it for...?" The Chief Steward squeaked thrusting his elbow into the startled official. "Cheap booze!. .hee hee Cheap clap!...hee..hee"

I stepped sharply back the Chief Steward's words ringing in my ears; loud shouts and harsh laughter sounded all around me.

"Shore pass. . .!"

"Your Shore-pass. .!"

"Forgot yer Shore-pass!"

I felt myself shoved roughly back and stood once again in front of the smirking, unctuous Chief Steward playfully dangling a slip of white paper between thumb and fore-finger.

"You won't get far without this .." He squealed amiably.

I snatched at the slip of paper and to roars of amused laughter rushed to the open door and out on deck.

Perhaps I won't even go ashore after all, I thought gloomily crossing over to the rail. Better to stay on board like Old Paddy....

But how humiliating to be spoken about like that.. 'No need to say more. . .' What did *that* mean? How I loathed him.. So why then didn't I tell him what I thought of him to his face? 'Now listen you f-----g, fat arsehole.. see we've all worked very hard for this money and. . . .'

I shook my head self-pityingly knowing I could never do it.. just puerile fantasizing .. One squeaky jibe from him and I would be reduced to an imbecile dumbness... But what gave him such power over me? Did he instinctively guess my secret desire to sleep with a woman.. ?

Perhaps I should go sight-seeing with the Sec. after all, I mused, looking idly down at quayside below; my attention insensibly drawn to the frenetically busy scene below. Amongst troops of dock workers in blue boiler suits, small three-wheeled lorries were zipping back and forward raising clouds of fine dust; further along the quayside wire ropes suspended from the ship's booms were whisking aboard bulging cargo nets; beyond the warehouses; pointed curved roofs glimmered silverly in the hazy glare ..

I took a deep breath, the humid air heavy with sweet burnt spice odours mixed with decaying smells from the harbour waters; I squeezed tightly the roll of banknotes, a deep ache throbbing within me; my destiny.. waiting for me... . . . . I thought with a fearful, joyful shiver.

CHAPTER TEN

"Coming…" I yelled back pausing at the top of the gangway to tie a loose shoelace. 'This is it. ... 'I whispered to myself before bounding down the swaying gangway onto the dockside; solid land at last, I thought excitedly, stopping short. I had been warned it would take time to get my land-legs..

Is something wrong?" I demanded, my legs braced, wavering slightly; seeing Billy and Tad and Norrie standing laughing at me.

"Come on matey… Let's go.... "Billy grinned sardonically flicking back his quiff, turning away down the dockside.

Righto matey "I laughed self-consciously, taking a few clumsy first steps; how odd it felt to be wearing shoes again.. and how strange my new clothes felt against my skin; the air too seemed denser ..more heavily scented..

I turned to look back at the ship rising square and solid against the blue sky quite as if it was permanently joined to the land.. and yet just a few days before it had been far out to sea.......

"Hey what are they for?" I wondered pointing at saucer-shaped metal disks, circling the top of the hawsers running from the ship's bows to the iron bollards on the dock-side; glinting mirror-like in the afternoon sunlight.

"Rat-catchers ain't they." Billy explained pityingly. "To stop the f-----n' rats running up the ropes."

"But zee don't ..!" Tad squealed, contorting his bony face into an ugly grimace.

"Yeah… sees 'em down in bilges dontcha, bigger n' f-----g cats." Norrie beamed knowingly.

"Really? Did you know it was rats with fleas carrying the plague bacillus that brought the Black Death to England." I said excitedly "Makes you almost feel part of history doesn't it…"

"Save yer f----n' 'istory lessons fer the Sec." Billy jeered. "We just wantsa good time eh mateys?..

"Yeah! "Norrie and Tad chorused.

I flushed regretting I had told Billy about the Sec.'s offer to take me sight-seeing; when would I learn to keep my mouth shut, I sighed, following the others over to a booth just before the dock gates; standing at the door was a Japanese official in a neat uniform with peaked cap and wearing white gloves.

I waited, as one by the one the others presented their Shore-Passes to the official; what does he make of these foreign seamen? I mused. Tad, eyes starting from a gaunt pock-marked face, arms and legs sticking out of his loud-checked suit, like a scarecrow; Norrie, grinning smugly, his stolidly squat body filling to bursting a pepper and salt outfit and then Billy, in tight black trousers and a maroon jacket with a black velvet collar, a habitual scowl on his face; the tallest of the four; clearly the leader....

And what about me? I wondered catching a glance from the official as I handed over my Shore-Pass for inspection. Did he recognise me as another sailor on shore-leave. Or did he detect something false...a pretence.. a pose ?

"Thanks.." I smiled taking back the slip of paper; unsmiling the official made me a formal bow.

At once I bowed in return.

"Did you see that; I bowed just like the Japanese. "I boasted catching up with the others.

"Yer a f----n' jammy show-off..." Billy scoffed, slapping my back.

"Who cares .. We're ashore...! "I cried dancing forward, the road passing through a web of railway tracks, the polished steel, glinting fiercely in the sunlight.

"British Tars ashore ya mean.." Billy grinned.

"Yeah.. British Tars ashore. "Norrie boomed out.

"And zee Pole too! "Tad squealed.

"You mean a Tarry Pole?" I giggled. Billy and I began to laugh hysterically, watched by a gawping Norrie, reeling wildly about the dusty roadway beneath the dazzling sun; how wonderfully, strangely, amazing it all was..

"Zee all crazee .." Tad yelled furiously glaring at us.

We had come to a stop; the ground trembling beneath our feet, the air heavy with burning oil; hissing and clanking, with ear-piercing screeches of metal on metal, belching black smoke, a shunting-engine was moving ponderously towards us.

Uttering a wild shriek Tad darted forward.

"Wait.. I didn't mean.." I gasped sprinting after the gangly figure, glimpsing a small face staring incredulously down at me; a thunderous quaking ran through my body, hot oily air filling my lungs.

"Zee 'im shaka his fista? He one angry engine driver.." Tad shrilled excitedly hopping from foot to foot.

"Your'e mad.. both of ya..Ya coulda been killed.." Billy remonstrated coming up.

"We'ze do whata we wanta! We'zz Free! Free!" Tad howled his face waving his arms.

"Yeah! Free! Free! "I yelled joyfully; free from what though? I wondered staring at the black square engine puffing black smoke, slowly trundling away into the shimmering distance. Could it really have killed me? Surely not.. But what if I had slipped or tripped.. ? How often had I read newspaper reports of similar accidents.. . And yet I still couldn't believe it could happen to me..

But where had the others gone? I looked around, feeling quite giddy. Was it the heat? How could they have disappeared so quickly? Perhaps they had crossed the road. Before me lay a waste-land of sun-bleached grass and small dark green bushes. I plunged recklessly forward following a narrow path through the soft sandy soil, the feathery tops of the grass waist high. Could it be this is where the atomic bomb fallen? I thought suddenly; vaguely remembering some first-hand accounts I had once read.. a blinding incandescence lighting up the day, a furnace-like heat vaporizing steel and flesh, fusing the bodies into the concrete.. hurricane gusts of wind blasting and shredding..

and then in the awful silence of utter destruction, the soft patter of radioactive ash.... How unimaginably terrible it must have been....

All in the past, I thought walking on down the path; just history... like the Middle Ages.. or Ancient Rome..; nothing to do with me.. Phillip Wight.. now ..ashore for the first time with his ship-mates. Looking down I saw that my shoes had become coated with a fine white dust recalling the time when first coming aboard the ship thick with a floury powder and seeing the heaps of golden wheat in the ship's hold I had the overwhelming sense of being part of history and then seeing the rat-catchers earlier... ..

I gazed around at the empty expanse of bleached grasses hazed by the glaring light; and yet I was just one amongst the millions and millions living in this moment in the world..

I walked on coming to a stretch of still water lying between, banks of withered bushes, the path leading to a slender foot-bridge, the criss-crossing slender piles weakly reflected in the wrinkling milky surface. I stared hard at the flimsy wooden construction, the faintly etched outline washed in the afternoon light; overcome by feeling of having seen it all before.. perhaps a picture? or a photo? I shook my head.. No.... But how then? Could it be from another existence.. ?

From the other side of the bridge I heard voices calling; three figures stood waving at me.

I hesitated, conscious of an strangely disembodied feeling.. as if I didn't belong to this place or time....

"C'mon Phil." "Hurry zee up..!" The voices were insistent.. urgent..

The bridge shook under my feet as I crossed over; large gaps in warped planking gave me sight of the silky water below; yes, exactly as if I had been here before..

The others crowded around me as I reached the other side.

"Where d'ya go?"

"Stick with yer mates.."

"Really weird .." I giggled waving back at the bridge. "Sort of Deja? vue feeling ..." I glanced doubtfully at the puzzled faces; why couldn't I be more like them?

"The Sec.'ll f------n' kill me, if ya gets lost." Billy grumbled as we walked on down roadway

So that was it, the Sec. had told Billy to look after me; as if I was a child, I thought absently all emotion lost in the stifling hot air.

A little further on we found ourselves in the middle of a mixed crowd moving steadily towards a long row of canvas booths; between them ran a wooden walkway echoing to the clatter of feet, mixing with an unceasing prattle of shrill voices; quite oblivious to our presence it would seem and yet even the old women in dark-coloured kimonos, hobbling along, kept a distinct space about us. Four abreast we walked freely on, indifferently passing the numerous stalls with displays of strange, colourful food-stuffs and then others with tottering pyramids of shiny aluminium pots and pans, alongside others with massed displays of table-ware and pottery of all sizes and shapes.

And all this goes on, day after day; another world complete in itself of which I have no part, I thought feeling ever more detached and remote....

"Look at 'em will ya.." Billy hissed suddenly jabbing me in the ribs.

I turned feeling a sharp spasm as I rudely stared at the four figures walking two by two.. twittering just like little birds, utterly separate from the passing motley crowd, exquisite doll-like heads perched on kimonos of glossy gorgeous materials, they tripped along with sharp clacking sounds, white toes showing at each step, black hair neatly coiled and pinned behind, to show porcelain-smooth necks.

Must be the geishas, I marvelled with a ache of longing, vainly trying to make eye contact and then moving abruptly to keep them in sight and almost bumping into a passer-by who stepped away from me with a fearful look.

And won't it always be like that? I sighed, thwarted .. nullified; watching the slim, colourful forms swallowed up by the teeming crowd.

Norrie and the others were looking over a stall displaying transistors radios in a variety shapes all in bright plastic colours; unable to make up his mind Norrie kept picking up one then another, with the stall-owner nodding and smiling with genial patience.

Becoming bored I wandered off towards several large shed-like buildings further along the road; made curious by the unremitting, percussive din coming from the open doors I went to look inside.

As my eyes adjusted to the shadowy interior lit by flashes of coloured lights, I made out multiple rows of upright pin-ball machines reaching away into deep interior. Before each machines stood single figures, childlike faces, set with impassive intensity watching the blinking lights in front of them; oblivious to the incessant pinging of the machines multiplied to a deafening clangour.

For a minute or two I stared in stunned amazement at the nightmarish scene, the solitary figures seeming-eternally fixed in front of the flashing coloured lights amongst the incessant, unremitting dinging ..clinking …chinking.. … .

"Really awful.." I exclaimed as I met up with the others feeling as if I was lucky to have escaped. "Huge sheds full of pin-ball machines.. like a hell…."

"Pachinko Parlours ya calls 'em." Billy said shrugging. "Some of Japanese is crazy for 'em.. ."

"Hey listen to this will ya Phil. "Norris chirruped gleefully holding out his new transistor radio for me to listen to tinny incomprehensible squawking.

Yeah.. Great.." I murmured, as we walked off through the hot dusty afternoon; following blindly along, I found ourselves in a maze of closely-packed buildings of weathered wood, the air pungent with rich earthy smells, the narrow alleys between overhung by grey-tiles and festoons of wires, every now and then I thought I caught a glimpse of faces watching from a shuttered window. I remembered Old Pete had warned me about robbers who preyed on foreign seamen lurked in the alleyways and I looked nervously at the dark gaps between the buildings.

Some of the doorways were hung with coloured cloth, marked with Japanese script.. What lay behind I wondered almost fearfully, my heart beating faster. Could it be that there were geishas like the ones I had seen earlier waiting inside.. .. holding out a tiny soft hand.. leading me ..

"Hey Phil .this way.. ." Billy called sharply turning through a narrow doorway shielded by coloured plastic strips. I glanced up at a strip of wood nailed to the lintel reading *Bar America* in faded letters.

A bit ironic, I thought entering the gloomy sour-smelling interior my eyes slowly adjusting to the half-light, a row of bar stools in front of the grey zinc-topped counter revealing itself; the rest of the narrow space lost in shadows.

We all took a seat and Billy ordered beers from the Japanese bar-keeper an old man with a gentle dignified face, thick silvery grey hair swept back over his head.

Tad thrust a cigarette pack towards me and Norrie scratched a match, the tiny flame at its tip glowing supremely bright as I met it with the tip of the cigarette; the writhing coils of smoke drifting upwards into the black, cobweb-festooned rafters above.

Billy slid a glass of beer in front of me and I watched the bubbles rising through the column of golden liquid to the white -crested top.

"Cheers matey…" Billy grinned at me through a haze of cigarette smoke.

"Cheers, matey.." I echoed raising the slim-waisted glass, the light shining through the globules clinging to the glass, like dew-drops I thought absently; the slightly bitter liquid burning an icy path down my throat; instantaneously absolving the oppressive humidity of the afternoon.

I smiled around at the others, grinning widely as they wiped specks of white froth from their lips with the backs of hands.

"My turn mateys!" I cried slipping some of my new Japanese bank-notes out of my wallet; dimly marvelling that these crisp slips of dark paper could transmute the hours of toil at sea into the four frothing glasses dripping with golden droplets along the gun-metal grey counter.

"Cheers, matey!" Norrie bellowed; Tad and Billy echoing him as they all raised their glasses.

"Cheers !" My voice rang in my ears, the ice-cold flushing my throat; the moment brimming... extravagant... splendid..

I looked boldly around the shadowy bar-room, the light filtering in through the plastic strips showing up at the yellowish stained walls, bare except for an glossy beer advertisement showing a woman's oval face with a gentle smile, just visible in the gloom. How lovely she is, I mused dreamily; the voices of Billy and the others a low murmur.

So it is happening to me.. I thought here I am in a bar in Nagasaki and just beyond the door lay a maze of tiny streets, the entrances obscured by dark cloths and .. soon... surely soon it would all be known to me ..my imagination yielding to vague, softly-rounded images .. I tapped the grey ash from my cigarette end into the tin ashtray.. yes soon .. very soon..

"Here ya go.. matey "Billy grinned, slipping a golden foam-crested glass across the zinc topped counter towards me.

"Cheers matey.." I chirruped taking a long draught of icy beer my mind falling back to the moment just before I had crossed the footbridge; as if I was dissolving into the vacuity of infinite space. Was that why those individuals shut themselves away in that oppressively artificial world of noise and flashing lights? What had Billy called them? Yes.. Pachinko Parlours.... .All of them possessed of a desperate need to a blot out the emptiness of existence?

Absently I picked up one of grey-green banknotes from the counter studying the engraving of a severe-looking man in a dressing gown. Who could he be? My mind drifting back to the time I had got my shore money and vaguely recalling something the Chief Steward had said? What was

it? Something about the Cabin-Boy I had replaced....
something unpleasant... ..

"I've been thinking ... something Chief Steward said.."
I said startled by my own voice "About the Cabin-Boy who
jumped ship.."

"Less said about thaat the better eh Mateys "Norrie
boomed back winking at the others and they all laughed;
slightly malicious sound echoing around the bar.

I flushed and shrugged.. what did it matter? Did anything
matter...? I took another long swallow of the exquisitely icy
beer, numbing... annealing.. smoothing.. perfecting...

I ran a finger through the film of condensation on
battered zinc, yes it was all wonderful.. everything ..the
sour-smells, the shadowy bar-room, the different shaped
bottles lining the shelves behind the bar.. .

Absently I studied the old Japanese bar-tender, a benign
look on his worn face as he methodically dried glasses with
a white cloth.

"You know something .. mateys this old chap here reminds
me of my grandfather .." I announced suddenly. "Stoker on a
battleship you know.. stationed for years in the Far East with the
Royal Navy. Looked half Chinese so they called him Chinkee.
Never learnt to swim so they kept throwing him overboard but
he just sank .. so they had to pull him out again. "I laughed and
choked and laughed again.

"Firsta tima zee'ad skin-full eh?" Tad giggled wrinkling
up his face.

"Maybe ..." I laughed draining the glass with a flourish
watching fragments of foam slip back down the inside of
the glass.

"Not only thing...first time...huh." Norris bellowed a
beaming smirk on his fat round face.

"A genuine Cherry Boy aintcha Phil?" Billy grinned,
blowing out puffs of cigarette smoke.

I smiled mysteriously; a tingling, burning iciness spreading
slowly though me as I delicately drained the glass.

"Same again eh Mateys.." I sang waving several
banknotes towards the kindly old barman.; such a lovely
old man ..

Curiously I watched my hand as if propelled by some exterior force reaching for the shiny glass brimming with pure white froth; yes it was all astonishingly amazingly wonderful... .....

"Hey Phil yer comin'?" Billy called from the doorway; Tad and Norrie stood beside him. How had they got there?

Carefully I let the last watery drops slip down my throat without the least sensation of cold or wet. How queer..

"Coming.." I said carefully getting off the stool and almost falling over; we all laughed; how funny it all was...beautifully, seriously funny..

Halfway through the doorway I glanced back at the dusky interior inhaling the damp sour smells; surely I would always remember this time and yet .. wasn't it already beginning to fade from my mind...?

Now.. always now.. I thought solemnly, pressing after the three shadowy forms further down the alleyway; letting the warm air push me along. Only was it *me*? I felt myself dissolving into innumerable particles.. becoming part of everything ..the pavement under my feet...the skein of overhead wires criss-crossing the darkening velvety sky...the lights in the innumerable shops that streamed past.. the smell and smoke of traffic ...the unending passage of pedestrians and cyclists.. and yet at the same time I was almost nothing...without form or direction.. floating helplessly in a languorous vagueness ..

"Hey wait for me.. ." I begged marvelling how easily the words slipped from my lips, dimly aware of a powerful grasp waltzing me effortlessly through the thronging, jostling streets.

"Where's Tad and Norrie?.." I wondered suddenly aware that there was only two of us walking along.

"Don't worry about 'em.. matey.. Us Cabin-Boys gotta stick together.." Billy growled marching me boldly through the long shadows that stretched over the fiery metal rails.

"Yeah.. Cabin-Boys .. Ship-mates ....Pals.. Mates.." I giggled; smiling at the Japanese official as he politely waved us on from the door of his little hut.

"You said it ...." Billy laughed tightening his grip on my arm.

I pulled Billy to a stop, tears coming to my eyes. "Perhaps you think...I'm drunk well perhaps I am ...but I know what I'm saying....it's like Damon.. and P...pp.. Can't remember ..You know David and Jonathon ..you know what I mean..

"F-----n' right, I does.. it means yer f-----n' pissed." Billy chuckled, gently tugging me on.

Stride for stride, we crossed the shining dock-side toward the ship silhouetted against a pure golden light streaked with orange and red fading to glowing tints of purple and rose.

Once again I stopped." Look at that Billy ... "I whispered.

"We.. we're .. you know.. immortal......"

"What ever you say, Phil..." Billy said ushering me forward and up the absurdly swaying gangway.

I think I might be sick." I heard myself murmur the stifling acrid air of the Companionway engulfing me.

"You'll be OK. . just have a kip.. I'll cover fer ya.." Billy said guiding me through the cabin-doorway and pushing me backward into the musky gloom of the lower bunk.

"Thanks.." I said feeling my shoes being pulled off. I opened my eyes to see a shadowy form bending over me, the teeth showing white.

I tried to smile but yawned instead; tears ran down my cheeks.

"Billy, I.. I .." I whispered, but the cabin was empty and I swooned into an infinitely soft darkness.

CHAPTER ELEVEN

"Hey board's up!" Norrie bellowed and we all turned and looked back up the gangway.

I stared hard at the scrawl in white chalk on the small blackboard hanging from the ship's rail. *"Dep: 0800 Hrs.",* slowly understanding that we were sailing early tomorrow morning and so this was my last time ashore in Nagasaki.. . .

How unfair of the Sec. to punish me by docking a day off my shore-leave.. . ..

Why was it these things only happened to me? wondered moodily, pausing to glance back at the ship a dark block bright with spot-lights outlined against the evening sky... Was it my fate then to always be thwarted?

I sighed hurrying to catch up with the others already showing their Shore-Passes to the Japanese official at the Dock Gate.

In silence we marched across the silent, sparsely-lit railway siding, the railway tracks gleaming faintly. How different to our first time ashore, I mused remembering, how we had laughed and shouted for sheer joy at being ashore.

Our footsteps rang out dully we hurried along the metalled roadway towards the clustered lights; like soldiers on a secret mission deep inside enemy territory, I thought grinning to myself.

"Zee gonna get zee eh Phil!"

Tad's shrill bray echoed with startling loudness along the close-packed buildings.

I shrugged diffidently, glancing at the others, the skin on their faces lurid under the flashing neon lights; sensing a grim nervous excitement; four shadowy forms propelled relentlessly through the hot, smoke-scented air trapped in the narrow alleyways.

A little further on Billy lead us toward a white oval sign marked *BAR* in black letters shining brightly in the evening light; as one we moved toward the light gleaming beneath the cloth hanging over the doorway thrusting it aside.

The bar-stools scraped noisily across the floor as the four of us sat up at glass-topped bar. Billy ordered beers from the blank-faced barman.

I sat stiffly my hold on my beer-glass tightening; out of the dim recesses at the back of the room came a muted tittering.

With casual deliberation I turned to look; at a small table at the near the end wall sat two women, talking in low voices, utterly oblivious it seemed all around them.

"Right cow that 'un...." . I heard Norris chortle my eyes settling on the woman seated facing us, her round puggish face framed by severely cropped grey-black hair, before moving to the companion; feeling a deep ache, at the sight of her delicate profile, her dark hair gathered in a neat bun, a slim neck rising from a pale green kimono. Such loveliness. I mused, flushing angrily at Billy's low growl.

"Other' un aint bad.."

As if sensing our interest, she turned towards us, her small nose lifted slightly, lively dark eyes glancing swiftly around.

'Me.. look at me..' I whispered but already she had turned back; a slender arm appearing out of a wide sleeve she put her hand over her mouth. There was an audible ripple of laughter; like the tinkling of wind-chimes, I thought in a despair of longing.. .

"To 'ell with 'em both.." Billy snapped abruptly standing up. "I knows a f-----n' better place.."

I jerked to my feet the room spinning; was I drunk already? Absently I put my hand to my temple, my eyes still fixed on the seated figure sitting perfectly still, a faint flush on her cheeks, her exquisitely curved lips slightly parted, now calmly meeting my gaze.

'She likes you....' I urged myself giving a reassuring touch to the bulge of my wallet, conscious of a stiff awkwardness to my walk.

Struck speechless I stood before her, overwhelmed by her composed loveliness, distantly seeing the green cloth of the front of her kimono rising slightly with each breath.

"I…I have er.. money.." I finally croaked my eyes drawn to where the kimono, edged with a gauzy undergarment, parted to a V of moist ivory skin. "You see… I.. well Cherry Boy.. so well.."

Absently she stared back at me dabbing a handkerchief at the drops of perspiration on her forehead then darted it over her mouth; there was a muffled sputtering, the slim body moving convulsively.

"Please.. anything.." I said in a last desperate appeal, my eyes falling to the tiny white socks, poking out beneath the hem of the kimono.

A frown etched her small forehead and then came a proud dismissive twitch of her small head.

I nodded, choking back my shame; what a brute I was.. unforgivable..

"She like you..velly much"

For a moment I stared uncomprehendingly, following the movement of her hand, the palm open, fingers elegantly angled, towards the woman across the table; stolidly immobile she stared blankly ahead, her worn, tired face expressionless.

I gave an angry, despairing shake of my head, flinging myself back to the doorway, giving a final pleading, resentful glance back; seeing as in a photograph, a slim arm up-raised, smoke spiralling slowly upwards from a cigarette; dark eyes watching me with amused curiosity.

My footsteps beat harshly down the narrow lane flecked with light and shadows; hopeless… hopeless…. just hopeless.. But hadn't I always known it would be?

From out of the dark gap between buildings I caught a glimpse leaping shadows that suddenly grappled at me from all sides. So it was happening to me.. just as Old Pete had warned, I thought distantly, not even struggling.

"Ha! Ha!" A voice shrieked in my ear, deafening me.

"Tad!" I groaned.

"Gocha ya there matey."

"F-----n' scared ya t'death eh!"

"Nah! Not really. .." I lied shaking myself free, trying not to show my resentment and my relief and strangely something like disappointment; had I wanted to be a victim..?

Together we moved on down the alleyway lit by garish neon signs; other men, striding determinedly, followed by blunt shadows all around us. I gulped at the close air heavy with sickly-sweet odours, flinching at shrill laughter mixed with the faint sounds of dance music coming to me; feeling a grim, anxious excitement.. ..

"Watch yerselves.. Russkies....." Billy warned in a low voice as the four of us approached neon sign flashing *CLEOPATRA CLUB*; the lurid yellow and violet lights colouring the faces of the mob of heavy-set, belligerent-looking men milling around outside.

We went through the open doors flanked by gold painted plaster sphinxes chipped on the edges and entered a large room hung with a line of huge glass chandeliers and large-bladed fans tirelessly whisking the smoky blue air.

I hesitated rather repelled by the hubbub from the close-packed mass of men, glasses in hand, all talking and laughing noisily. Should I go back to the ship I wondered distantly, my blood pulsing as I became aware of numerous small, pretty women in colourful skin-tight sheath dresses, long slits down the sides giving glimpses of flesh, mincing boldly around laughing and smiling; coyly brazen.. . .

So at last.. I thought eagerly pressing forward through the jostling press of bodies, gasping in the stifling hot air, inhaling the sweat and sickly perfume smells.

"Hey Mr.. Mr... ."

I stared at the tiny girlish woman, her bright black eyes fixed teasingly on me.

"You buy me drink.." Her bright red lip-sticked lips opened to show small white teeth.

"Oh sure .." I murmured feeling a wonderful lightness; a deep relief.. at last..

"Money.. Mr.. .Give me your money... "She tittered archly putting out a small hand.

Hastily I pulled out wallet and watched fascinated as her nimble fingers deftly removed some notes handing the wallet back to me with a sweet smile.

"Take a seat.. over there .." She ordered pointing to a bench seat beside a low partition. I threw myself onto the black vinyl seat staring at the wiggling bottom of her shiny tight-fitting dress disappearing into the crowd. What if she just kept the money? I suddenly thought, wondering vaguely too where Billy and the others had got too. Perhaps I should have stayed with them.. yet it had all just happened without my will or intention..... ..

"I back... now..." I started at the shrill lively voice; watching with fascination the doll-like little creature, her rounded figure outlined by her shiny yellow-satin dress embroidered with swirling red dragons; my eyes fixing on her soft, plump arms, bared to the shoulder, as she set down a tray with two glasses.

"Me called Betty ..." She added slipping onto the seat beside me and curling up her legs, her tight dress riding up to show her plump calves.

"Nice to meet you ..Betty. "I grinned a fearful joy pressing through me.

"You drink Japan whisky velly good." Betty cooed her long bright red nails neatly plucking a cigarette from the pack I had put on the table.

"Cheers!" I laughed taking a long swallow ; the darkly amber coloured liquid burning a fiery path down my throat. I gasped and grimaced; tears coming to my eyes.

"You velly funny.. What you do..?" Betty giggled pertly.

"I'm off ship in the harbour.. Me.. and my mates that is.." I said glancing guiltily around; still I really hadn't meant to desert them.

"What you do on ship.." Betty asked leaning forward the cigarette stuck between her plump red lips.

"I'm er a Cabin-Boy.." I admitted, vaguely wondering if I should have pretended to be an officer. I scratched a match and held out the flame to the tip of her cigarette.

"Leally ? you velly Good Cabin Boy I think "Betty simpered blowing out a cloud of smoke; her dark eyes brightly admiring.

"Yeah? Well.. .she's a good ship ... "I said manfully swallowing down the whisky, suppressing a shudder. "We always call a ship 'She'...like a woman." I added with a knowing smirk.

"All women like you I bet..." Betty laughed, pouting teasingly. "You need more whisky .. I get for you...."

Dazedly I watched as she took the money from my wallet and then wiggled her way through the crowd. I gazed around, everything a soft blur, over the shouts and laughter came faint sounds of slow, pulsing music with a woman singing about love in husky American voice.. tears came to my eyes ..

I smiled genially as Betty slipped back beside me. We touched glasses with a faint clinking sound; how easy it all was.. I thought complacently joyful; my destiny.... ..

"You velly big hand." Betty tittered taking up my hand and placing her small palm against mine.

"You very small hand.." I murmured feeling giddy; slowly squeezing her soft hand, conscious of my immense strength.

"Hurt very much..." she whimpered; her eyes gloating bright.

I relaxed my grip her hand going limp in mine; my eyes wandering to her softly rounded bosom revealed by the tight fitting sheath dress.

"Betty...." I crooned gazing into her bright black eyes. "I .. you know.. you.."

"You drink whisky..." Betty cooed patting my knee, nibbling her upper-lip, her tiny white teeth stained red.

'Your last chance.. ship sails .... .' I thought absently, urgently; pressing closely against her warm body, greedily inhaling the cloying perfume.

"Cherry Boy you see...see...that means.. well.. I never... so ..." I stammered gulping the whisky, the alcohol piercing my brain like sharp needles.

"I get more whisky.." Betty said frowning, wrinkling her snub nose.

"No!.. no! "I burst out pathetically, swaying forward.

Betty pushed back at me and stood up, "I go.. freshen up. Come back quick.. ... "She bleated pettishly, frowning tiny cracks showing in her thick make-up.

Dizzily I watched as she smoothed out the wrinkles in her dress, her hands seductively sliding down her hips and thighs, shuddering, as casually she reached up an arm to push at her hair, showing a dark hollow.

Stifling a yawn she turned quickly about, her tiny womanly figure disappearing into the multitude of bodies.

I stared at the ash-trays full of ash and cigarette butts, two of them ringed with red; hearing the harsh shouting and laughter all around; soon.. soon I thought vaguely ..only wait.. surely it was my destiny .. wasn't that the key to life after all? just to wait and it would come of itself....

"Hey matey where d'ya f----g go? Billy right narked at ya bunkin' off. But ya got yerself a real hot one eh.." Norrie smirking broadly, had planted himself in front of me; swaying slightly he gawped vaguely around the room.

What did he want? I wondered resentfully; suddenly painfully conscious of time passing.. my life .. passing ..passing.

"Telly ya summat matey. She ain't coming back no more.."

I heard Norrie chortle, managing to shrug indifferently; knowing suddenly the awful certainty that she had abandoned me; a despairing gulf gaping inside me.

"Just after ya lolly anyway.." Norrie chuckled, abruptly pitching his broad bulk beside me, washing my face with sour whisky breath.

"Blood-suckers ain't they? squeeze ya dry like a orange n' chuck yer away....."

I nodded absently; was this how it was meant to be then?

"Oy have a dekko at at this..matey .." Norrie gurgled cheerily, pulling up the sleeve to show a tattoo of a heart with an arrow through it and on a ribbon twined with red roses: *MOTHER*. "What d'ya reckon.. Nice ain't it.?"

I nodded; how absurd it all was, Norrie's slurred, voice burbling in my ear.

"Done in Valetta weren't it? Put me in the nick cos I had no money to pay fer it. Say hows about ya coming hoam to meet me mam? Woants me to give up the sea doan't she. Get married settle doun loike. What yer say Phil matey? You wanta marry be faithful loike..No more taarts. Some on the ship never goes wi tarts yer knoaws..Daon't want to risk gi'n' wife the f-----n' clap. Wot yer say Phil? D'yer faancy coamin' home every day to a cuddle froam yer lovely. Get it when yer wants it? I dunno.. meself.. I loikes me freedom. Like now... Us'ns ashore together..ship-mates eh...." Norrie suddenly flung out an thick arm and squeezed me tightly against his chest. "Oy! Whaor ya goin matey?"

I yanked myself free and stood erect, the room spinning and swaying then without a word I was brutally pushing my way through the slowly shuffling bodies; flinging myself past the chipped, plaster sphinxes and into the alley, the paving stained by the neon lights. I staggered across to a wall, pressing my head into the hard surface.. Was this my destiny.. to be denied .. rejected.... endlessly humiliated..?

Footsteps clattered re-echoing along the alley re-echoing off the walls; at once I recognised the thick-voweled, tipsily cheerful voices; they're from the ship I thought recognising some of the faces as the small phalanx clumped past.

'Go with them 'I urged myself but a stubborn indecision kept me stiffly unmoving; the last echoes died away and I was alone in the shadowy darkness.

Where am I going? I wondered as I plodded through the vaguely menacing dark shadows thrown by the bare light-bulbs hung across the alleys; on and on.. my footsteps ringing out as I passed through one deserted alley after another; without purpose or direction. What did it matter? It was all empty .. meaningless.. hopeless..

I came to an abrupt halt, my heart thumping, gazing wonderingly at an illuminated white oval with *BAR* in black lettering, halfway down the alleyway. Had I meant to come here all along or was it just pure co-incidence.. or was nothing really a co-incidence?

A spasm wrung me, as I saw the empty chair at the back of the bar, yet I kept on towards the figure opposite, wearing a shapeless garment, motionless as if carved from a block of wood. What on earth was she doing still sitting there? I wondered irritably; was she waiting for something or what..?

Impassively she turned a sallow, flat face towards me, her flat cheeks badly pock-marked I noticed, staring unashamedly at her; a fierce triumph rising in me as obediently she got to her feet, an acquiescent gleam in her dull gaze.

My heart beating heavily I followed the lumpy figure through a side door, a puddle of water gleamed underfoot, a strip of night sky showing, the stars twinkling dimly; I gulped at the pungent, acrid air... yes.. I thought .. it all real..

But what is she thinking? I wondered the insistent scraping of her wooden clogs the only sound. How unreal.... absurd.. Scuff, scuff.. scuff, on and on such a feeble, pathetic sound and yet somehow indomitable....

Where was she going? With never a look back; perhaps she was leading me to be waylaid.. robbed.. murdered even, I thought smiling wryly. Did I hold my life so lightly?

A light touch on my arm turned me; a faint gleam shining out into the narrow passageway; dreamily I stooped to enter the small doorway; gasping at the mouldy, musty air.

Out of the chaos of shadows, a wizened, spectacled face peered out of a tiny glassed-in booth; the woman inclined her head and passed deeper into the gloomy recesses, reaching a low platform of squared-off logs, shiny from use.

I watched curiously as she took off her clogs and placed them into one of the small open square boxes lining the wall and then paused, dully looking at me. Slowly I understood that I had to remove my shoes too. But why? Was it somehow to render me helpless, perhaps prevent me from getting away?

'Now.. get out.. while you can ..' came the desperate thought, conscious of the figure waiting patiently in the shadows.

With an anguished shudder I sat down and violently tugged off my shoes and shoved them into one of the square boxes.

As if it was inevitable, pre-ordained... I mused distantly following the dim shape up the unlit, narrow stairway; one hand on the wall, the narrow wooden steps glassy smooth under my stocking feet, a creaking and groaning at every step; as if the flimsy, rickety structure was about to collapse around me.

Cautiously I stepped out of the stairwell, cracks of light from under the tiny doors on either side of the narrow corridor.

With a fast-beating heart I padded along the rough bare-wooden floor towards the shapeless figure waiting for me at the other end, my ears catching at sudden creaks and rustling noises from all sides.

Just like some weird dream I thought absently looking through the small doorway into the tiny room, a single electric bulb dangling on a long flex, glaring harshly on the bare walls only just above head height.

I stepped in sending huge shadows leaping about, registering the black metal bedstead with a brown mattress, a chair with a broken back, the wooden seat pitted with cigarette burns.

"Moneey.. . moneey.. pliss.."

The faint murmur seemed to come from out of the swaying shadows. My eyes averted I dragged out my wallet, turning away to extract the last note and eyes-closed press it into her palm.

Then I was alone.. with a sigh I sat down, the bed sinking beneath my weight with a twang, the rustling and creaking noises fading away to intense silence. I yawned nervously staring blankly at the bare floor-boards, starting at the sharp snick of the door being shut.... my blood pounding...

Dimly I became aware of a determined repeated plucking at my sleeve, looking up the broad shape before me, the thin cotton robe gaping to reveal the nipple on a drooping breast, my heart constricting so I could hardly breath, fixing me to the bed.

A knowing look touched the plain features; there was a shadowy gesture and an almost inaudible click.

Out of the sudden darkness, faint gleams of light marked the four corners of the room; my blood throbbing in my ears, collapsing onto the floor I began to tear off my clothes, my fingers stiff and clumsy, finally frantically pulling off my socks.

Blindly I scrabbled onto the clammy softness, breathing in the rancid body scents, thoughtlessly, ruthlessly piercing the gaping moistness; my body gasping and bucking to an exultant crest, finally to slip back, dropping limply to a shuddering, exquisite passivity ....

Slow exulting waves of sensation rippled over my motionless body; distantly there came a muffled shuffling and a momentary gleam of light before an implacable stillness fell on me.

I struggled to open my eyes, a vaguely mothering presence at the edge of my consciousness; the clear sound of trickling water, half-rising, I fell back into a shameless submissiveness; murmuring incoherently at the wet, rough caressing of my genitals.

Then I was alone again, stretched out in voluptuous nakedness in the musky gloom. So that was it.. I thought complacently, faintly conscious of a dull nagging ache, pressing through me. A dim light glimmered briefly into the dark room and I boldly flung out an arm to snatch at the loose robe.

"Again....again." I begged commandingly holding tightly to thin material, pitilessly suppressing the knowledge that I had no more money.

A joyful spasm ran through me, hearing the faint rustle of her garment falling to a shadowy heap on the floor.

"I.. I......." I gasped incoherently the bed twanging violently as I gleefully flung myself onto the flaccid body, desperately thrusting myself into the slippery wetness, reaching infinite depths, hearing a harsh, wild cry in my ears as I faltered and then broke, collapsing feebly onto her soft, flaccid breasts, vainly struggling to rise, a feathery darkness ruthlessly sweeping me to a dizzily blissful torpor.

Shards of light splintered the shadowy darkness; indolently I listened, the scuffing fading away into a suspenseful silence

'Get away .. now!.' I groaned feebly; galvanised by guilty, nervous tremors I fell off the bed onto the floor and struggled into my clothes. My shirt unbuttoned, trailing my jacket I cautiously pushed open the door and quickly tip-toed along the creaky corridor; half-falling, giggling, down the narrow slippery stair-case; emerging into the darkened vestibule; at once recognising the overpowering dank, musty smell.. Yes it was the same place...

'My shoes.. my shoes' I muttered imagining having to walk barefoot all the way back to the ship, fumbling into the dark square boxes and dragging them out; a supreme elation welling up within me as I tied the laces.

The small door gave at my touch and I was out into the narrow lane, a starless pale grey sky above. I took a deep ecstatic breath. Which way? Somehow it didn't matter in the least; my shoes clumping steadily onward without the least hesitation; my mind busy with stray thoughts: what about the poor woman? I had grossly deceived her... perhaps she would go to the Police.. But how could she prove it. ..? but how despicable of me.. how could I have behaved in such a dishonourable way? was I completely amoral? And what if I had caught the 'Clap' that I had been warned about? Wouldn't that be a deserved punishment? And how would I find the ship? What though if it had already left...what time had been written on the departure board...?

I came to an abrupt halt in the middle of the empty alleyway, before me the single dangling light-bulbs glowing dimly; in my mind came the scene at the dockside: the hawsers unloosed from the bollards… flung carelessly into the water… the ship moving with slow, irresistible momentum away over the gleaming dark waters .. abandoning me .. forever.

But from deep within rose irrepressible bubbles of pure elation……… how little it mattered… nothing mattered but my selfish contentment.. ..

I started off, striding powerfully, possessed of superhuman energy quite as if I could walk to the ends of the world pulsing with effervescent sensations.. so incomprehensible.. shame and fear and.. and.. yes.. joy.. fierce unyielding joy..

Coming to the end of another lane I looked up and saw the wide blue-black sky streaked with pale light.

'Dawn… 'I breathed coming to a complete stop, tears in my eyes. "Dear God who could have thought life could be so wonderful?" I murmured fixed with awe.

I moved thoughtfully on, a little relieved at seeing the now familiar network of dockside railway lines shining dimly in the faint dawn light.

Leaping from rail to rail, I tripped lightly forward, finding the dock gates ajar and slipping through unobserved. Deliberately slowing to a leisurely pace I strolled across the deserted quay-side, chuckling to myself as at some inexplicable, amazing secret; before me the gangway sloping upwards to the ship's superstructure spotted with the sickly glow of the deck-lights; above all a dark funnel stabbed a radiant pink dawn sky.. .

Chapter Twelve

Pressed against the fiercely vibrating stern rail I stared down at the froth-stained glassy mounds welling up from below, marvelling at their endless disintegration into a myriad of seething, frothing vortices…

Could I have caught the "Clap…" ? The question rose un-thought into my mind and at once panic seized me…….

.. . . perhaps even now as I stood here, gazing idly at the ship's wake the disease was inexorably eating away at me..? I stared helplessly into the foaming, churning maelstrom; wouldn't it be a just punishment for my sins….? But did I really believe in such retribution….?

Raising my eyes I saw how the churned up froth waters became a sparkling, lacy ribbon that floated peacefully away on the calm waters, a sudden joyous affirmation rising irresistibly through me. Somehow I just *knew* it couldn't be so.. my whole being a living protest against such an idea…. .. No it wasn't meant to be. .. my destiny was here.. now.. the living present moment.. body and mind subsumed into the unending shipboard routine, one with the ship, laden with wheat, passing resolutely through burning days and sweltering nights.. indomitably forging a passage through the Yellow Sea…

Yes, the Yellow Sea, I thought elatedly, seeing in my mind the brightly coloured map of the world that hung on the wall of the Geography class wall.. remembering how the Korean peninsula hung down across from the Chinese mainland, and picturing the ship, a tiny dark chip with a white tail in the a blue sea sailing steadily towards a port in Northern China….And with me aboard.. quite astonishing really…

All the talk now both in the Crew Mess and the Pantry was about China…… and what it would be like.. . Communist China I reminded myself, glancing at the frayed, faded Red Ensign fluttering spasmodically, thinking how the day before a plane had circled over us several times before flying away..

"Ca' canny loons.. jest maaking sure o'us." Jock had said with a chuckle.

"Better not f-----n' bomb us…" Ronnie had retorted. "F-----n' Reds.. Don't allow no tarts do they, ain't 'uman.."

Yes.. Red China, I thought gazing at the grey line sketching the horizon, the faintest of intimations of the vast land mass beyond with it's millions on millions of people.. And soon I would be among them.. How hard to imagine… ..

And what kind of place exactly was it we were sailing to? I had heard the Crew name the port several times. Ching Wang or something … Ching Wang.. Tao.. yes, that was it. None of the crew had been there which made it seem a little threatening and yet intriguing.. .Ching Wang Tao .. I repeated to myself.. like a name from a Chinese fairy story.. 'Once upon in the small town of Ching Wang Tao lived a poor couple who had an only daughter who they loved very much; now the years passed and she grew into a beautiful woman.. 'I shook my head and turned to Billy stretched out between rail and a broken-down chair, his eyes half closed against the glare, a cigarette smouldering away between his fingers…

"What time do you think we'll dock?" I asked casually, since leaving Nagasaki I had been conscious of a distance between the two of us; remembering the time when our friendship had seemed perfect. What had I done to spoil it? I kept asking myself.

"Dunno.. tomorra probably… "Billy muttered sitting up, flicking his cigarette butt over the rail. "Better get back eh,,.."

Side by side we walked down the heaving, trembling afterdeck, towards the engine's roar, the booms were still lowered and we had to step over pulleys and coils of rope and other gear left lying around the deck. Was that why the plane had come to look us over, I mused attracted by our slovenly appearance; recalling how I had heard some of the crew bitterly grumbling about it, blaming the Officers who had decided it wasn't thought worth the trouble to stow them away with our next landfall so near..

"What d'you think this Ching Wang Tao will be like?" I persisted glancing a little nervously at Billy.

"From what I 'ear a f------n' 'ole.." Billy scowled. "It ain't no Nagasaki.. ." He added with a sharp look.

"No.... I suppose not... "I smiled, gazing over the flat water glittering like polished steel; smelling again the musty odours of the shadowy interior, climbing again the narrow stairs, my socks skidding on the steps glassy smooth steps, passing along the narrow corridor with the sudden creakings and rustlings and seeing again the tiny square room the corners streaked with light, becoming dizzy at the thought of the infinitely soft, yielding body..

"N' next time ya 'ave to do it f-----n' proper like... "Billy said jeeringly.

"Really. ." I muttered weakly, gasping for breath.

"Yeah, right way is t'get 'em from behind." Billy said with a harsh, mocking laugh.

"Oh.." I murmured pretending an indifference, a deep sadness overwhelming me. Mechanically I carried on walking on down the deck, my mind reeling .. so I had failed after all then. .and just when I had thought I had proved myself... I stopped short, hearing a faint echo of the triumphant cry torn from deep inside me, conscious of a glow of pure, shameless delight burning within.. undimmed .. un-dimmable . ..

With a last look around the Pantry, the crockery chinking spasmodically, I hurried out on deck, to join Billy, both the Cooks, Old Pete and Mitch lined up along the ship's side to watch us dock. Already the ship's engines were reduced to dull throb as we moved ever closer towards a grey, flat land, shimmering dully beneath an overcast sky.

China.. China.. I echoed silently suddenly remembering how once my brother and I had frightened each other lying in bed with the lights off, hinting at one of my grandfather's Navy yarns about China ..

"Death by a Thousand Cuts.." was his name for it; the hapless criminal stripped naked and tied to a post before the executioner using a great bladed razor-sharp sword would commence by making tiny cuts ... again and again .. larger and deeper until the victim criss-crossed with slashes, streaming blood .. the last cut striking off the head in a single sweep of the sword.....

But it was China of long ago.. .. nothing to do with the modern reality that was before us .. slowly revealing itself to our eager eyes...... .

And yet even as the ship drew ever closer, the deck vibrating fitfully beneath our feet, the shore seemed to retreat before us, the grey featureless land fading away under the darkening sky; obstinately resisting our presence even at this time of greatest need, I mused a little fantastically.

Several of the Deck Crew came past, their boots scuffing along the deck.

"D'y a see them tugs! Coal burning.. Thought them had gone out with the Ark.." One them exclaimed indignantly in thick vowelled accents.

"See them spaarks fly out the fuunnel! Like bloody bonfire night. Then broake down. .didn't it... dead luucky we didn't smaash 'er.." Another chortled wryly.

"That's yer f-----n' Communism fer yer. "One of the others guffawed winking at me as they all passed on down foredeck.

There was pause and we all looked to Jock.

"At least theres nane o' they bum-boat loons swarming o' the ship yammering at yer t'buy..." He snapped, glaring around.

"Cos they ain't got f-----n' to sell..." Ronnie said a smirk on his doughy white face.

"N' ya can leave yer cabin unlocked without fear o' thieving .." Jock insisted, his face going bright red.

"To scared ta... steal that's why.. Live in fear .. Beat ya t' death fer nothing or send ya to some helluva prison... .."

Old Pete wheezed out. "I hears they're gonna have armed guards onboard..."

"Betta not put no f----g gun near me.." Mitch growled in a menacing tone.

I gave a quick glance at the small, bloated Assistant Steward a vicious scowl on his puffy face; vaguely conscious of being proud to be associated with his fearless intransigence.

"Quiet ain't it, by Harry.." Old Pete gasped out. "No seabirds..ya see.. Killed off everything that weren't no use as food....by Harry.. rats.. birds .. flies.. you name it.. a regular campaign.. exterminate all the parasites .. same with society.. workers encouraged to report on each other.. what they call er elitists.. pullin' themselves up.."

"So what dy'a say to that Jockie?" Ronnie sniggered, Old Pete wheezing to a breathless stop.

"Hoot maun.. what d'ya expect?" Jock retorted stoutly. "Just like the Russian Revolution.. overcoming all them centuries of mistreatment and exploitation.. bound to be a few mistaks yer ken.. Am I richt laddie?"

At once all eyes were turned on me.

"Yes.. well. ..French Revolution.. of course... and Russian.. and American.. ultimately maybe a good thing.." I stammered.

"Just so they don't try it on me..." Mitch growled and we all laughed; the sound instantly absorbed by the dense, humid air; the sky growing darker too.

Like Cortes and his men, I thought, no one speaking, the small knot of men all gazing with wild surmise towards the land.

Steely sheets of rain swept over the milky-brown water peppering the surface with tiny explosions; the ship barely moving we edged past steeply sloping mud banks green with dried slime; the ship's bow-wave, chafing the dirty froth clinging to the waterline.

A row of low shed-like buildings with shaggy, thatched roofs visible behind the filmy rain, looking as if freshly brushed on coarse wet paper, I thought, casual strokes leaching into a sepia-coloured ground. Do people really live here? I wondered dully.

Abruptly as it had started the rain stopped and the sun blazed down, raising dank earthy smells; along the top of the glistening, steaming mud bank appeared a line of slow-moving blue figures, all in cone-shaped wide-brimmed straw hats..

"Hey ..Look at me...look at me' I ordered mentally 'Me, Phillip Wight, Cabin-Boy on the good ship *MS Grimethorpe* bringing wheat from Canada to feed your famine-stricken multitudes.' Rather hoping for a sly, sideways glance from one of the figures but even as I had the thought, the entire line was swallowed up by the dried-out, dun-coloured land.

How lifeless.. worn out.. exhausted.. it appears, I thought rather despairingly ..as if long ago drained of all purpose or endeavour...

The ship's engines faded away, the hawsers tightening across water, the colour of milky tea pulling us towards a crumbling concrete jetty, the pillars covered with dirty white barnacles, coated with green slime..

"Built by the... Germans... yer knows.." Old Pete huffed with a wave of a fat hand toward the jetty. "Part of their.. er Concession.. until Brits got the Japanese to chase 'em out..".

On the dock was a large crowd, all with cropped black hair, all dressed in the same dark blue serge of loose tops and baggy trousers, all perfectly still, lidded black eyes blankly staring out of identical-looking round sallow brown faces.

"A f-----n' welcoming Party." Ronnie chirruped sarcastically and we all laughed, glancing at each other as if startled at the unexpected sound.

As one the crowd abruptly shrunk back and several soldiers in khaki uniforms pushed roughly through; awkwardly clutching old-fashioned looking rifles with wooden butts they formed a single line to face us, their sallow, round faces expressionless under their forage caps, a red star in the middle.

"Not exaactly the f----n' Grenadier Guaards." Mitch jeered and again we all laughed, a faintly defiant echo coming back from the buildings on the other side of the dock.

Still the crowd remained perfectly immobile, the tense silence broken by the harsh scraping noise as the gangway was run out over the concrete surface. Now the soldiers hesitantly stepped towards the gangway while the crowd quickly parted to allow a single person to pass through. A severe frown on his rather babyish face, bare-headed in a khaki uniform with red shoulder flashes, a holster at his belt, he marched up the gangway, a new-looking leather briefcase in one hand.

"Letters frae hame, dootless.. ......" Jock muttered.

Surely there must be one for me I mused; joyful hope mingling with a dread of disappointment.

Stepping out of the of the Officers Smoking Room I blinked against the harsh glare, the sun shining through the grain-dust rising like smoke into the clear blue sky; from all sides came a whirring of motors with metallic screeches more faintly a distant thudding, and a continuous sing-song screeching from a loudspeaker on the dock buildings ; a oily floury smell filled my nostrils.

Absently I noticed how the canvas cover on the hold had been removed and the steel hatch-covers folded back leaving the amidships hold wide open to the sky above.. .for the first time since leaving Vancouver, I thought, even now feeling the bitter disappointment that there hadn't been a letter for me; my eyes following the steel wires glinting in the sunlight running from the pulleys at the tips of the booms, before vanishing into the hold... ..

This is your life.. here ..now.. seeing all this.., I argued mentally, letting my gaze move along the booms hinged to the bottom of the King-posts, admiring the arrangement of steel guys running through a series of block and tackles secured to the bulkhead. A letter wouldn't make any difference to this reality, I continued now studying the blue-clothed Chinese Workers perched on metal seats at the base of the King-Posts busy working the two levers that controlled the electric winches, sending the oily wire-coiled drums noisily whirring first one way then the other. From conversations in the Pantry and Crew Mess I knew that the operatives were relatively inexperienced, recklessly racing the electric motors so the armatures continually were burnt out.

Yes.. I knew all this.. was part of all this.. part of history really .. Billy had merely glanced at his letter from an aunt in Wales and then crumpled it up and thrown it away with contempt. Why should it be any different for me and after all I would be back home in a few weeks. I mused going down the stairs and onto the afterdeck, stepping carefully past the guy-wires giving tension to the boom, connected to a block and tackle secured to rings set in the deck, as the boom swung the steel wires whipped viciously back and forth; like shiny-steel snakes striking out.

Going over to the hold I looked in, my eyes following the steel cables running down into the light and dark shadows below. Through the shining haze of dust I made out dozens of workers in the regulation blue serge, white cloths over their faces, standing on the heaped grain that sank beneath them. Using bamboo scoops some of them were busy filling woven bamboo mats with wheat, once filled one of them gathered up ropes attached to each corner and attached it to the dangling hook. A wave of the hand and with a whirring and the screech of steel on steel the swag moved jerkily upwards, grains of wheat raining down in the dusty sunlight.

I shaded my eyes the bulging swag swayed uncertainly high above my head, a dark blur in the glare watching as it was swung jerkily about and abruptly dropped onto one of the small wooden-sided railway wagons beside the ship. Standing in them were more of the blue-suited workers ready to tip the swags and release a flood of golden grain; puffs of dust rising up into the scorching hot, windless air.

All about the ship and dockside were troops of blue-coated workers armed with brushes and shovels sweeping and gathering so not a single grain was lost; always working without the least pause or idle glance around with the continuous shrill sing-song harangue from the loudspeakers.

But how did they bear it, working without a break in the stifling heat, noise and dust, I wondered returning back up the stairs to the lifeboat deck .. . Some of the workers I guessed, catching at a slight roundedness under the loose clothing and a fineness in their faces, were actually women and yet I thought with a sigh, denied all womanliness, just workers, neither male of female; like so many worker ants in their indistinguishable baggy blue garb.

From the vantage point of the life-boat deck I was able to see the long line of small wooden wagons piled high with the pale golden grain even as an ancient-looking steam train, belching sulphurous coal-smoke from it's narrow funnel, clanking and puffing furiously began pulling the squealing wagons through the dock-gates. I turned and climbed up onto one of the lifeboat stanchions straining my eyes to follow the train, wavering in the glare, before vanishing into the heat haze; a small dark smudge of smoke persisting in the bleached sky ..

Food for the starving, I murmured.

"Wight .."

"Sorry Sec. just .. having a breather .. ." I said turning back.

"Yes.. well.. never mind that.. a couple of things.. you're getting shore-leave tomorrow.. and I'm afraid.. ."

I nodded smiling inanely, the Sec.'s words booming in my head and yet somehow not quite making sense..

"So get a letter written and let your folks know.. and I'll see it gets off. And when you're ashore behave yourself .. we're having enough of a problem with Mitch and that Officer chappie.."

Again I nodded a dreadful excitement bubbling within me and yet somehow deadness that made me stare back dully at the Sec. who stayed in the doorway watching me and then with a shrug turned and disappeared down the companionway.

My hand shaking slightly I took up my pen..

Dear Mother and Father,

I'm writing this from China and well I have to tell you

I've just been told we're not coming back to Vancouver this trip..

A bit of a shock I have to admit but..

I paused staring around the Officer's Smoking Room.. hearing the Sec.'s words echoing in my head.. 'Not going back .. not going back..' I frowned.. trying to recall the rest of what he had said.. yes.. Australia.. that was it we were sailing to somewhere in Australia instead. I took a deep breath.. so that was my destiny then.. surely I should embrace it .. and yet a throbbing anguish tore at me.. and yet I must let my parents know, I thought slowly writing on.

We're at a place called Ching Wang Tao but I don't think you'll find it on a map.. just a harbour and a pier and some huts.. terribly dry and barren.. not a bit of green in sight.. No birds either ..they've all been killed! All the flies too.. awful isn't it !

I was rather hoping for a letter from you when we got here but so far nothing .. The Sec. blames the Chinese Authorities.. their very suspicious of us.. We have soldiers with loaded rifles! in the spare cabin next to us. They sit around all day playing cards while the workers dressed in these identical blue outfits.. slave all day in the dust and this unbearable humid heat.. Actually I had a bit of a run in with their officer he's always slinking around the ship, Mitch the Scouser I mentioned in my last letter nicknamed him "The Polecat" he hates him. The Sec. is worried it might give us problems with the authorities. The officer looks very smart in sharply creased uniform with leather straps and a gun-holster. I bet he thinks I'm terribly scruffy! There's several loudspeakers on the roof of the building opposite to the dock we're berthed and all day long a high-

pitched, sing-song female voice screaming. So I went up to this officer and asked him what she was saying.." *Work only to work.. Work for the Motherland.* "he told me quite straight faced. What a joke! The poor workers never stop, from morning and late into the night in the heat and dust and noise I was told some of them had suffocated in the hold.. buried by the grain.. So I told him that if it was me, I would jolly well refuse to work if I was going to be screamed at to work harder all the time.. though probably they are so used to it they don't even notice it.. or maybe so indoctrinated they even agree with it ..

The Officer told me in very precise English that it was a great joy to follow the guidance of Chairman Mao such a wise teacher and leader.

I told him that was rubbish and that the reason there was a famine was mainly due to Mao's foolish policies. He became very upset, stared at me in kind of horror then turned around and stalked off. Actually I felt a little sorry for him.. the look in his eyes....pure fear that what he always believed might not be true.. .

Goodness know how long we're going to be stuck here, Mitch calls it the "armpit of the world". They keep running out of freight wagons.. such small wooden ones a fraction of the size of our boxcars and pulled by ancient steam trains.. the smell of sulphurous coal-smoke everywhere and the Chinese winch operators haven't been trained properly and keep burning out the winch motors.. Lecky that's what we call the ship's electrician is being driven crazy replacing the armatures and there's only a few spare ones left. The dust from the wheat (like dirty flour) is everywhere so it's absolutely impossible to keep the ship clean. It gets everywhere the watch you gave me on my last birthday has stopped, clogged up with dust.

Though that doesn't stop the Sec. from insisting we keep cleaning just as if we were at sea.. So far we haven't been allowed ashore though we've been promised a coach trip to the Great Wall of China so I'm really seeing the world..I'd better finish this so it can be posted .. Love Pip..

P.S I miss you all..

I stopped writing feeling the grief rise irresistibly dry-eyed.. great silent sobs wracking my body.. .. How could I survive? Day after day of the same tedious toil with no end in sight.. on and on.. really it was unbearable..

Absently I heard a subdued, intermittent yet persistent buzzing and turning around saw with surprise a large fly crawling up the glass of the porthole. So they hadn't managed to kill them all yet, I thought with a wry smile; closely watching the little creature calmly cleaning it's tiny, bulbous head with minute hairy front legs...conscious of something like fellowship; to survive .... endure... was all..

CHAPTER THIRTEEN

"You'll get us all shot you f-----g arsehole!" Norrie yelled as Tad dashed down the gangway and past the two startled guards at the bottom, then began wheeling crazily about the dockside.

The three of us followed after him, laughing excitedly. Ashore at last. But might we be arrested or mistreated? No.. somehow I couldn't believe such a thing..

I wandered a little further down the dockside attracted by a Donkey engine, thudding away with ponderous monotony. Watching the tall smoke--stack belch out thick black smoke shot with glowing sparks I remembered how I one day on deck I had met Chips and expressed my contempt for such antiquated equipment only for him to tell me with a gentle, knowing smile that it would out-pull any electric winch on the ship..

The steam engine was coupled to an equally primitive-looking crane angled over the ship a steel cable running from it's tip down into the No.1 hold. With a terrible screeching and grinding every so often it would hoist the bulging swags just clear off the ship's side and with a ferocious clanking noise, spewing wisps of steam turn slowly about and add them to a heap of wheat now accumulating on the dockside due to a shortage of wagons.

Standing there in the heat of the sun, the mingled coal--smoke, oil and wheat--dust smells reminded me of a time when as a small boy in a farmyard, somewhere in England I had stood watching a steam-powered threshing machine at work, forgetting all about dinner until my mother had come to fetch me.. .. and now, here I was far away on a quayside in Northern China, .. the two experiences linked by the invisible thread of my life.. how amazing that was... ..

"Are ya coming Phil. ." Billy shouted from halfway across the dock.

I turned and sprinted towards the three of them, my legs stiff and clumsy feeling, the rush of the burning hot air on face.. this is what it is to be alive, I thought almost dizzy.

Together we approached the huge double-wooden gate, topped with spikes and blocking the entrance to the harbour compound, On one side was a small guard--house and beside it stood a number of stocky, grim--looking soldiers, rifles slung over their padded jackets, soft round caps with a red star, a sleepy, Mongolian cast to their features. Two of them marched towards us and began to closely examine our Shore--Passes. I glanced back, seeing the ship, through the clouds of dust, the fore and aft decks choked with booms and running gear, the white superstructure dribbled and spotted with orange-brown rust, revealed in the harsh glare of the afternoon sun

MY home now, I thought with a quiver of emotion.

Our passes finally approved one the guards opened a side-door we clambered through to be met by a bright red banner with black Chinese characters on it hung between two poles.

We stopped to stare up at it.

"Some saying of Mao.. I bet "I declared. "The same as that loudspeaker screeching out.. 'Work.. only work.. for the Motherland.. that sort of thing..'

"How d'ya know all that "Billy asked frowning suspiciously.

"That soldier Mitch calls the "Ferret" told me. "I explained. "He's a bit of a fanatic but then he's been indoctrinated since a child.. brain-washed.. ."

"Zee dirty Chinks.. need wash." Tad squealed.

"Who cares what 'e t'inks. "Billy snapped irritably . we moved on, walking four abreast down the empty dirt track passing through flat bare earth that stretched away on all sides into the shimmering silent glare.

A little way further on we passed a straggling line of thatched huts, like mounds of blackened hay, the ground of bare earth beaten smooth.. A movement caught my eye. An old man appeared out one of the doorways, blinking at the sunlight; deeply wrinkled, bald except a few long single hairs, he gave a toothless yawn then meeting my stare, a sly, amused look came to his age-worn face.

Probably mad or senile, I thought but smiled back, turning and running after the others, the three figures dark shapes in the sunlight. The road rising slightly, I began to sweat heavily; why was everything such an effort in this place? Even the air seemed thicker.. heavier.. .

A little further along we came to a plain narrow building weathered grey above the small porch was with a wooden sign that read: *Seamans Rest Club.*

One after another we stomped up the steps and into the shadowed musty interior, the tall windows on each side of the bare, discoloured walls pasted over with yellowing paper. I glanced up at the row of carved wooden roof beams. Was it a church once I wondered ..

At the far end was a long table covered with a cloth and behind a shelf crowded with green bottles with bright coloured labels. Staring impassively at us were two barmen neatly dressed in white short-sleeved shirts and black bow-ties.

"Some bar this" Billy grumbled and we all laughed; our voices echoing harshly around the empty space.

Billy and Norrie went over to the bar and brought back four of the green bottles and glasses set them on one of the whitish marble-topped tables; we pulled out the ornamental cast-iron chairs the legs scraping noisily on the bare wooden floor and sat down.

"Doan't think much of this Chink beer." Norris growled crashing his glass onto the marble top in disgust.

"Zee f-----g cabbage water.." Tad squealed.

Frowning I sipped the pale beer, not sure what to think.

"Yer goes fer the Chinese stuff dontcha Phil?" Billy said.

"Chinky.. like a chinky.." Tad sniggered pulling at the edges of his eyes with his fingers.

"Soapy water .." I sneered pushing away my glass with contempt.

We all got up, condemning the beer in loud voices, our footsteps clumping loudly on the wooden boards; as if asserting the very fact of our existence I thought. At the doorway I looked back at the two bar-tenders watching impassively. What must they think of us? I wondered suddenly ashamed.

Beside the door was a small room was a number of display cabinets and we went in to have a look. I gazed through the dingy glass at the carved wood and jade figurines of a squatting fat grinning old man along with fans and painted scrolls faded and water-stained and thought of buying something to take home but was overcome by a sense of futility and could only stare helplessly at the scanty display of dusty souvenirs.

"Go on buy summat Phil.." Billy urged jeeringly.

But I shook my head stubbornly and we all went on out into the dense humid silence passing along the road lined with naked trees a few withered leaves adhering to the bare branches..

Billy and I stopped as Tad and Norrie began squabbling over something, shoving and pushing at each panting and swearing at each other as they scuffled half-heartedly.

"Go on Tad .. sock 'im one.." Billy idly encouraged them, lighting up a cigarette.

Listlessly I kicked at the road stirring up clouds of fine dust; as if I was evaporating into the dense humid silence.. How utterly pointless.. meaningless it all was.. I gazed dully around the featureless ground dissolving into a haze; beyond lay the sea a leaden strip reflecting the sun's glare...

With a sudden movement of my legs I began walking away through the wiry dried grasses down the long steep slope to the sea; distantly hearing the shouts of the others. At the edge of the sandy beach I paused allowing the others to catch up and together we started out across the soft white sand passing a small group of Chinese women with small children all busy digging in the sand. As one they lifted their heads to gawk at us.

As we advanced, long wavelets snaking forward in frothy curves reached towards us across the hard wet sand; fascinated by the foam-spattered glinting tawny waters sliding invitingly to our feet, hesitantly drawing back we came to a halt..

For a minute or two we stared daringly at each other; then in a sudden impulse we were all pulling off our clothes in reckless abandonment; white bottoms gleaming against tanned skin shouting and laughing joyfully we sprinted through the gently foaming surf, the sun blazing down on us out of the blue sky...

Knee-deep I flung myself into the gleaming opaque water, revelling in the pure sensation of the water's slippery caressing of my naked body I paddled slowly around, looking around out for the others.

"Ya!" Tad screamed, waist deep, hitting the water so sheets of spray flew in all directions.

"Get'im mates; duck the mad Pole!" Billy shouted, emerging from the water, flicking back his quiff rivulets of water streaming down his sun-brown body.

There was rush of bodies through the placid waters; a confused sudden entanglement of arms and legs; gasping and spluttering amongst the frothed up water, lungs bursting with hoots and wild yells; Tad's flailing gangly limbs jerking and slithering from the our fiercely grasping hands. Finally he managed to break free and stood swearing and splashing water toward us from a safe distance.

"Stuff it.." Billy gasped and breathing heavily we staggered back to drop down into the bath-like shallows.

With my finger-tips resting on the sandy bottom I delicately balanced my floating body, my penis waving slightly below; the sun's rays touching my skin just beneath the water's surface; the gently undulating waves washing over my neck; eyes half-closed, immersed in pure bodily sensation; my arms smarting from the fierce struggle; distantly hearing Norrie bawling, "Why dya think it's called the Yellow Sea? .. ..Cos it's full of piss!" .. I smiled despite myself; dimly wondering what was going to happen to me; would I ever get home? Was it all predestined.. my destiny or just chance.. who had decided we shouldn't return to Vancouver? Perhaps some office worker.. utterly ignorant of my existence .. perhaps on the top floor of some office building somewhere in the world.. Chicago.. London ..Sydney .. New York...perhaps meeting a colleague at the water-cooler.. . 'Hiya Dave..Got this loada wheat in Australia to shift.' Yeah? How about the *Grimethorpe*.. should soon be finished unloading I hear' 'Yeah? Good idea.. thanks..'

And so quite by chance we were being sent to Australia ..and my life changed forever.. and yet somehow I couldn't believe it was mere chance.. But why not? I sighed opening my eyes and catching at sudden glittering from high above. What might it be, I wondered vaguely

"Looksa zee ..! "Tad yelled excitedly.

A small knot of children stood at the tide-line pointing at us and squealing to each other in shrill voices.

"Lets give the little buggers a scare... "Billy laughed. "One...Two....Three!"

In an explosion of froth the four us burst out from the water, like white-banded sea-creatures we charged through the gently rolling surf, splashing and shouting; spray sparkling around us, a vastly extravagant scattering of diamonds.

Like a flock of tiny birds, the children turned as one and fled shrieking and were soon hidden by the sand dunes.

Laughing and coughing we reached our clothes, scattered over the churned-up sand.

I began to get dressed, from the corner of my eye seeing Billy standing casually smoking; his lithe body, sun-tanned except for his white loins, the pubic hair and genitals exposed in the bright light; just like a classical bronze statue I thought.

"Looksa Phil.. zee fancy Billy!" Tad suddenly squealed hysterically, nakedly leaping up and down; his thin arms and legs making him look like hairless baboon.

"Now yer ain't gonna home, Phil "Billy grinned brushing sand off his legs. "Gotta know what yer really likes. What yer say mateys....."

"Yeah.. afore Bo'sun do "Norrie chortled, squatted on the sand, pulling a shirt of over his head the rolls of fat on his body reminding me of one of the figurines in the gift shop.

"What do you mean?" I wondered anxiously struggling to pull my trousers over my wet skin stuck with sand grains.

"Ya see Phil.. when ya at sea for months.. it's different." Billy said looking up from pulling up his trousers.

I fixed my eyes on the foaming wavelets endlessly sweeping forward and backward over the sand, my fingers suddenly clumsy as I tried to do up my shirt buttons; had I been expecting this moment in some way perhaps, I mused anxiously from one to the other; clutching my shoes to my chest, the three figures pressing closer. .

I jerked back struggling violently as the three leapt forward and grabbed me pining my arms to my sides.

"Get off me.. ! "I raged, struggling violently.

"Put 'im down .." Billy yelled and I was shoved brutally forward downward, turning my head at the last minute to avoid swallowing sand; feeling my trousers and underpants being dragged down to my ankles.

"Nice arse.., Phil.." Billy laughed hoarsely.

"Hey stick this up 'im.." Norrie croaked to raucous shouts.

A burning softness pierced me flushing my thighs and my back; how shameful.. .

"Ya Pheel youze real good man ...." Tad sniggered coarsely and the others laughed knowingly; a flush of pride perversely springing up.

"No.." I screamed thrashing ever more wildly. Suddenly I was free; scrambling madly forward on all fours, then turning and frantically jerking up my trousers and underpants.

"Ya a real scrapper, ain't ya Phil.... "Billy said grinning at me, taking a comb out his pocket and running it through his hair.

"Yeah.." Tad and Norrie chorused gaily.

I sat down to put on my shoes, choked with shame. How had I let this happen? Was I naturally perverted? Absently

I noticed at the top of the ridge of land that ran steeply down to the beach, a flickering dazzling light. Was that what I had attracted my attention when lolling in the surf?

"Why don't we go up there." I said trying to pretending as if nothing had happened. "I think there must be some building up there. Worth a look"

"Nah. Don't fancy that." Billy said indifferently blowing out cigarette smoke.

Norrie and Tad grinned and shook their heads. I hesitated and yet felt as if I had to prove my self. .. my independence..

"Don't forget to write.." I heard Billy call out and the others laugh loudly. I kept on my feet sinking into soft sugar-like sand, my head aching under the hot sun ; my eyes aching from the light reflected by the sea. Perhaps the others were following after all I thought and gave a furtive backward glance but there was no sign of them. I rubbed at my arm aching from where I had been held and felt again their combined overmastering hold on me.... how utterly humiliating, yet perhaps I had asked for it.. ? No matter how hard I tried I wasn't one of them.. All I could do was keep walking, following a faint path up the gravely slope spotted with clumps of dry grass, conscious of the pull on my calf muscles as the slope rose steeply and then catching at a roof-line edging into the deep blue sky. What building was it... Was I trespassing perhaps .. at any moment I might be challenged by a soldier with a gun.. and yet how little I cared.. let them shoot me, I thought indifferently.

Near the top I paused for breath and looked back down at the beach; a few minutes ago I had been a small figure plodding along the empty beach beside the white-frilled waves.... Like Cain I thought, marked out as different from all those around me..

I scrambled up the rest of the narrow path and pushing through glossy green bushes found myself looking at a large two storey villa enclosed by the remains of the remains of a wooden fence. One glance told me it was deserted; dry grasses growing up against the pastel-grey stucco walls; the curtain-less windows staring crazily back at the blinding glare of the sun. Under the pointed red-tiled roof with squat chimneys at each end it fallen from the clear blue sky into this withered desiccated landscape.

Was it perhaps the home of Resident of the German Concession? But why didn't the Chinese Communists make use of it?

I looked at the severe rectangular front.. square windows on either side.. wasn't there some lingering spirit of the colonial regime.. stern.. methodical...

A little nervously I went down the concrete path tall dried up plants growing out of the cracks, to one of the low windows and put up a hand to shade my eyes... making out a large room the bare dusty floor strewn with yellowed papers, faded wallpaper peeling from the wall; caught in the glare of sun against one wall lay an elegant dining room chair with a broken leg the only furniture....

I drew back; the windless heat of the afternoon like a vacuum draining me of any purpose. I went back and sat on the low step leading up to the narrow porch, with my elbows on my knees resting my chin in my hands. Why had I come here? What did I hope to find? .

Before me the ground sloped into a rectangle carpeted by pale grey mosses surrounded by dark green shrubbery reflecting the sun light.. Could it have been an ornamental pond, with water lilies and golden carp rippling the surface as they came goggling up from the muddy depths.. .. or a rose garden perhaps.. imagining a willowy figure in a full length dress, her face hidden by her wide brimmed straw hat decorated with flowers, moving slowly about her arms full of rose stems.... speaking in crisp commanding tones to the Chinese gardeners bent over weeding....and then the voices of children in the shrubbery.. strident, spiteful.." Don't do that.. It hurts.. ... I'll tell mother.."

Only of course it would have been in German... How long had they lived here? How many time had they watched the sun rise from out of the Yellow Sea? But had they been happy? Wouldn't the man have been a red-face bullying brute with a pith helmet and swagger stick? Perhaps not.. who knows he may have been a scholarly type.. interested in Chinese antiquities .. devoted to the welfare of his workforce.. wearing himself out in an effort to bring improvements.. in the face of superstition.. distrust.. ignorance...

And then the events of world history in far away Europe.. rumours.. and confusing reports.. and the realization it was all over.. last-minute packing .. the journey to the dockside.. and a last look back.. and what had been the point.. all those years of struggle and toil and effort .. and now all that was left was an abandoned house mouldering away the garden already obliterated .. I sighed weighed down by a sense of futility of life..

Out of the silence came a harsh, shrill noise.... then silence. Was it a bird or insect? Was that something moving in the dense shadows of the shrubbery? Again the noise, harsh and somehow cruelly jeering. I stood up my heart beating, unwilling to pass through the blackly writhing branches and pointed shiny leaves of the massed shrubbery..

There must be another way down to the docks I reasoned, quickly passing beside the house, past a wide stretch of barren ground the old kitchen garden or so I guessed and through a grove of silvery leafed trees with tall smooth grey trunks .. and along a smooth worn strip that ran straight ahead .. Surely the road that was used when the house was occupied..

I glanced back at the house, the back in shadow, the sun already below the roof line, long shadows reaching out. I hurried intent now on getting back to the ship before it became dark.. Regretting I hadn't stayed with the others?

Always I was doing the wrong thing.. ...

I stopped short the smooth track petering out into bare open land stretching away to the hazy horizon, behind me the sky glowed a fierce red.

A panic seized me and I stood trembling uncontrollably looking fearfully around at the empty land, slowly, inevitably sinking into a grey shadowy formlessness. What was that. A low whistle .. two notes, the second lower .. just the way my father called my mother when they became separated.. A bird..perhaps? Again ..it must be someone looking for me. But who? I turned around and around listening intently, waiting ..the minutes passing by. Nothing .. utter silence.

'Dear God..' I murmured, 'Help me.. help me..' I shook my head angrily How weak.. spineless. just like a little child... What had happened to the intrepid adventurer? If the sun was behind me the docks must be to my right..

I turned sharply, forging my own way across the dusty earth, valiantly suppressing the lurking doubts that I might be going the wrong way entirely; the last faint orange glow fading from the sky.

I stumbled and almost fell, giggling at the sense of the absurd; how had I come to be here .. alone in the empty darkness of Northern China;

I moved slowly my eyes staring intent on the ground before my feet.. yes.. alone...... utterly a tiny, warm-blooded organism moving through the evening dark....Of no real significance... what if I were to fail to appear back at the ship.. Of course there would be a search party.. a little stir.. but in the end.. a few shrugs ..blank looks and the ship would sail away.. my parents would grieve of course... my mother especially but in the end...

I paused, breathing heavily; out of the inky blue darkness, a star was shining brightly.. the evening star.. so clear and bright.. and somehow enduringly vital.. no, not alone I thought with a sudden sharp ache, moving slowly along, not alone and there in front of me was a sickly yellowish aura rising into the dark; the floodlights around the dockside, I realized with a sudden joy... hastening eagerly forward, crossing a shallow, empty ditch and gaining the road.. But what was that? Out of the darkness swelled a black shapeless mass and a strange, thrushing sound...

I stepped back into the ditch, anxiously waiting as the dense mass of bodies moved steadily past, silent except for

the combined scraping of their feet on the pressed earth ..
Workers returning home, heads bowed, the lampshade
hats hanging down their backs ; human-shaped husks,
I thought, sucked dry of life.. meaning..

Finally the last stragglers scuffed past, dark moving
forms, empty shells, how awful I thought, starting at a
whispered giggling and out of the shadows a glimmer of
bright eyes...

I smiled to myself, stepping back onto the road and
gazing wonderingly after the retreating multitude.. until the
faint scuffing stopped and all was lost in the darkness..

The large double door was still open and I presented my
pass to the dough-faced guards and stepped into the
dockside compound, strangely dark and silent, the air still
heavy with smells of coal-smoke and grain dust. From
behind came a scraping and crashing and rattle of chains as
the gates were closed and secured. What had it all meant?
I wondered distantly. Was it just a sequence of events..
impressions .. experiences.. like atomic particles endlessly
rebounding and colliding ..

I shrugged stepping eagerly forward over the railway
lines set into quayside, empty of wagons, before me the
ship's superstructure rose up out of the darkness, picked
out in bright lights, the flood-lit decks criss-crossed
with dark shadow from the cables and booms; the dull
thudding of the ship's generator coming clearly out of the
silence.

But who was that? At the top of the gangway a figure
was leaning out looking over the.

"Where have you been ?" The Sec. said, a slight frown
masking his annoyance, I guessed as I reached the top of the
gangway.

"Nowhere really. ." I said shrugging perversely obtuse.

"Well .. I added the Sec.'s frown deepening. "I went up
to have a look at this house at the top of the beach looking
out to sea. The Residents House I guess from the time this
area was a German Concession, completely abandoned.. a
bit spooky.. then I got lost coming back."

"What happened on the beach. Billy said you got into a funk and went off by yourself" The Sec. said, rocking slightly on the balls of his feet; watching me closely.

I looked away, feeling my face go hot and yet somehow it was all so long ago; almost as if it had never happened.

"Not really.. just wanted to do a bit of exploring, but they weren't interested." I explained looking down.

For a minute or two neither of us said anything; both caught up in conflicting emotions. I gestured back across the dockside." Why aren't they working?"

"Run out of wagons, it seems.." The Sec. said frowning. "They all suddenly stopped and left. Captain not pleased. That reminds me the Red Guard Officer was looking for you, to give you this "The Sec. held out a small red booklet. "He's gone too, don't think he'll be back somehow....You two were getting friendly were you?"

I shrugged, looking wonderingly at the bright red cover. "Not really.. we had one short discussion.. Perhaps ..." I shook my head; had he wanted to befriend me?

"Another thing coach trip to see the Great Wall had been cancelled.. no reason given.. Inscrutable Chinese and all that "The Sec. said rubbing his chin. "Better get changed and start work."

Strange the Sec. wasn't at all angry I thought stepping into the Amidships; the steel bulkheads echoing to the shouts and crashing of pots from the Galley, gladly breathing the familiar acrid, burnt-food smells.

"What f-----n 'appened to ya matey?" Billy grinned coming out of the Pantry and slapping me on the back.

"Got f-----n lost.." I laughed back; yes, we were ship-mates no matter what, I thought hurrying along to the cabin.

CHAPTER FOURTEEN

In the pale dawn light I made out a small figure at the ship's side gazing steadily out over the darkly shimmering waters, while I hesitated Chips turned to me.

"Lovely morning…. "I smiled, breathing in the fresh salty air; the muffled thud of the engines breaking the stillness.

"Thee says right sonny." Chips chuckled contentedly. "Lively ain't she? Kinda eager you could say."

"Yes.." I laughed; now the holds had been emptied the deck rose and fell much more vigorously; moving to the rail the sound of water rushing along the hull seemed much louder; perhaps in exultation at being at sea, I mused.

Chips raised a sinewy arm to point to the luminous grey vastness above the darkly gleaming water.

I stared hard into the luminescent grey-mauve sky.

"Stella Maris.. Star of the Sea .." Chips explained patiently. "Protector of Mariners.." "Let's hope so.. ." I murmured uncertainly.

"Tha'll be missing home, eh sonny. "Chips said rubbing his chin.

"Home?" I echoed as if to give the word definition.. meaning…

I gestured out towards across the ruffling water towards the glowing dawn sky. "This is my home now.." I declared boldly, conscious of the sea-breeze brushing my face, stirring my hair around my neck.

"Heh Heh. . Thee says well sonny. ." Chips chortled approvingly, his bright blue eyes on me. "But to be right thee needs a hair-cut."

"Yes.. I guess.." I laughed flushing as the ship's carpenter reached out a hand and ran his fingers lightly through my hair. "I haven't had one since Vancouver.."

" Come thee to No.2 Hatch Block some Sunday afternoon n' I'll clip thee a mite…" Chips said his eyes crinkling in a smile before moving away down the deck.

For some time alone now I stayed at the ship's side looking out at brightening sky, the morning star fading as a vast pink and orange glow flamed across the sky, a swathe of glittering golden scales reaching over the water towards the ship. Yes, I thought solemnly it *is* true.. this is my home... my life.. now..

Leaving the muggy air of the Officer's Smoking Room I went quickly to the rail and gazed around.. yes to be out to sea again.. the sparkling blue water all around and the clear skies above.. How wonderful that was.. and how happy the crew were even Mitch seemed pleased, a crooked grin on his face he waddled around crooning tunelessly: *"You'll never get me on Slow Boat to China.."*

Looking down on the After-deck, I felt almost dizzy remembering how just a day before it had had been crowded with a myriad blue-costumed workers toiling in the sun the incessant screeching of the winches, the shrill jabber of the loudspeaker mixing with the jangle and crashing of wagons and puffing, snorting steam trains.. the scorching windless air thick with the sulphurous reek of coal-smoke and fine floury dust that coated everything.. .. ...

Now order and calm are ours again, I thought contentedly, remarking how the steel hatch-covers rolled flat and covered with the familiar faded, green tarpaulin secured with wooden wedges hammered home with sledge hammers; the booms pulled upright and secured to the King Posts with bolts.. the complicated array of blocks and tackles and pulleys with all the cabling all taken down coiled and sorted and put away in the store-cupboards in the Hold Blocks.. A kind of magic I thought surveying the empty deck though I knew the deck-crew had laboured under arc-lights late into the night as soon as the ship had left port.. readying for the long sea voyage to Australia. .

Australia.. how amazing it was to think of it! Me .. Phillip Wight bound for Australia... the Antipodes, the other side of the globe, my mind flushing with hazy recollections of the voyages of Cook, Darwin, Tasman ... so many intrepid explorers .

I pressed against the vibrating rail, gazing idly down as the Day Gang appeared to finish sweeping up the piles of dust lying over the deck; their voices ringing cheerily across the calm water.

Now two of them came to the ship's side holding a piece of old canvas heaped with dust and other rubbish.

"One. . !. Two …! "They called out.

"Three! "I joined in as the load went flying over the bulwark to splatter into the water and slowly sink into the shining water, staining it a pale brown; wisps of dust drifting away to vanish in the brilliant sunlight.

At the sound of my voice all of the Day Gang looked up at me.

"We'll maka f----n' sailor of tha yet." Hobbsie bellowed jovially and the others roared with laughter .

I grinned back, rather envying them working out in the open air rather than in the stale oven like heat of the amidships; watching the four stripped to the waist their tanned bodies gleaming as they moved about cheerily tossing pieces of broken wood and other odds and ends overboard to slowly bob away over the gently swelling ocean. Bringing to mind the times when moodily patrolling the tide-line of a Vancouver beach I wondered about the strange objects washing up by the foaming wavelets.. Now the mystery was revealed.. it came from sailors gleefully throwing rubbish overboard after leaving port....

"N' f----n' good riddaance!" Hobbsie hallowed throwing a last piece of wood to splash down with white foam onto the blue waters.

"Finished here are we Mr Hobbs.." A voice came from just below where I was standing.

I recognised the voice of the 2nd Mate .

"Certainly Sirr." Hobbsie drawled with good-humoured insolence.

"Let's see shall we.." The 2nd Mate said in rather boyish voice moving into full view. A slim figure, clean-shaven with fine gingery hair, dressed in smartly creased white trousers in a short-sleeve shirt with gold barred shoulder flashes he seemed to me to belong to a different species to the hairy, bare-chested, sun-burnt Day Gang in their torn shorts and sandals.

The 2nd Mate pointed out various places where small drifts of grain dust remained. "I trust you are taking this seriously Mr Hobbs. "The 2nd Mate chided gently. "A dirty ship is a dangerous ship. .."

"Veary true Sur. Bet they' larned ya that at Naval College."

Hobbsie answered in faintly sneering tone winking at the others of the Day Gang who stood around grinning.

The 2nd Mate's brow wrinkled with irritation. "Enough of this Mr Hobbs.. Take your men for'ard. Help the Bo'sun get the hawsers in order."

"But Surr.." Hobbsie protested moving forward until his broad hairy chest almost touched the 2nd Mate's white shirt. "Youse juest said yerself loike w'se aint finished here amidships." He glanced up and winked at me.

The 2nd turned and looked up too.

"Just take your men for'rd Mr Hobbs. "He said firmly, without the least change of tone.

Hobbsie didn't move, a belligerent look on his face, his massive arms partly raised; like a gorilla about to reach out and crush to death a hapless victim I thought surely Hobbsie wasn't about to refuse to obey an order? That would be mutiny....

"What ever you say Surr.. ." Hobbsie boomed out, jerking his head at the others and they marched away together, laughing uproariously as if it was all some hilarious game.

The 2nd Mate stayed just below watching them pass along the amidships to the foredeck. What gave him such authority? I wondered. Was it simply his rank, as shown by his smart uniform? Or was it the man himself....?

The next minute to my surprise he had bounded up the stairs and was in front of me.

"Mr Hobbs certainly er, seems to appreciate your er, notice." He said with a slight smile.

"Yes.. .er.. Sir.. ." I stammered, wishing I had got away while I had the chance, stealing a glance at the 2nd Mate; one hand was resting lightly on the rail looking out over the freshly swelling ocean gleaming so brightly in the sunlight; how self-confident he is, I mused.

"So you wont be getting back home er Vancouver, this trip.." He said turning and looking thoughtfully at me.

I gave a quick shake of my head, flushing slightly, was the whole ship talking about me then?

"But you like the life er at sea..?" The 2nd Mate went on, absently tapping at the rail, the ring on his finger making a dinging sound. "Get on er, well with the rest of the Crew eh ? Some er real characters.. eh like Mr Hobbs.."

I shrugged evasively.

I wonder er if you'd like to er a get on Deck.. You must get fed up washing dishes and cleaning floors I bet.." The 2nd Mate voice came to me out of the dull roar of the engines.

I stared down at the deck, surely that was what I really wanted? And yet now I was quite unsure. . .

"It could lead er.. somewhere you know.." The 2nd Mate went on sympathetically. "Ever thought about a career in the Merchant Marine?.. Go to a Naval College... become a Deck Rating. Navigation now that is a real skill, you know no er, no road signs or street names.. out here .." The 2nd Mate made a quick gesture over the vastness of shiny blue--green watery hills and valleys flecked with foam. "Learn how to read charts... plotting a course.. even with radio fixes as much an art as a er ..science."

"Well perhaps .... "I responded doubtfully conscious of a rising excitement and yet worried too what might Billy think.

"You don't seem too keen." 2nd Mate said frowning; was he annoyed I wondered.

"Well no.. I mean.. yes.." I stammered flushing hotly. "Only well Billy and I.... we're Cabin-Boys.. ship-mates you see... ".

"Of course .." 2nd Mate said frowning thoughtfully. "Well anyway think about it.."

"Yes.. yes.. .. thanks.. thanks a lot "I murmured eager to sound grateful.

With a thoughtful nod the 2nd Mate turned sharply away; his footsteps clattering down the stairs.

Back inside the Officer's Smoking Room I picked up the polishing cloth my mind seething with thoughts. Was this what was meant to be? My destiny? To go on deck .. act as look-out.. perhaps save the ship from colliding with another vessel.. how impressed the rest of the Crew would be with me.. And then after Naval College to take my place on the Bridge.. skilfully navigating the huge steel bulk of a freighter across the trackless oceans of the world..

Just like the deck officers out in the open facing the eternal vastness of sea and sky.. on the bridge, legs wide apart, in my sharply-creased uniform.. .. 'Easy as she goes... Steady. Steady .. Some dirty weather on it's way.. I'll plot a new course.. 'Perhaps I would save the ship from grounding on a sand-bank or hitting a submerged rock... later to be summoned by the Ship Owners to a ceremony to be presented with a special award.. how modest I would be.. and afterwards a reception .. beautiful women with lovely bare shoulders rising above silky floor-length ball gowns, the plunging necklines giving glimpses of the curve of their breasts.. all of them clustering around me their eyes full of admiration ..

I blinked and looked blankly around the shabby room, breathing heavily the hot air redolent of stale cigarette smoke and beer smells. Could I really learn how to navigate? Hadn't I struggled with mathematics in school.. especially geometry and trigonometry .. And even in simple arithmetic I often made stupid mistakes. What if my faulty calculations put a ship onto rocks.... or some other disaster.. how awful to be the cause of loss of a ship .. the loss of lives, of men with families, wives, children....

I began to polish the brass portholes in slow desultory movements.. my mind slowly trying to resolve my thoughts. Did I really have the courage to face down men like the overbearing Hobbsie or a Murdoch who rejoiced in having smashed the skull of a scab; rebellious. . violent.. dangerous men.... Men like Mitch even trembling at the thought of his cold vicious stare ..

I gave a long sigh; how foolish, childish really to let my mind rush into such self-deluding fantasies... I knew nothing about ropes and knots.. and how to rig up blocks and tackles.. Couldn't I just imagine the contempt that the Deck Crew would feel towards me.. Really admit the truth all you are good for is washing floors and dishes; anything else was sheer vanity.. absurd fantasizing.. far better not to think beyond the present moment.. the daily routine..

Yet despite this stern resolution at odd moments during the day, my senses dulled by the repetitive toil, I would suddenly start in dismay my mind having fallen into plotting fantastic daydreams .. there I was in the Chart Room plotting a course around dangerous shoals to the admiration of the other officers.... or out on deck in the midst of stormy seas... rallying the men.. inspiring them with my coolness and fortitude ... But then at night more than once I woke sweating, from some confused distressful dream, guilt-ridden at having committed some stupidly careless act..

Soon though the monotony of the unchanging shipboard routine as the ship sailed on through dazzling seas and glittering starry nights deadened my imagination and having kept the 2nd Mate's offers of working on deck a secret from Billy it had became not wholly believable; like the distant sightings of land.. indistinguishable to my untrained eyes from the low clouds that sometimes lined the horizon..

The door from the Amidships deck clanged dully behind, it's faint echo ringing through the whispering silence of the foredeck; announcing my new adventure at sea, I thought still not quite able to understand how one minute I had been at the sink looking out of the Pantry portholes watching the king posts jousting with the brilliant blue sky; and now here I was striding purposefully down the lifting deck glancing up at the glinting windows of the Bridge, guessing that the officer of the watch would be looking down at me.. perhaps thinking the 2nd Mate was wrong to give me a chance ..

Away from the amidships a warm breeze gently buffeted my face.. on all sides lay the sparkling blue ocean flecked with gleaming white.. But I would show them I thought.... And what would my mother think if she could see me... or Marta.. How impressed they would be... .. the one chosen to excel ..

And how long the Foredeck seemed, rising on a upward slope that pulled at my leg muscles then, as in a dream, suddenly dropping away.. forcing me to walk faster.. faster..

The 2nd Mate was waiting for me just before the fo'c'sle, wearing a boiler suit over his uniform, a tie and collar showing at the neck.

He nodded at me in friendly yet serious manner, my heart beat quickly; was this some kind of test?

"See if we can make a real sailor of you.... "He said pointing towards an open doorway giving to a flight of metal stairs to the bows.

Holding tightly to the rail I made my way down the steep stairs towards the square of daylight at the bottom, still holding the handrail the deck dropping sickeningly beneath my feet, I peered into a cavernous shadowy space; picking out several figures moving about.. How hot it was, not the slightest draught of air; as my eyes adjusted I made out bulkhead lights shining on the welded steel angles and groins; for a moment I was puzzled by a dull rumbling noise then realized that it must be the sound of water passing the bows as the ship ploughed steadily through the Pacific.

"The Bo'sun'll see you right "The 2nd Mate said casually with a nod and abruptly went back up the stairs, a flicker against the brightness above and he was gone. So it's up to me I thought anxiously, breathing the dust-filled air detecting a stagnant smell; swallowing hard against a distinct queasiness; the deck now rising alarmingly.

"Come to bloody help us have yer.." The Bo'sun smirked affably in his sing-song Welsh accent, coming forward. "Ya can join them bloody useless..skiving so-called Deck Boys.. . Here's a bloody ..broom fer ya.."

"Thanks.." I smiled with pretended enthusiasm, an increasingly uncomfortable swelling in my stomach.

You'll soon adjust, I told myself letting go of the handrail and pushing off into the shadowy depths.

"Whatcha dooing here.?" Norrie bawled jeering into my ear, as I joined him and Tad desultorily pushing brooms towards small heap of dust.

"2nd Mate.. er wanted me … "I said began making a quick stab with my broom; a hot prickling all over my body.

"Amazing to think..eh We're actually in the bows.. ." I remarked steadying myself and staring into the darkest point; thinking that beyond the steel-plate surged the immensity of the Pacific.

"But youse aint no Deck Boy.." Norrie insisted pushing up to me.

"Just to see.. if....and then perhaps after Naval College.. deck rating.." I gasped feebly; fighting to keep down the mounting nausea.

"Wezz zee f-----g Deck Boys.." Tad squealed indignantly doing a shuffling dance with his broom. "You'za f-----g Cabin-Boy . .ya...."

Incomprehensibly the shrill voice faded away, hot and cold waves swept through me I concentrated all my energies on staying upright, my stomach heaving, 'Please God... Don't let me fail' I moaned inwardly, shadowy shapes spinning around faster and faster.. ..

Norrie's voice boomed faintly in my ears. "Ya..look like ghoast chum."

I grabbed at him, holding grimly against an overwhelming faintness; black and white shards flashing before my eyes.

Hauling at the handrail I felt myself being pushed up the stairs dazzled by the glare, collapsing onto the deck.

Distantly aware of the hot, hard steel beneath me yet feather- light I was floating away into a mysterious flickering darkness; as if I had died, I thought, smiling to myself; imagining the 2nd Mate and the other Officers gathered around my lifeless body.

'Yes, dead' The shocked faces stared at each other. 'He would have made a good officer.'

Chips keen blue eyes were looking down at me a gently smile on his leathery face, a long needle glittering in his hand. Had to come to that then? The men gathered bare-headed at the rail 'Commend his soul' intoned a deep voice as the canvas shroud slid into the blue water with a splash of white foam; a gentle blissfulness submerging me..

"How's yer bloody feeling youngster?"

I opened my eyes; the Bo'sun was squatting beside me, a strange fuzzy shape in the sunlight.

"That there 2nd Mate's a bloody duffer.." He went on soothingly. "Sending a chap like yer to fo'csle .. Ship's up and down like a shuttle cock.. no cargo .. fuel tanks almost empty. Bilge pumps not working proper either....."

I nodded absently; feeling strangely content; beginning to remember what had happened to me; I had failed miserably and yet how little that mattered; to feel my body returning to normal; the awful overwhelming nausea fading away.. seeing the sun and sky above.. as if I had come back from the dead, I thought dreamily.

"O.K now are ya ? The Bo'sun asked reaching out a hand and tousling my hair

"Yes.. thanks .. afraid I'm not much use on deck...." I heard myself say remorsefully; flushing at the Bo'sun's intent stare; probably he secretly he despises me, I thought uneasily.

"What do you reckon the best bloody things at sea?" The Bo'sun asked with a sly smile grasping my arm.

I shook my head; getting to my feet; the Bo'sun still holding my arm.

"Books that's what.. The Bo'sun said gleefully.

"Really "I mumbled, pulling my arm free. "Somehow I've stopped reading since coming aboard." I added looking at the deck; was I becoming a different kind of person then?

"I've one or two'll interest ya I bet.." The Bo'sun smirked knowingly.

"Perhaps.." I said shifting awkwardly, . "Still books aren't life.."

"Just what I always says Phillip." The Bo'sun chuckled gleefully." Bloody books ain't bloody life.. Bet you'd like a turn at the bloody wheel eh..?"

"Yeah sure.." I muttered vaguely turning away.

"Heh .heh I thought so.. up on the bridge is where ya belong.. not the bloody fo'cosle.." The Bo'sun grinned smugly.

"Maybe .." I sighed moving back down the deck; probably I should have never have come to sea in the first place, I thought moodily looking over the smoothly rounded glistening waves, spattered with gleaming white lacy patches; once again I had been humiliated, not daring to look up at the bridge imagining that I was being observed by the officer on duty.. soon the entire ship would know of my failure....

"Told ya shouldn't go.." Billy jeered as I entered the pantry

"Yeah .. I guess... "I grinned shamefaced. "Hey.. !" I shouted flinching, a bright red welt appearing on my arm.

"That'll teach ya..!" Billy sniggered flicking again at me with a tea-towel.

"Missed … "I laughed jerking aside and grabbing a tea-towel from off the counter.

"Have at you..! "I cried a sudden rage breaking through my dulled mind.

In the bright glow of the declining sun shining through the port-hole the two of us moved slowly about the pantry, raising shadowy gestures as we snapped our tea-towels at each other .. darting and parrying .. feinting and striking.. grinning and laughing as we scored hits or neatly evaded them .. a silly, boyish game and yet somehow more than that for me .. like Roman gladiators, I thought my life at stake, utterly indifferent to the red wheals marking on my arms.. gasping for breath, my strokes becoming fiercer and more reckless blindly advancing on Billy with a mad flurry of snapping flicks.... conscious of several faces in the doorway.. and murmur of voices..

"Go it.. Phil.."

"A richt fighter yon laddie.." .

"O.K... O.K. .." Billy finally conceded panting heavily. "Better stop afore the Sec. comes along.."

"Yeah.. you bet .." I gasped out happily.

CHAPTER FIFTEEN

So this is what it means to be in the tropics I thought
remembering the lines drawn across the world map in the
geography class wall,.. just lines .. to be glanced at .. never
had I ever thought it would mean that I should have to
suffer so much .. Even after a cold shower except the water
was lukewarm, my body was immediately streaming with
sweat, and first thing in the morning I watched the dark
brown liquid dribbling down the steel urinal with faint
horror.. surely this wasn't normal.. Everyone seemed to be
withdrawing into themselves.. hardly speaking.. so as to
save energy.. only the Sec. seemed unperturbed reminding
us to take salt-tablets after every meal to maintain the salt
in our bodies and anti-malarial tablets.. Surely I can't go on
like this though, I thought; every morning staggering along
to the pantry, the air trapped in the heated steel-box of the
companionway a viscous acrid-smelling substance.. not so
much to be breathed but to swum through .. .

And as I gave my exhausted body to be unmercifully
drawn and racked in the sweltering darkness of the cabin
the remorseless thudding of the engine vibrating through
the steel bulkhead beside me I knew it was hopeless .. that
nothing would ever change.. that I was doomed to be an
automaton, an unthinking mechanism blundering about
half-dead my movements more like vague gestures than
purposeful actions.. .

Perhaps I'm going mad.. I wondered looking around the
crew--mess the sailors at the tables, so much immobile statuary
amidst the haze of cigarette smoke, Old Paddy continuing to
silently mouth the words and yet surely the dull thud .. thud ..
thud of engines had become hesitating . uncertain ..

"Sounds like something's wrong with the engines.."
I said rather surprised at the sound of my own voice.

"We'se be bunkering "Came a voice from across the
room.

"Bunkering.. ?" I questioned uncomprehending.

"Taking on fuel-oil.." Another voice said. "Sarawak.. yer calls it ..No tug or pilot neither.."

"Sarawak.. Sarawak...." I repeated, a faint recollection pressing at the dulled recesses of my mind; was I forgetting everything I had ever known?" Where's that?"

"Just some f----n' fuel depot on t'edge of the jungle "Billy said dealing out the cards; his face half hidden by a curling cigarettes smoke.

I half-rose the engines abruptly stopping, a tense silence holding the ship.

"Yer playin' or not..?" Billy demanded irritably.

"Just have a quick look .." I said pushing back my chair and going out of the room, followed by the eyes of the seaman.

Was I making a fool of myself again? I wondered stepping out on deck, the shadowy darkness embracing me; dense swarms of insects dimmed the bulkhead lights; a hoarse rasping noise faintly audible.

As if the night was alive, I thought crossing over to the ship's side; flapping vainly at the shadowy wings brushing my face.

At the ship's side I stopped short feeling as if I had just awoken from a deep sleep, across the glistening water rose an intensely black mass like some immense creature risen from the depths and resting lightly on the crested back, a full crescent moon of shining pale gold...

'Oh God.. how lovely.. oh how lovely ', I exclaimed the faint scratchy sounds rising and falling like some harsh music; the silvered, bristling land rising steeply over the dimly gleaming shoreline; the rippling water washed with a pearly luminescence

'And so real ! So real!' I shuddered holding tightly to the iron bulwark the faint breeze bringing rich earthy scents stirring a vague longings; reminding me of my fantasies lying out in the back-garden.. imaging myself ship-wrecked like Odysseus.. swept ashore on some island beach .. to sprawl naked, exhausted helpless in the ebbing water ..the darkly fronded bushes parting. glimpsing bare-feet sinking into the sand, brushing the long dark strands of hair from her face as she stoops over my prone body.. dark eyes smiling eyes her small hand reaching out to gently touch my bare shoulder...

I shook my head angrily; just a silly fantasy.. a self-indulgent day-dream .. how far from the reality of life.. why couldn't I just accept what was happening to me now .. at this moment..? I leant out over the ship's side, long hawsers, faintly shadowed on the water, stretched out towards the distant shoreline; alternately slackening and tightening, twin black lines slowly but steadily pulling the ship towards a cluster of dim lights.

How had the crew managed to secure the ropes to the shore? I wondered, thinking that if I had succeeded in becoming one of the deck-crew I would have been a part of this masterly display of seamanship, rather than a mere onlooker...

The faint pricks of lights grew brighter as the hawsers pulled the ship ever closer, to what now I could make out, was the end of a slender pier of criss-crossing poles, stretching out over the shiny waters from the distant shore.

How alien it seemed, I thought looking at the shadowy skeletal structure, the uprights burning in pools of pale green-blue phosphorescence; an ugly intrusion in the vast tropical night, faint with stars, the moon floating clear of the land, stippling the dark water with pale gleams.

I flinched at the spasmodic roar of the ship's engines rupturing the intense silence followed by the sound of shouts through a loud-hailer, then from over the water metallic clangs echoed harshly in the velvety darkness.. Why are we doing this I wondered .. why are we breaking into this unblemished primeval tranquillity.. the world before man was.. . of course.. we need fuel to continue to Australia.. to fetch wheat for the starving Chinese people.. yes, it was all to the world's good.. and I was part of it. . Even so I felt a sadness, turning back to the amidships.. .

Billy had left the crew-mess I had sat blinking at the glare of the florescent light surveying the seamen through the wispy smoke their grizzled heads bent as if for all eternity, over their cards; indifferent to the wonder of the moonlit scene just through the door; my eyes settling on Old Paddy, watching the old greaser, slowly traced by a single bony finger across the open page.

But what was the point? I wondered, ultimately they were just black marks on a white paper. What did they have to do with the real world? imagining myself marching across the Crew-Mess snatching the Bible from out the feeble old hands and then running outside and flinging the Bible as far as I could, a faint splash signalling it's disappearance forever into the dark waters...

With a start I turned around and went quickly out on deck; pressing my forehead against the steel of the Amidships bulkhead. How could I think of such a thing? I wondered deeply ashamed; why did I want to torment such harmless old man ...I was worse than Hobbsie.. Did some irredeemable evil lurk within me..? I stiffened, an ominous, thundering ripping apart the deep stillness of the night, the deck trembling around me.

For a minute I stood fixed, staring up at the glittering stars, realizing it was just the ship's anchor being let go...

How distant it all was from me.. . as if I was on board by accident.. a stowaway .. an intruder, I thought passing aimlessly along the row of portholes in the amidships, fuzzy yellow gleams in the shadowy darkness. At the first porthole I mentally pictured Old Pete in his cabin lying on his back peacefully wheezing away.. the next would the Sec's .. perhaps repeatedly thumping his hand against the block of wood he used for his karate exercises and then Mitch's .. of course he would be up with the Chief Steward drinking themselves into a blissful alcoholic stupor; next in line would be Jock's cabin.. what would he be doing..? Sipping some of his precious Scotch . reading over one of his much thumbed collection of *Scots Magazine* then Ronnie's porthole.. probably he would be smirking away at one his dog-eared girlie magazines he sometimes left lying around the galley.

All of them quite happy to have the chance to rest .... Only me out of the whole ship, I thought dissatisfied .. always striving for something more .. even though I didn't know what it was..

At the last porthole I reached up to peer in; the ceiling light lighting the bare narrow space, both berths empty. Where was Billy I wondered thinking how empty the cabin looked in the harsh light and how different to my bedroom at home, my eyes resting on the Billy's blonde starlet pin-up above the sink, a faint ironic smile on her scarlet-red lips.

For several minutes I returned her unflinching gaze; just a colour photograph from a magazine I thought and yet I couldn't deny a some kind of vague longing .. to be appreciated.. admired. .desired.. how impossible that seemed.

Restlessly I turned carried on down the afterdeck, deep in shadow, as I neared the stern I could hear through the darkness the intermittent whirr of a motor and loud cheerful voices and occasional laughter from the men operating the stern capstan. I stopped unwilling to go closer.. afraid almost of being recognised.. Really I wasn't really one of them .. just pretending to be seaman....

The door to the accommodation block stood open casting a rough square of light onto the deck.. perhaps Billy had come down here and was visiting some of the crew I thought stepping inside, stifled by the acrid sweat smells as I moved cautiously along the short companionway between rows of blank cabin doors.

Halfway down I stopped short, a pair of boots stood at the open cabin door, inside the ceiling light shone on the bare walls; my eyes coming to rest on a broad figure squatting on the linoleum floor, a shaved head rising from a short neck and broad shoulders, heavily muscled upper arms resting on broad thighs, his legs folded under his body; open eyes staring intently ..

I went quickly on and out into the shadowy darkness of the Afterdeck walking slowly back towards the Amidships.

It must be Wonner, I thought remembering how Billy had told me about him; an A.B. he kept himself apart from the rest of the crew when off duty... eating his own special food by himself.. his cabin scrupulously clean and bare.. a disciple of some oriental martial arts that included hours of meditation as well as rigorous physical exercises. Yet really what was the point? Wasn't it just like Old Paddy .. immersed in his Bible.. shutting themselves off from the real world around them...

Back at the Amidships on impulse kept on up the stairs to Life-Boat Deck; passing the portholes of the Officer's Smoking Room, the curtains drawn, glowing red. I moved closer, the clink of glasses and thud of darts sounding through the chatter and bursts of laughter.. .

How could I ever thought I would make an officer? I thought gloomily; more than ever possessed by a conviction that that I was a thing apart from the ship and her crew.... .

Fearful that one of the officers might come out and find me skulking about I went on past the lifeboats, two sepulchral shapes looming out of the shadows, and climbed up the ladder to the deck above; the broad mass of the funnel splashed with light hanging over me.

Moving carefully along a narrow metal grating I came to a bank of skylights above the engine-room; broad fingers of light speckled with insects, rose high into the night-sky.

Kneeling down I peered over the edge, at once a gush of hot oily air blasted my face, I pulled quickly back just glimpsing pallid forms moving around amongst the complex of machinery in the depths of the engine-room. Just like everyone else on the ship, I thought sadly, all of them confidently carrying out their appointed tasks, while I roam about the .... wandering around like a ghost.. purposeless.. useless.. I thought coming down to the lifeboat deck and hesitating before keeping on down the stairs to the main deck.

For a minute I hesitated possessed of a deep weariness. .and yet for all my tiredness the thought of going back to my cabin . And yet I felt myself drawn across the deck to stand once more at the ship's side; a dull hammering sound coming to me over the water; straining my eyes I made out a cluster of tiny lights in the darkness; perhaps that's the accommodation for the workers for the oil-bunkering company, I thought, wondering what kind of life they lived, marooned in this remote spot on the edge of the tropical jungle; sensing something faintly hostile in the silvered darkness, the shining moon now risen high above the land dispensing a cold light over land and water .. merging all into a icy frozen waste... .. ..

Abruptly a tinkling metal sound rang out through the darkness, followed by loud laughter; one of the workers must have dropped a tool, I thought, seeing several shadowy shapes moving around the pier-head; yes, fellow humans I thought.. giving life.. meaning to this eerie, alien world washed by a pale moonlight.

Really I should go back to my bunk bed I thought and yet lingered on the ship's side, starting when with brutal insistence a clanking reverberated through night; the anchor being raised, I thought trying to block out the clank, clank, clank.. that seemed to go on forever echoing off the nearby hills... soon drowned out by the roar of the engines we must be ready to leave I thought thinking of how on the bridge the helmsman would be standing his hands on the wheel his face lit by the greenish light from the binnacle the officers speaking in low voices .. and down in the engine room, the greasers their white skin streaked with oil stains would be standing by amongst the complex of casings, pipes and wires.. attentively watching the gauges and dials waiting for the word of command; the massive pistons glinting in the glare of arc-lights poised to respond.. to thrust and thrust again tirelessly turning the propeller shaft.. the propeller blades smashing the placid water into frothy atoms . .. pushing the ship irresistibly through the waters of the Pacific Ocean ....towards the equator.. and Australia..

High above the moon like a gauzy silver boat was drifting up towards stars even as the deck and bulkhead began to tremble urgently through me.. the lights on the pier-head becoming blurred.. fading into the surrounding blackness and then vanishing. ..a nostalgia taking home of me.

'Goodbye.. dear.. dear land.. Good bye..' I crooned before hurrying back inside, scratching absently at the insect bites on my neck and cheeks.

CHAPTER SIXTEEN

Lulled by Chips's deft touch, I felt my eyes closing; the men sitting in the shade of the Hatch block, blurred forms against the glittering water; the regular click, click of the scissors at times the only sound in the whispering silence of the Foredeck; the rich scents of burning pipe-tobacco wafting over me on the strong breeze.

Sporadically one of the men would portentously clear his throat or make some laconic remark; just like the village elders gathered in the shade of some old tree, I mused feeling myself almost slipping into a doze.

"Aye,aye Suunday right enough.."

Was it Sunday then.. .? I thought with mild surprise; the days so like each other to have become identical.. anonymous. .

"But none o'Chaapel for us'ns ... Sinners all . ." One of the men added with a chuckle.

"Nay, nay.. this be our Chapel.. bright sky be our roof ..shiny sea the floor." Chips declared from behind me, the click of his scissors unfaltering. "And God above .."

"Amen. . Amen. . "Came the gruff response.

Sleepily I imagined the chorus of amens wafting upwards into the infinite brightness of the sky ..

"Almost finished sonny.." Chips said in my ear.

I gave a slight start; the men's voices abruptly louder.

"Mind yon Bo'sun on t'*Cleethorpes*.. Can't mind the name."

"Reeps weren't it..? Youngest Bo'sun I ever knew'd."

"Skye man weren't he? Tall with fair hair.. like a Viking.. gentle as a girl times .. but get him drunk.. Heh..heh Look tha out Bobbies!..."

"Aye the very one.. Saw him once knock over a Russkie in Valparaiso with a single blow.. Mind too though that toime in port.. Where was it? Hong Kong?"

"Manila comes to mind....."

"Aye you're right there.. Mornin' comes of course he'd been on the bevy loike all night.. insisted on going down to a staage where the laads were painting the hull.. fell and pulled the paint-pot over himself ..red-lead of course.. then fell into the waater.. What a sight.. when we pulled him out.. dripping with red paint and waater... laughin' his head off...could'a easily drowned.. yet he thought it were the funniest thing in the whole world.."

"What became of him then?"

"Liver packed-up.. so I heard... .. One day right as rain ..next rushed to hospital.. barely lasted a month.. .."

"Aye he liked his drink.."

"Aye and the ladies ....No wonder! How they went after him! Fight loike cats for 'im.. heh heh.. every port the same.."

"A good seaman though...He'll be surely missed come bad seas.."

There was a long silence and I imagined the grizzled old faces solemnly contemplative as they considered the fate of the Bo'sun. Imagining him... tall blonde.. so attractive to women.. and still a man's man .. hard-drinking .. ready with his fists ..like a hero in a Norse saga, I mused.

"Did I ever tell that abaat yon Lascar Cook on the *Scunthorpe?*"

Another voice began in a low tones.

"General cargo .. bound for Baltimore.. mid-Atlantic.. pretty rough.. Didn't some A.B. grumble about his cooking.. Well.. Cook went crazy.. chasin' about with a cleaver loike.... took six of us to get'im down.. 'ad to lock 'im in Brig till landfall.. Raving soomthing awful. .."

"Aye summat had stirred 'im.."

"Bad luck that ship doan't care what they says.."

There was another long silence; were they thinking that our ship might be unlucky too I wondered.

"Chief Mate almost swept to his death mind.."

"Aye..some things 'appen loike. No saaying how or why.. .."

Again there was a pause; the regular clipping of the scissors broken by the scrape of a match and a harsh sucking sound.

"Soon be The Line, I guess…."

"Aye.. soom things ..aye come.. aye pass.."

My eye-lids flickered. So soon we would be crossing the Equator.. but surely it was just an imaginary line across the globe, only the navigation officer would know when we were crossing it… and really what difference did it make? None at all . ..and yet the entire crew were possessed by the idea.. As if somehow the act of crossing we were all affected in some way.. passing from one life to another ..

"Sure that 'll do thee sonnie.." Chips said pulling the bit of canvas from off my shoulders and shaking out the hair clippings.

I stood up stiffly, blinking at the glare reflecting from the glittering ocean; smiling vaguely around at the small group of men in singlets or stripped to the waist, trouser-braces trailing down; grizzled, weather tanned faces; yes sea-farers I thought, as in ancient times, out on the open deck .. braving the vast oceans.. far from home.. ..

"Like a new shorn lamb…" Chips said flicking a brush over my shoulders, his eyes bright.

"Thanks.. Chips… "I murmured glancing shyly at the old Ship's Carpenter; feeling strangely light.

"Need t'give tha a wee shave now." Another of the men said gesturing at his chin to approving chuckles from the others.

I smiled absently stroking the soft down on my chin; as if it wasn't quite part of me….

"Reckon t'Aussie lasses 'll fancy thee summat." Another of the seamen laughed taking a broom and beginning to sweep the hair into a pile.

I grinned self-consciously and looked down at the clumps of hair; how fair they were; were they really from my head?

I nodded at the little group before setting off down the deck back to the Amidships.

"First toime fer 'im Crossing the Line, aint'it?" I heard one of the seamen say behind me as I carried on down the Foredeck stretched before me, steadily rising and falling; sea and sky fused into one shimmering entity. What am I? I mused feeling myself dissipating into the glittering vastness....

A scuffing sound made me look up, starting at the sight of grinning faces, first amongst them Hobbsie, all of them shouting and laughing uproariously as if it was a festival or celebration; sweeping me before them.

"Hey.. watch it.." I protested my voice lost in the babble of voices finding myself beside a greaser grinning self-consciously as we were pushed along. What was happening I wondered excited and anxious as I was pushed between the Hatch and the Hatch block and between them a faded canvas hatch-cover draped over a wooden frame. Where had it come from? Had Chips made it? What was it for? I glanced at the greaser a genial smirk on his broad face; like a lamb to the slaughter, I thought but not me.. and on . an impulse I darted forward.. out onto the other side of the Foredeck, followed by loud shouts..

"Catch 'im..!"

"Catch the nipper.."

"Cut' im off!"

The open deck stretched before me as I hesitated whether to run back to the Amidships.. but already someone was coming towards me.. . my escape was towards the bows.. I raced away.. a clatter of footsteps behind me.. but I knew I was faster.. nimbler than any of them with their heavy boots .. .. 'Run run you'll never catch the Ginger Bread man..' I panted gleefully my thongs making a loud thwacking noise as I sped up the long slope, seeing myself a single figure on the broad deck beside the dazzling sea the sun burning down on me from a clear blue sky. A large dark shape loomed out of the sun's bright glare..

'Murdoch. . !' I cried in dismay recognising the grim-faced Irish A.B making to dodge around him but in a single sweep of his arms I was lifted high; sun and sea and ship all spinning around.

"Gotcha, ya f-----g little bugger..!" He growled in a strong brogue grinning complacently holding me in a powerful grip; loud gleeful shouts rang about as the other men now surrounded me; hard calloused hands roughly grabbing at me.

"Hold 'im!"

"Slippery as a worm. ain't 'e!"

Flailing impotently I felt myself borne back down the deck to beside the Hatch block my shorts were pulled off and I was tossed casually forward to land sprawling in a pool of warm salty water; a loud roar in my ears. I struggled up dripping wet, my feet stabbing into the loose canvas, intent on getting away, suddenly doused by flood of water.. half-blinding me..

"Neptuune King of the Oceans welcoomes tha!" I heard Hobbsie boom loudly. .

"Hey.. That's enough! "I gasped petulantly, sitting back down into the pool of water as another full bucket-load flushed over me, I brushed at my eyes, a rusty-salty taste in my mouth; the fiery sun burning down my naked body. 'This is you .... 'flashed through my mind as in a moment of revelation..

"Ya!" I cried stumbling elatedly about; laughing crazily as another torrent of water half-drowned me. A calloused hand take my arm and I was dragged out; my shorts thrust into my hands.

"Cheers mateys!" I smirked gazing around at the grinning weather-worn, sunburnt faces before waving my shorts about my head as I hobbled gingerly down the hot steel deck; squinting up at the laughing faces looking down from the Bridge. 'Yes! it's me.. Phillip Wight.. Cabin-Boy.. Crossed the Line.. a real sailor' I thought exultantly.

But perhaps it was all delusion I mused as the days passed without any noticeable change; perhaps the ship wasn't really moving at all on all sides as far as the eye could see lay a glittering watery emptiness, merging to a cloudless blue dome; the ship's engines roaring out a frayed dark grey swag, to fade away into the vast sky; at night blowing a black plume towards the distant stars; and so night to day to night.. a thudding, vibrating mass of steel eternally lost in endless time and space..

And even leaning against the stern rail during our afternoon break, my eyes idly following the foamy wake into a dazzling oblivion, it seemed quite possible the ship was merely churning up the water, fixed eternally in the midst of the vastness of the Pacific Ocean.. .

But surely there had to be something .. anything really to break the awful sameness .. the endless sameness .. I glanced at Billy, his taut, tanned body stretched out as usual between a chair and the rail, smoking calmly I should be more like him I thought like the other seamen.. .. living in themselves.. stoically accepting the monotonous uniformity of this existence....

Unable to deny my restiveness though, I prowled around the stern without any real purpose and then looking in cubby-hole amongst all sort of odds and ends I spotted a coil of old rope and pulled it out. But what to do with it? Impulsively I turned to the rail and with gleeful defiance threw the coil as far as I could out over stern...

"There. .!" I exclaimed with a deep satisfaction as the coil slowly unwound before settling on the frothed-up waters until finally becoming sodden with water disappeared beneath the swirling, foaming waters..

"Watcha yer f----n' up to now Phil?" Billy said with a grin, joining me at the rail.

Together we pulled back the rope, hand over hand; water-droplets flashed and sparkled about the jerking line

"Great eh ! "I laughed picturing the two sun-bronzed figures, shoulder to shoulder, engaged in an heroic battle with some mysterious force hidden below the foamy water....

Soon though that wasn't enough and turning to the stack of old dining- room chairs it was the work of minutes to tie one to one end of the rope..

"One! Two! Three!" We shouted merrily and together flung the chair far out over the stern rail.

Gripping the rail with elation I had watched the chair sail through the air and then smash violently down into the frothy swirling water; the padded red seat dramatically flying off, the black metal frame vanishing momentarily, then as the rope tightened, breaking free and skipping and bouncing though the foaming wake.

How I had rejoiced! At last here was something out of the daily routine...

Though it wasn't long though before the chair-back came loose and floated away and then the metal-frame too broke apart, leaving the rope trailing tamely through the foamy wake. What a shame, I had thought conscious too of a vaguely guilty feeling as I watched the two reddish blotches drift away amongst the white froth.. . . .

Each day we flung the chairs over the rail and watch as they hit the water and began to bound and skip.. leaping madly skywards before tumbling back only to flip up again ..eventually, inevitably, breaking to pieces; the red seats and backs floating away; the metal frames vanishing beneath the foam.

Until one afternoon here were no more chairs to throw overboard.

"I knowas howsa about we's catch a shark! "Billy exclaimed one afternoon adding he'd seen it done on other ships.

Really.." I responded gazing out into the shining waters, was it possible that somewhere beneath the surface lurked one the most ferocious of all the world's predators.. capable of ripping a man to pieces in seconds, endowed with the uncanny ability to home in on traces of blood or slight disturbances in the water from immense distances?

As one of Billy's duties was to clean in the Cold-Store, for which task he was allowed a tot of rum, he was able to remove a shiny steel meat-hook and an ox-tail for bait without difficulty and it was with great excitement that we tied the baited hook to the rope and with all our strength flung it over the side of the stern ..

Every time we pulled up the hook I felt something pulling strongly, imaging a dark shadowy mass rising up through the water, and then foaming eruption of blunt snout gaping with rows of white teeth and coldly vicious eyes.. only to know a mingled relief and disappointment as the hook plopped out of the water.. the bait untouched..

Lying in our berths Billy and I talked ourselves to sleep with fantastic accounts of possible titanic battles and ultimate triumph over some great grey-skinned dorsal-finned, torpedo-shaped, evil-eyed monster dragged struggling and bloody from the shiny waters.. ..

But only once was the bait missing and in the end without any discussion we gave up allfurther attempts; neither of us saying anything.. and never thereafter referring to it.. as if the failure was too painful to even talk about .. It would have been better if we hadn't even tried I concluded gloomily.

"Like going camping.." I giggled as we dragged our mattresses up to the Lifeboat deck; finding it exciting in being out in the night-time; so glad to be away from the stifling hot air of the cabin; the dull roar of the engines greeting us as we reached the top of the stairs to the lifeboat deck..

I laid down on the mattress a steady throbbing coming into my body through the deck; Billy a shadowy hump beside me; above our head a monstrous white wraith pouring from the dark mass of the funnel, endlessly burying itself in the black depths of the night, strewn with innumerable brilliant stars.. marvelling how bright they were and yet how distant.. .millions of light years away.. countless fiery balls of incandescent hydrogen gas.. moving through infinite empty space.. so how could there be a God...?

"I wonder which is the Southern Cross..?" I murmured my eyes watering as I stared around. "So many .."

"'ow many d'y reckon? .." Billy gave a loud yawn.

"Millions I guess.." I murmured,

"And just think some of them don't even exist any more.." I mused out loud.

"Watcha mean…" Billy objected after a pause. "We c'n f----n' see' em can't we . ."

"I know but some of them are so far away that it takes millions of years for the light to reach us and by that time the star itself might have exploded.. become so much interstellar dust…"

"Howda f----n' know that?" Billy grumbled.

"Well from books .. I suppose." I answered finally;

Yer can put anyt'ing into a book "Billy objected sleepily.

"Yeah.. I guess so . "I sighed unable to argue; thinking how Billy had told me that Chips had been shipwrecked somewhere in the middle of the Pacific.. what would it have been like to be alone on a raft bobbing about in the dark looking up the stars and not knowing if you would be saved or not.. and yet never losing hope.. . .

I felt myself slipping off to sleep, seeing in my mind the seat-covers from the chairs we had casually destroyed; small red patches bobbing tirelessly across the ocean until they were flung by the foaming waves onto some distant shore.. Really we shouldn't have done it.. still as long as no one knew about it surely it didn't matter?

CHAPTER SEVENTEEN

Coming out on deck to empty the "Marie "I shivered violently, pausing to look out over the expanse of grey-green water marbled with white foam; the rolling masses of dark grey clouds pierced by a shafts of brilliant sunlight... How suddenly it had happened. ..like a scene change in the theatre .. the blue Pacific glittering eternally beneath a cloudless blue sky swept away in a single day. Yes.. quite amazing I thought inhaling the fresh, salty air; fascinated by the tiny rainbows shadowing the sheets of spray blown from the tops of the jagged waves by the fierce wind.

For days now we had been crossing the Great Australian Bight famous for rough weather; now and then black smoke was blown down from the funnel filling the air with burning diesel smells; beneath me the deck rolled and plunged making me faintly nauseous. Still I had longed for change hadn't I?

"Mair hame-like "Jock chirruped emerging from the Amidships to join me at the ship's side.

I nodded;

"Pleased I bet to have het dinners again..eh laddie.." He added smugly

"I guess.." I temporised, swallowing hard; remembering too that when the ship's cooks had refused to light the stoves in the galley because of the extreme heat the Greasers had chorused with good-humoured sarcasm. 'Whaat t' gaalley too hot..? Tha should try t'engiine room..

"Och aye, Phil laddie" Jock mused leaning against the ship's side .

"Always a braw thing ye ken to see land afta a lang syne at sea."

"Yes..it is.." I murmured earnestly studying the dark smudge on the horizon; so that was Australia.. the antipodes.. the bottom of the world.. remembering how once digging a hole in the back garden my mother coming out and smiling remarked that I would soon be reaching Australia…. and now it was coming true if not in the way she had meant.. ..

How amazing life was….

In a single motion I brought up the "Marie" to the top of the bulwark and deftly tipped and tipped it over the side; watching the slurry of kitchen waste flying briskly away down wind.

"Aye aye, a richt sailor the noo.." Jock commented approvingly reaching into his apron pocket to pull out a pack of cigarettes.

"At sea and on land…." he added with a smile making as if he was going to offer me a cigarette but then thinking better of it.

I took out one of my own and Jock gave me a light and together we looked away over the white-spangled green water; the smoke from our cigarettes instantly blown away. The distant coastline now buried under vast mound of white clouds, piled high on each other, a gleaming, billowing, wreathing mass on mass creased and ravined with dark shadows.

"Aye, it's a bonny warld..fer a'that…. "Jock crooned.

"Yes……. …" I murmured absently, gazing at the shifting, drifting, snowy cloud-mountains; imagining myself sliding down the crevasse, rolling deliciously around in the soft feathery whiteness.

"Yer first Aussies were aye convicts yer ken." Jock said importantly, his thumbs pushing out his apron. "Transported fer steeling a bawbee yer ken or speakin' oot agin injustice…. .like yon crouse loons frae

Dundee…"

"Really .." I responded turning to the craggy faced Scots cook, strands of gingery hair blowing around his mottled scalp; marvelling how confident he was.

"As the man said all property is theft.." Jock said gravely censorious.

" N' the law is used t' keep it .."

"But better than no law at all… ." I suggested hesitantly.

"And Australia seems to have done quite well out of them...in the end..."

"Ane wrang will never mak a richt laddie." Jock intoned sanctimoniously

"As ye'll learn in time I doot .."

"Yes.. I suppose "I sighed.." But it seems there will always be rich and poor.."

"Them that hast, maist gie to them that dinna.. .." Jock insisted sternly.

"They just help themselves. .." I laughed pointing as seagulls, in a flurry of glossy white wings and loud cries, stooping low over the water squabbled over the floating scraps.

"What yer f----n' moanin' on about now, Jockie?"

Ronnie appeared out of the Amidships doorway; a habitual smirk on his pale doughy face.

"Of nae interest to daft sachannach like yersel.. .." Jock declaimed haughtily. "Speirin' with the loon o' the injustices o' this warld. ."

"A lot of bullshit. "Ronnie scoffed. "A hot-blooded young buck like 'im wants some tail to get 'is love-juices go'in'. right Phil?"

I shrugged embarrassed and yet secretly flattered.

"Geelong ain't Nagasaki.. though Phil." Ronnie leered gloomily rubbing his chin dark with bristles.

"Geelong..?" I said surprised. "I thought we were going to Syndey.."

"Nay.. nay it's Geelong we're landing.. the port for Melbourne yer ken...

" Jock said "A richt place fer a dram.. .."

"I see.." I murmured rather nonplussed; Billy and I had spent hours after hours talking about how we would meet up with some girls on Bondi beach .

"I doot there'll be some post waitin' for us.." Jock added flicking his cigarette butt over the side.

"Yeah..?" I murmured turning back to the amidships doorway and then glancing back at the towering mass of cloud covering the coastline; the twisted, churning flanks now inky black.. the light too beginning to darken; how quickly it all had changed. .that was like life too… .

With the afternoon light slowly fading from the heavy grey sky, I stood on deck outside the Pantry to the ship's side; keeping back from the showers of salt-spray blown by fierce gusts of wind; dressed now in jeans and a jumper and shoes with socks feeling quite strange, almost like another person..

Not far off a black tug-boat with a red funnel was tossing wildly about on the rough sea, rags of smoke torn from it's snub funnel, the roaring wind snatching at the sound of it's engines while on it's madly bucking deck the men moved casually around; as if they were on a dance-floor I thought admiringly. Already several lines had missed the tug-boat and through the whistling of the wind and the roar of ship's engines I could make the megaphone bellowings of the Chief Mate.

By sheer force of character he believes he can overcome the elemental forces of wind and sea I mused just as a line finally reached the tug was quickly hauled in by the tugboat crew. A hawser sprang free of the foam-spattered, blackly-green waters and the ship was irretrievably joined to the powerful tug-boat a flattened plume of smoke tearing from the funnel as it turned astern.

Will there be a letter for me? I wondered the thought coming of itself as I gazed at the indomitable tug-boat, a long streak of black smoke bent from funnel, appearing and disappearing amongst the spray-blown waves. Somehow I felt I couldn't bear the disappointment.. and yet really it was such a trivial thing .. just sheets of paper with black marks on it.. I scoffed defiantly.. How much I had longed to an end to the days at sea with their unchanging routine starting with the deadly knock on the cabin door tearing me from sleep.. each task.. each moment like the day before and the day to come.. without end yet now it had come to end.. and once again I would have land under my feet.. be able to walk out in my shore-clothes .. going drinking with Billy and the deck-boys ..and .. perhaps.. perhaps ..

I closed my eyes losing myself in an intense reverie soft and urgent until a shower of stinging rain and spray drove me back into the amidships.

Coming out on deck later I found the ship was alongside the dock and the gangway had already been lowered.

"It be oor luvely poet laads.." Brownie boomed out as the Day Gang came clumping past me, all of them wrapped up in heavy coats up so I barely recognized them as the same half-naked, sunburnt men

I had watched toiling under the tropical sun.

"So hows tha loike Doawn Uunder?" Brownie drawled, pausing in front of me."

"Cold and windy..." I laughed suddenly self-conscious.

"Tha'll have to watch tha self. They'll have nowt o' tha' hanky-panky here. Eh mateys?" Brownie leered knowingly before leading the men away all laughing noisily.

Why are they laughing at me? I wondered dully looking across the quayside; a few dockers mere thickly rounded forms, were moving slowly about; on the periphery rows of blurred orange points retreated into the misty gloom; fortress–like a massive grain silo drove a dark wedge into the yellow streaked violet sky; the chill air tasting gritty and smelling of coal-dust..

'Australia. . the other side of the world.' I thought with a shudder; how did I come to be here? It was all such a mystery..

Breathing out white puffs Billy and I strode side by side over the empty quayside; dust and black grit blowing around our feet..

In front of us the grain terminal rose starkly into the dull winter sky.

Was it just my imagination or was there something.. resistant .. unwelcoming. .. in the air? I wondered vaguely.

Near the dock-gates a gang of burly longshoremen in thick navy-blue donkey-jackets stood about stamping and banging their arms, blunt, unfriendly-looking faces, brick-red from exposure to the wind; their breath drifting away like smoke. I looked away not daring to meet their hard looks.

"Howsa'ya doin' Pommies.." One of them called out in a twangy jeering drawl as we passed.

"Missing yer mams I bet.... ?" Another of them bellowed to hoarse laughter.

"At least we f-----n' got 'em." I retorted unthinkingly.

"Shut it ya dope .." Billy grinned grabbing my arm and hurrying me on; explaining that the dockers were forced to hang around in the cold, not earning anything while their Union looked into a complaint by the Seaman's Union, that the ship should have returned to England.

So we might be going to England after all ? I posed excitedly but Billy shook his head, it was just Murdoch and Hobbsie stirring up trouble, for the fun of it. a way of their getting their own back.. .

"Really.. . "I murmured as started up out up the long slope from the dock-side wondering how it was that two men purely from spite and devilment could interfere with such an important enterprise.

We walked on the bitter wind blowing between the low buildings, penetrating the thin cloth of my trousers and jacket. Now and then we passed by other pedestrians hurrying along raised their heads to stare at us suspiciously.

To them we are strangers.. to be distrusted.. unwelcome intruders into their world, I thought giving a sideways admiring glance at

Billy in his short jacket and narrow tight trousers and pointed shoes, his hair slicked back.

Several times we turned down wide empty streets lined by shabby industrial buildings, the passing vehicles the only movement.

Was Billy lost I wondered remembering he had told me he had only been here once before but I didn't like to ask and we kept on walking down the deserted streets not speaking.

Perhaps we should just go back to the ship, I began to think my ears and nose hurting from the cold, as we entered a street of square two-storey grey concrete buildings; how much I had looked forward to getting ashore I thought sadly running to catch up with Billy as he stopped suddenly and pushed open through a door.

In an arc across the square plate-glass window large letters in red and blue read : *MISSION TO SEAMEN*.

For a minute or two we stood inside the door grateful for the warmth of the warm fuggy air. What a dreary place I thought gazing around the interior, bare fluorescent tubes glaring down on sets of formica-topped tables and metal-framed chairs ranged in rows; the only occupants two men at one of the tables who didn't even bother to turn to look at us.

I followed Billy between the tables staring greedily at the iced cup-cakes and biscuits in the plastic display box while Billy ordered two cups of tea from the woman behind the counter

Wearing a faded pinafore, thin grey hair straggling around a drawn, tired face; she stood in front of a steaming urn drawing mugs of tea vaguely reminding me of my mother.

"Yer off some ship are ya dearies?" She asked with a faint smile putting the mugs on the counter taking the money from Billy and handing him some change.

"Yes *MV Grimthorp* actually.. British .." I began feeling an overwhelming need to speak.." We're loading wheat or will be when the dockers decide to start work. For China you see there's a terrible famine there.. It's my first time in Australia.. It's terribly cold for us here. we're used to the tropics you see.. so terribly hot .. you have to take salt tablets.. to stop heat exhaustion.. and quinine against Malaria.. We've been at sea for more than three weeks.. Just getting our land-legs.."

"I'm sure.." She murmured giving the counter a wipe. "My husband was a sailor. All over the world.. Lost at sea…. Five to bring up on my own…. ."

"Really ." I muttered embarrassed. "That's terrible.."

"Long time ago now.. You forget mostly.." She added with a wan smile.

"Yes.. I suppose.." I murmured feeling the weight of her sadness settle on me.

Something else dearie?". She asked her dull eyes sunk in purple sockets fixing on me.

"A cup cake please .." I asked pulling out my wallet, feeling awkward.

"Fancy 'er do yer?" Billy laughed lighting up a cigarette as I joined him at one of the tables.

I shook my head angrily. "Of course not.. just felt sorry for her that's all... she seemed.. well so sad.. lonely.."

"Bet yer t'ink it cos ya never got no letter from 'ome."

Billy grinned blowing out a plume of smoke

"It doesn't bother me. "I replied haughtily; gazing around the long bare room, long dribbles ran through the misty condensation on the large window; it was true.. I didn't care at all.. Live only for the moment I thought taking the paper of my cup-cake, salivating slightly.

"It was 'ere in Geelong, that 'e signed on...the Cabin-Boy ya replaced.."

Billy remarked. "Tad and me met 'im 'ere .. looking for a berth."

"Really .." I said picking up the last cake-crumbs with my finger tip;

"What was he like?"

"A real mummy's boy, 'ated 'is dad..some big-shot with a 'ouse in

Melbourne. Wanted to get away from 'im.." Billy said tapping out another cigarette from the packet.

"What was his name anyway?" I asked casually.

"Forgot .. 'Billy said frowning. "What d'ya care anyway?"

I shrugged. "Just curious.... Sometimes it seems to me that he didn't really exist a sort of phantom.... doppelganger.. ." I laughed .

"What f----n guff ya speak sometimes." Billy said staring hard at me.

"Good afternoon lads... . .Jessie tells me yer off the *Grimethorpe* loading wheat for China.. terrible business ..the famine.."

A short heavy-set man with a chubby round face a dog-collar showing at the neck of his rumpled black suit had come to stand beside our table.

I'm the Chaplain here "He went on smiling affably, his eyes watchful slightly anxious.

"We have a Prayer Services on Mondays and Friday and Divine Service on Sunday.. That's if you're interested of course.."

"Not our kind of thing Padre. "Billy grinned winking at me, stubbing out a cigarette "Eh Phil..?"

"Just a f----g waste of time.." I sneered my cigarette shaking between my fingers.

The Chaplain nodded thoughtfully, stroking his dimpled chin. "I understand you don't quite see the point.."

"Of course not "I snapped strangely angry. "Look at all the awful things in the world.. wars and diseases and famines and.. and earthquakes and storms .. millions killed every year.. ."

"Ah, The Problem of Evil..." The Chaplain said nodding "Yes.. very hard to understand sometimes,, how an omnipotent God a God of love allows such things happen."

"They've all got a scientific explanations.." I argued hotly. "You don't need a God to explain all the bad things that happen in the world.. ."

The Chaplain smiled blandly down at me.

"Of course He endowed us with Free Will.. to deny Him if we so choose. .."

"So if we can deny Him he's not omnipotent.." I crowed, glancing triumphantly at Billy frowning .

"You favour a Manichean view of good and evil..?" The Chaplain mused a deep frown crossing his forehead.. .

"Who cares what it's called.." I blustered. "That's just a lot mumbo-jumbo.

. Like all religion... 'The Opium of the People' Just a way of keeping people quiet...."

"C'mon let's get out of here." Billy grumbled pushing back his chair back, with a screech.

"And you in a job. ." I added jeeringly, getting to my feet.

"Let's hope so..!" The Chaplain laughed cheerily, coming to the door and holding it open.

"Your welcome anytime, Geelong doesn't have a lot to offer.. there's a pool table next door help you from getting bored.. or lonely."

"F-----g stupid ass ..." I stormed as we went down the steps the last gleams of the setting sun lighting up the street. "Who does he think he is?"

"Bad luck.. arguing with likes of 'im. Billy said angrily.

"Ya worse than Hobbsie ."

We walked on heads bent, hunched into our jacket collars down the wide deserted streets towards the docks; now and then tiny flakes of snow gusted around us.

Surely everything I had said was true, I thought and yet at the same time I bitterly regretted having spoken out.. as if I had betrayed myself in some deep way.. when would I learn to kept quiet.

"When Tad and Norrie get their shore-leave we'll go into Melbourne. .."

Billy said as we got near the dock-gates;.

"Yeah. great.." I murmured absently conscious of a deep isolation; really it was all just words.. ..

Before us the dim lights outlined the ship, reminding me forcibly of the inescapable daily routine; above a spectral half-moon showed in the feathery grey sky.

Yes, perhaps I was bored and lonely I thought as we clumped up the shaking gangway but it didn't make any difference; what I had said was still true.. of course there was no God.

CHAPTER EIGHTEEN

With a grating of gears followed by a violent shaking the bus, reeking of exhaust fumes, pulled away from the curb; the street lights glowing dully through the pale dawn light. Looking down the narrow, bright-lit tube lined with seats, it came to me that I could be on a bus on my way back home ..

But of course not.. I was on bus journey with my ship-mates for a day out in Melbourne .. Australia.. ..the other side of the world..

I nudged Billy, nodding at the heads of Tad and Norrie in front of us; Norrie had surprised everyone by returning from Geelong with a Mohican-style haircut, the shaved scalp making his large ears even more prominent.

"A Cockatoo crossed with Dumbo.." I whispered.

Billy grinned and yawned, twisting his body trying to find a more comfortable position on the hard bench seat, his eyes closing.

After a little while Tad and Norrie settled down too, the damp warmth of the bus and the low hum of the engine acting like an anaesthetic, I thought yawning myself. Recalling how excited we had been running down the gangway, shouting to each other as we crossed the darkened quayside but after waiting for what seemed forever in the chill air at the bus-stop, our excitement had evaporated and now sitting upright in the gently swaying bus, I was only conscious of a gnawing unease..

'Yes.. it's you,' I reassured myself, glimpsing a momentary reflection in the dark window glass, wondering how the Sec. was getting on in the Pantry by himself, was he regretting his suggestion that we make an early start to get the most out of the journey? I imagined him in the white T-shirt and creased trousers, moving swiftly around the Pantry .. each movement deliberate.. precise .. Of course a lot of the Officers would be absent on shore-leave..

Perversely I almost envied him in the familiar surroundings..
the usual routine… fixed… definite ..without any fear of the
unknown ..

I leant back resting my head between the window and
vibrating metal trim, through my half-shut eyes the bus
became a hermetically-sealed rocket, shooting through the
dawn light, propelling the slumped bodies towards some
nameless destination…

A lurch of the bus pushed me against Billy and he
sleepily growled something.

"Sorry matey.." I murmured realizing that I had dozed
off, glancing at Billy, a long quiff fallen over his faces, his
saturnine looks softened by sleep; how defenceless he looks
I thought, prompted by a vague foreboding. . ..

Don't be silly, I told myself turning my head and rubbing
a circle in the misted glass with my sleeve, observing as
through a camera lens, the rows of suburban bungalows set
in open ground with a scattering of bushes and spindly trees;
blurred crayoned outline against a glowing opal sky. And
within those faint shapes, I thought even now people were
waking to the new day, yawning and stretching.. even
without the Sec. to brutally rouse them.. impelled by some
unfathomable impulse to rise and begin all over again…. .

Several times the bus shuddered to a stop and some
passengers got off to be replaced by others. I stared at they
newcomers as they moved towards me, their eyes meeting
mine for a split-second before looking instantly away; they
couldn't care less that I had left home and gone to sea,
I thought resentfully.

Looking back through the misted window I saw that the
bungalows of the outskirts had changed to impressive
stone-built mansions, each of them set back in large
gardens, with shrubbery and mature trees obscured by a
drizzling rain. Perhaps the cabin-boy I had replaced had
come from one of these houses I speculated, remembering
how according to Billy his father was a prominent citizen…
But what had prompted him to leave the ship so suddenly?
Would I ever find out? Or would it always remain a

mystery? Perhaps there was no clear reason? A momentary impulse and then it was too late.. But why should I care anyway it was all in the past.. nothing to do with me .. here .. now ..

The bus swung around another corner and wallowed to a juddering halt.

The four of us clattered down the bus steps the rain falling steadily; momentarily transfixed, we stood marooned in the flood of pedestrians and umbrellas swirling around us. I grinned nervously at Billy, conscious of a slight panic.. unused I thought to seeing so many people at once all of them rushing blindly on heedless to all around them. Is this why Chips prefers being on a ship at sea? I wondered absently.

"C'mon mateys." Billy ordered, turning about and fearlessly cutting a swathe through the crowd with Tad and Norris close behind, I tried to keep up, dodging the mass of pedestrians endlessly flowing between marble and glass facades.

Billy turned away from the crowded main street with the three of us close behind.. Tad his head and arms sticking out of khaki great coat he had bought in an 2nd Hand store in Geelong and beside him Norrie his Mohawk crest bobbing up and down. I too felt rather a little odd in the overlarge raincoat the Sec. had lent me. Like a circus troupe come to town, I thought smiling, hurrying so as not to get left behind.

At the end of the street a green and red neon sign flashed *Natty's Diner* and we hurried forward pushing eagerly into the large bright lit room. We all went over to an empty table and dropped into the chairs. Sniffing the warm air rich with cooking smells, suddenly faint from hunger I stared almost disbelievingly around at the bright space with its glass and chrome fittings and luridly colourful placards advertising a variety of meals. Could this be the same world as the open expanse of wind-swept ocean beneath vast blue skies.. ?

"Oi.. Phil your turn.." Billy called out and the others laughed.

I grinned looking up to see smiling waitress, shapely plump in black skirt and white blouse, her hair in a neat bun, standing patiently, pen and pad in hand.

"What it be chuckie.." She drawled in a twangy languorous voice.

After taking my order she turned away and my eyes followed her full rounded body moving rhythmically, crossing the room to put in our orders.

"Phil fancies a go with her.." Norrie guffawed.

I shook my head flushing hotly conscious of deep ache of longing.

An excited murmur rose from us as the waitress returned and put down the plates with huge steak oozing juices, two fried eggs and a heap of thick golden chips; a rack of toast and cups of tea soon followed.

"Howsa about this mateys!" Billy crowed and we all smirked joyfully.

Was there anything better in the world, I wondered feeling slightly dizzy.

We began to eat, except for the occasional grunt, the only noises loud slurps and gulps and the clink of cutlery on china; like the seagulls swooping on the scraps, I thought greedily intent on one thing.

But then Tad pushed away his plate the meal unfinished, and lit up a cigarette and Billy soon did the same and I too to my surprise found I couldn't eat anymore. Only Norrie kept on, eagerly shovelling food into his mouth and even helping himself from left-overs on Tad's plate.

"Youza peeg!" Tad squealed and we all laughed.

How splendid it is to have a full stomach, I mused blowing out cigarette smoke looking complacently around the large bright-lit room.

Once more out in the street, full of new energy we paraded down the wide pavements, now almost empty; the sky a bright blue strip between the buildings tops; a cold wind in our faces.

"British tars ashore! Billy called to us and we shouted back

"Yeah British tars ashore.!"

And yet for all our shouting and swagger, I sensed we were ill at ease ..a bit lost .. like country yokels arrived in a big city for the first time; half-fearful of the soaring concrete walls, the row on row of windows glinting coldly down at us.

"Try in here .. mateys.." Billy said turning through a door of a run-down old-fashioned building sandwiched between large office blocks..

The large dark bar-room was almost empty, I glanced around at the panelled walls taking in the marble-topped tables and bent-wood chairs; the several men lining the bar giving us wary glances.

"G'day t'ya sports. What yer havin'?" The portly bald-pated barman turned reluctantly from his conversation with one of the men at the bar. I thought I detected a faintly sarcastic note in his loud cheerfully twangy voice .

Norrie ordered four beers and we retreated with our glasses to a table against the wall; through the frosted glass of the street level windows I noticed shadowy forms slipping endlessly past.

"Cheers..! "We called out raising our glasses the sound ringing around the room; like a challenge I thought uneasily,conscious of being watched by the men by the bar. I took a long swallow, charting the course of the cold liquid down my throat to my stomach; eagerly waiting for the numbness to reach my brain.

My mind insensibly going to back to the ship and the now familiar daily scene on the dockside when at the blast of the hooter, a solid mass of dockers swept through the gates breathing out white plumes, like an invading army taking possession of ship and dockside; the various machines suddenly, violently battering away in the early morning silence, the gangway shaking under the heavy deliberate tread as down on the dockside and at the bottom of the holds they took up positions, wielding viciously pointed curved hooks with skilful abandon, shouting to each other in loud twangy bawlings as they plucked and flung the heavy sacks of wheat about. As if, I had thought watching them, it was some kind of game.. a fiercely competitive sport with timed breaks that allowed them to sprawl or walk about eating and drinking looking around with superior indolence as if they were on a holiday picnic then at an invisible signal to begin again with the same grinning reckless energy until the hooter sounded and with undiminished energy, jostling and halloing noisily they would stream out into the evening gloom.

Surely I wasn't sorry not to be back aboard I mused draining my glass, wondering distantly if I become so deeply attached to the ship I couldn't enjoy being away from her. I grinned at Billy who pushed another full glass towards me and took a long swallow; feeling my unease slipping from me; what if I was becoming an alcoholic though?

Suddenly we all rose, scuffing over the floor to the door; looking back my eyes meet the unfriendly stares of the men at the bar..

No, they don't like us, I decided as we stood undecided outside in the cold sunshine. But surely I hadn't expected that we would be hailed as brave voyagers from over the seas, garlanded and paraded in triumph along streets lined with cheering people?

And yet I couldn't quite get rid of the resentful feelings as we moved away down the street; surely we deserved better than to be rudely stared at.. treated like misfits.. outcasts.. not proper members of society …

"My turn mateys.. .." I insisted pushing the crumpled notes over the gleaming mahogany bar "Whiskies for us all .." My voice echoed around the narrow bar-room; a faint tawny light seeping through the windows set below street level. Had we been here before? I wondered surveying the tables crowded with foam-smeared glasses and overflowing ashtrays… .

Yes, we deserved better, I thought bitterly, frowning severely at the tall fair-haired bar-tender as he pushed the small glasses of amber liquid toward us.

"Here's to us mateys..! "I sang out shuddering as I sipped the harsh burning liquid ; everything in the bar acutely magnified and yet at the same time strangely blurred.

Standing in front the crazed china urinal I tried to understand how I came to be here, absently studying the copper water-pipe coated with verdigris; water plopping incessantly into a cistern above my head. Was it mere chance or was there some plan.. some purpose to it all.. My mind groped clumsily around .. images flashing past.. climbing the shaky steep slippery unlit narrow stairs .. the shadowy passageway with mysterious noises and then the box-like room with the single light bulb.. the sudden darkness and the flabby soft body yielding to my impetuous plunge ..Was that what I was seeking? Only that..? You're drunk, I thought solemnly possessed of certainty that I could explain everything.. .

The thin door to the gents flew open at my touch, pitching me into a crowd of heavy-set men in workman's clothes all talking loudly in brash, confident voices. I squeezed through to join the Billy and the others pressed against the bar talking their voices barely audible above the din of conversation.

"Cap'n 's coward.. ." Norrie was mumbling tipsily, shaking his head so the stiff crest jerked about. "Murdoch n' Hobbsie knoaws it.."

"We'ze ready !" Tad grimaced, his face twitching wildly.

"Are you planning something.. ?" I wondered vaguely. "A protest .. a mutiny?" my words echoed in my ears.

"You f----n' said it Phil." Billy responded with a sardonic grin. .

"No bizzeeness of zee cabin-boys. "Tad shrilled turning on me indignantly, his eyes staring bright.

"Bloody Poms. . "Came a deep voice from out of the buzz of talk.

I turned about, meeting the stare of a large wide-shouldered man in a bright checked shirt further along the bar; loud chuckles came from the others standing around him.

I'zz Polack!" "Tad screeched back, standing back from the bar, red spots showing on his hollow cheeks.

"Don't give a 'roo what yer are! "The same man responded, evoking a loud roar of mocking laughter.

Now at last I thought, my heart pounding, I could make them understand; explain how much we had endured, far from land.. the endless days and nights the ship alone in the vast expanse of sea and sky…

I stepped back from the bar, the grinning faces crowding forward .

I gestured towards Billy, Tad and Norrie.

"We're ship-mates…" I shouted almost tearful.

A roar of derisive laughter filled the room.

"Yer making an arse of yerself." Billy hissed in my ear taking me by the arm.

"Just make them understand.. we crossed the Pacific.. ship-mates ..together "I muttered as we stumbled out of the door into the street; the light fading as we straggled along on the street the lighted shop-fronts casting dim fires onto the wet pavement. My mind churning confusedly. But really it was absurdly funny.. the men gawping suspiciously at us as if we creatures from some other world when really we were the same as them.. . .

"A man's a man for all that n' all that "I gasped out hysterically.

"All for one.. one for all ! "Billy laughed slapping me on the back.

"British Tars are best … "Norrie bellowed.

"And zee Polish! "Tad shrieked.

Our cries echoing off the tall buildings strangely excited us; I became aware of a fierce resentment so suddenly we began aiming wild kicks at the passing walls and making violent feints through the air as if attacking some invisible enemy…. I felt my blood pounding in my temples driven along by a burning indignation. 'We'd show f----n show 'em!

I then we came to sudden stop in front of one of the brilliant-lit windows of one of the department stores glaring angrily at the blank-faced mannequins, somehow incensed by the artfully arranged displays of household goods. .towels, sheets and blankets, pots and pans and crockery.. as if the colourful array of goods somehow humiliated us.. excited a violent antipathy.. an abstract hatred of all material things.. ....

Suddenly a voice shouted out, "All property is theft.!" It must be me I thought, my throat hurting; watching Norrie step up to the glass and smash his forehead .. a large forked crack appearing . .. like a dream.. I thought.

"Peelers.... "Billy hissed and we stood stiffly immobile the deliberate echoing steps becoming louder as the two large figures, with matching shadows under the sickly-orange street-lights paced slowly towards us; giant forms in dark blue great-coats and over-sized peaked caps, idly whacking long batons into their gloved palms.

I gave a sigh of relief as the two gigantic silhouettes turned and paced slowly back down the street..

With a single loud whoop, we turned as one and ran, our footsteps ringing down the deserted street; instinctively keeping the same direction, running effortlessly, tirelessly; both pursued and pursuers.. one of us slowing briefly only for an other to find new energy and sprint past the others, shouting encouragement.. until we had came to a sudden halt.. winded.. breathless.. staring wildly at each other as if we'd just woken up from a deep sleep.

"We gave the f-----n' peelers the dodge eh ?" Billy yawned leaning towards me. "Tad 'ates all Police fer what they did 'is dad .... "

"Yeah.. .." I murmured glancing at Norrie and Tad collapsed into dozing heaps feeling myself sinking irresistibly into spongy depths; the steady thrumming of the bus like a sedative; through the window lights repeatedly flashed out of the night.

'But you see officer.. it wasn't me.. .well not exactly ..' I looked around the square tiled room.. somehow not like a Police station at all. 'You see we've been to sea for weeks and weeks .. 'I went on feebly 'Being ashore after nothing but sea and sky .. you feel this anger .. against ..against everything really ..' But I knew it was useless the stern faces showed no emotion.. no sympathy.. and really I knew I didn't deserve it.. I'm irremediably bad.. evil.. criminal.... I thought even as the fierce grip on my shoulder marched me down the narrow corridor the tiny cell with a slit window, the iron-barred door crashing shut behind me; what would my parents say. really I had failed them.. . .

"Hey .. Phil.. Phil..! We's 'ere... Wake up matey!"

I opened my eyes seeing Billy standing over me his hand on my shoulder and struggled to my feet .

"I was having this dream .. thought I'd been put in a Police cell.." I laughed.

"Yeah.. ?" Billy yawned indifferently and I followed him down the steps of the bus

"Home sweet home.. mateys.." I sniggered as the four of us, crossed through the orange glow of the empty dockside towards the bright-lit ship; faintly conscious of guilty feelings.

CHAPTER NINETEEN

What now? I wondered irritably turning from the sink to face Pete's fat, round pink face tiny eyes bulging, his massive shoulders pressed through the Pantry Hatch.

"Helluva ship... Phil.." Pete gasped, his face going bright red.

"Treat ya like. . . a Coolie by Harry. Ya knows Officers invited some Student Nurses? Hah! Ain't right... They wants me to be huh waiter having some kinda party.. on board jest like a cruise ship. Ain't on my Articles, no sireee. Had enough. Getting out.." "Really..?" I mocked, how often had Old Smelly threatened to leave the ship?

"Howsa about you com' with us hey? Been to see Canada High Commission Melbourne I has.. says he'll help us." Pete puffed. "Get ya home... ..No time..by Harry.."

"Me?" I frowned my heart thudding; wasn't this what I longed for .. to escape from the oppressive, ceaseless shipboard routine..?

"You betcha.. It ain't right what they done t'yer. Yer signed on jist fer one trip.. didn't ya? No sayin' when she'll go back to Vancouver Look at ya.. skin n'bones.. own mother wouldn't recognise ya...We'se slip away early morning gone afore they knows it.." Pete wheezed.

"Slip away? Jump ship you mean.." I muttered; just like the Australian cabin boy, I thought agitatedly.

"You said it son 'afore this old tub goes down." Pete groaned breathlessly.

I looked up at the porthole above the sink, a flicker of a scowl in the dark glass, hearing a jeering whine 'Admit it.. you're finished.. .a failure....get away while you can..'

"What yer say son.." Pete goggled pleadingly.

"Just mind your own business will you.. ." I shouted with sudden ferocity, surprising myself. "It my life.. I can do what I want with it. . ."

For a few minutes Pete stared back at me, his mouth opening and closing before sadly shaking his bullet-head he jerked himself out of the Hatch into the Officer's Dining Room.

For a minute or two I looked down at the sink-full of grey scummy dish water; my heart thudding. Why had I become so angry? Was it because I was tempted? Almost as if I was ready to betray myself

"C'mon Wight! Stop dreaming n'finish off here and get yourself up to the Officer's Smoking Room. Needs to be given a good clean.." "Sure thing Sec.." I chirped, strangely relieved to be shouted at; guessing that the Captain had been onto the Chief Steward about the arrangements for the party and he had in turn taken the Sec to task.

And so now he takes it out on me, I thought bitterly as I went up the stairs.. the bottom of the heap.. the lowest of the low..

Yet shut-away in the stale-smelling Smoking Room busy vigorously polishing the brass rims and catches on the Port holes I wondered if my spirit was inevitably being worn down grinding and abrading me so as to become a smoothly-working part of the whole?

Perhaps I Should have taken up Old Smelly's offer to get away, thought before all individual spirit was rubbed out of me.. before I became a mere shell.. a husk …. like the workers in China..

But surely I am still capable of free spontaneous action, I thought frowning and yet was I ? Wasn't everything I did fixed.. determined .. ordered.. inevitable….

'Dear Mother and Father,
I'm writing this in my bunk-bed in the cabin as it is much too cold to be out on deck anymore. It's strange how you miss the ship not rolling around and the noise and vibration from the engines, We've been berthed in the docks at Geelong the port near Melbourne for over a week now and ever since we arrived a bitterly cold wind has been blowing. And we thought we were going to get to be able

to sun bathe on the beaches!.. It just shows you shouldn't let your imagination run away with yourself.!

Geelong is very dull.. almost the only place to go is the "Mission for Seamen" We did go to Melbourne once but it was cold there too and the people not very friendly .. so I don't think we'll go again .. This time I managed to get my land-legs almost immediately..

The loading is going pretty well. The wheat is in sacks this time which means a lot of handling but the local Dockers are all great big men with loud voices with Australian accents. Some times it feels like they've taken over the ship! I think most of the crew resent them.. so big and noisy it makes us look quite feeble by comparison.

They love disputing.. about almost anything.. ..I was out on deck one day when two of them began this argument about which of two seagulls perched on a roof top would fly away first. It all got very heated finally to settle it they ended up betting on it and so one of them had to pay the other and that pleased both of them tremendously!

They aren't working at all today because there is a Cup Final in Geelong and they all just walked off .. they only work if they want to and I was told quite openly help themselves to the cargo if they want .. even deliberately breaking open crates.. but they do work very hard, for them it seems almost like fun.. I was told by the Bo'sun though that they really know what they are doing as it's vital the ship is loaded properly otherwise she might begin to list and even capsize. Which has happened on other ships. I've learnt how to appreciate what seems very simple is actually complicated and needs skill to do it properly.

Still no letter from you.. I can't quite understand it.. Everyone else practically has got one. ... Still it doesn't really matter..'

I let the pen fall from my fingers, really what was the point.. all of it so trivial and I didn't even know if a letter would even reach them.. Like talking to yourself.. I thought gloomily.

"Where ya f-----n' goin? Billy demanded as I slipped down to the cabin-floor.

I turned at the door, his face just visible in the shadow of the lower berth watching me closely over the top of a War Comic.

"Just get some fresh air." I explained "So fuggy in here.."

It was true the porthole was thick with condensation and yet it more a sense of claustrophobia.

"Goin' see them nurses come aboard I bet.." Billy jeered. "Some of the Crew is dead against it. Reckon brings a ship bad luck. Just f----n' bint ain't they."

I nodded and left, feeling a little as if I was escaping from something.

Out on deck I went up the stairs to the lifeboat-deck, the wind had dropped; the sky a uniform pale grey; an eerie stillness hanging over the dockside; the only sound the faint throb of the ship's auxiliary motor.

From the rail looking down on deserted space I recalled seeing the dockers going off in high-spirits, shouting and laughing like schoolboys on an half-day holiday and now I imagined them crowded together in the stadium, enthusiastically cheering on their team; extravagantly exultant at each gain and just as extravagantly despairing at every setback. Didn't I admire their reckless enthusiasm for everything around them? So unlike the carping, cynical Mitchie and Hobbsie and others of the crew.. But hadn't I become infected by that same cynicism? Viewing life as an obdurate routine .. regulated.. unyielding. . to be endured more than enjoyed..?

But what was it Mitch had said about the Dockers? 'F-- ----n' babbies the lot of 'em..' And I had smirked in agreement. And it was true.. wasn't it? Like adult-size children blissfully ignorant of the harsh reality of life. . .it's miseries and cruelties.. the ache of being alive.... life passing .. moment by moment by moment.. inexorably ..irretrievably ... alone here on the deck in the still cool greyness.. on the other side of the world far from all that was known and familiar..

The squeal of brakes made me look down. A small bus had just pulled up on the dockside close to the gangway; my heart beating faster at the sight of the swirl of red-trimmed dark blue cloaks with wide hoods, catching a glimpse of ankles as they one by one they stepped carefully down from the bus. They must be the nurses I thought with strange joy, their excitedly cheerful twangy voices filling the air as they milled around uncertainly. Like a flock of birds, that might at any moment take flight, I mused, gazing rapturously at the flushed, soft skin of their faces.

Loud shouts made them all looked towards the ship. I leant over watching the hoods moving up the gangway with anxious cries, small hands grasping tightly to both the guide-ropes, until they had vanished from my view..

Nothing to do with me, I thought gloomily even as suns rays broke through the monotone greyness, flooding the ship and dockside with a brilliant winter sunshine.

Really I should get back to the cabin I thought and yet I lingered on revelling in the sun's faint warmth. Slowly I became aware of the sounds of tinny dance music, mixed with the chatter of voices broken by shrieks of excited laughter.

How unfair life was, I thought conjuring up a vision of the cheerful party scene; the superior-looking Officers in their navy blue uniforms with gold braid, the Student Nurses disrobed of cloaks and hats, in filmy dresses, chatting excitedly, sipping cocktails dispensed by leering Mitch and smirking old Pete.. the dancing couples, close-pressed bodies swaying to the rhythmic dance music... .. Always I would be an outsider, I mused self-pityingly.. looking on full of envy and self-contempt.. and yet

I felt my eyes closing; my mind swirling with vague fantasies.. slim sun-brown arm. and bare shoulders. ... .small hands lifting strands of hair from a smiling mouth.. warm breath.. shining eyes eager... passionate...

"Hello... you . there . .."

The plangent twang made me look up, staring rudely at the flushed, radiantly lovely features, tumbled about with wonderful rich auburn curls

"Hello .." I muttered finally, breathing in the sweet-scented flowery perfume. .

"Stuffy in there.... . ." She murmured with a quick glance back; my eyes at once fixing on the fine gold chain crossing the fine collar bones, the heart-shaped locket resting lightly on the swelling scoop of glistening skin. How lovely she is I thought dazedly.. .

"Don't know why I came at all." She went on in the same full tones. "Some of the others were very keen.. Sure a party on a ship, should be a bit of a giggle and all that. Didn't go home even.. changed after our shift was finished.. no one there anyway...." She gave a slight shake of her head, a wry smile coming to her full bow-shaped lips.

"So tell me, you're a fella.. what's so wonderful anyway about watching over-grown men with hairy legs and nobbly knees chasing a ball around a muddy field eh?" She gave an impatient huff, the rounded curves of her bodice heaving.

I flushed helplessly caught in her calm searching gaze.

"Who are you anyway?" She posed teasingly so I felt my heart swell.

Me..? I'm a Cabin Boy. ..." I stammered self-consciously.

"Cabin-Boy..?" She gave a snort of laughter. "How very funny.."

"Yes.." I agreed eagerly, revelling in her amusement

"But what's your name?" She gave an encouraging smile, her clear brown eyes watching me closely.

"Me? Well er.. Phillip..." I answered, words tumbling excitedly. "Though I usually get called Phil by the crew, or Pip by my mother.." I stopped suddenly conscious that I was gabbling.

And did your mother mind you going to sea?" She wondered tiny frown lines creasing her forehead.

I shook my head. "But it's my life anyway ." I added flushing hotly.

"Of course. .but mother's always worry. I hope you answer her letters? I'm sure she writes regularly" She wagged a finger with playful severity.

"Well but I haven't received any actually." I countered my eyes resting on the gold ring on her middle finger.

"I expect they're held up somewhere.." She murmured sympathetically

"I guess.." I sighed. "Originally we were meant to go back to Vancouver straight away that's where I joined the ship you see, but they sent us here instead.. now we don't when if ever we'll ever get back there.. ."

"I see.." She mused thoughtfully.

"But I like being a seaman.." I boasted flushing hotly.

"You do .. ?" She laughed gaily. "But don't they have a bad reputation? Drinking and fighting. a girl in every port ?"

I bit my lip; looked away suddenly ashamed.

"Somehow it changes you.. being at sea.. for weeks on end.." I muttered gruffly.

"Yes.. I'm sure.." She soothed. "It must be quite ..well.. boring at times."

"You can say that! The same jobs day after day and the food's so bad too and everything is so old-fashioned. We have to do the washing-up in cold water and for detergent they use this shredded bars of yellow soap but .. so you never get anything properly clean.. in the pantry where I work there's a line of hideous black sludge at the back of the counter.." I stopped short was I so desperate for her sympathy?

"See this.. ." I exclaimed suddenly turning to a stanchion and pressing one of the cracked blisters on the painted metal; flakes of paint fell away bleeding drops of water and showing the rust .

"No matter how much they scrape and paint, the rust comes back .. lurking just beneath the surface .." I looked down catching a nervous, almost hysterical note in my voice.

"And did you always smoke?" She asked, gently taking up my right hand to show my nicotine-stained fingers, her firm grasp flaming through me.

"Just since coming to sea.." I stammered. "Once we're in international waters cigarettes are duty-free. So almost all the crew smoke. It's becomes second nature... Like swearing.. everyone does it .."

"I see...." She murmured, amused lines forming around her eyes.

"Of course I know it's wrong.. I try hard.. .." I pleaded.

"I'm sure you do.." She murmured distantly, looking away over the dockside. "We all do.."

I nodded, deeply moved; so she had known suffering and yet still could be so graciously kind.

"I'd better get back.." She said with a sigh. "You are very sweet.. I could get to like you a lot."

I nodded dumbly, imagining myself sinking to my knees before her, in pure admiration.

"'Bye Pip. Don't worry so much.. You'll be O.K....." A moistness pressed my cheek, a flower-scented warmth suffusing me.

I stayed still, stiffly pressed to the rail hearing the click of her shoes on the deck abruptly cut off by the thud of the door to the Officer's Smoking Room closing.

Looking up, I saw that the sun had become a corroded disc slipping in and out of clouds, a misty greyness closing in. I shivered in the air suddenly feeling an icy chill hearing the sounds of dance music and sudden girlish shrieks of laughter. I bet now she's in there I thought with a sharp ache, chatting and smiling to the Officers forgetting me completely.

Surely not the Irish Sparkies, I groaned, going down the stairs to the main deck; the lights on the dockyard beginning to glow through the gathering gloom. I will never see her again, I thought dully

"Where ya been ...?" Billy demanded from the lower berth, putting his legs out and yawning.

"Just up on the lifeboat-deck." I said casually; my beating faster.

"Been spying on them nurses eh?. Right f-----g Peeping Tom ain't ya." Billy grinned staring fixedly at me.

"No... not at all.." I retorted glaring angrily.

"Hey what's that!" Billy exclaimed leaping to his feet and holding me by my shoulders. "Lipstick! Yer f----n' jammy so and so...."

I wiped the back of my hand across my face and looked wonderingly at the red smear.

" Ya shudda got 'er down 'ere. Askin' for it weren't she.." Billy said shaking his head pityingly

I dragged myself up onto my berth, my head reeling. Could it be I had missed my chance? Of course .. it was so obvious.. at the very least I should have asked her where she lived.. but all I could think to talk about was the black slime in the Pantry.. How astonishingly stupid..

"Tell'us what she was like, Phil?" Billy called up from his berth. "Fancied ya I betcha.. Didna I tellya their was some right crumpet ..How d'ya meet 'er"

I squirmed uncomfortably.

"I was sitting up beside the lifeboat and suddenly there she was beside me... "I said my throat feeling rough.

"Nice body 'ad she, with big tits ?" Billy leered looking up.

"Mmmm.. I think so.. ." I murmured, strangely my mind was a compete blank; only the rich scent of perfume persisting.

"What was 'er name anyway? Maybe we can look her up.." Billy insisted. "Them fancy birds really goes fer tars like us.. ."

"Name.? Yes what was her name..." I puzzled. "I don't think she told me.. I mean I didn't ask..."

"We'll go to the Hospital.. get 'er there." Billy chuckled knowingly.

"I think she was married though.." I added with a sigh. "At least she had a ring on her finger."

"That don't mean nuttin.." Billy scorned. "Them are the ones to go fer.. experienced.. Ya a still gotta lot t'learn me old matey."

"I guess so. . "I sighed sinking back onto the mattress, suddenly exhausted, eyes wide-open, staring at the ceiling just above. Would I ever learn? Or would I always end up failing to be harried by bitter regrets..

I closed my eyes, feeling again the feather-like brush of her lips on my cheek... such a warm, contented feeling. .already fading leaving a faint sense of loss..

"Ya comin' or what Phil?" Billy called from the doorway.

"No choice really .." I groaned, sliding down from the bunk; so this is the reality of your life, I thought inhaling the familiar stench following Billy down the gloom of the tunnel-like companionway.

CHAPTER TWENTY

Wringing out the thick floor-cloth, the dribbles plopping into the pail of dirty brown water, I made another wide sweep over the floor; the companionway stretching away into a shadowy gloom, the deck-door kept shut against the bitter wind.

Will we ever put to sea again? I had begun to wonder. If only we could put to sea, that was now our only thought. To be sailing through unruffled blue waters beneath a cloudless sky with the sun blazing down on us and all would be well..

And yet how vain that wish seemed, the loading continuing, the ship's holds seemingly bottomless; above our heads the pale grey sky often darkening as showers of icy rain pitted the green-grey harbour water; the ship's great bulk heaving fitfully against the moorings. Just like us, I mused eager to leave these dull skies and bitter winds even as the days passed and there was no sign of departure.. as if we were doomed to a stay moored to the dockside for the rest of our lives...

Billy and I had almost completely given up braving the icy winds blowing down the deserted streets of Geelong; our one attempt to find the nurse I had met on the life-boat Deck a humiliating failure when the grumpy old porter at the hospital threatened to call the Police if we didn't leave at once.

The *Mission to Seamen* was our only refuge and for a time Billy and I, sometimes with the two Deck Boys, went there every afternoon to play cribbage or pool or dominoes. Only once did we meet the Chaplain and rather despising myself as a coward I restricted myself to the banal pleasantries. Was I even a little afraid of him? I wondered abstractly; cowed by his hearty, genial bluster; as if life was simply a matter of being cheerful and friendly.. .. . .

After awhile though we began to find the mission even more wearisome than being on the ship and spent our free-time in our cabins, away from the dockers; lying on our berths reminiscing of those charmed days lolling at the ship's stern our bare skin hot in the sun's rays.. the frothy wake unrolling endlessly over a blue sea…

Instead we were caught in an indeterminate existence .. like creatures stranded by the tide neither of the land nor of the sea ..

What bad luck, we continually moaned, that we should end up in Geelong..of all places so far from the bars.. the weather so bitterly cold and no women.. No wonder then that the crew were increasingly resentful of the Aussie dockers with their loud, voices and good-natured disdain for us scrawny Pommies.

Coming out on deck I had heard one of them bellow out 'Call 'em Pommies more like apple-cores.. Ha! ha! Badly need some feedin' up yer ask me.' And it was true I thought beside the broad-chested, hale and hearty Dockers we did seem a weedy, ill-nourished lot.. ..

"G'ona be a right bust-up one of these days.." Billy told me in a low voice, telling me how Murdock the Irish A.B had snatched up one of the needle sharp cargo-hooks lying around and had threatened to slash one of the dockers for making some jeering remark about the crew.

Like a scene from a film I thought picturing the looming shadows in the depths of the hold, the angry voices and violent gestures .. and didn't I feel deep within myself the same violent urgings? To strike out.. wildly .. without real cause .. to smash and shatter that infuriating assumed superiority..

Adding to the general discontent was the belief that the Captain hadn't been on the ship for over a week, resulting in various rumours. One that was that he was busy arranging for another crew to be sent out and we would all soon be returning to England. But hardly anyone took that seriously… .. 'Too bloody good to be bloody true' was the usual observation with a fatalistic grin.

The favourite of Ronnie, was that he had taken up with a local woman and had forgotten about the ship altogether.

Jock for his part speculated sagely on the premise that both the Captain and the Chief Steward who also had been absent for a few days had been arrested and charged with defrauding both crew and ship owners..

Wheezing tediously Old Pete had confided to me that without doubt the Captain had been committed to an mental asylum.

"Hah...madder n'hatter by Harry. no wonder ship's falling apart.. a goner.. ..."

As I washed my way slowly along the companionway floor I considered how surprising it was that the crew who habitually took great satisfaction in deriding the Captain as a useless old woman, incompetent and lazy, so deeply resented his absence; as if without him, even as a unseen presence, they lacked something vital to their daily lives.. .

Did I feel that too.. ? I mused or was I just so bored with the waiting.. without any end.. yes.. utterly bored even more than when I was at home I admitted during the afternoon breaks; Billy and I now often joining the two deck-boys in their cabin.

Was this why I came to sea, I mused, sprawled out on the floor the air thick with cigarette smoke, smelling of sweat and unwashed clothes; my eyes drawn to the glossy pictures of skimpily-clothed women and pinned to the cabin walls, smiling and pouting, their satiny rounded bodies in provocative poses fascinating and at the same time shaming me.. just pictures I thought averting my eyes .. listening enviously to their boastful accounts of going ashore and getting drunk and fighting and going with women of all races; while all the time I was living at home and going to school with occasional family outings and church on Sundays....

One time Tad, his sharp bony face flitting with grimaces, had begun to speak in his uncouth English about his boyhood, at times muttering fiercely in what I assumed to be Polish. Out of the flood of words, tinged with a bitter pathos, I had picked up the outlines of his life .. a story at once incongruously brutal and ludicrous, darkly shadowed by fear and suspicion: describing a ruined apartment block in Warsaw stinking and dirty, his mother dying of cancer with untreated, suppurating ulcers, while he and an older sister fought like dogs for scraps of food in back streets until he was sent to a juvenile labour camp barely surviving on the scanty rations, and treated so harshly that he had decided to kill himself but then miraculously was befriended by a guard and managed to escape to wandering through the countryside living off the land; describing how he slept with some half-mad woman in a ruined out-house in the hope some food.. always without qualms or regrets or doubts.. or so it seemed. After some time in Italy ending up in Genoa where he had stowed aboard a ship bound for Liverpool though he had no idea where that was .. when discovered he had been treated kindly by the crew and allowed to work as a deck-boy.. and so had begun a career at sea.. never settling anywhere ashore...

What an unhappy life, I had mused studying the thin, bony figure lying on the lower berth, without family .. home .. or country.. .

I knew the deck crew regarded him as a bit mad and often made him the butts of their jokes confident that they would get a vehemently exaggerated reaction adding to the fun; almost always in a state of nervous, irritated excitement .. ready in a flash to construe some chance remark into a deadly insult..

Only Norrie seemed to have any real regard for him .. yet how different they were I had thought looking at Norrie sitting with his back against the door like some overgrown humpty dumpty his shaved scalp now sprouting tiny black hairs; he had grown up with the sea coming from a village on the Norfolk Coast his family had been fishermen or seamen for generations... One day he had told me smugly he was sure he would get to be an A.B..

And yet perversely Tad frequently vented his spite on his fellow Deck-Boy but nothing seemed to upset Norrie ... the grin on his moony face only growing broader.. even Tad's shrillest revilings failing to penetrate Norrie's placidly affable exterior.. They were deck-boys.. ship-mates.. best mates.. and that was all that mattered .. just like Billy and me I wondered doubtfully again pausing to wring out the cloth, near to the end of the companionway aware of a brightness coming through the open door of the officer's smoking room.. noticing a strange brightness inside the officer's smoking room... What could it be?

I got to my feet and wrenched open the door and stepped out on deck.

"Snow... it's snow.." I chuckled blinking at the dazzling reflected light, the sun clear of the roof tops shining from a clear blue sky;

Blowing out white smoke into the icy air I went to the rail marvelling how the multitude of projections and angles of the ship had been smoothed to a unblemished, gleaming whiteness.

Suddenly stopping I scooped up a handful of fluffy flakes and pressed the soft flakes into a snowball and turned and threw it against the bulkhead watching with glee as it stuck momentarily then slid slowly downwards; my mind crowding with boyhood memories of snowball fights. Was that why I felt such an overwhelming joy, I wondered, looking around again and again seeing how ship and dock-side buildings were moulded into one lustrous, white marble sculpture beside the dark harbour waters..

I turned and retraced my footsteps leading from the open doorway, staring in amazement at the dark holes plunged deep in the sparkling crystalline white mass of snow; had I really made them I wondered dazedly pressing a supreme gladness to myself; surely anything was possible?

When I next went out on deck, water droplets sparkling like diamonds were dripping steadily from the overhanging snow and from all around me came faint gurglings; ragged dark holes had appeared in the white surface, the snow now too watery for snowballs. Later in the morning the snow had almost all gone only a few streaks between walls and on the rooftops remaining as a reminder of what had been; the sky once more a dull grey; the air chilly and damp. And yet the shock of the dazzling whiteness in the morning sunshine stayed with me... a talisman.. a comfort ... yes. anything might happen.. suddenly without warning.

And so lying on our bunk beds that afternoon when a sudden tremor tore through the cabin and a dull roaring broke the silence, the steel cabin walls vibrating ecstatically I jumped down to the floor.

"The engines!.." I cried doing a little dance. "We're going to sea.. going to sea.."

"Nah! just engineers testin' t'new bearings.." Billy grinned from the gloom of the bottom bunk.

"Really?" I murmured crestfallen and almost at once the thudding shuddering vibration stopped.

How foolish I am, I thought grimly pulling myself back onto my bunk; so easily deluded and yet .. . surely it was possible...

Several times during that afternoon there were again sudden roarings and the cabin walls vibrated fiercely but wiser now I knew it wouldn't last... Out in the companionway I twice encountered junior engineers wearing boiler-suits streaked with oil stains, exchanging nods and grunts their faces marked with determination.. purpose...and I imagined them crawling amongst the complex of machinery in the depths of the engine room.. fitting and tightening. .scraping knuckles and forearms against sharp steel edges.. the skin abrading ..oil mixing with blood.. . While all I could do was wait impatiently, tantalized by the repeated starts and stops.. despairing of ever leaving this grey world and yet still I remembered the wonder of the freshly fallen snow sparkling in the brilliant sun..

Perhaps it's Sunday.. I mused coming out on deck from the Pantry and finding the dockside deserted; the machinery silent Where the dockers were on strike again..?

I wandered on down and through into the foredeck, under the ragged clouds the ship a sleety rain blowing in from the sea; along the quayside the spidery cranes bent stiffly motionless; the faint pounding of ship's auxiliary motor and the splash of bilge water the only sound. I stood shivering in the cold wind as if waiting for something....

Out of the still air came a ringing sound.. and again. like the rhythmical striking of a clock .. clink.. clink.. clink. . I moved forward the sound growing louder .. And there were some of the deck Crew wielding sledgehammers driving in the wedges that secured the canvas covers over the hatches.. the sound ringing out over the flecked green harbour waters.. echoing around the dockside; striking of our chains.. I thought grinning .. .

And then the ship's engines abruptly roared out; a roar of sheer defiance to the mysterious forces keeping us in a chill clammy embrace.. and looking up I saw a column of black smoke rising far into the sky .. signal for all to see that it was happening at last.. yes we were going to sea.... and all around me the steel bulk vibrated triumphantly..

But where we sailing for? As usual there was no certain knowledge.. just shrugs a few guesses and wishful conjectures.. But what did it matter? We were going to sea.. that was all that mattered. Passing each other in the companionways or out on deck we exchanged contented looks and winks; fellow initiates of a great mystery..

Waking suddenly that night into the pitch dark of the cabin I was immediately conscious of the triumphantly brutal drag and shove on my stretched-out body tingling to the vibrating steelwork, the unhesitating thud of the engines pounding my senses.

'So we were at sea.' I murmured gleefully immediately falling back to sleep.

Gulping at the tangy salt air the blustery wind pulled at my clothes and hair as I came out on deck; the Australian coastline retreating to a hazy outline; it was true .. .we were out at sea...

I stared up into a piercingly bright blue sky through which puffy white balls tore themselves to shreds in their eagerness to outrace each other. Going to the rail I looked down at the rolling mounds of water gleaming like green glass in the clear sunlight; the ship with her cargo of Australian wheat in the holds, rising and falling with ponderous majesty. But would my joyful feelings last? Wouldn't the daily routine in the tropical heat soon wear me down? I wondered, my eyes attracted to several seagulls, swooping and wheeling uttering sharp cries. This is their home, I thought as one by one they folded their wings and settled on the water, their smooth white shapes slipping effortlessly up and down the steep-sided waves; such perfect oneness with the natural world, I mused .. while we are just passing through.. visitors.. intruders

"Pheel!.... Phell !"

It was Tad waving madly at me from the doorway to the foredeck and then before I could move he ran and grabbed me by the arm.

"Your mad crazy.. ... I cried struggling to free my arm from his fierce grip.

"Lookzee ! "Tad shouted into my ears, jabbing his free arm out across the water.

I stared out over the foam-flecked grey-green seas, my eyes watering in the wind.

"Kosciusko! Kosciusko!.." Tad shrieked grinning and nodding. releasing my arm. I shook my head uncomprehendingly; rubbing my arm really he was crazy.

"Mountain.. .Zee mountain.. Kosciusko.." Tad wailed despairingly.

I stared across to the distant mainland now able to see a range of mountain crests, rising into the pale blue sky, one more prominent than the rest, it's snowy flanks and top glittering in the winter sunlight.

"Yes…. I can see it!" I cried excitedly.

"Kosciusko zee greatest, bravest Polish hero.." Tad exclaimed breathlessly, his eyes bulging out of his sharp, pock-marked face.

"Really .." I laughed looking wonderingly at the ungainly bony figure hopping about the deck; all the time the ship pushing resolutely through the rough seas beneath a bright sky.

"He nevaa.. gives up..even zay keels 'im.. Neva...." Tad sobbed, tears dribbling down his hollow cheeks.

"He must have been a real hero.. ..." I murmured moved almost to tears myself.

Tad turned and seized my shoulders, his lips wet on my cheek and then in an clumsy stumbling gait ran back down the foredeck.

"Whaat's with t'Pole thean?"

It was Hobbsie followed by the rest of the day-gang all of them looking curiously back at Tad now near the fo'cosle.

I pointed out across the expanse of foam-streaked waters to the distant shoreline, the snow-tipped peak now veiled by sunlit gauzy clouds.

"See that peak it's called Mount Kosciusko. A Polish patriot..."

"Whaat 'e do fer em?" Brownie demanded lowering at me.

"I'm not sure exactly, but he died bravely trying." I retorted angrily.

"Another f----g useless Pole!" Brownie roared out before they all moved off laughing raucously.

Wiping my cheek, I walked slowly back down the deck gazing as I went over the slate-green water, the wind effortlessly sculpting it into mounds and hollows, streaked by blackish foam, vast shadows sweeping over the surface like, great cloud masses moving swiftly over the sun's shining disc. Did it matter if men were brave or cowardly.. ? Surely all human effort was as nothing before the elemental forces of this world.... air .. water... light ..

Passing through into the amidships I found Chips looking out to sea, the crest of his white hair ruffling in the wind.. his head a finely modelled profile; like an ancient seer, I thought smiling to myself.

"You're pleased to be out at sea... "I said rather doubtfully guessing at something uncertain in his manner as he turned to me. "Or is there something wrong with the ship...."

"Nay.. nay.. we'll be alright .." Chips a faint smile stretching the crazed leathery skin.

Perhaps he is a bit crazy after all I thought turning inside beneath me the ship heaving and trembling, pressing indomitably through the wind-tossed waters towards the shining vastness of the Pacific Ocean beyond the horizon.

CHAPTER TWENTY-ONE

And so day after day the sun's fiery disc emerged from the dawn-dark sea incinerating the ragged wisps of clouds streaking the horizon, mounting ever higher into the brightening sky until the ocean became a vast blazing furnace .. the ship a floating crucible.. .. boiling and roasting us ..evaporating all our energy as we struggled out of our sweat-soaked beds, already exhausted we plodded zombie-like through the day's appointed tasks, barely conscious of the sun's slow decline, the dying rays, marking the horizon with premonitory red streaks before the final plunge into the evening blackness allowing the myriad stars to glitter brightly forth, the close night-air swamping us in a steamy, enervating heat. .the blustery winds and choppy waters of the Great Australian Bight long since obliterated from our memories..

"Het as the deil's girdle eh, Laddie." Jock wheezed faintly, with sketch of a grin as I stepped through the amidships doorway.

"Surely now we've crossed the Equator." I speculated wearily, moving over to the ship's side, pressing against the vibrating steel bulwark, dazzled by the mirror-like glare of the water..

"All the f----n' same ain't it "Ronnie whimpered testily.

"I guess.." I sighed turning around. Both the Cooks were sprawled out, beside the Amidships doorway their backs against the Amidships. Like two rag-dolls I thought an attempt at a smile cracking my lips. Once again they were refusing to serve hot meals and passed a lot of the day sitting out on the deck, hardly moving. Willie looked most the pitiful, strands of hair plastered on the pink scalp, feebly dabbing at his craggy face, flushed scarlet.

While Ronnie was as pallid as ever the only sign he was suffering from the heat were the beads of sweat on his forehead and the bad-tempered scowl. His ankles were stuck out of the bottom of the checked cook's trousers and for some reason I was faintly revolted by the sight of the coarse black hairs pricking the pure white skin.

A squelching noise brought my head around. It was the day-gang, led by Hobbsie filing slowly past, their rubber-thongs sticking to the hot deck. Bare to the waist, their bodies sun-blackened, red sore eyes staring forward they trudged slowly past; bone and muscle in motion ; as if the dead had come to life to run the ship, I thought as they passed without any of the usual banter along deck and out of sight.

"Working on your tan are we Wight?"

I grimaced at the Sec's sarcasm, glancing at the trim figure holding to the jamb of the Amidships doorway; how did he manage to be so fit and lively?

"Maybe in for some bad weather. So no sleeping out on deck." He said curtly before turning about and vanishing into the shadows of the Amidships.

"He makes it sound serious.." I snarled feebly.

"No mair than we deserve I doot." Jock croaked as I crossed the sill back into the Amidships. "We maun dree oor weird.."

"What ever that might mean.." I muttered wearily going back to the piles of dirty dishes clinking fretfully beside the hatch; no.. nothing ever changed..

Dazzled by the sun Billy and I made our way down the afterdeck towards the stern for our afternoon break, above our heads the engines roared unceasingly, a pale grey plume rising high into a cloudless blue sky; on either side the unchanging glare of the Pacific.

Dragging out the old dining-room chairs we moved into the shadow of the Poop Deck, a hot breeze fitfully playing over our slumped, stripped bodies.

Why do we come here? I mused dully; just from habit .. wasn't that the whole of life really.. doing the same thing over and over again without any clear reason . .But surely it couldn't go on like this indefinitely ..

"What a fuss-pot the Sec. is.. saying we can't sleep out on deck." I complained stirring myself and going to the rail. "It's our choice.. you think we were convicts.."

"Yeah.. ." Billy yawned indifferently, flicking ash off his cigarette.

Shielding my eyes against the glare I felt the steady vibration through the steel deck passing through me; the ship's wake like a ribbon of white lace floating serenely away across the gleaming water towards the distant horizon. Was there anything out there? I mused gazing into the silent glare.. nothing.. nothing .. yet conscious of a faintness; my heart beating as if I had been running hard.

Just your imagination I scoffed, catching at a low keening sound that rose and fell; frothy little water-spouts broke the silky smooth water surface, materializing out of the bright shimmering air.

'Can something come from nothing.. . .? 'I posed abstractly to myself gripping the rail tightly feeling my skin prickling.

"Hey "Billy shouted as a violent gust of wind blasted over us s sweeping our cigarette packets across the deck and over the side; jagged white flecks ripped up the flat ocean and dark shadows swept over the surface like the wings of monstrous birds..

"Look at that "Billy shouted against the noise of the wind, a lurid green glare flickering on the darkening horizon.

"Weird isn't it.." I giggled a little anxiously.

Pushed by the wind we walked quickly back down the afterdeck; a flurry of rain-drops abruptly exploded around us smashing into the sun-heated deck wreathing it with white smoke; rain mixed with hail stung our bare backs; whipping us forward. The sun was now a pale disc, racing away from fleets of menacing ragged black clouds, appearing and disappearing until it was abruptly blotted out.

Across the dark waters whitish gleams swarmed towards us; like an avenging host bent on our annihilation I thought, water running down my face; the deck rising and falling erratically so we struggled to keep our balance.

Reaching the amidships a bright light gashed the darkness, the brilliant flash illuminating huge curling waves riven with spume racing towards us.

Suddenly I found myself cowering against the deck, my hands pressed to my ears, a deafening boom ringing in my ears.

"Look! …Look! "Billy yelled his teeth showing white in the gloom, throwing up an arm.

I stood staring in awe at the electric-blue flames dancing along the wireless aerial around the rim of the funnel and down the wire stays.

"C'mon.." Billy shouted.

Heads down against the driving rain and blown spray we struggled across the amidships the deck tilting abruptly at steep angles; repeated thunder-claps above our heads seeming to rock the ship, wiping my eyes I saw the Sec. in the doorway waving us, just as the deck slipped from under my feet.

'Now I'm in for it' I thought absently glimpsing a marbled white and green wave, breaching the ship's side and sweeping down on me.

Sputtering and splashing in a pool of sea-water, I made a determined effort to get to my feet, just as the deck awash with water tilted abruptly away from me, leaving me sprawled helplessly, another wave already frothing over me.

A claw-like grip dug into my arm, a bright yellow carapace hanging over me and I was jerked to my feet..

"On yer way…." "the Bo'sun chortled smugly from out of the his yellow oil-skins as I pulled out of his grasp and shuffled clumsily away

From the safety of the amidships doorway I looked back; vast serried ranks of darkly foaming waves were pressing steadily towards the ship, spray blasted off the leaping crests merging with the driving rain; in the distance sheets of garish yellow lighting glimmered against the darkly lowering sky.

A watery hell I thought perturbed; wondering if the ship was in danger of being swamped.

"Good thing ..Bo'sun got you.. could have been swept overboard. "The Sec. remarked tartly shutting the door after me; cutting off the rising roar of the wind.

"Really?" I said watching him securing the catches; the first time I had seen them in use; a banshee wailing persisting.

"Understand this is a Cat.4 storm "The Sec said. "So don't go out on deck until it's over. And that's an order." banshee wailing persisting.

Inside the cabin the floor fell away before me and I grabbed at one of the bunk stanchions to save myself. Tumbling around the floor struggling out of my wet clothes it felt as if I was engaged in single contest with the brute forces of nature.

Clutching the hand-rail, for the first time since coming aboard I made the steeply slanting companionway, the familiar stale smells and the reverberating thud of the ship's engines reassuring me. A modern ship is more than equal to any storm I told myself, made a little uneasy though by the sudden dimming of the bulkhead lights.

Through the door to the galley came a metallic cacophony as pots bounced and skidded about the tiled floor; in the pantry the crockery in the dresser was clinking and chinking madly.

Billy his legs wide apart, was standing braced against one of the counters, smoking a cigarette.

This is f-----g crazy.." I grumbled clutching the door-jamb against the suddenly pitching, rolling ship.

"Gonna get worse afore it gets better..." Billy grinned casually blowing out of cigarette smoke.

I let go of the door-jamb and dropped across the steeply tilting floor to end up on the other side holding to the sink. Steel covers blocked the view through the port-holes, the wind shrieking and whooping with every now and then there were loud thuds

Really this is crazy, I thought grimly as Billy and I began fetching the plates of cold cuts from the galley; one minute sliding downwards and then abruptly forced to struggle up; dodging and manoeuvring as if it was some ridiculous game.

Inside the Galley the two Cooks were desperately trying to keep everything in place as they prepared the dinners; their angry shouts punctuated by metallic crashes.

Back in the pantry looking through the hatch I could see the Officers now and then grabbing at the plates threatening to slide off the tables. Old Pete despite his top-heavy bulk showed himself surprisingly nimble, pirouetting and rotating; like a dancing elephant I thought. Mitch perversely appeared in a cheerful mood, humming and grinning as he waltzed about serving the tables with what seemed to me exaggerated flourishes.

Despite the unceasing heaving and rolling of the ship the dinner hour proceeded as if everything was as it should be; how surreal I thought thinking that just the other side of the steel plates of the bulkhead a storm was raging ..a storm that might sink the ship.

Bracing myself against the sink I ran the dirty dishes through the wildly slopping dishwater and gave them to Billy to dry and put them safely back in their racks. Now and again a plate or cup as if determined on self-destruction would fling itself over the edge of the counter and explode into fragments on the floor tiles.

Billy and I grinned at each; who cared if the Chief Steward docked our pay for breakages as he was always threatening; it was all a kind of madness anyhow..

The crew-mess was deserted when Billy and I entered for our evening game of cribbage. Only Old Paddy was in his usual seat, his wire-rimmed spectacles slipping off his waxy nose, the open Bible held firmly in place. Was he reading I wondered cynically, the story of Jonah?

Billy and I had to take turns holding down the cribbage board, bracing our bodies against the table, keeping hold of our cards anything on the table immediately began to slide away.

I found it hard though to concentrate on the game, a continuous roaring and rumbling mixed with shrieks audible through the bulkhead, at times so loudly that the throb of the engines was lost and I waited in suspense for the familiar slow thudding beat to reassert itself.

Soon we gave up playing and left; sliding the door shut I gave a last look back, the old Irish Greaser still reading a wan smile on his aged face.

What does he have to smile about? I grumbled lying stiffly in the pitch-black of the cabin, listening to the wind howling sensing the ship mounting ever higher .. higher and then. . . after a seemingly endless pause, plunging irreversibly downwards .. down.. down.. Only for another interminable pause before reluctantly the steel-work groaning and creaking in protest another slow shuddering, laboured ascent; every rise and fall violently distending and compressing my weary body quite unable to fall asleep.. Listening intently to the dogged thudding of the engines, my mind perversely fixed itself on the bow plates, imagining how the constant battering would inevitably cause a rupture in the welds, the fine spray turning into powerful jet and . .then a calamitous onrush of water. . . .followed by a frantic shouting 'Abandon ship..! Abandon Ship!' . But then hadn't I been told that running gear on the lifeboat davits was fatally corroded and the boats themselves un-seaworthy ? And really did I care if we sank? Surely anything was better than lying in the dark with each downward plunge convinced the ship would never rise again.. and just as I had given up hope the slow juddering ascent.. only in time for the inevitable downward movement.. Yes.. better just to give up this insane futile battle with the elements .. just acquiesce .. let the ship and all it's crew sink beneath the raging waves.. to drift slowly down through the calm depths .. stillness .. peace... .. at last..

I sat up upright, hearing at once the dull beat of the engines, a dim light showing at the port-hole.. So the night had passed and perhaps the typhoon had blown itself out..

but immediately I felt my feet being roughly dragged downward.

So it wasn't over yet, I thought resignedly, bracing myself for the inevitable juddering and groaning as the ship strove once again to rise from a precipitous downward thrust..

"And remember don't go on deck "The Sec, added to his usual wake-up call. "Some big waves coming over the side."

"But surely it can't last much longer. . . "I wailed hanging onto the bunk stanchion struggling to get dressed as the cabin floor tilted steeply.

"Don't yer f-----n' bet on it." Billy laughed quite as if he was enjoying himself.

They're all mad, I thought gulping down the slabs of bread smeared with margarine and jam, the bright lit square pantry like some fairground ride endlessly tilting and dropping in sickening manner. Out of the growl of voices I picked up something about sea-water into the fo'cos'le and the aerials had been blown away making radio-fixes impossible. But how complacent almost smug the nods and head-shakings as if perversely they rather admired raging wind and water... Or was it perhaps their way of concealing their unexpressed.. inexpressible fears... .. Yes .. I decided clutching tightly to the banister dragging the pail of water up the stairs, the water slopping in all direction.. ..it was just a pretence ..a denial of reality.. and so here I was facing the companionway alternately steeply upwards and then abruptly reversing so I was in danger of falling forward. How impossible.. And yet by sitting down and pressing my feet against one wall and my back against the other, one hand holding the pail I found I could slowly wash my way along.

On reaching the top deck landing holding tightly to the banister I watched with fascinated disbelief as the pointer on the clock-face of the Roll Indicator swung almost horizontally and then stuck before slowly swing back to the opposite side of the dial. Any minute the ship might any minute roll completely over I gasped fighting down a panic

.. imagining how water would flood in .. trapping all the crew inside .... what a terrible way to die..

Abruptly with the door to the bridge burst open and the 2nd Mate coming to shut it saw me, hesitated and then beckoned me forward .

Inside I glanced around at the several figures in the dim-lit narrow space, quite oblivious to the roar and shrieking of the wind and furious battering of spray on the bridge window, their legs wide apart braced against the violent pitching and rolling.

I slid nervously forward grabbing at the rail running beneath the window, through a wide arc made by the wipers.. glimpsing darkly foaming waters beneath, only the king-posts visible.. Is this it then.. is the ship about to founder I wondered absently.. ..

"Ah.." I murmured with relief, the ship's bows breaking clear of the seething, all-conquering ocean; slowly rising ever higher and sending a foaming wall of water surging down the foredeck, to smash violently against the amidships, the spray flying against the bridge windows, to be calmly swept aside by the wipers. But already I saw that a dark foam-flecked chasm was lying in wait and how unquestioningly the ship's bows plunged into the gaping monstrous void to allow the foaming grey-green waters to flood exultantly forward to cover the foredeck.

Again I gripped the hand-rail, in suspense .. doubtful.. surely. .. though .. perhaps this time .. and again felt a deep relief as finally the ship's bows broke free of the watery mass, spewing foam and spray, rising.. rising victoriously, triumphantly upward..

But for how long? I wondered the faint day light slowly passing into night, the bulkheads shuddering and jerking and creaking as the ship rolled and pitched outside the wind rumbling and shrieking in shrill malevolence. And then lying in the dark of the cabin my body being ruthlessly stretched and compressed I realized that it was inevitable the ship must finally succumb to the unending onslaught of water and wind.. an onslaught that never slackened or paused confining us to the amidships; like doomed prisoners I thought.. waiting .. waiting. . so wearily ..so hopelessly.. ..so desperately.. .

And then on an impulse, flouting the Sec.'s command not to go out on deck I was sliding back the bolts on the door of the officer's smoking-room door and pushing it open...

Only for it to be torn from my grasp by the force of the wind. stepping recklessly out, gasping for breath the clotted spray blasting my face.

Bent almost double, I fought my way against the unrelenting wind to the rail, salty water streaming down my face into my mouth, half-blinding me. Grasping tightly to the rail I straitened, my eyes watering and bleared, my heart failing as I gazed out at the serried ranks of monstrous glassy blackish waves skeined with white froth, curling tops wreathed in blowing spray, sinking only to rise ever higher, jostling and pressing with menacing fury, possessed of one purpose to overwhelm the ship..

And the waters lay over the earth, I muttered glancing down at the great mounds of blackish green white-flecked water beside the hull, swelling and leaping upwards in malicious watery graspings that touching my feet eager to claim a first victim..

Turning away I glimpsed a figure far down the afterdeck. Who could it be? I wondered as the figure moved slowly forward, holding tightly to the ropes that had been strung between the accommodation block and the amidships moving slowly and carefully hand over hand. I wiped my eyes recognising through the sheets of blowing spray, Wonner the A.B I remember I had once glimpsed meditating cross-legged in his cabin. His trouser bottoms rolled up, shoes strung around his neck he paddled through the water lying on the deck like a week-end holiday maker, I thought; my mouth opening in alarm seeing a massive curling mound of water racing towards the ship .. for an instant it hung a green glossy watery curtain, streaked with white, over the deck, just as Wonner glanced aside, a look of terror coming his face.

238

My hand locked to the rail, barely conscious of the howling of the wind and stinging spray, I saw the watery avalanche come crashing slowly down onto the deck, burying the solitary figure in a frothing deluge.

In terrible suspense I watched the slavering green waters rushed with a greedy violence around the Afterdeck, spewing jets of frothing water into the air, scouring and cleansing, the deck leaving a pool of crystalline green spotted with foam, only the hatch block and King Posts reminders of what had been there, seconds before. . .

A groan passed through me as I realized what had happened, the ankle-deep water rippling gently away over the deck as the ship rolled.. the line empty. I stared blankly out over the pitiless grey-green waters restlessly heaving and spouting, preparing for more violent watery assaults ... I had often read about such things hadn't I? Seaman ..swept overboard.... body never recovered. And now before my very eyes......

I wiped my eyes .. seeing in astonished relief just below me, a single figure moving slowly forward, head bowed, stripped of his T-shirt and shoes, his broad muscled body dripping with water, like an exhausted swimmer coming up the beach....

Slamming the door of the Officer's Smoking Room shut behind me I fell onto the settle almost faint, my face and hands stinging; seeing again in awful immediacy the look of sheer terror on Wonner's face, the great seething mass of water hanging over him and distantly sensing.. How could it be? Something implacable and .. purposeful...

I lifted my hand from the cribbage board amazed that it was not immediately sliding away.

"Do you think..?" I said looking at Billy slowly becoming aware that the incessant howling and screeching of the wind had ceased.

Old Paddy's glasses almost fell off his nose as he looked up suddenly as with a shout we scrambled towards the Crew Mess door.

Out on deck we paused, hardly believing, the wind making a low sighing sound rising and falling over the steady thud of the engines; the deck slowly rising and falling under our feet.

It must have blown itself out at last.. After all it couldn't go on for ever, I thought as we crossed to the ship's side.

"How many days.. has it been "I wondered looking up the sprinkle of faintly glittering stars and then low down in the luminous mauve sky a gleaming slip of a moon; freshly scrubbed, I chuckled to myself.

How amazing it all is I thought half-delirious.

Out in the dark water banks of mist, like ghostly icebergs came drifting past. Yes wonderful I mused scraping at the layer of salt coating the iron bulwark; a faintly putrid smell rising out of the water. What could that mean?

I looked up to see the stars and moon had now vanished. I shivered, an icy dampness creeping over me. White confetti began drifting down out of the darkness.

"Snow!" I exclaimed, the flakes melting on my upturned face, thicker and thicker yet instantly vanishing.

From far away came low rumble of thunder, a sudden flash lit up the sky showing the water creased with steep ridges marled with white.

So it's not over .. I thought the wind rising as we turned and ran back to the amidships.

Back in the violently pitching and rolling Crew Mess we attempted again to play cribbage. Perhaps we are doomed to this forever.. I mused absently too worn-out to care anymore; indifferent to the groaning and creaking of the steel around me above the dull roar of the wind; a plaything of some incomprehensibly immense power. In my mind I saw the raging seas sweeping violently down the foredeck grasping the ship in another foaming embrace.. but always the valiant upward thrust of the ship's bows .. stubborn.... resolute .. . . But for how long? Yes that was the question; for how much longer.. and would we survive to know the answer?

CHAPTER TWENTY-TWO

"Ya! "I cried out defiantly and leapt boldly into the flickering blue water below; my head broke through the surface, droplets spattering out of the sunlight all around.

For a minute I stood chest deep spitting out the chlorine-tasting water, rubbing my eyes; seeing again the darkly menacing mountainous seas, heaving and spouting, advancing ominously towards the ship.. .

But that's all past, I told myself, swimming over to the pool-side and taking hold of the tile-edge, the ship now berthed safely in Singapore harbour.

And now I am here, I thought, jerking myself out of the water and standing in the burning sunshine, water running in streams down my legs forming puddles on the tiles. Yes.. here .. how amazing..

I picked up my towel and rubbed myself glancing over at Billy his sun-tanned torso thrown back, a quiff fallen over his forehead, cigarette smoke curling from one hand, a tall glass in the other; just like the hero in a film, I thought admiringly.

"Hard to believe isn't it.. all this.." I waved an arm at the rattan chairs and tables shaded by large white parasols arranged around the shining blue pool; seated at the tables were a scattering of well-dressed people who occasionally turned to stare critically at us; little imagining what we had been through I thought.

"Especially I mean after the typhoon.." I added sitting down and picking up my glass; hearing again the roar and shriek of the wind, remembering the endless downward plunging and the slow shuddering ascent; would I ever get over it?

"Yeah real bad 'un ..." Billy remarked blowing out neat smoke-rings.

I nodded, thinking of when I had ventured forward for the first time; feeling like one newly risen from the dead in the silence of the foredeck, the sea shining serenely, gazing around in awed amazement at the bent and torn metal; whole lengths of rail twisted into abstract modernist sculpture; some of the canvas hatch-covers in shreds; strands of seaweed lay strewn about as if in a whimsy of decoration; the metal surfaces marked with orange rust and streaked with salt. Near the foc'sle I had come across a ventilator-hood bowed over, and near it another sheared off completely, leaving a circle of mangled bolts and a gaping black hole in the deck..

I took a long swallow of the sour drink; such an overwhelming power solely bent on our destruction it seemed.. and yet we had survived ..

"Murdock 'ad to go forward with a rope around 'im to get t'ole blocked.. almost washed away weren't 'e.." Billy chuckled.

'ell of a sea-water got in a n' lot of wheat spoiled. Deck Boys won't get no shore leave 'till it's cleaned out"

'Murdoch .. I echoed inwardly gazing across the sparkling pool water to a strip of grass backed by shrubs thick with waxy pink flowers.

Was it possible that the brutal, violent Murdoch had done such a brave thing.. and saved the ship ..?

I stared at the bare trunks of palm trees bearing stiff green top-knots against the blue sky; so without his courage I wouldn't be here,

I concluded, my heart beating heavily. But no I just couldn't accept that... ...it couldn't happen to me.. not to me.. I was beyond death..

"How long do you think it will take to do the repairs.." I wondered out loud, lighting up a cigarette.

"Dunno.. A f----n' lot of damage.." Billy grinned "Means we gets ashore t'ave good time."

"You bet an ill wind as they say.." I grinned. "Same again.?"

I twisted around to the colonnade of white Grecian-style pillars fronting the club building and beckoned the Malay waiter.

242

At once he came obediently towards us; the same age or younger than me I

Guessed wearing creased black trousers and a white coat with a high collar, his dark eyes bright; like a shy woodland creature I thought, admiring the silky smooth milk coffee skin and black bright eyes but was that a curl of disdain on the full lips beneath the smudge of a moustache?

We gave out orders and I followed with my eyes the slim figure walking quickly back inside.

"Fancy 'im .do ya Phil?" Billy grinned noticing my long intent stare.

"Of course not.." I retorted angrily. "Just wondering what kind of life he has."

"Don't get yer f-----n' danda up.." Billy said coolly, picking a shred of tobacco from his teeth. "Ain't nuttin' wrong t'fancy a bit of t'other. Lotsa sailors does.."

I studiously looked the other way as the Malay waiter returned carrying our drinks on a silver tray. Was I becoming perverted, I wondered, flushing at the thought of the taut, smooth body beneath the waiter's uniform.

Sometimes I noticed him watching us intently as we played around in the pool splashing water at each other before swimming lazily around and hauling ourselves out, water streaming down our bodies, to lie on a towel on the hot tiles. What was he thinking I wondered. He seemed happy enough but perhaps inwardly he was seething with resentment at having to wait on noisy foreigners? Perhaps he had communist sympathies.. how hard to know what lay behind those dark bright eyes ..

And then one day he wasn't there at all. Was I relieved I wondered as we showered and changed back into our clothes. But the walking stiffly down the steps of the club into the steamy heat of the afternoon I was conscious of a sense of loss. I gazed down the neat green verges of the boulevard lined with palm trees.. how empty it seemed ..unreal.. .would I ever know what I really wanted from life?

Cars swished past as we ambled across the road towards the taxi rank on the other side.

A horn sounded and tyres squealed as a car swerved around us.

"Go to 'ell!" Billy shouted making a rude gesture.

No one really cares about us I thought sadly glimpsing a woman's angry face glaring through the car window.

At the dockyard gates we got out of taxi and made our way to the ship. I pictured us two small figures walking beneath the towering cranes, picking our way through hot dusty air amongst the confused activity of the dockside.. lorries and vans coming and going.. piles of crates and boxes spilling out in all directions.. a chaos of noise and movement to which we were utterly incidental I felt.

Back on the ship we found it occupied by a small army of workers, slight dark-skinned, bare-legged men; an insistent hammering, echoing off the dockside buildings; the air full of acrid burning smells; out on the deck, fountains of red and yellow sparks, like Roman Candles, sprayed into the hot air, the blinding glare of acetylene torches piercing the bright sunshine; acrid blue smoke wreathing the deck.

Such unceasing activity to make the ship sea-worthy also made us feel of little significance and yet even the workmen themselves were only a means to an end it seemed. I'd overheard talk of two of them being been badly injured and yet how little that seemed to matter; the work carrying on without pause as if there the world knew only one purpose .. one goal: to prepare the ship for sea..

Think I've had enough of the Club.." I said as we came down the gangway at the end of the week, vaguely wondering if I wanted to avoid meeting the Malay waiter again.

"Yeah.. nuttin' but stuck up toffs.." Billy willingly agreed.

So instead of taking a taxi we crossed over a wide street and entered an area of narrow alleyways overhung by rickety looking wooden buildings. Soon we were pushing our way through the dense crowds of Chinese men and women mostly in loose trousers and colourful blouses shouting cheerfully at each other in shrill sing-song tones

Old wrinkled faces looked down from balconies hung with lines of washing; in the doorways below tiny sallow-skinned black-headed children were playing. On either side of the alleyways ran steep-sided open drains, the trickling scummy water buzzing with flies, the rank smells mingling with pungent cooking odours.

This it real life, I thought excitedly, comparing it to the dull formality of the club and the wide boulevards lined with palm-trees, deserted but for speeding cars.

A little further on we came to a street market and had to push our way through the dense crowd packed between stalls piled with vegetable produce the roots and leafs and stalks and fruits in greater abundance of colours and shapes than I had ever seen before; anything falling to the ground being ruthlessly squashed under the feet of thronging passers-by.

Amongst the stalls prowled wolfish-looking dogs, ribs visible through their thin coats, snarling over scraps, to be kicked and screamed at. But what if I had been born here? Would I have revelled in this vigorous activity of daily life or would I have found it as familiarly tedious as life in Vancouver, I wondered pausing to look at some chickens their heads, dangling pink combs, stuck out through the bars of slatted crates.

I watched in grim fascination as the top of the crate was jerked open and vigorous hands were plunged in to pull out a scrawny fowl, squawking and flapping wildly, to be held up by their yellow scaly legs, beady eyes glaring indignantly; a curt nod from the dour-looking woman customer and it's neck was put onto a block of wood, and with a single blow of a cleaver it's head was cut off with a gush of bright red blood, spattering the stall-keeper, the small feathery body continuing to jerk and twitch.

That's the reality ..one minute alive and then dead, I thought with a shudder turning back to join Billy. The two of us swept forward by the noisy jostling crowd, like twigs or leaves on a flowing stream I thought beginning to feel weary; now passing a succession of booths selling steaming hot food, a heady mixture of burning charcoal and spicy, sweet smells wafting over us, the vendors tirelessly bawling invitations to the passers-bys; around about their customers sitting at small tables or squatting on the street were eating from small bowls, eyes glazed as they vigorously plied their chopsticks, expertly stuffing the food into gaping mouths.

But it's life too, I thought rather appalled by the blank ferocity of the eaters, stepping quickly aside to avoid being hit by vendor, bawling loudly as he rammed his cart with a large shiny metal tea-urn through the press of bodies.

Then came booths displaying of varied chunks of raw meat impaled on hooks, the sellers making perfunctory sweeps with fans at the ever present swarms of flies; beyond were other stalls selling an assortment of marine life, shell-fish tiny crabs and dark prawns squirming and bubbling, fish staring out of glass tanks, or laid out in boxes or baskets in gleaming ranks or dried, hanging on string like brown card-board cut-out.

Helplessly we were thrust on by the press of the crowd on past stalls displaying squares of brown paper neat cones of bright coloured powders and then endless-seeming display of dried stuffs, stalks, seed-pods, leaves of various shapes and colour and other mysterious odd-shaped dried objects; pungent earthy animal scents diffusing into the hot sticky air.

Who would have thought there were so many edible things in the world, I thought beginning to feel oppressed by the crush of bodies the noise, sticky heat and smells.

"Hey what's that?" I exclaimed rhythmic clangings and shrill piping noises reaching to us the unceasing hubbub of the crowd.

A sudden rush of bodies many of them bowing low pushed us back and between the crowd came a slow-moving procession; first men in long robes with square hats, carrying lighted tapers and swinging brass vessels of smoking incense; their faces set; moving with regular even paces. Behind them borne high on the shoulders of men wearing loose white tunics girded by brilliant yellow sashes, their brown faces and chests gleaming with sweat, was an ornately-carved red and black palanquin picked out in gold, it's sides draped by a richly patterned gold and green cloth. Following on came more men in long dark robes, some beating metal gongs dangling from black wooden frames, others making ear-piercing sounds on long bamboo pipes.

"What a f-----n' din ." Billy growled as we went on the crowd already reforming in the wake of the procession.

"Yeah.." I grinned wondering if it was a funeral or perhaps a celebration of some local god, the colourful scene persisting in my mind even as the sounds faded away; remembering how some of the crowd had bowed almost to the ground, a rapturous.. ..euphoric look on their face but surely that was just primitive superstition. . .?

I looked up above the grey-tiled roofs, a skein of cables cut across the strip of brilliant blue sky, reminding me of the vastness of sea and sky far away from the noise and frantic bustle around me. Perhaps Chips was right.. perhaps that was where one was truly at peace..

But where was Billy? A sudden panic went through me; the jostling crowd hemming me, imagining darkly hostile eyes watching me, reminding of a time when a boy I had briefly lost my parents in a crowded street on a day-trip to London. I began pushing vigorously through the crowd, my heart beating.

"Thought you'd disappeared "I laughed, conscious of a swell of relief as I came up to Billy ; suddenly ashamed of myself; would I never learn to be self-reliant?

We went on through the maze of narrow streets and lanes; moving determinedly through the close afternoon heat until we came to a large building with an ornate façade; a red-neon strip proclaiming: *The Alhambra Dance Hall.*

Together we passed into a red plush foyer, threadbare and water stained in places I noticed; strains of dance music coming to my ears. Billy went over to a counter in one corner, behind a glass screen perched on a stool was a solemn Chinese cashier, in a white shirt and black bow-tie perched on tall stool; like little boy dressed for the part, I thought feeling superior.

Holding my two tickets I followed Billy through the padded door into a large ballroom full of couples circling around the to the sounds of a slow waltz, the men pressed closely against the women in tight-fitting sheath dresses all with red or yellow flowers in their short black hair. Overhead large ceiling fans turned slowly through the hot, smoky air. But what was that sour odour I wondered as we found seats at a table near the dance floor.

A waiter, a twin of the cashier in a white shirt and black bow-tie instantly appeared and impassively took one of our tickets.

Sipping the cold beers and smoking, Billy and I faced the slowly gyrating dancers the women with fixed red-lipstick smiles on their faces; the men grim and staring; more like a some weird ritual than proper dancing, I thought.

Then a bell rang and the floor was suddenly deserted.

"Go on ..your turn.." Billy grinned.

I looked up swallowing hard at the sight of a heavy-set woman in a close-fitting shiny red dress; bright red lips painted on a heavily rouged face.

With a quick movement she plucked the ticket out of my hand deftly tucking it inside the scoop of her bodice. Impatiently she fluttered long black eye-lashes, crooked a finger beckoning me forward.

Nervously I stepped out onto the dance floor, once more full of slowly shuffling couples; so now I am part of this arcane ritual, I thought absently.

Locked in close embrace with her solid, stocky body we moved around and around in hobbling circles, her thigh pushed into my groin.

"You good dancer "the woman murmured showing large white teeth, her breath hot on my face.

248

I nodded numbly, retreating from the rhythmic pressure, looking away past her helmet-like head; the other dancers, a coloured, swirling blur the music almost inaudible.

"You good dancer too .." I managed to gasp out, sweat pouring down my body; round and round we went, as if we were eternally bound to each other; at times just avoiding a collision with other slowly circling couples.

"Finish now "The woman said abruptly, frown-lines cracking her thick make-up abruptly pulling free and walking away through the milling couples.

I slunk back to the table, dazed and numb.

"F----n' teasers matey" Billy said as we passed out of the foyer.

Like some weightless shadow, as if hollowed out inside. I walked back with Billy through the crowded alleyways slightly less crowded and back into the docks.

"Watch it.. !" Billy yelled as a fork-lift truck bore down on us between piles of boxes.

To hell with them all, I thought conscious of a dull anger as we mounted the gangway, breathing in the acrid smells of burning metal; looking across the deck the acetylene torches made splashes of dazzling glare in the fading light, the hammering of the repair work still echoing around the dockside; perhaps I should stay on the ship like Old Paddy I thought ruefully.

"Ronnie says we should try *The Golden Mountain Bar*" I said with a strange hoarse laugh; the moist hot night air almost sickening with its rich pungent smells.

"'Es don't know nuttin' "Billy jeered without slackening his steps.

Already we had left the docks behind and were more making our way through the narrow streets lit by dangling light bulbs with a shadowy halo of insects.

How different I mused to the afternoon when we had let ourselves be swept casually along by the thronging crowds; now we walked quickly with hardly a word exchanged as if wary of each other.

Billy stopped in front of a shadowy building just off one of the larger alleyways. I could just make out a dimly lit sign showing a faded yellow vaguely pyramidal shape against a green background.

"Is meant to be a Golden Mountain?" I giggled nervously.

Billy grunted something and pushed at the large double door and I followed him inside through an outer room, into a large room squared with heavily-carved dark wooden galleries. What kind of building could it have been? I wondered gazing around at the high walls the plaster cracked and fallen off in places. Huge round ceramic pots with large fronded palms stood around the black and white tiled floor. Perhaps the home of some affluent family fallen on bad times, I mused sniffing at the strong smell that reminded me of mothballs.

A squat cross-eyed, old Chinese woman, dressed in a shapeless black garment, waddled out of a curtained doorway, a scowling grin showing several black teeth on her fat, heavily jowled face. What ugly creature, I thought glimpsing a face at the doorway that immediately drew back. So we were being watched... perhaps we were going to be robbed... .. murdered.. hadn't Old Pete continually warned me.. vague thoughts flicked inconsequentially through my mind.

"Ave to pay .." Billy grouched as the old woman stuck out a hand exposing an arm with rolls of fat.

I watched the old woman deliberately lick her nicotine-stained fingers before counting over the bank-notes; like a miserly shop-keeper, I thought as she shuffled away gurgling to herself.

I sat stiffly beside Billy on one of the old leather sofas; like a waiting for a hair-cut I thought incongruously, glancing at Billy, calmly smoking a cigarette; distantly I heard high-pitched female voices, shrill angry shouts and shrieks of laughter. What could it all mean?

Without warning a number of women, chattering noisily wearing loose, brightly patterned house-coats, all with black hair and brown skin, came clattering through one of the doorways and seated began fanning themselves; occasionally glancing over at us between giggles. How small they are, I thought feeling as if I had suddenly grown enormously.

Would they like me? I wondered but then it didn't matter I reminded myself complacently I had paid hadn't I? Unless it of course I was being defrauded.. .. surely not ..

"Some cat house.." Billy glowered bitterly. "Ronnie's full of shit ..as usual.."

"Yeah...." I murmured, weak with nervous excitement.

"Who d'ya fancy..?." Billy asked with a brusque movement of his head.

"Dunno...." I muttered, pretending to look at the seated women; glimpsing smiling lips and eyes and gestures, shy, sly looks and frowns; the giggles and girlish shrieks of laughter ringing in my head.

"Here's the old dragon.." Billy grumbled standing up.

I stood up too; the room full of confused movement, the old woman shrieking, pushing roughly at the different women.

A sudden panic took hold of me.'Now..! now ..! Leave before it is too late' I urged myself but wouldn't that be deserting Billy?

There was a touch on my arm and feeling like a clumsy giant I allowed myself to be led across the room by the tiny figure with black hair.

'Too late.. too late' I moaned despairingly joyful as we all went up the bare narrow stairs to the second floor. I wiped at the sweat running down my face, the air even more suffocating hot than downstairs. Billy was already passing along the narrow passageway and through a doorway, a woman by his side. I hesitated but the firm grasp on my arm turned me after him; despite the torn blinds the narrow room was glaring bright, the only furniture small metal beds in a row.

Surely we aren't to be in the same room? I thought despairingly; wishing I had stayed on the ship.

I hesitated at the bed-side, absently watching tiny fingers deftly unbuttoning the top of thin cotton shift, glimpsing narrow bony shoulders and the curve of tiny breasts before turning away.

"Come on you boy" the woman whimpered pettishly, glancing coyly at me with bright eager eyes.

I looked down; the thin, naked sallow body exposed on the bed; my eyes catching at the dark patch between her thighs and two bright red nipples.

"Me no wait.." She twittered gaily.

"What yer f----- do'in' Phil.." Billy shouted from across the room. There was a sound of a loud slap and shriek of laughter.

Yes.. of course.. now .. now, I thought bemusedly, agitatedly struggling out of my clothes.

The small, thin body writhed rhythmically beneath me; a hard-boned softness, eel-like, moist, slippery.. evasive... moving further and further away.. I lunged feebly.. hopeless uselessly.. conscious of a sticky wetness. I stared blankly down at the small, sternly frowning pixie face,

"You too quick.... "She said wrinkling a snub nose. "You come again.."

I lay staring dully at the wall; incapable of response; remote.. disembodied.... empty.. .

"Maybe next time ." Her voice chirruped from far away; muted shufflings and scratchings faintly penetrating my fatigue.

"Hey Phil....'ad enuff ain'tcha? Billy's asked his voice strangely muffled. "Go get a drink meet up with Deck Boys..Toilet thata way" He paused in combing his hair to point out the door.

"Yeah....sure... ..you bet." I muttered, forcing myself into movement, gathering up my shoes and clothes against my body and down the passageway finding a tiny room without a door. Inside was a cracked hand-basin before an open window; the sound of voices from below. I stiffened recognising the nasal whine. It was the Ronnie the 1st Cook from the ship, and I imagined his round face smirking complacently surrounded by the women, their shrill giggles and shrieks of echoing about the room below.

They're all laughing at me, I thought absently splashing water at my genitals, the lukewarm water trickled down my legs onto the floor, reminding me of the swimming-pool at the Club. When was that? How simple it all was then, idly sipping drinks and smoking and larking about in the pool; now I only felt a guilty dreariness.

As if I had actually killed someone, I mused, imagining accusing eyes staring at me from the dark shadows as Billy and I walked back through the dim-lit alleyways; finally stopping at narrow building with several mullioned windows across the street from the docks.

Perhaps I should kill myself, I thought absently looking up the signboard just visible in the street light, of a crudely painted picture of a man with a big nose with a cocked hat and breeches and underneath in large black lettering: *The Duke of Wellington.*

I forced myself through the open door and into the smoke-filled room with dark-wood panelling around the walls; electric imitation candles on black iron wheels hung from the low-ceiling shone down on the tightly-packed men all talking and laughing loudly.

I pushed after Billy to the bar where the two Deck Boys were waiting for us.

"What's wi ya matey? Ya looks right gloomy "Norrie bellowed sliding a tall glass of beer towards me.

"Nothing.. nothing "I muttered defensively, gulping down the ice-cold beer;

"Hey.. look there's Mitch n'some others from the ship."
Billy said nodding across the room.

We all turned to look my eyes meeting Mitch's knowing, jeering stare. He knows I'm a failure, I thought flushing with shame and looking quickly away.

Tad shrieked something in my ear sliding another full glass towards me.

"Cheers shipmates..! "Norrie rumbled boozily.

"Yeah.. cheers.." I murmured eagerly draining my glass.

"Hey this way.." Billy laughed steering me around a corner.

"Yeah.." I laughed amiably, stumbling and catching myself.

From behind us I could hear Tad and Norrie singing loudly their voices echoing along the street.

"Need a slash.." Billy said suddenly turning aside; the dockyard gate now in view, lit by flood-lights atop high posts.

We stood side by side in the half-lit shadowy space a trickling sound audible, two rounded dark stains appearing on the wall.

"Betta' than a bad screw.." Billy sniggered hoarsely.

"Sure . "I murmured looking up; vast dark clouds blotting out the stars; it is what it is, I thought dreamily.

CHAPTER TWENTY-THREE

The plate glass door swung forcefully shut behind me, instantly slicing off the sweltering heat and noise outside.

I shivered in the chill air-conditioned air waiting while Billy bought the tickets from the cashier behind the glassed booth; Tad and Norrie behind him sniggering and jostling each other excitedly. I had already seen the film once with Billy and I wasn't sure why I had agreed to come and see it again. Was it because I felt guilty I was spending so much time with Marie? I mused gazing idly around the gleaming shiny foyer.. like a modern cinema anywhere in the world really.. yet just outside .. a short distance along the narrow crowded alleyways...... . ... I shook my head; better not think about it, I told myself turning to stare at the garishly coloured poster advertising the film: across the top in fiery red letters was written *THE SECRET OF COYOTE BLUFFS* ; beneath it two men, one clean shaven in a white cowboy outfit faced the another dressed in black with a moustache both with revolvers in their hands, behind them stood a slender woman with fair skin, blue eyes and blonde curls in a gingham dress; flung melodramatically between the two men was a shapely dark-skinned woman in flounced scarlet dress her deeply cleaved bosom pushing out of the low-cut frilled bodice.. I shuddered moving my eyes to the caption; *a Film of Savage Passion.. Hate .. Greed.. and LOVE! Starring........ ..* How stupid.. I thought disdainfully, gripped by a sudden desires. Why was I here? Why wasn't I with Marie?

But I merely took the ticket Billy handed me and padded down the deep piled carpet along the narrow corridor behind the others; the sound-proofed door shutting silently behind us as we stepped into the cavernous darkened space, shot with two long beams of white light, illuminating the writhing spirals of cigarette smoke.

Following the dim circle of light from torch held by the shadowy figure of the usherette we found our seats; Tad swearing at something and evoking a chorus of shssss from all around.

I sank into the soft velvet seat; the ranks of seat-backs with silhouetted heads falling away in the semi-darkness to the flickering brilliant screen below. I half closed my eyes seeing Marie looking flatteringly up at me, reaching out her thin arms, with her odd twitchy smile.

"'Ates this newsy guff. "Billy grumbled, scratching a match to light a cigarette; I blinked at the brief flare of light and turned to the bright screen now showing a rapid sequence of news events from around the world; a clipped British accent booming out sardonically over the grainy black and white pictures; a wall of water flooding down a street with people on roof-tops, and cars buried, trees bowed to the ground and the ripped off the roofs of building blowing away ; then small figures in shorts running around after a ball.. .. a funeral procession .. a glamorous wedding with a large wedding cake... a volcano erupting .. *CHAIRMAN MAO WARNS THE WEST* read the heading superimposed upon row upon row of soldiers stiffly marching in front of a huge government building covered with gigantic posters of a round smiling face.

"These pussies will say Meow to Mao .. not just paper tigers either they have real teeth! "The voice joked in a growling voice as fighter jets, with a star insignia on the tail, took off in quick succession from an aircraft carrier.

"And here's some chaps that will say amen to that." the voice went on cheerfully mordant the caption reading *POWs HOME AT LAST* On the screen a line of weary, blank faced men in army fatigues came down the steps of an airliner.." They might have been brain-washed but they know home when they see it.. .

THE END flashed up in large black letters, a movie camera swinging it's lenses towards the audience. So that's the news I thought indifferently, sinking down into the seat, in my mind seeing Marie.. smiling wryly back at me, a blanket around her thin naked body ... smoking a cigarette.. such a tiny girlish figure so ..vulnerable.. desirable...

"Film's starting .." Billy hissed, elbowing me.

I pulled myself upright, momentarily registering the bright Technicolor desert landscape with a line of giant green cactus reaching spine-studded arms into a blue sky silhouetting a horseman galloping furiously towards distant ochre coloured bluffs, even as my mind took me through the crowded alleyway drawn by some seemingly irresistible force, deliberately pausing to look up at narrow sign board of *The Golden Mountain Bar,* above the lintel of the ornate heavy wooden door eager to fix the sensations of this moment in my life for all time..

But how familiar it had become.. and so quickly as from a distance watching myself stepping inside the once grand now decrepit building, the repulsive old Chinese madam, appearing like a jack-in-a-box, her knowing leer showing a glint of gold; like a slimy leech swollen with blood, I thought shamelessly ignoring my complicity.

Revelling in my throbbing anticipation listening for the muted voices interspersed with girlish shrieks; turning expectantly at the slap of sandals on the tiles to be suddenly surrounded by talking, giggling women, my heart beating at the glimpses of legs and arms as they moved in their colourful shifts, inhaling deeply the warm scents of their bodies pressing close around me.. knowing.. knowing .. all the time.. knowing with such perfect certainty. ....

Even as I with casual munificence bought drinks for everyone and handed out cigarettes to eager hands as sipping and smoking all eyes on me as I.. talked .. talked .. the words seeming to come of themselves, imaging myself a wandering knight of old recounting his adventures to the chatelaine and her ladies I talked boldly about the ship.. Billy and the Deck Boy and Chips and the Bo'sun and the Captain such a ninny.. and the Sec. such a bully knocking on the door when it was still dark.. and the awful food.. how that delighted them to hear me tell of the bread that thrown overboard sank like a stone and the tea like brown glue.. And then of course all about the typhoon: 'You see I was out on deck..' The words echoing with new force. 'There was these huge waves bigger than this house all around the ship and what do I see but this sailor.. a strange chap.. shaved head .. does meditating .. eats by himself.. coming down the deck hanging onto the life-lines when there was this really huge wave.. a mountain of water ..' I recalled how I had paused delighting in the admiring wondering looks of the women around me. But had I really said I had waded into the flooded deck and rescued Wonner? Had I with guileful modesty smiling demurred their exclamations of admiration?

In the dark of the cinema I felt my cheeks glow with shame. Why had I done it? Did I so much want to be seen as a hero? Admired by all.. ? How pathetic.. And yet how they had loved it.. .. shouting and laughing and pulling and clutching at me in some joyously malicious girlish game.

That was how I ended up with Marie, wasn't it? It was all so confused I wasn't sure .. I remembered how I had my eye on Rosie, such a pert face and slim curvy figure so I could hardly breath as she bent over me for a light for her cigarette. Or Patty who shrieked at everything I said my eyes fixing on her full plump body clearly outlined beneath the thin shift.

Yet none of that counted it seemed.. each time it was Marie who came forward and claimed me.. And how could I refuse .. and how wonderful was the way she excitedly pulled me after her.. as if I belonged to her in some deep way; her eyes so admiring and that sly, furtive smile as if she knew something I didn't.. Yes that was so exquisitely wonderful... Why then was I nagged by the thought that she was so plain; her thin hair straggling down over a tired-looking face, a slight squint in one eye. And how ashamed I was one night over drinks in the *Duke of Wellington* Billy had joked: 'A bit of a scrag ain't she?'

For a minute I stared vacantly at the shimmering brightly coloured screen: a woman in a red dress with black hair on horseback was riding through trees along side a river.. a man in black buckskins, steps boldly out, and grabs the bridle; the horse rears as he pulls her off the saddle; "Not so fast ya little pole-cat.."

She struggles fiercely; with overwhelming strength he pulls her closer, presses her lips to his, her body stiffening then going limp; "I loves ya Joe.." She whimpered exultantly.

How false I thought, my mind slipping back.. Marie lying beside me I watched the wispy blue smoke rise from my cigarette, as she idly ran her fingers through my hair and suddenly tears began to trickle down her cheeks.. and my heart had swelled with pity, and I had leant towards her my lips brushing her coarse hair, a sweetish rancid scent as I tried to kiss her ..

She had whimpered turning her head. 'Me bad girl...'

'No.. I'm bad too...maybe even worse." I had groaned falling back.

She had looked down at me a sly, gentle smile on her face, bending hesitantly over me, touching my lips with hers a quick, nervous kiss.. a child's kiss..

"You're .. you're beautiful.." I had said a rapt look lighting her face. And it was true wasn't it .. ? Or did I need to believe it .. for my own satisfaction..?

And why had I confessed that I was attracted to the exotic black haired Mexican film-star in the cowboy film?

"You pretend I her.." She had murmured bowing her head.

At once I had felt ashamed and yet pleased too.. living out a fantasy .. a nostalgic aching tenderness for her sallow bony child-like body taking hold of me... .

I frowned steadily at the screen, absently noticing the credits were sliding down the screen. Was I in love with her? Would she marry me? What would my parents think? 'This is er.. Marie . I met her in Singapore you see..'

I turned at the rough push at my shoulder; the lights coming on Billy frowning down at me.

"Ya sleeping Phil.. .?"

Unsteadily I got to my feet; but did I really love her?

"Ain't Jack Palance the greatest. He shoulda f----n' kill'd that other un when 'e 'ad a chance..." Billy chortled happily as the four of us reached the door. I glanced back at the screen now a faint pale grey rectangle.

Outside the cinema; the heat and light struck me a stunning blow; I walked along with others talking and laughing with happy delight; as if the film was more real than life, I thought dazedly.

"Bang! Bang! Ya dead..!"

"No I aint.. yer missed!"

Ducking and weaving the four of us ran down the gangway dragging our shadows in the floodlit dockside; our voices echoing hollowly off the surrounding walls.

Darting behind an empty crate I crouched down my heart thudding, thinking back to boyhood games of cowboys and Indians .. but surely I was different person.. a man.. crossing the Pacific.. getting drunk.. going with women..

"Behind ya !.. Phil.. Behind ya! "Billy yelled suddenly and I spun about.

"Pow.. pow.." I yelled shooting my imaginary revolver at Tad creeping towards me.

"Izz shot.... ." Tad shrieked clutching his chest and staggering around in circles stirring up the dust but then suddenly straightened.

"Bang .. Bang .." He screeched pointing his finger at me. "You dead now.. I trick zee.."

"That's not fair.." I objected .

"Just like a deck-boy.." Billy jeered in disgust.

"Itza stupeed game .. .." Tad screeched back.

Yes, I sighed wondering why we had begun it, looking back at the ship, now ready for sea, large swatches of red-lead paint on the hull and superstructure visible in the bulkhead lights.

"Hey mateys...." Norrie panted coming up his broad chest heaving. "We sails tomorra doan't ferget .. Betta not waste no more toime."

Of course, the ship was sailing and I had to admit I was pleased.. my last visit to the *Golden Mountain Bar* had left me feeling unsatisfied ..almost bitter.. Marie had seemed diffident, almost perfunctory refusing to linger with me for a shared cigarette. Billy was right of course she just did it for the money.. and some other man was waiting.. perhaps another favourite customer.. I thought grimly; even so I knew I wanted to go with her one last time.. almost as in revenge somehow .. I thought and yet even so a deep emotion welled up when I thought of her .. perhaps it was love after all..

"Hurry up Phil.. we'se as dry as dust.." Billy urged and I hurried on to follow through the gates posts, the iron barred gates with spiked tops pulled back and so into the streets with it's passing traffic.

How amazingly real it all is, I mused, as laughing and shouting to each other we dodged past the cars, headlights blazing and yet I considered as we reached the other side by tomorrow morning we would be far out to sea.. and all this.. the crowded streets, the market with it's hectic buying and selling and the *Golden Mountain Bar* and Marie would cease to exist . quite as if it had never been..

Just live for the moment, I urged as we passed under *The Duke of Wellington,* and pushed our way to the bar through the buzzing press of men, the air thick with cigarette smoke and the mingled smells of sweat and stale beer.

"Here's to a life on the ocean waaves!" Norrie bellowed raising his glass as we settled around a table together.

"Cheers.." We all cried; the clink of glass ringing around the room.

What could be better than this, I mused, directing a spume of cigarette smoke out into the room; to be drinking with mates.. And yet still I felt restive.. . Was it because of Marie..? Perhaps it was all my fault .. maybe she guessed that I was ashamed of her. .guessing that the crew were all talking about me.. How cowardly I was.. really I had to meet her and explain..

"Took six of 'em didn't it.." Norrie chuckled.

"Zee fight like zee devil.." Tad squealed.

"Is that Wonner you're talking about?" I asked recollecting some of their conversation.

"A real nutter .." Billy laughed.

As if I was in some way responsible, I heard how Wonner had been acting very strangely in the last few days, laughing out loud for no reason and talking to himself, he began accusing the Bo'sun of stealing from his cabin and then out on deck suddenly attacked him. The Chief Mate had persuaded him calm down an ambulance was called and he was taken away him to a mental hospital.

"'Appens all f----n' toime doan't it.. 'member that Taffy greaser Tad? ..Went starkers didn't 'e off the Cape weren't it... "Norrie took a long swallow, smacking his lips with satisfaction

I stared at the table top recalling Wonner's face at the moment he was threatened by the monstrous wave. Was that the reason? Had fear unbalanced his mind…fear of the unknown .. the unexpected.. threatening him with total oblivion? But why should I feel implicated.. as if I should have done something .. and even now how little sympathy I felt for him..

I got to my feet, seeing as if for the first time the crowded room, at one table the men were all tall men with broad shoulders and fair hair and beards, in eager conversation, animated, vivid; shouting and laughing with the pure joy of being alive. Surely that was how life was meant to be lived.. not like me, unable to make up my mind.. a ditherer.. feeble.. I must go to Marie. .

"Sit down.. Phil.. mate.." Billy ordered amiably . "We'se ain't finished yet drinkin' .."

I slumped back into the chair; yes it was best to stay and drink until I couldn't think anymore. How many had pints had I drunk? I mused looking blankly at the table covered with empty glasses streaked with foam.

"So whaat abat yon f----'n t'taart o yars'?" Norrie bellowed suddenly, his eyes starting from his round red face.

I smirked stupidly; finishing off my glass as if it was an answer.

"Sweet on yer is she.. get's it fer nuttin' does ya.. Norris persisted, winking at the others. "Like Billy .. with thaat floosy . .. Freetown wern't it..?"

"Ope zee don't get zee clap....." Tad sniggered; making an ugly face.

Once again I found myself on my feet, rather admiring my ability to keep such perfect balance.

Where ya goan..Phil?" Billy growled.

I smiled mysteriously; serenely ignoring the shouts and jeers; pushing my steadily my way through the crowd of men room to door.

Outside I paused looking questioningly towards the sky; wasn't there a moon ? A small group of men came towards me and with a distant horror I recognised Mitch amongst them.

I fell back against the wall; my heart beating faintly.

"'N where's our little Pansy off to ?" Mitch drawled fixing a cold stare on me. "Gonna to mummy are we.."

I nodded and then shook my head. The other men roaring with laughter.

"Don't get f-----n' lost ..." Mitch shouted as he turned through the doorway.

I wandered off down the street. How I hated Mitch. . .

"One of these days.." I snarled, making a violent lunge into the air and finding myself sitting on the pavement.

"Your drunk .." I grinned wryly struggling to my feet; a gust of hot air swept over me stirring up the dust and papers.

I opened my arms to embrace the humid night air heavy with cooking smells and burning charcoal.

"Marie… My Marie" I whispered passionately not sure if I was serious or not; my legs seeming to carrying me on of their own power. Yes drunk, I told myself but so what.. wasn't it splendid to be drunk.. 'Pansy .. Mummy's little boy' .. I'd show him..

And there, just as I knew it would be was the *Golden Mountain Bar* the pointed roofs emerging out of the shadowy darkness of the street.

I felt my heart beating steadily, my hand confidently resting on my wallet in my jacket.

Strangely though, the heavy door stayed firmly shut despite my determined pushing. Surely I wasn't to be denied .. somehow I couldn't bear it.. I began hitting the door with my fist strangely weak.. a feeble thudding the only result.

'Please God.. don't make me suffer..' I groaned staggering back; but I didn't believe in God.. perhaps for now though.. but how shameless.. despicable.. I jerked back at the sound of a bolt being drawn and the rattle of chain.

I pushed violently at the partly open door and stumbled inside; the camphor smell stronger than ever; vaguely aware it was strangely silent and dark; a squat black shape shuffling towards me.

"Marie. . . Marie .." I insisted catching the glint of gold in the shadowy form. "Or Rosie or Patty.. . "I groaned, despairing, ready to use violence to have my way..

There was a callous shake of the head and an impatient movement towards the door handle.

"But there must be .. someone.." I hissed fiercely frantically pulling out my wallet lest the moment be lost; an appalled delight at seeing the hand grasping eagerly at the bank-notes.

This is what you wanted isn't it? I jeered inwardly following the squat black figure through doorway and down an unlit corridor through another door and down some steps into finding myself once again outside in a narrow alleyway there was some mistake? I thought recoiling at the foetid smells and yet still ruthlessly determined to have my way.

A few steps and a cave-like space appeared, lit by a wavering dull gleam; hesitating at the insistent rustling noises I peered down at the recumbent fleshy mass a head with eye holes nd vacuous smirk. What are you doing? I demanded even as my hands undid my belt and dragged down my trousers and underpants; stumbling forward onto the sprawling clammy flesh, brutally entering the wet oozing vacuity; a despairing cry burning my throat at once recoiling back in sheer horror...

Don't think,, don't think I ordered noticing that the fine rain falling through the aureole about the streetlights. What had I done.. ? Was I so drunk..? I stopped to listen to the gurgling watery noises; noticing the steep-sided drains seething with water bearing dirty foam; this is what is real.. only this .. I thought nothing else.. Head down, down one narrow lane after lane, indifferent to my wet clothes sticking to my skin, my shoes sloshing with water; to the ends of the earth I thought anguishedly.. and beyond.. to nothingness... oblivion.......

Flood-lights beamed out through of the blackness, illuminating the slanting lines of rain. Without the least surprise I realized that somehow I had found my way back to the docks.

I took hold of the bars of the gate running with water and shook them. "Shut.." I muttered looking up at the spikes ranged along the top; thinking that by the time the gates were opened for the morning, the ship would have sailed; imagining the silhouetted stern slowly moving away in the faint dawn light.. without me.. I shook my head; so what. .. nothing really mattered anymore...

I began to walk along the high brick wall pushing through the tall dried weeds heavy with raindrops..

A lean-to appeared in the faint light; a workmen's shed, I guessed, the door hanging off the hinges. I pushed into the pitch black interior smelling of newly dug clay. At least I was out of the rain, I thought, hunkering down against one wall. I stared into the inky darkness. What an terrible thing.. how could I? Don't think.. don't think..' I begged myself; an abyss of self-loathing opening in front of me; feeling my head dropping onto my chest slipping into a vast aching fatigue.

I stirred, yawning hugely; stiff and wet .. as if I hadn't washed in years.. I must have fallen asleep, I concluded ; a faint light seeping into the dark grey sky. But how did I come to be here? A faint moan rose to my lips; bitterly shameful memories pressing into my dulled consciousness.

Perhaps it was all just a hideous dream, I proposed, walking through the faint light to the dockyard gates.. Yes that must be it.. befuddled with drink I had fallen asleep, it was all in the mind.. not real at all. But at once an undeniable disgust welled up. . .over-powering, beyond any imagining. How could I have done it? 'The wages of sin are death' Where did that thought come from? Yes .. sin.. black. . hideous sin... .. Before it had seemed just word .. without depth or real meaning... But now .. a groaning sigh tore through me.. How could I live with myself?

The flood-lights made a yellowish glow through the mist hanging over the quayside, the sheds and cranes forming broken lines in the light. I paused to have a cigarette, extricating the pack out of my pocket only to find it a soggy pulp mixed with tobacco shreds, staining my fingers. I shuddered throwing down the sodden packet..

The dock gates wide open, I walked quickly over the quayside, a dull roaring filling the air, the great steel bulk of the ship, rising solidly out of the brightening mist. I guessed at the scene in the Pantry; the men gathered for the start of another day; and then noticing I wasn't there exchanging knowing grins. How I dreaded meeting them and.. Billy. I stopped and looked down at the down at the bits of flotsam bobbing on the black-green harbour water iridescent with waste oil; just make up some story I thought.. how you got lost or something. I gave a groan.. more deceit .. lies.. more sin..

"Be this early morning or late night sonnie?"

I looked up to see Chips leaning over the rail at the top of the gangway.

"Late night.. I guess.." I said choking a little; starting up the gangway.

"Looks like thee had a fall." Chips chuckled as I moved closer.

"Really.." I glanced at my jacket and trousers streaked with a yellowish clay.

"Must have slipped.." I muttered not able not able to meet the keen gaze of the old ship's carpenter.

"Never mind thee sonny. Shortly be out to sea. Ye'll get comfort then." Chips said with a kindly smile.

I nodded; if only it was true, I thought sadly; stepping down from the gangway onto the deck the familiar vibration passing through me; at once gnawed by fierce hunger pangs.

Chapter Twenty-Four

'*Dear Marie..*'

I began and then hesitated, chewing on the end of my pen, staring at the undulating silky blue-green water overlaid by a gleaming white ruffled strip reaching to the horizon. Why was I bothering really ? I didn't have a proper address just *Golden Mountain Bar..* not even the street name .. and even so I felt such an irresistible impulse to write to her.. to tell her of all my shame and suffering and longings…

I began again the pad on my knees, the vibration from the deck coming up through my feet and making the writing shaky.

'*Now we're sailing through the South China seas far from land and back to the usual routine so it feels like months ago since we left Singapore except you seem so very close to me.. .* 'Again I stopped writing shutting my eyes against a swooning sensation. Was it true..? Yes ..I breathed eagerly. Oh yes.. really it must be love.. such anguish yet at the same time such a deep joy, so at times I was ready to cry…

Yet it was impossible I could ever see her again. Surely I should forget all about her.. but still he memory of those days ashore wouldn't leave me.. whatever the task I was about I found my mind reverting to those times.. drinking and smoking with the girls in their loose shifts close around me.. their small soft forms the sweet scent of their bodies.. and the times with Marie .. especially in the darkness of the cabin before I fell asleep .. and yet worryingly I couldn't exactly recall her face.. only a dim round shape and a curious wry smile. Somehow I had never asked her about her life.. How she came to be in such a place.. . perhaps if we had more time together.. if I had spent the night with her I had heard Ronnie boast that he did that with some women. How perfect it would be to wake up together... and chat about our lives.. instead of suddenly finding myself alone with an empty.. lost abandoned feeling.

I sighed taking up the pen.

'Once we get to Shanghai I will be able to post this. But I must tell you about what happened my last night ashore in the pub down by the docks one of our crew an Assistant Steward called Mitch got into a fight with some Swedish sailors.. and during the fight he cut one of them in the face with a glass.. the Police had to be called.. there was blood everywhere.. and the Swedish sailor will be scarred for life. My cabin-mate Billy(you'll remember him) told me all about it.. I wasn't there you see because I came to the Bar to wish you goodbye only I was terribly drunk and .. well you weren't there.... none of you were and so the old woman took me out through the back and I was terribly drunk you see ..... '

My pen seemed to stop of itself, my heart beating heavily; a dark stain seeping through my mind.. how could I have done such a thing.. would I ever get over it..? And yet

Billy had merely grinned when I had briefly told him about it "Appens sometimes .." He had said shrugging. "Just betta 'ope ya ain't got the clap I says.."

Somehow that didn't worry me; a wave of self-disgust covering even my fear of disease.. only perhaps if I could tell Marie and yet..

For a long while I stared fixedly at the scribbled page and then in a sudden impulse tore the page off the pad and twisted it into a screw.

"Betcha pissed off writin' t'ya folks 'cos ya not yer not getting letters back." Billy said grinning.

"Something like that.." I muttered ashamed to admit that I was writing to Marie and then going to the rail and dropping the scrap of paper overboard and watching it float down. 'The past is past ..I thought and yet still the shame lingered indelible stain that nothing would remove.. I thought the scrap of paper vanishing before my eyes; a sudden sharp ache on one side of my face.

I looked up at the thin white clouds drifting across the vast pale blue sky, massaging my aching jaw. Surely I couldn't be getting a toothache so far from land? With a feeling of relief I felt the pain subside looking down t the swirling, frothed-up water churned out by the propeller below I was conscious how vulnerable I was so far from home and family..

'Don't be such a coward' I told myself as Billy and I walked back to the Amidships on both sides of the ship a serene glittering vastness; thinking of Wonner just before he had been overwhelmed by the monstrous foaming wave and remembering the look of fear in his eyes.. . Yes.. fear itself can destroy you.. I thought anxiously as once again a stabbing pain made me wince again fading away to a persistent dull ache.

Could it be a punishment? I wondered. yes .. God was punishing me but really .. such a trivial thing? No it was just coincidence.. life was simply a succession of coincidences wasn't it? In any case I wont give in to it I vowed, the mariners of old must have endured far worse without complaining. . now I could show that I was as brave as them..

But after slowly the constant nagging pain undermined my defiance; reducing me to state of abject self-pity. 'Please God.. please God..' I whimpered inwardly. But there was no relief.. the pain continuing throbbing relentlessly .. ruthlessly... ..

And yet as always the ship's engines thudded away a plume of black smoke pouring from the funnel rising high into the cloudless blue sky, pushing the ship steadily through the flat, dazzling waters, irregardless of all else....

How can I go on living? I despaired unable to settle during the afternoon break pacing up and down, massaging the swelling in my gum with my fingertip.

"Why don'tcha ask the Sec. He's got a whole medicine cabinet.." Billy suggested watching me calmly through wisps of cigarette smoke.

"Really? Do you think ..?" I muttered surprised to think that I didn't have to inevitably suffer.

"Take two twice a day The Sec." said coming out of his cabin where I had followed him and putting the large white tablets into my hand.

"Codeine .. very addictive.." he added sternly. You'll have to see a dentist, when we get to Shanghai... I'll get the Sparkies to radio the line's agents."

"Sure.. Thanks Sec.. Thanks a lot.." I muttered gratefully looking at the tablets in my palm a little sceptical.

But within a few minutes of swallowing the tablets the pain faded away. away. Never would I complain about anything I vowed, thinking how wonderful merely to be free of pain.

From then on each day I went to the Sec. and as I waited for him to bring me the tablets I felt the dull ache returning.

"But Sec.." I wailed feebly my complacent expectation turned to horrified disbelief as one evening he curtly shook his head.

"You're becoming addicted." He explained sternly "We'll be in Shanghai in another couple of days anyway. You can see a dentist then."

"But Sec.. Sec.." I argued. "The pain is pretty unbearable.."

Pitilessly the Sec. waved me away.

"Toothache won't kill you.."

Was I addicted? I wondered dazedly returning to the cabin to complain to Billy; surely it was just the unbearable pain.. nothing else..

"Yer just 'ave to f----n' put up with it.." Billy replied cheerfully indifferent.

Pressing my hand as hard as I could against the piercing ache in my jaw I lay curled up on the bunk barely aware of the slow rhythmic rise and fall of the ship or throb of the engines; my body soaked in sweat. Was it really worse than before I wondered or was it because I knew I was being denied certain relief ? Think of other things.. think of being with Marie I urged but the unremitting pain shut out all else.

'Please.. please. God. stop the pain' I moaned silently but even as my lips formed the words I knew it was hopeless.. I was doomed to lie all night and suffer.. without the least hope of relief.. and tomorrow.?

But then before I knew what I was doing I had dropped onto the cabin floor and was out in the companionway making my way towards the open deck-door.

Above the vast array of glittering stars; indifferent to all human suffering I thought; moving across to the ship's side and looking down at the dimly gleaming blackness below. Now.. now, I thought, now is the moment to free yourself.. from all the misery and anguish and pain.. . I hoisted myself up onto the rusted bulwark; shutting my eyes; the faint swish of water below reaching me.

'Fool!. .. Fool!' A voice cried within me and startled I slipped back down onto deck. 'Go and make the Sec. give you more tablets' I ordered myself possessed of a calm rage.

Standing in front of the Sec.'s cabin door I absently watched my fist repeatedly striking the door.

The cabin-door opened abruptly and the Sec., naked except for briefs, his muscled torso just discernible in dim bulkhead light, stood frowning sleepily at me.

"Sec. I know you think I'm addicted but believe me it's just the pain it's unbearable. Give me tablets or I'm going to jump overboard,, ." I grinned fiercely; how absurd it sounded but it was true wasn't it.?

The Sec. hesitated then nodded and turned away, leaving the door ajar; allowing me to see inside his cabin for the first time, catching sight of a framed photographs of a pleasant faced woman with two boys beside her.... So he must be married I thought distantly.. yes of course .. he wore a ring too...

Strange to think he has a life apart from the ship I mused greedily swallowing the tablets and immediately turning away.

"Thank you God .." I murmured dragged myself up into the bunk bed the pain already fading and slipping almost at once into an exhausted sleep; only of course it wasn't God was it.. just the codeine tablets. .. .

"Like the f-----g Dark Ages betcha... Yank it out with a pair of rusty pliers.. .Give ya blood poisoning. .." Mitch jeered.

I nodded indifferently; getting dressed to go ashore I had felt as if I was clothing a wooden dummy; my mind trance-like floating away on it's own; could it be the codeine ?

"Mair o' yer Capitalist lees.. . "Jock snorted. "Jist like the newsreel in the Picture Hoose in Singapore ye telt me aboot. Am I nae richt Phil laddie?"

"'e 'ad more to do than f----n' Pictures .." Ronnie sniggered.

I nodded indifferently glancing over the dockside, deserted in the pale morning light, the gangway already in position; conscious of the faint warning throb in my jaw. Where was the car to take me to the dentist the Sec. had promised was coming? Had there been some misunderstanding? Already several severe faced Chinese men in blue double-breasted suits had come aboard and then left again. Why was this happening to me.. how unfair.. or did I deserve it. .?

"Yon Shanghai is nae like yon backward Ching Wang Tao. Top city in China." Jock went on complacently.

"The Peoples Republic of China ya mean. .." Pete boomed out in his usual absurdly pompous way. "The Great Helmsman.. that's what they call him Chairman Mao.... has a system Maoism .. like Marxism ..."

"Nae matter .... "Jock interrupted impatiently. "Afore the Communists took over yer Shanghai was famous fer deevilish Opium dens gambling and brothels run by gangsters, cut yer throat fer a bawbee."

"Triads yer calls 'em." Peter puffed. "All yer businesses had to pay protection money to 'em.. Special initiation .."

"A few Royal Marines 'ud soon settle their f-----n' haash.." Mitch drawled; his blotched face flushing red.

"Hoot maun! "Jock burst out indignanty. "Yer Majesties loyal British Government sent in the gunboats to shell the Chinkies to force'em t'buy opium."

"Grown in India. "Pete declared knowingly." For trading companies like Matheson and Jarndyce.. heh. heh Scottish.. Claimed Opium war was for free-trade.. not opium."

"It was whaat the Chinks f-----n' wanted weren't it.." Mitch snapped giving a hitch to his trousers sagging over his protruding stomach. "Can't blame us fer giving 'em what they f-----n' waanted."

"Nae nae.." Jock objected vigorously. "Wrang is wrang.. and richt ..is richt.. nae matter what the situation. Am I nae richt Phil laddie?"

"Well.. I suppose.... "I stammered only conscious of the growing ache in my jaw

"That's the car for you now Wight "The Sec. said sternly coming out of the amidships. "Good luck.."

"Aye guid luck t'ye laddie.." Jock chortled and there was a murmur from the others.

Watched by the others at the ship's side I walked deliberately down the gangway; as if I was going off to be executed I thought grimly giving a nonchalant half-wave before stepping into the old-fashioned black saloon car with running boards and large round headlights mounted on the sweeping wings; like something out of an American gangster film..

Without turning or speaking the driver engaged the gears and the car sped off down the dockside. I looked around at the shiny wood and leather interior, the musty leathery smell reminding me of a boyhood car journey, wearing a pageboy outfit complete with skullcap to the fashionable wedding of a uncle.. with my parents and brother and sister beside me..

But now I was all by myself.. in Shanghai.. Communist China.... .going to a dentist. But what did Mitch know about it? He just wanted to frighten me. I thought suppressing my fears.

The car slowed as we approached the dockside gates but the soldiers in khaki on duty sternly waved us on. Obviously I'm seen as a person of importance I congratulated myself; relaxing into the leather seat; of course they will want to give me the best treatment possible.. .

"Is it er far .?" I thought to ask, glimpsing through the windows a double boulevard line with tall buildings but there wasn't the slightest response from the broad shoulders with a round head topped with a flat cap in front of me.

"We are going to the dentists are we?" I tried again after a little while noticing we had left the wide streets with large buildings and were now passing through a maze of narrow streets thronged with pedestrians and cyclists, almost all wearing the regulation blue serge, but again the driver made no response. He must have been told not to speak to me I concluded, my jaw beginning to ache ever more strongly. The car had slowed moving almost at a walking pace, bumping and swaying down narrow streets full of moving bodies. I looked through the car window at the sea of black head bobbing utterly oblivious to the car pushing through.. for them I simply don't exist I thought conscious of being more alone than ever in my life before. Why hadn't the Sec. let Billy come with me?

Without warning the car stopped, the engine still running, the driver got out and without a word disappeared into a building. I sat nursing my jaw wondering what was happening. Was he asking for directions perhaps?

I closed my eyes, trying to ignore the throbbing; vague fears seeping into my consciousness. Perhaps there was a cunning plot to abduct me .. take me to a prison .. and brain-wash me imagining how the cheerful brash voice in the Movietone news would declaim: 'Vanished Cabin-Boy makes Public Appearance to Denounce Capitalist Ship Owners.'

Was that why there hadn't been any letters for me again? Was it all part of the conspiracy to isolate me.. make me vulnerable for suggestion...? I shook my head.. that was crazy How possibly could they have known I would get a toothache and need treatment..?

I opened my eyes at the sound of the door opening and watched as the driver got behind the wheel and drove away; it's all utterly absurd.. meaningless .. I thought shutting my eyes again.

I sat up realizing the car had stopped, the engine turned off; the broad blue suited shoulders rigidly unmoving. Was this it then?

I got out almost dizzy shielding my eyes against the hot sun; my fresh shirt already sticking to my skin with sweat. Could this be the dentist? I wondered looking up at the run-down old fashioned looking three-storey building the square windows covered with blinds staring blankly down at me.

I glanced back, the driver was now sitting on the running board smoking contentedly. At least he's waiting for me, I thought pushing going up the steps and through the tall doors of patterned glass into a black and white tiled vestibule, sniffing at the faintly medicinal smell. Nothing for it, I thought my jaw aching ever more painfully starting up the staircase with curved wooden banister and wrought iron balustrades rising in flights to a domed skylight high above.

And I thought I was going to be being treated like a V.I.P., I thought bitterly pulling myself up the stairs; each step seeming to add to my humiliation.

On the second landing I noticed a small square of white paper pinned to top glass half of a door and below the Chinese characters: DR WANG. Was this the dentist then? I stopped and looked back down the stairwell hearing a creaking noise from below. Was I being followed perhaps? Was I about to be ambushed? Chloroformed .. taken into one of the rooms....? I shrugged the pain making me indifferent to all else; pushing open the door and entered a small square room with old bent-back chairs ranged against one wall. No receptionist not even a counter. Could it all be a artfully contrived hoax, I wondered wiping the sweat off my face. But to what end?

I crossed to another door and looked in; a single narrow window covered with bamboo blinds, leaked light into the narrow room; a ceiling fan moved slowly around the hot air, heavy with disinfectant smells. In the middle of the room was an old-fashioned dentist's chair the stuffing coming out the padding in the head rest. A museum piece I thought in dismay; beside it was an antiquated-looking drill of complicated set of pulleys and wires. Perhaps I should go I thought conscious that the throbbing had stopped completely.

A small stooped Chinese man, in a white-coat silent appeared through another door; his thin hair a pure white, a wary look on his worn lined face.

"Are you the dentist?" I ventured despairingly.

He gave the slightest of nods.

"Sprechen die Deutsch?" He enquired in a mournful sing-song voice pointing to the chair.

"English .." I replied gloomily hesitating then going over and sitting in the chair under a light bulb dangling from the ceiling, the rusted metal reflector spotted with flyspecks. I put a finger in my mouth to point out at the tooth and gave a stifled moan to show it was hurting me .. how ridiculous.

Closing my eyes I waited with my mouth open, my mind going back to my last visit to the dental clinic in a Vancouver office block recalling the gleaming modern equipment and the broad-shouldered, business-like dentist and the smiling blonde dental nurse with shapely legs, her full bust pressing out her gleaming white nylon dress and here I am in a dusty room in back street in Communist Shanghai.. all the equipment old and worn with a dentist that doesn't speak English and is probably incompetent, just as Mitch predicted.. . My destiny I thought grimly, jerking violently at the touch of the sharp point of the stainless-steel probe.

"Ja...Ja..." Dr Wang murmured a gleam of satisfaction on his worn face. I felt the needle expertly, gently pierce my gum, nodding as Dr Wang held up five fingers .. Yes of course... time to let the anaesthetic work I thought; my fears falling away; a deep gratefulness suffusing me...

Really I had to thank the Sec.. I mused and the Sparkies too for radioing the message... But surely more than just them.. they were part of a complex of communications that spanned the globe.. the electrical pulses motivating anonymous workers in offices around the world.. hidden from my sight and yet working entirely for my personal benefit.. really a kind of blessing from above..

A thick finger pushed into my mouth to prod the frozen gum, I smiled amiably then pulled back in dismay as I saw the steel pliers he was holding and realized that the intention was to extract my tooth..

No! No.! Not that!" I cried, half-getting out of the seat.

Dr Wang looked at me in astonishment, a deep fear in his eyes.

"If you're any kind of dentist.." I bullied. "There must do something else you can do.."

Dr Wang shrugged and then nodded, unhooking the drill-end and switched on the motor, the ragged wires running slowly through the complex of pulleys. I shut my eyes, trying to shut out the grating noise vibrating through my head. But I have saved my tooth I thought joyfully, as I washed out the bitter taste of oil of cloves spitting into a steel bowl held by the old dentist.

"Thank you, Herr Doktor. .." I condescended getting stiffly out the chair and holding out my hand; the handshake limp... .

Then I was leaping down the stairs, rushing into the sweltering heat of the morning.. Free of pain for good, I rejoiced .. how wonderful everything was.... the sky .. the burning hot sun.. the whole world. .. how grateful I was for life.. the past forgotten ..

"Home James.. and don't spare the horses." I ordered gaily clapping the broad blue back of the driver; exhilarated as at some great achievement; looking with awakened interest through the window; the narrow streets still crowded with humanity; this time I occasionally picked out a pretty face cycling or walking amongst the uniform serge, flaunting a pony-tail, and dressed in bright colours, in blatant defiance of the regulations, I presumed. Like wild flowers growing in a monotone field, I thought poetically, waving to them, exulting when they smiled back.

"Wait to I tell Billy," I chuckled. "Real lovelies ..just waiting for us.."

I smiled genially at the guard who peered in the car as it paused for inspection at the dockyard gates. Really everyone was so good to me.. .. but didn't I deserve it..?

"Thanks me old matey.." I chimed as the driver pulled up on the dockside not far from the ship amongst waiting lorries; rather to my surprise he turned and grinned at me, showing large gaps in his teeth.

As I approached the gangway I saw that the unloading was well underway hatch-covers rolled back and the dockside cranes were bent over the steel cables plucking up slings bulging with sack of wheat. Wheat harvested in the vast fields of Australia the other side of the Pacific.. I mused moving up the gangway and considering how like my dental treatment, the wheat being unloaded was only the visible sign of a complicated web reaching back to the workers at their desks in towering office blocks...... in Chicago .. London.. Sydney .. Toronto ... Or in dingy back streets; indefatigably telephoning, telexing, telegraphing through different time-zones and currencies .and languages,.. .And not only in offices of course but in fields and workshops around the world; men with strong arms and backs .. lifting and driving.. pushing and pulling.. skilfully twisting and tightening and hammering.. intently watching dials.... adjusting gauges.. hour after hour....no matter what the weather or conditions.. day after day.. year after year.. individuals and yet joined to form a complicated organism reaching into the furthest parts of the world.. and now here in China delivering wheat to the starving millions.. ..

I turned and looked down from the ship's side at the dockside from all sides came the whirr and screech of machinery; the floury dust and shrill cries rising into the burning hot air the over-arching cranes were dropping the slings loaded with sacks onto on the dock-side, while one of the waiting blue-clothed workers rushed to free it from the slowly swaying hook and allow the heaped-up sacks to sprawl out, at which with a loud shout others ran forward to load them on each others shoulders before staggering away to pile them onto the waiting flat lorries.

How little any of them understand the complexity that allows the crane to casually dump this bounty onto the dockside I considered, proud to think how I was in a small way part of this life-giving enterprise.

Absently my hand went to my jaw aware of a renewed throbbing.. just the anaesthetic wearing off, I decided but then as the day passed even as I busied myself with my usual tasks I had to accept that the pain had returned .. as bad or even worse than before. Despondently I wandered out on deck and going to the rail looked down on the Chinese labourers on the afterdeck How little they think of themselves I mused my hand pressed to my throbbing jaw seeing them working with such tireless energy in the dust and heat. The clink of footsteps made me look around.

It was Chips, coming rapidly up the stairs the familiar faded green hold-all at his side.

"Won't listen no way... will they?" He said with a shake of his silvery head. "A couple of them Coolies killed.. pulling sacks down any which way."

He absently rubbed his chin, his bright blue eyes fixed thoughtfully on me.

"What's two out of so many millions? Is what they think. But a life is a life.."

"Yes I guess they suffer, just as much as we do ." I sighed, pressing at the unrelenting ache in my jaw.

"Nothing more true. "Chips said looking at me closely. "Sommat wrong sonny.."

I nodded "Toothache.."

"Better pluck it out if it offends thee.." Chips said thoughtfully before moving away in his usual easy rolling gait.

Easy for him to say, I thought morosely..

"It's just one f----n' tooth" Billy laughed when I told him the pain had come back. "Norrie lost two in a fight in Rio..."

So why was I so upset at the thought of losing a single tooth? I wondered lying in the strange stillness; the Sec. having consented to giving me more codeine tablets on the strict condition of my returning to the dentist the following day to have the tooth extracted . It was just one tooth after all ... true it would be the first one since losing my baby teeth and yet still just a single tooth.. but somehow it signified to me something far worse.. the beginning of something too awful to think about.. And why I should it happen to me? What had I done to deserve it? So. . so.. unfair.. Or was it? Did anyone deserve illness or pain.. or injury..? The Chinese workers crushed to death.? Wonner going mad ? And how many of the crew had missing teeth.. like the Chinese chauffeur. It was just life.. to be endured.. bravely or despairingly made no difference .. to be endured ....

My jaw still anaesthetized, a blood soaked cloth clenched between my teeth, I reclined exhausted in the back seat of the car.. Yes.. it was all over... I had nothing now to fear; the gentle throbbing clear proof that the source of the pain had been removed .. Dazedly my mind went back to when breathing the musty smells I had reluctantly pulled myself up the stairs.. finding the waiting-room deserted.. all just as before ..Dr Wang abruptly appearing from the side room, utterly impassive as he gestured to the chair but then the violent wrenching that had pushed the side of my face brutally into the headrest .. the sharp crack as the roots gave and the sheer relief hearing the clink of the extracted tooth dropping into the steel dish.... ..yes relief and also a bitterness.. one inescapable conclusion pervading my thoughts: I had lost a tooth..

And yet the as the car lurched slowly through the crowded streets back to the ship, nauseous from the blood I had swallowed came the conviction that the pain.. the misery, the suffering and anguish ..the bitter grief at losing a tooth.... .must in some way unknown to me have a purpose.. .a meaning . ..

CHAPTER TWENTY-FIVE

Talking and laughing the two deck-boys, Billy and I squeezed into the back seat of one of the old black saloon cars waiting in a line just outside the dock gates.

Without a word the driver started the engine and drove off.

"Say where we going anyway Billy?" I wondered excitedly.

"Special place fer us tars.." Billy grinned.

"Betta be good afta waitin' so long.." Norrie said wagging his round head dolefully.

"Zee Commies guards f-----n' 'ate us... "Tad screeched out.

"That's because you scare them.." I laughed. "Let's hope they aren't so touchy in this place.."

"Nah.. Us'd to be right swanky though "Billy chuckled. "A club for toffs no Chinkies allowed in."

"Really .." I mused looking out through the car windows; the tip of my tongue touching the gap in my gum; remembering the time I had been driven to the dentist; somehow the streets looked completely different or had I just forgotten?

The car came to a halt beside one of the large buildings lining the wide boulevard. Billy paid the driver and we all got out and passed through a set of ornate wrought iron gates towards a classical portico; draped across the line of pillars was a banner with *Sailors Palace* in yellow letters blazoned on the shiny red cloth.

"Some place eh mateys.... "Norrie chortled. as we entered through the tall, wide doorway into a semi-circular atrium; our footsteps echoing and re-echoing we walked down the long reddish marble floored hallway stopping as we reached a large circular area lit by a glass dome. We all stared curiously at the small display lit by coloured lights; into a semi-circular plastic basin edged with plastic flowers a single jet of water splashed; above it was a banner with the slogan: *WORKERS OF THE WORLD UNITE!* with a crossed hammer and sickle at either end.

Leaving the others I went over to investigate a screen of green baize framed in a light wood.

Under the heading the *Great Patriotic War* were a series of black and white photographs one showed a crowd of bemused looking soldiers American I guessed, receiving some parcels from jovial Chinese in quilted jackets. On a strip of paper was a typed. "*Warmongering Imperialists gratefully accept presents from Peace loving Socialist Worker-Soldiers Defending the Motherland.*"

As well as the photographs there were newspaper clippings cut from . "*Miners Worse than Slaves.*" was one of the headlines with an account of how coal miners in the American State of Virginia were obliged to buy their supplies from Company stores and so never were able to free themselves from debt. Another from the *Daily Worker* described the awful conditions of immigrant textile workers in the East End of London under the headline: "*Bosses Gets Fat on Sweat of Oppressed Workers.*"

Do they really think anyone will be interested in such crude propaganda . I thought turning away to catch up with Billy and the others.

"This very must pleass you "A giggly sing-song voice made me look around; two Chinese women, in army fatigues had come up behind me.

"Not so very interesting really.." I said, smiling back at the small pretty face, two pig-tails tied with pink ribbons stuck out either side of her small round face; her black eyes mischievously bright.

"The International struggle against the Capitalist Imperialists *must* be interesting." The other older woman intoned in a heavy foreign-sounding English; wearing thick glasses; a severe almost angry look on her squarish face.

"Sorry .. not me.." I responded repelled by her grimly assertive manner.

"Workers of World must unite to defeat Capitalist Imperialists." The older woman chanted resolutely.

"Yeah..? Meantime you need Capitalist wheat?" I sniped glancing at the younger woman who was busy chewing the end of her pigtails.

"Marxist-Leninist Historical dialectic means final Victory of Proletariat is inevitable." The older woman declared, her face fixed, only her lips moving.

I shrugged . "Says you.. but that doesn't mean we can't enjoy ourselves does it" I grinned winking at the younger woman, who looked away two red spots glowing on her cheeks. "You know.. have a drink .. go dancing.." I did a quick pirouette.

"Typical corrupting Western decadence." The older woman scorned, jerking her head and stalking away towards one of the corridor; the younger woman obediently following her, stopping to look back and smile cheekily at me before disappearing around a corner.

I moved thoughtfully across the wide atrium towards the main corridor thinking to follow Billy and the others; could it be though that the grim-looking older woman was right though. Communism was so logical in away.. everything shared equally.. and now so many countries in the world were devoted to that system.. perhaps there was something inevitable about it.. an irreversible historical process.. regardless of individuals. . or their feelings.. hopes.. desires...

But no.. somehow I just couldn't accept that .. individuals made history.. great men like Wellington and yes.. Napoleon and even the brutal Stalin and tyrannical Mao.. even if they managed to convince everyone they were a product of some inevitable historical force then I remembered the cheeky smile of the younger woman; I bet she isn't fooled I thought with a grin.

At the end of the corridor I came to a set of tall doors with frosted glass panels and pushed them open, entering a large, square room with large wall mirrors reflected the ornate bronze wall-lights ..the steamy air heavy with fragrant soap-smells.

"Where ya been Phil..?" Billy called from one of four leather and chrome barber chairs set on a raised platform, only his head showed over a white cloth. Tad and Norrie were in other chairs their heads covered with foam. Chinese attendants in white jackets with high collars stood behind them patiently massaging their scalps.

I mounted the platform and sat myself in one of the black leather and chrome barber chairs. How luxurious it all is, I mused complacently gazing around at the iridescent green tiles and elaborately framed mirrors, thinking how once it was a club only for the wealthy and important yet here was I, Phillip Wight, a mere cabin-boy deigning to surrender my jacket to the Chinese attendant bowing obsequiously to me.. .

"Who were ya talkin' to.." Billy asked only his eyes and nose visible under the thick lather

"These two women army types.. one of them spouting a lot of Commie propaganda . the other was nice though."

"Trust ya…" Billy laughed. "Ya always sniff out some bint don't'cha."

I flushed hotly; gazing up the square mirrors set in the ceiling, the reflection blurred by the swirl of the fan-blades attached to long brass stalks; surely it had just happened of it's own… ..or had I somehow caused it to happen? Another of the white-coated Chinese attendants now came forward, bowed low and placed a steaming cloth over my face; something touched my feet and I lifted the edge of the cloth; kneeling in front of me was an old man in a brown jacket using his fingers to work polish into my shoes; he glanced up a toothless servile grin on his wrinkled old face. I suppose he's happy enough I mused shutting my eyes thinking how seductive it was to be treated like a superior being.

After a while the cloth was whisked from my face and a large cape placed around shoulders; the chair tilted back and I glimpsed a hand flourishing a shaving brush and then my cheeks and neck were quickly plastered with a creamy lather; just like Billy I thought complacently.

Out of the corner of my eyes I saw the Chinese barber flourish a single-bladed razor, reminding me of my grandfather stropping a blade on a long leather strap attached to the wall... A cut-throat razor wasn't it? With deft strokes the shaving foam was swept away the blade comfortably grazing my face; the first time I have ever been shaved I mused dreamily.

Once again I closed my eyes submitting to the strong fingers massaging the strongly scented shampoo into my scalp, distantly conscious of a faint unease. After all what had I done to deserve such pampering? It is what it is .. I told myself my head rocking as it was gently towelled.

The steady click of scissors took me back to the time that Chips had cut my hair; remembering the subdued murmur of conversation from the gathered sailors and beneath me the foredeck slowly rising and falling into the vast blue sky above.. how long ago that seemed.. and a vague feeling of loss rose in me.. tears filling my eyes.. how sad life was.. even at the best of times.. .

A tap on my shoulder, made me start. I stared back at the face reflected in the wooden framed mirror held before me. Who was this other looking quizzically back at me, so fresh and neatly groomed I wondered, nodding approvingly to the attendant. Yes that's me, I thought strangely moved, as powerful finger tips massaged my neck and shoulders.

"Hey Phil! We'se going for a drink. Up the stairs.." I heard Billy call from the doorway.

"Right-o.. ... "I called back slipping into a voluptuous daze under the rhythmic pressure on my shoulders and neck ; distantly uneasy that I was losing myself in the sensuous feelings.

I put my arms into my jacket held out by the attendant glancing at the round flat face, the dark eyes blank, unseeing; as if don't really exist I thought wryly, the soft brush flick rapidly over my shoulders and arms; for him I'm just so much raw material to be lathered, scraped and rubbed..

I went over to the pay-desk, a glassed-in wooden cabinet beside the door taking out a wad of the odd-looking bank-notes remembering how the sailors had made jokes about them until the Chief Steward had become angry and threatened to stop issuing our subs.

Inside the cabinet an ancient-looking Chinese cashier, perched on a high stool blinked dully at me from behind wire-framed glasses; strands of fine white hair hung over his bald pate blotched with dark stains.

Probably he'd worked here when this was an exclusive foreigners-only club I thought watching his scrawny hand groped around the brass plate and despite everything that happened wars.. revolutions.. purges .. he was still here.... surviving by sheer passivity.. like a barnacle on a storm ravaged rock..

"Keep the change "I said impulsively pushing back the flimsy aluminium coins.

The old cashier hesitated for a second and then a gnarled hand hastily, jerkily scraped the coins towards himself.

Who knows what hideous things he has witnessed I thought, my footsteps ringing out on the marble floor of the hallway as I retraced my way to the atrium. Shootings and disappearances ...surely to survive with a trace of dignity was a triumph, I decided pulling myself up by the brass banister up a broad flight of stairs sweeping overhanging balcony with ornately carved balustrades.

At the top of the stairs I paused looking up at the elaborate plasterwork ceiling with a painted oval showing a pastel-coloured scene of diaphanous-clothed nymphs bathing; in the middle hung a cluster of opaque globes on wreathing brass stalks; palms in large white marble urns stood at intervals in front of the walls panelled in pale wood patterned with a dark inlay.

What did the peasant soldiers of the Red Army think bursting into all this extravagant opulence, I wondered crossing over to the padded leather double door on the other side of the landing. Did they feel a hatred for it or perhaps they were awed by it; anyway they hadn't vandalized it .. or burnt it to the ground.

I pushed through the heavy doors to find myself in a cavernous space, the tall windows draped in heavy red curtains, bronze wall-lights like antique torches reflected off the dark panelling; the air permeated with the smell of cigars and noisy with talk and laughter. Like a baronial hall I thought moving forward my feet sinking into the thick-piled carpet; on the far side ran an enormous gleaming mahogany bar and behind it a massive pier-glass, the tiered shelves reaching to the ceiling gleaming with bottles in a variety of shapes and colours.

Noticing Billy I moved towards him passing through the tables crowded with men who I guessed must be foreign sailors.. some heavily bearded and wearing uniforms with gold braid all of them engaged in loud conversations while drinking and smoking. Chinese waiters, in white starched jackets and black ties, bearing aloft silver trays, glinting with bottles and glasses threaded noiselessly between the tables.

Sinking into a high-backed red leather armchair, I gazed wonderingly up at the brass-bladed fans slowly rotating through the bluish air. Was I really meant to be here? A mere cabin-boy? Almost at once one of the immaculately-dressed Chinese waiters appeared and I ordered a beer. In a few minutes he had returned placing bottle with a label of red and green dragons and a glass in front of me; producing a bottle opener with a flourish he flipped of the cap and half-filled my glass, the foam rising to the top of the straw-coloured beer.

Thanks matey.." I said to the waiter who bowed impassively before retreating.

I raised my glass to toast the others and took a long swallow of the cold beer; how splendid it all was, and how easily I had become part of it. Or was it all just an illusion?

Leaning towards each other the four of us talked in excited loud voices; of when we were likely to sail; what our next port of call was likely to be; clouds of cigarette smoke curling upward from our cigarettes, repeatedly gulping at the shining golden liquid while the white-coated Chinese waiters silently came and went, clearing away the empty bottles and putting down fresh ones; the red and green dragons on the labels writhing mysteriously under the watery dribbles.

Slowly I felt myself floating free of the hum of conversation and clinking of glasses, my eyes straying idly around the immense bar-room, the small groups at the rows of tables deep in conversation, now and then one of them would throw back his head to roar laughter such a good-natured, generous, hearty sound. And now I am one of them . sailors.. seamen.. mariners. . seafarers .. courageously braving the open sea far from home and family and now enjoying a drink with their shipmates... just like me and Billy and Tad and Norrie. . Ship-mates.. what a wonderful word.... yes.. ship-mates..

Distantly I heard my name? What were they saying about me? I stared suspiciously at the two grinning deck-boys opposite..

"You're deck-boys.." I began patiently "And we're cabin- boys but .."

"Ya doan't knoaw nowthing about deck-boys." Norrie bellowed back.

"Cabin-boys zee f-----n' wankers." Tad screeched loudly getting to his feet.

"A bit noisy aren't we lads? What ship are we off?"

I looked up, a tall, slender man with a tanned, fine-boned face, in a naval uniform with gold rings on the cuffs, stood over our table, fixing me with a clear gaze.

"Er.. *MV Grimthorpe*.. er Sir.." I piped up, noticing Billy's frown but somehow unable to stop myself. "Bulk Carrier .. registered Hartlepool.. Cargo of wheat from Australia.."

"The devil you say...." The officer raised sharply-defined eyebrows.

"Because of the famine.." I added thinking he must be a very senior officer, perhaps a captain; he certainly had an air of authority about him, like our 1st Mate, only more refined, not blustering or bullying.. Perhaps I could be like him some day.. . .

"But are *you* regular crew.? The officer asked doubtfully looking closely at me, an amused look on the narrow elegant face.

"You bet, cabin-boys, aren't we Billy?" I chirped looking to Billy who was silently studying the slowly dissolving smoke rings.

"You're no Geordie.. .I wager .." The officer posed thoughtfully with a faint smile.

"Er no sir.. signed on Vancouver previous cabin-boy jumped ship they say.." Again I looked to Billy but he was frowning into space.

"Jumped ship eh?" Deep frown lines creased the officers broad forehead.

"A mystery that.." I burbled on. "No one talks about it, do they mateys?.. Sometimes I even wonder if he existed.." I reached for my cigarettes, wondering if I wasn't making a fool of myself.

"A ghost story eh.." The Officer laughed, long fingers caressing his pointed chin. "But what made *you* decide to go to sea?"

"Just looking for a bit of excitement.. I suppose." I said airily "It was only meant to be return voyage but then ship-owners sent us Down Under.. and now were going back there again. Anyway I guess they've forgotten me..no letters but that suits me let's me life my own life...." I gave a hoarse laugh.

"I wonder if I shouldn't try to arrange a passage back to Vancouver for you..." the Officer said smiling kindly.

"Vancouver.." I echoed; my heart thudding. Is that what I really wanted?

"Yes.. exactly.. . get you back home .. family ..where you really belong. "The officer eyes flickered critically over Billy and the others sitting dumbly. "Not waste your life eh?"

For a minute I hesitated; home.. yes.. proper food and ..all those things I had taken for granted.. Was this my destiny? Just like the telephone call from the Harbour Master's office all that time ago. . ..?

Abruptly, defiantly I shook my head.

"Can't leave my ship-mates.." I muttered clumsily waving to the others around the table.

"'e's wit' us.. We'se shipmates.." Billy growled, reaching forward to stub out a cigarette.

Norrie and Tad grinned and gawped and nodded approvingly.

The Officer stiffened frowning sternly.

He isn't used to being refused I thought suddenly nervous, thinking perhaps he had authority to make me leave the ship.

"Anyway keep it down ." The officer said severely. "I expect you feel yourselves as superior to the Chinese .. and it doesn't matter what amount of silliness you indulge in"

"No sir.." I protested feebly.

"But really your're just letting down our side.." The officer went on ignoring me." I'll tell you something that might surprise you.. one day the Chinese will lead the world.."

"Really?" I sniggered stirred by an obtuse spirit. "And in what way will that be I wonder.. ."

The officer frowned angrily; the fine lines about his eyes tightening. "Just keep it down.." He snapped turning to stride rapidly away to a table at the far side of the room.

For a minute or two the four of us sat in complete silence.

"Let's get out of 'ere.." Billy frowned getting to his feet.

The padded leather doors thudded softly behind us.

As if escaping from something we ran down the grand stair-case and across the atrium blithely ignoring the alarmed stares of the Chinese attendants. Led by Billy we passed through an open door and into an old-fashioned shopping arcade. Out of breath and moving more slowly we passed down the patterned tiled floor beneath roof-lights supported by decorative cast-iron pillars and rafters. Every once in a while we paused to look in the shop-window most of them displaying identical-looking souvenirs; really I should buy a presents for the family I thought dazedly yet would I ever get back home..? Perhaps I was fated to wander the world's oceans for ever ..

Reaching the main entrance we pushed through the heavy doors and stepped outside, the sky already darkening.

How had it got to be so late? I wondered the past few hours a dim blur of sensations; conscious of an underlying sadness; was this how life was meant to be?

Together we jammed into the back seat of one of the waiting identical black saloon cars. I peered out at the wide streets sweeping past in the fading light, thinking of the officer; what had he said to those at his table when he got back?

Perhaps something like: 'Off a grain carrier it seems .. usual riff-raff you get at sea these days... one of them a real greenhorn .. .romantic notions about going to sea.. now regretting it ..but too stubborn to admit it.. cocky little so and so. He'll get his comeuppance though.. 'I sighed to myself; how would it all end?

Getting out of the car just outside the dockyard gates we stretched ourselves after the press of the car.

"Ya talks too much Phil.." Billy said abruptly his face dim in the half-light.

"Zat officer. .." Tad squealed accusingly.

"You mean about the other Cabin Boy?" I mumbled flushing.

"T'ings yer knows nuttin' about." Billy snapped back.

"Doan't speak t'officers.. ." Norrie rumbled portentously.

"You're all crazy. ." I muttered, walking quickly away, vaguely realising I was going in the wrong direction. What did it matter?

At the sound of footsteps coming after me I increased my pace. I'll show them I thought with sudden elation finding myself walking close to a railway siding, between the tracks swathes of dried grasses showed under the faint glow of single light-bulbs hung between spindly poles.

I stepped aside walking clumsily along the sharp stones; where did I think I was going?

From behind I heard shouting and looked back, seeing three dark shapes coming after me. I grinned sardonically becoming aware of a dull clunking sound; the ground shaking beneath my feet.

With faint squealing a square-shunting engine pulling a line of goods-wagon moving slowly began to pass me by. I walked faster and faster in an attempt to keep up; suddenly in an unthinking reflex action I took hold of a stanchion and pulled myself up onto a ladder on the side of a wagon. Gripping tightly to the stanchion I hung out looking back at the three figures, watching me in amazement.

"See you in Peking!" I cried twisting around, warm gritty air rushing past my face.. a sense of being borne triumphantly through the twilight, .faster and faster.. to the ends of the world. . ..

With brutal force the darkness smashed against my shoulder, sending me tumbling .. Far above me dim stars whirled, a magnetism pinning me down; a faint rumbling passing through my prone body. Am I still alive then? I wondered calmly.

The sudden clashing of feet on gravel and excited voices came to me with intense clarity. I opened my eyes to see Billy's face close to mine.

"You OK, Phil ?" He demanded kneeling down and raising my shoulders.

"Sure thing, matey.." I grinned, shutting my eyes as if to go to sleep.

"Yer a f-----' arsehole. Get up! "Billy hissed in my ear, dragging me to my feet.

I struggled to catch my balance, pressing the dull ache in my arm; gazing with stupefaction at the railway lines and beside them a line of concrete pillars; dimly realizing it was one of them that had knocked me down.

"We'se thought ya a gonna." Norrie guffawed.

"Zee helluva crazzey man!" Tad shrilled leaping about.

"Someone up there must be f-----n' looking after ya."
Billy grinned.

"Yeah.. I guess so…. "I laughed, feeling strangely happy as we walked on back beside the railway line; the only sound in the shadowy darkness the crunch and clink of stones beneath our feet, passing another of the concrete pillars. ..if I hadn't been leaning so far out, I would have been badly mangled .. perhaps killed.. I thought absently.

We passed into the dockyard gates, showing our passes to the impassive unsmiling official and into the glare of the floodlights lighting the deserted quayside.

In single file we thumped up the shaking gangway; halfway up I paused to look down at the gummy clumps of blue-green phosphorescence burning on the waters of the harbour; amazing to think they are living organisms, I mused gazing up at the faintly gleaming stars in the inky dark sky above. Absently I rubbed at my sore shoulder and here was I .. alive.. yes alive..

Chapter Twenty-Six

"So itsa goodbye to ha...The Peoples Republic of China... and the great Leader..ha.. great deceiver.. ha ha... "Old Pete wheezed out, the Shanghai shoreline vanishing behind a thick curtain of fog. "Be back. . I reckon we knows it.. by Harry.." he added between gasps.

But there was no response from the others lining the ship's side all of us it seemed entranced by the brightness filtering through the damp whiteness swirling around the ship, giving sudden glimpses of the shimmering waters outside the harbour.

Is there anything more wonderful in this world than putting to sea, I thought, my hand on the trembling bulwark wet with condensation; the slow beat of the engines running up my arm.

Yes, no doubt after a few days at sea the unchanging routine would become wearisome again but at this moment I could only exult; the steady roar of the engines from above merging with the thrashing sounds of water passing the hull below, the ship moving steadily towards the veiled brightness gleaming enticingly beyond.

Now at last we could forget the monotony of those days spent in the *Sailor's Palace*, our only entertainment ashore..

How we had begun to loath the grandiose building with it's dead echoing marble floors; resenting even the trickling fountain and lurid coloured lights amongst the plastic flowers and the screens with the propaganda and above all the banner insistently demanding: *Workers of the World Unite.*

Settled with glasses of foaming beer around a table in the vast stuffy ornate bar-room, now grown tediously commonplace, confident that the Officer that had cautioned us before wasn't in the room, we scoffed with savage glee at the very idea. Why would British Tars likes us want to unite with the Chinese or Russkies or Yanks.. or Japs.. or any others for that matter.… ? In low conspiratorial whispers we hatched various plans to sabotage the display .. only for our ingenious plans to dissipate in a beery daze; leaving us to wander back down the stair glaring impotently at the propaganda banner and dribbling fountain and plastic flowers and then carrying on into the shopping arcade salving our ill-humour by making loud sarcastic comments about the displays in the windows of the little souvenirs shops; occasionally entering to stare stupidly at the shelves crammed with jade and wood statuettes and fans and painted scrolls..

"For my mother.." I had grinned tipsily to the smiling fat-faced shop-keeper on a sudden impulse picking up a set of table linen embroidered with what I recognised was the Willow Pattern. "She's got a silver tea service with that pattern.. I had to polish it every Saturday .." I had added confidentially, immediately thinking how absurdly sentimental I was.

And then what had I done? I jeered silently gazing into the luminous mistiness left the brown paper parcel, neatly tied with string, in the taxi.. hadn't I.. Perhaps it was meant to be.. I mused grimly all that really mattered was that I was a member of crew on a bulk grain-carrier sailing across the Pacific .. ..

A sudden spasm rippled through the bulwark was followed by a low muttering from the men lined up against the ship's side.

I peered into the dull brightness picking out a short pointed silhouette, bristling with aerials, lying close to the water not far away.

"Navy.… huh patrol-boat.. Chinese .." Old Pete gawped.

"Really?" I said finding something menacing in the narrow grey shape, even as a swirl of fog blotted it from view.

Inexplicably the ship's engines died away leaving a spasmodic trembling, the harsh rush of water failing; the splashing of the bilge water audible. What was happening?

Were we being intercepted? There had been various rumours about some ship's being detained by the Chinese Authorities because of some breach of protocol by ship's crews. Perhaps Mitch had deliberately insulted some official. It would be just the sort of thing he would do. I stole a glance at the pudgy Assistant Steward, his swollen belly pressed against the bulwark. As if guessing my thoughts he jerked around.

"Summat on yer mind Pansy... "He leered, sidling menacingly towards me.

"No Mitch .." I stammered, my heart thumping, caught in his coldly vicious stare.

"So whatcha f----'n starin at me fer.." He snarled softly reaching out a tattooed arm and gripping my chin.

"Sorry.. .. sorry...... "I murmured abjectly; choked by an intense hatred; my legs trembling.

"Willie... !."

We all turned towards amidships doorway, Mitch releasing his hold on my chin. The Sec. stood balancing the soles of his feet on the sill of Amidships doorway; his voice stern and using Jock's name made it even more serious sounding.

"The captain wants you in his cabin smartish..."

Without a word Jock shuffled off quite unlike his usual combative self.

"Oh yes.. this is for you Wight.." The Sec produced a brown paper parcel tied with string. "It came aboard with the Pilot.. .. one of the taxi driver's handed it in it seems."

Absently I took the parcel, recognising at once my purchase from the souvenir shop in the arcade. So it had come back to me.. without my even making an attempt to get it back .. How strange.. my present for my mother.. and I suddenly felt an intense nostalgia.. .. my mother.. home .. yes home.. oh, how I wished I was going home.. So why had I spurned the offer from the officer in the Seaman's club to arrange my return to Vancouver? Yet even now I pressed myself the ship's side gripped by homesickness, I knew I would refuse again; quite as if

I had no will of my own and could only blindly follow some predestined path...

But what was happening with Jock? I wondered hearing the excited buzz of voices growing louder; some of the deck-crew having joined us at the ship's side.

"Dropping 'is kilt t'Chinks I bet. "One of them said to a roar of laughter.

Before long though Jock was back, a scowl on his craggy face shaking his head and ignoring all the excited questions he crossed to the ship's side, like a man in shock mumbling to himself.

"Aye aye.... Pack o' rogues o' a nation.. runnaagate shopkeeper. jest fer a kist..hoot maun..siller .. aye .siller that's what maks the warrld tick nae doot.. ."

We all followed his gaze to see a narrow black shape emerging from the shining curtain of mist, trailing a white froth across the harbour waters and heading directly towards us.

What can it mean? I wondered pressing hard against the ship's iron bulwark as if to convince myself I was really participating in these strange events.

Slowly a sampan, gunwales low on the water, pushing a white wave the clattering sound of the motor breaking the stillness of the morning, drew near the ship; clearly visible in the middle of the open deck was a square block wrapped in thick bundles of straw. How utterly mysterious.. And yet there must be a simple explanation surely; there always was, wasn't there?

But just then the Sec. came to the amidships doorway and ordered Billy and me back into the Pantry, sternly waving away my protests.

Through the pantry walls we could hear dull bangs and thumps .. and then muffled loud shouts .. the 1st Mate I guessed bellowing orders over a megaphone. No doubt they were unloading the crate from the Sampan.. What *could* it be? I recalled the grey, slim Patrol Boat; surely there had been a gun-turret on the forward deck.. if we had failed to stop would they have fired on us..? Perhaps it would have been known as the "The Shanghai Incident.." a Chinese Navy gunboat shelling a British registered grain carrier. .. hadn't there been something of the sort just after the end of the war?

"So what.." Billy grinned. "Don't make no difference to us do it...."

"I just would like to know .. that's all.." I sighed, just as the a shudder went through the Pantry walls followed by the familiar thudding; the crockery in the dresser clinking violently. We were under way again.

Quickly I went out of the pantry to the amidships doorway; all traces of mist had vanished; the sunlight glinting on the unbroken water. For a minute I stood still staring into the empty blue brightness before us lay the Pacific and somewhere far beyond the horizon, Australia.. suddenly aware of tears in my eyes, feeling strangely light; was I happy or sad? Both somehow..

"What a f---n' nutter Tad is.." Billy grumbled deftly flicking his cigarette butt over the stern-rail. "Who'da thought 'e done summat like that.."

I glanced aside at the lithe body hung between chair and rail, exposed to the burning sun, a grimace darkening his face. "A real nutter.." I muttered slipping back into a sun-dazed muse. Really though it was because we were so bored with the stultifying daily routine.. Desperate for something.. anything to break the monotony.. So in our imaginations we had made the oven-like steel hulk stuck somewhere in the midst of a blinding glittering, windless, cloudless Pacific into a make-believe world taken from Billy's war-comics where we were intrepid British Commandoes fighting a ruthless enemy.. the deck-boys variously Jerries or Japs or Eyties. Ignoring the puzzled looks and grins from crew and the oppressive heat we gleefully dodged around the afterdeck and up on the lifeboat deck shooting at each other with broken broom handles for make-believe guns.. being shot at and wounded .. and dramatically dying only to get up and begin again..

though eventually that had become to seem boring and we began thinking of other things we could.. Almost I thought as if some power was working in us to do something more exciting .. more extreme ..more violent ..

It had been me who had spotted the two deck-boys holystoning the wooden deck running alongside the Officer's Smoking room.

'How about water bombs.. they're sitting ducks' I had suggested that night and Billy at once had come up with the idea to fill condoms with water.

How gloriously hilarious it all had been, creeping up the stairs and out of sight of the Deck Boys on the other side of the smoking room and then exchanging farewells.

'Best of British..' 'Give Jerry hell old man..' We had joked grinning hugely and yet hadn't there been something deadly serious as we shook hands? Affirming an unspoken bond.. brothers in arms.. I had thought as I shimmied up the ladder on the outside of the Officer's Smoking Room.

'See you in Blighty..' I had giggled leaning back down to take up one of the water-filled condoms my voice almost lost in the roar of the engines.

Barely able to suppress my giggles I had crept over the roof of the Officer's Smoking Room; the smoke streaming from the funnel, the heated air shimmering in glare; in every direction a vast glinting sheen; the sun glowering fiercely down on me .

Looking down on the two kneeling figures, their forearms outstretched transforming the dirty brown planks into shining white then with guilty delight I had watched the water-filled condom wobbling through the sun's glare smashing down and bursting in an explosion of glittering droplets, just as Billy appeared around the corner to lob his. How funny Tad had looked staggering to his feet soaking wet from two direct hits, his thin, pocked face convulsed with a frenzied rage.

And Norrie still on his hands and knees dripping wet, dazed and bewildered ...

Excitedly I had made my way across the roof and back down the ladder to meet up with Billy.

"Caught with their pants down .." I grinned as we shook hands though secretly I was a little anxious thinking that Tad would be sure to seek revenge.. Well let him.. we would be on our guard..

But the days passed and Tad and Norrie seemed to be avoiding us cabin-boys if anything... and so we gave up any idea of further attacks on them and our make believe war-games; abjectly submitting to the unchanging daily routine; moving slowly, dully around, soaked in sweat, eating just enough to give us sufficient energy to move about ..

So it was that I nodded indifferently when the Sec. informed me that from now on I would begin my daily duties by first cleaning the Chief Engineer's Day room; a task ordinarily carried out by Old Pete but who was finding it difficult climbing the stairs to the top deck. Billy predictably gasped out a vague protest when I told him but really what difference did it make to me? Hadn't I long ago given up all self-determination ..self-will ..inner purpose..? No longer a thinking, feeling being I had become an automaton, a wind-up mechanism that could be set to work, to wash and wipe and wash and wipe until I was utterly worn out.. like the Chinese dock workers.. a husk of a human being..

With the indigestible ship's bread and sickly-sweet tannic tea swilling around my stomach, I now began my day by dragging a pail of water up the four flights of stairs and passing around the stair-well to the first door next to the Bridge.

As if magically I had been transported from the ship to an elegant sitting room on land was what had come to my mind the minute I had stepped inside; my eyes adjusting to the dim glow shed by two brass wall-lights; the engine's thud barely perceptible, breathing in the faint scent of cigars and leather a faint breeze stirring the gauzy curtains covering the glass doors the height of the room on the other side of the square room. I had gazed wonderingly around at the glossy parquet floor with a scattering of dark-red Persian rugs; one wall was completely covered by a glass book-case the shelves massed with dark green books with gold lettering that I on later examination I found out read: *The Proceedings of the Society of Marine Engineers.* Arranged around the wall of pale striped wallpaper were framed prints of English country scenes; a large pale wooden sideboard ran along another wall and above it was drinks cabinet lined with bottles of spirits and glasses securely held by chrome-plated clasps; beside a luxuriously soft white leather sofa was a glass-topped coffee table strewn with magazines.

How different my life at sea would be if I was an officer ..and this was my cabin I thought wistfully yet of course I knew it was impossible.. I was just a cabin-boy.. I belonged to the struggle and squabble of the crew in the suffocating, thudding world below decks; it was only by chance that I had been allowed to glimpse this other kind of life. .

'Just get on with it!' I had muttered echoing the Sec. but in despite crossed the room and pushing aside the floor-length gauze curtains I slid open the heavy glass doors.

Standing on the narrow balcony, my hands resting on the wooden rail with only the occasional spasm of vibration a faint salty breeze playing on my arms and face; never would I be able to escape from the burden of endless repetitive toil.. how dreary .. how pointless it all was.. I gloomed, staring blankly into the pale emptiness. A gasp came from my lips as a fiery red globe erupted into the shadowy vastness... Fixed by an awed delight I stayed watching as brilliant blood red streams pierced the firmament radiating over the glossy black waters; such splendour of dawn.. how blessed I was to witness this moment I mused distantly, shielding my eyes against the dazzling orange-red circle disseminating a blazing golden glow over sea and sky.. Without light and warmth of the sun, I considered nothing in this world could exist.. animals .. humans.. plants.. all would wither away in the cold eternal darkness.. really it was a blessing .. a beneficence to the entire world.. a universal goodness.. And everyday without fail.. for ages past and for ages to come the sun filled the darkness with light.. So I thought as I left the balcony and started dusting the room .. for me and all the other living creatures.. really I should be grateful for everything in my life. though even as I left the dawning sky with the joy pulsing through me I knew I would quickly let myself be worn down by the heat and fatigue... but tomorrow .. surely tomorrow and for days to come I would know again the pure joy at being alive witnessing the red fiery disc rising out of the dark horizon.

It was almost time for our afternoon break and I was giving a last weary swipe to the scratched counter-top when something made me look up. Two eyes stared fiercely at me through the open Pantry port-hole the bony face contorted in revengeful glee. Tad! Before I could say a word he raised his arm; there was an shrill insane shriek followed by sounds of crockery smashing then an awful silence, before the dull thud of the engines became audible again.

"You madman "I gasped, helplessly watching the dark red paint dribbling down the front of the dresser, spattered with red drops, on the floor the tin of paint oozed what was left of it's contents into a dark red puddle.

"Such a crazy thing to do.." I had exclaimed still seething with anger as Billy I worked through our entire afternoon break to remove the last traces of the red-lead paint.

"We'll f----n' get 'im fer it.." Billy had vowed scowling.

"Yeah.. make him suffer "I had snarled and yet somehow we both knew it was just bluster and that we didn't dare provoke Tad to even more extreme action. Who could say where it would end? And weren't we responsible for starting it …. Better just to passively submit to the remorseless routine of shipboard life and yet… …

"Ya don't give up d'ya.." Billy laughed seeing me bring out my pad and pen.

I shrugged; yes, Billy was right really it was pointless so I thought gazing absently into the vast shimmering blueness and the white frothing wake wavering away into the distance. We might never even reach land .. and yet there flickered within me faint and feeble, the need to defy in some way the numbing monotony of the endless-seeming days of heat and sweat and toil..

'Dear Mother and Father,

I'm writing this in somewhere in the middle of the Pacific.. I think we've passed the Equator though none of the crew seems sure of anything as usual. Perhaps they don't care.. We're on our way to some port in Australia. It's the same old routine that never changes so you lose all sense of time, we're sleeping out on deck it's so hot… you wouldn't believe how bright the stars are and so many.. there's been no sign of land for ages.. just ocean and more ocean you don't realize how vast the Pacific is until you sail across it.. all of us are longing for land…… just the mere sight of it… ..nothing but blue sea and blue sky.. day after day .. and so hot..

But I have to tell you about something that happened just as we were leaving Shanghai out of the fog this Chinese Navy patrol boat appears, next minute the ship's engines stop and we stop dead in the water no one knowing what's happening.. I already told you about the 2nd Cook a Scot who struts around like a bantam cock crowing "I'm Willie McClucky frae Auchtermuchty' though everyone calls him Jock or Jockie. Well he was ordered to report to the Captain! So really serious… Then Jock comes back down looking rather crestfallen and after awhile this sampan appears almost swamped by this great big square crate bound up with straw which was hoisted onto the deck.. Such a mystery .. Later we found Jock had ordered this chest (he calls it a "kist.") from a shop in the Shopping Arcade in what's called "The Sailor's Palace" the only place foreign sailors are allowed to go to. Billy and I had seen him go into a shop piled to the ceiling with furniture ..all massive stuff tables .. sideboards .. wardrobes .. all in dark woods. Anyway Jock must have been tipsy there's a enormous bar on the second floor and he loves Scotch whisky and ordered the chest from the shopkeeper then

*forgot all about it. But the shopkeeper didn't and must of
gone to the Chinese Port Authorities and got them to have
the ship stopped and the chest carried out. Jock had his pay
docked to which didn't please him at all. Later Billy and I
sneaked a look in his cabin The chest is so big there's almost
no room between the bed and the wall. So he has to climb
over it to get to bed! Billy and I couldn't stop laughing.
Actually I think it's an ugly thing with this heavy carving on
top and sides. Can you imaging what it will look like in the
front room of his "wee hoosie" joked that maybe he'll
charge admission for people to admire it. At first Jock was
angry about it and the crew teased him mercilessly. But then
began to change his story and insisted he had deliberately
planned it to have it delivered like that . Now I think he
even believes it himself.. even though it's so obvious the
shopkeeper had outsmarted him, with the help of the
Chinese authorities probably delighted to have an
opportunity to prove their superiority over the British. I
joked that it might have started a war .. like the war of
"Jenkins's Ear" only the "War of Willie's Kist" but no one
knew what I was going on about. I suppose that's really
why I went to sea to experience things like this .. to feel in
small way I'm part of history except it turned out to be a
farce! But sometimes history is farcical*

*I've have a new job in the morning- cleaning the Chief
Engineer's Day Room. Pete the Assistant Steward used to
do it. He says he can't climb the stairs to the top deck
anymore Billy thinks he's just malingering. I've never seen
the Chief Engineer he's meant to be dying of cancer but
keeps working to get the best pension for his wife. One day
I was dusting away when suddenly there were this sudden
loud cough through the wall where his bedroom cabin .My
heart almost stopped. The coughing went on and one as if
he was coughing up his lungs.. I was so relieved when it
finally stopped but then I began to worry that he might
have died! I was just going to open the door to look in
thinking I might find a corpse when thank goodness the
coughing started again . Billy says he wont last out the*

voyage.. quite a thought isn't it.. that we're sailing with a man whose might die any minute. Billy says I'm stupid to do the extra work but it's very easy .. just dusting. As I said his cabin is on the top deck it's really big and luxurious you'd never guess when that you're in on ship at sea.. none of the diesel and cooking and bilge smells we get in our cabin and you can barely hear the engines .. and so very posh .. cocktail cabinet etc. On the far wall there's a sliding window which opens onto an outside narrow balcony every morning first thing I step outside and watch the sun come up such an amazing experience .. one minute this empty shadowy darkness and then up pops this fiery red ball.. and each time I feel such joy.. light coming into the world.. of course it doesn't last but at least I experienced it for a few minutes .. helps to keep me going ..

The other day I had a turn at the wheel the Bo'sun organized it for me, he seems to have taken a shine to me.. It seems an easy enough thing.. to keep the wheel steady .. .

I stopped writing thinking back to when I had nervously gone with the Bo'sun to the bridge even then doubtful of my abilities and yet the Bo'sun had been so confident that I would make a first-class helmsman; repeatedly patting me on the back and smirking: 'You'll bloody show'em Phil.. A born natural bloody sailor if ever I saw one...."

How I wanted it to be true. But when the Bo'sun after escorting me to the bridge door had left me, the door clicking shut behind me I was shaking with nerves; Billy was right. I should stick to being a cabin-boy.. Why .. .why had I agreed to this..

The 2nd Mate nodded distantly at me from across the bridge the other officers on duty were outside on the wings of the bridge. I hesitated glancing towards the gangly figure of Hank the Yank, raised on the wooden grating.. his legs apart, his large hands grasping the brass-tipped spokes of the wheel. From behind the droopy moustaches he had given me a sleepy smile which encouraged me but then I heard whispered giggles and guessed that it was the Irish Sparkies probably watching me from behind the curtain of the wireless room. "Perhaps ..I shouldn't.." I had murmured half turning but Hank had already stepped back and motioned me forward. Standing in front of the wheel, almost as tall as myself, I had grasped the brass-tipped spokes; smoothed by the calloused hands of innumerable seamen I had thought . 'Keep the lines matched up ..' Hank had explained in soft American drawl pointing to a fine red line above a broad dark line beneath the glass dome of the binnacle. "Don't jerk. Smooth and easy ." He had added and then stepped away leaving me by myself desperately clutching the spokes.

My eyes had watered as I had stared intently at the two lines on the binnacle, jerking at the wheel to keep lined up.

This was it.. a supreme moment in my life.. now I would prove I was a seaman; only my arms and legs were trembling and I felt dizzy and faint, sweat tricking down my face and back.

As in a dream I saw the two lines in the binnacle had diverged and I had jerked at the wheel. . . too much.. now back again... the wheel slippery... a roaring in my ears.. Already the two lines were moving apart again.. my legs and arms had lost all sensation ...through the Bridge window a dazzling emptiness glared pitilessly .. It was hopeless... yes utterly hopeless..'Enough.. that's enough..' I had finally muttered stepping back my arms hanging limply aching painfully. For a second I had stood dazedly watching Hank's big clumsy hands caressing the wooden spokes, then I had turned and fled, desperate to get away.

In a way I had done quite well... for a first time, I had consoled myself as I walked back down the afterdeck to rejoin Billy at the stern. Really I should think of becoming a sailor.

"Not so hard.." I had said nonchalantly coming around the corner of the poop deck.

"Says you .." Billy had laughed, raising his body to point over the stern. "Look out there .."

For a minute I had stared wonderingly, the gleaming white wake running straight from the ship before forming large ragged zigzags floating away on the glittering blue water clearly visible. No doubt the whole ship would be talking about how I had failed. I shouldn't have even tried.. it was all pointless..

"Hey watcha doing..?" Billy demanded.

"No point is there .." I said grimly throwing the crumpled up blue airmail over the rail and watching it flutter away and vanish into the frothing, swirling waters below. Yes .. pointless..... ..

CHAPTER TWENTY-SEVEN

"I still can't well.. believe it." I said to Billy. "It must have given the Sec. a real shock when he went into his cabin.."

"Yeah.. musta.." Billy frowned "We all gotta f----n' go someday... matey."

"Yeah I know.. but who'd a thought.." I gestured towards the Pantry Hatch. "I keep expecting him to shove his big head through and huff and puff about something. He kept telling me he was going to leave the ship once we got to Fremantle. Only now he'll never get the chance.. poor old Smelly. ."

I turned back to the sink. Was I really sorry? Wasn't I rather enjoying the excitement .. the drama of it.. a death at sea...... with everyone talking about it... shaking their heads.. and trying to look solemn. Jock shaking his head and invoking gloomily the 'Grrrrrim Rrrrreaper..' And Mitch making cynical comments that made me grin despite myself..

"Hey Phil ya wanta t'a see 'im?" Billy asked suddenly. "I got the key to Cold-Store fer later.. Unless yer scared .. .."

"Nah.." I laughed wiping my hands; the first time I've seen a dead body I thought following Billy out of the Pantry and down the Companionway.

"They should have buried him at sea... "I said my heart beginning to thump as I stood watching Billy fit the key into the padlock. "You know Chips sewing a shroud and putting a last stitch through his nose to make sure he's really dead.. Everyone on deck.. the 1ˢᵗ Mate reading the 'Funeral Service for Use at Sea' and then over the side and splash! Straight to the bottom. Food for the fishes. A lot of food!. I added with a giggle.

"You don't 'alf natter sometimes .." Billy growled finally opening the clasp on the padlock and dropped the steel bar retaining the zinc-plated door. "'Ave to be autopsy when we get to Aussie won't there.."

"It's cold! "I exclaimed as we stepped inside; the heavy door closing behind us with a dull clack.

"What yer expect.. f------n' Cold Store ain't it" Billy grinned switching on a light.

The fluorescent tubes stopped flicking and I could look around the small square white-tiled room, in the middle a wooden butchers block and rack with knives and cleavers; the chilled, stale air smelling of blood.

"In here.. Phil.." Billy called crossing to the far side of the room and pulling aside the heavy yellowing-plastic curtains.

Hesitantly I slipped through the curtains, recoiling at the touch of the clammy cold plastic against my skin. Shivering in the sub-zero air I peered through a wreathing mist; impaled on hooks attached to tracks running the length of the ceiling were rows of headless carcasses, legs sticking out, every part coated with a sparkling white fur.

"Over here.." Billy called pointing to a long mound on the floor at the side of the room.

My arms wrapped around my body I stared down at the bulky form wrapped in several layers of frosted plastic; trying to make out the features on what I took to be the head.. imagining the mouth wide open, sightless eyes staring regretfully up at me. No, I hadn't been very nice to him.. 'Sorry old Pete 'I murmured to myself..

There was a rustling crackling noise. Was he moving?

"Let's go.. .." I yelped turning away and plunging through the plastic curtain.

I stood aside shivering uncontrollably despite the heat of the companionway as Billy put back the bar and clasped the padlock

"I thought he was coming back from the dead.." I sniggered. "It's the first time I've ever seen.. anyone.. . you know.. well.. dead.".

Billy shrugged, "Me grandpa was like that fer days .. family arguin' about who'se ta pay fer his f----n' funeral. Us nippers kept go'in up t'ave a look at 'im, f------n' yella like wax, stiff as aboard on 'is bed."

"And we weren't very nice to him. Calling him Old Smelly… "I said as we went back down the Companionway.

"Well he f-----n' did! N' breath like paint. "Billy laughed. "Anyway no one gives a toss about 'im"

"I suppose not.." I sighed back at sink. "I remember he told me once his mother had died when he was a boy. father a heavy drinker I think.. brought up by a granny in some remote place in Northern Canada. He said he married .. then divorced children too ..hadn't seen any of them for thirty years or something …A real loner in the end.. I guess.."

"Yeah.. well it was 'is choice weren't it…" Billy growled.

"Yeah.. though I guess we all loners.. in the end.. Isn't that what they say.. you arrive alone and go alone.."

"Get a move on will ya.. we'll never get to the cribbage." Billy snapped irritably.

"Yes sir! "I jibed; through the porthole I could see some of the Deck Crew coming along the Foredeck, indistinct shapes in the fading light, talking and laughing loudly.

How little any of them cared that death had taken one of their own… and might again…. death .. so close ..at any moment I thought; shivering as if the chill of the cold-store was in my bones.

Hey that reminds me!" I gasped as I passed the Head on our way to the Crew Mess.." One day I came in Old Pete was on the toilet wheezing away to himself 'Gonna make it.. by Harry .. Gonna make it 'But he didn't .. did he ?"

Nah! Stupid old git.." Billy snapped. "Jest ferget 'im will ya.."

Out of the vicious hissing and cracklings a jazzy bluesy dance music, swelled and rang off the steel walls of the Crew Mess; blotting out the dull throbbing of the engines.

"Gershwin.." Hank pronounced solemnly one hand on the tuning knob of the small wooden radio-set fixed to the wall; a blissful look to his thin lined face as he turned towards the other seamen seated around the tables in the Crew Mess.

I stopped abruptly moving the matchstick peg up the cribbage board. Where had I heard that tune.. Yes.. the last dance at the Graduation Ball.. How long ago that seemed .. years on years.. and the anguish and misery of that evening almost forgotten.. rather a dim nostalgia. Yes.. how innocent I had been.. I thought pushing back my chair, stepping away from the table the music swaying irresistibly through me.

"Yer f-----n nuts Phil.." I heard Billy call out; my arms wrapped about my body, I waltzed dreamily around; the fluorescent-lit room slowly rotating around me; recalling the girlish stiffness of her warm body, the sickly fragrance of the Gardenia bouquet..

As I turned once more I glimpsed the Bo'sun standing in the doorway an admiring smirk on his face, slapping his hands together.

At once I stopped moving the music already beginning to waver and fade; the steel walls of the Crew Mess ringing to loud clapping and cheering.

"A dancer a tha....! "A voice boomed in my ears and before I could think Hobbsie had stuck out ham-like arms and lifted me off my feet.

"Hey......" I protested feebly, gasping at the heavy body smells.

"Daance.. daance my little laaddie.. Daance fer tha daddie.." Hobbsie bellowed as he ruthlessly spun me around like a rag doll, blood rushing to my head, a blur of grinning faces careering past.

"Easy does it Hobbsie!"

"Tha'll maak him siick.. maan.."

I heard a couple of the seamen shout and then ever more angry shouts as the dance music was overwhelmed by static cracklings, whistles and ear-piercing screeches.

"Tha can sit next one oout! "Hobbsie guffawed releasing me from his grasp to stagger dizzily back to my seat, feeling distinctly nauseous, the room still turning slowly; raucous shouts and harsh laughter echoed around the steel walls; the lined weathered faces staring gargoyles;

from the other side of the room I noticed Old Paddy was looking wonderingly at me; a benign smile on his thin lips. What had possessed me?

Once again we had taken our mattresses up to the life-boat deck to escape the stultifying heat of the cabin. Lying on my back I studied the dark smoke bulging and thinning as it rose from the funnel towards the distant glittering stars.

"Hey what was that?" I exclaimed my eyes catching a sudden flicker of white overhead"

"Dunno...." "Billy yawned.

"Amazing they can see to fly.. it's so dark out there.." I murmured. "Chips says they're the souls of the sailors died at sea.. Perhaps it was Old Pete.."

Yer f-----n' bonkers." Billy growled.

"Not fat enough ?" I giggled "Hey that reminds me Chips keeps a little bird you know. He found it on deck in the dawn one morning.. blown out from land by storm.. Half dead .. he nursed it back to life."

"So what?" Billy scoffed. "Don't know what ya does with that nutty old codger."

"Well he's showing me how to tie knots like a Turk's Head"

"Shut it will ya.." Billy snapped. "Get some f----n' sleep..."

"Sure ..yeah.." I murmured turning over wondering why Billy objected to my spending part of the afternoon break with the ship's carpenter. As a cub scout I had been fascinated that a line could be manipulated in so many different ways.. even now I remembered the adage: sheep shank shortens.. But it was more than just about tying knots wasn't it?

Once through the doorway into the eerie silence of the fore deck rhythmically rising and falling, I felt myself become strangely lighter.. all my worries falling away .. ..

Invariably I would find Chips busy with some work sitting tailor-fashion on a rope-mat in the shade of the No.1 Hatch Block where he had his workshop.

'All your tools so tidy ..! 'I had commented on my first look inside; above a much-scarred workbench with a vice and grind-stone were rows and rows of tools, each held in place by leather strap; along with hammers and screw-drivers I had noticed the barber's scissors and clippers and comb.

'Aye.. laddie ..thee can aye tell what like a man is by the way he looks after his tools.' Chip's had replied gravely.

How true I had thought, ashamed of my own careless ways.

Under Chips's guidance I was tying a Turk's Head threading the thin line in and out and around until it was a solid round ball, heavy enough to weight a throwing line; such an amazing thing I thought when with Chip's help I had managed to complete one. It was then I had become aware of an insistent rather metallic clicking sound.

Seeing my puzzled look Chips had reached into his overalls and taken brought out some bread. Perhaps he is mad, I had thought confusedly as he broke off a tiny piece and tossed it onto the deck. At once a small olive-brown bird with a pointed beak had fluttered down from the workshop bench and began pecking the crumbs, now and then cocking it's head to look up at the old seaman with bright eyes as if in thanks.

'Somebody who enjoys Jock's bread anyway.' I had joked as Chip's scattered a few more pieces; explaining how he had come across the tiny feathered body lying on the deck early one morning.

'Thought it were a bit of old tow or summat..' He had smiling added. "Then when I picked him good lord, he were warm.. eyes kept closing.. guessed he was a gonner right enough. Put him uner the shirt next my chest. Later fed him bread soaked in milk."

I had nodded touched that this hardened old seamen could feel such a kindness for this tiny feathery creature.

After that each time I visited Chips had enticed the bird out of the workshop by throwing crumbs and I had watched fascinated as if fluttered down to peck up the crumbs pausing to cock it's head on one side.

'What a shock he must have had! 'I had laughed. 'There he is flitting from tree to tree getting on with his life and then without warning a storm blows up and whoosh there he it out of sight of land.'

"How desperate he must have felt .." I had gone on encouraged by Chips's knowing smile. "Nothing but empty ocean below and he's getting weaker and weaker.. and finally falls down and lands on a ship .. and is found by you .. What astonishingly good luck. Of course bad luck to be blown away in the first place.'

'Aye thee says well Sonny .." Chips had replied. 'None of us knows what's acoming to us.. good or bad..or which is which..'

I had nodded remembering how Chips had spent weeks alone on the raft in the middle of the ocean before being rescued

'A bit frightening that isn't it not knowing from one second to another what's going to happen to us next.' I had commented watching the little bird boldly hop onto Chips's finger and begin to busily preen itself.

Chips had lifted his eyes to the sky .

'Beast or man we're all under Him above.' He had said rising slowly and putting the bird back onto the work bench.

Could that be true? I had wondered realizing that I had let the line I was knotting become tangled. How possibly could God know about every minute detail of every single life on earth? Surely that was impossible..

"It tangles itself. "I had complained finally surrendering the line to the old seaman and bemusedly watching his gnarled mottled hands deftly unpick the tangle.

'Aye laddie .. it do.. reckon there be some mystery there .. yer single line.. it'll kink.. and tangle and knot itself enough to drive yer mad.. yet somehow it be for some proper purpose I don't doubt"

"Perhaps.." I had murmured doubtfully.

What was the little birds name? Lying in the darkness I shut my eyes in an effort to remember; after awhile Chips's words came into my mind: 'Call's him 'Natty' don't I. After an old shipmate. Kinda reminds me of him.. small lively kinda seaman cheerful type always whistling some tune.. . 'Yes that was it Natty.. after some old shipmate..

'Did something happen..to your shipmate I mean..' I had asked guessing at something eventful.

Chips had slowly bent his silvery-grey head . 'Aye.. let's see.. all of ten years ago now that Natty was lost at sea.. freak wave.. one minute on deck working to secure the cargo.. next gone..' Chips had stared thoughtfully out over the vast glinting vastness. 'Body never recovered. Aye resting in the bosom of the ocean 'He had added after awhile

'Do you believe you know there's a soul.. a spirit in us… even after death .. that lives on..' I had asked wonderingly.

"And what be your opinion, sonny?" Chips had responded with a chuckle, his blue eyes fixed on me.

I had shrugged, staring at my completed Turk's Head; was it possible? Could a spirit survive the death of the material body?

"What do you think? Is there life after death?" I had appealed to the old ship's carpenter unable to commit myself either way.

"Can't really be otherwise can it?" Chip's had said smiling kindly. 'Too much tells us it must be so…'

It was then I had spotted white shapes skimming swiftly over the water surface.

"Chickens! "I had laughed when Chips had told me that sailors called them Mother Carey's Chicken and they promised fair weather and safe landfall.

'Some do say they're the souls of mariners drowned at sea..' he had added musingly.

For long while I had gazed after the white flecks until they were lost in the shimmering brightness.

Just a sailor's superstition, I sighed staring up at the wisps of cloud drifting over the vast dark of the night sky and then above countless, numberless glittering starry points in an infinite universe…. How insignificant we were compared to the eternity of time and space.. thinking of the ship forging a solitary path through the vastness of the Pacific.. To what end… .to make the ship-owners and grain-farmers rich? To give employment to the sailors..? To bring life-saving sustenance to the famine-stricken Chinese? But did it really matter if they all starved to death? How many had already died.. and since the beginning of the world how many millions upon millions upon millions had died of disease .. famines… plagues… wars.. So what did a few more or even a few million more matter..? The world was doomed anyway wasn't it . .On the brink of a worldwide nuclear conflict, bombs vastly more powerful than the ones that devastated Hiroshima and Nagasaki.. incinerating all living things in all-consuming infernos .. followed by a cloud of radioactive-fallout slowly but inevitably annihilating all living creatures.. . And even if that didn't happen.. the world would come to an end one way or another one day…. And yet still the stars would shine down ..utterly indifferent to the extinction of humankind… and individuals like me.. yes death was the only reality.. so why bother about anything..? Ultimately it was all pointless.. meaningless.. hopeless..

I pressed my face into the mattress oppressed by the thought of nothingness .. feeling an unbearable loneliness.. an utter hopelessness..

I stirred half-rising; thinking that I must had fallen asleep and had been dreaming .. vaguely remembering being in an empty street and not knowing where I was…. abandoned.. alone..

Just a dream I tried to reassure myself, turning to the shadowy hump a little distance away.

"Billy.. Hey Billy.. . "I whispered, but there was no response; perhaps he had gone to the head..

"Bloody feelin' lonesome Phil?… Stars does that to ya..out in middle of ocean .far from home.. makes ya feel like nothing sort of.."

"I guess so.." I answered calmly wondering how the Bo'sun came to be talking to me or was he part of my dream?

"Betcha bloody misses yer ma.. and pa.. Sea can be a mighty lonely place sure enough. Yer needs a friend to look after ya...."

"I don't know.. I just don't know.." I whispered sadly, raising my head to the small shape hunkered down beside me.

"See that Hobbs should never be allowed to fling ya about like that.." The Bo'sun murmured reaching out at a hand. "Yer needs someone to protect ya"

"Maybe..." I murmured indifferently, distantly aware of my hair being lightly stroked; soothing and troubling....

"Like I told ya Phil.. Gomer's always ready to help. Be a pal t'ya.. older brother.. heh..father more like.."

I felt my lips gape in response, the softly lilting voice reassuring, the firm, even stroking moving ever further down my spine. I trembled spasmodically, a piercing tingling ache.. glowing. . spreading .... insistently... thrillingly... exquisitely pleasurable....

"What yer say Phil? Hows yer come my cabin.."

"Sure.. Why not .." I murmured submissively; hadn't he saved my life once? I thought slowly getting to my feet and following across the deck and down the stairs, the glare of the arc-lights briefly illuminating the curly hair of the small figure his head bent, a few steps ahead.

Beside the shiny watery darkness, the after-deck stretched out into a shadowy gloom; really as if I'm dreaming I thought, only the rough, hot deck under my bare feet felt real..

"C'mon Phil.." The Bo'sun encouraged; a twisted look on his face as he passed by a bulkhead light.

"O.K. O.K.." I grumbled but why was I doing this? Was I really that sort? Perhaps I was .. a shudder went through me; what did it matter anyway. ..nothing mattered.. did it?

I paused, imagining foot-steps behind me. Had Billy followed me perhaps? I looked around but everything was subsumed in the black shadows.., the distant roar and thud of the engines the only sound... yet something had moved ..half-imagining a face peeping around the corner.. grinning knowingly..

Surely not.. Out of the darkness from the corner of my eyes I saw a flash.. shooting stars.. or lighting perhaps. I took a deep breath sucking in the hot air, rich with earthy, leafy scents.. We must be near land, I mused.. land yes, land.. picturing the tall leafy woods near my home, the broken sunlight the smell of ferns and mouldering leaves.. What was that? A faint sound; like someone calling my name 'Phiilliip !' just some seabird...

"Yar com'in Phil.." The Bo'sun's croaked impatiently.

I glanced at the small figure hidden in the shadows, a stubborn resistance rising in me; why should I? I thought with sudden contempt.

I turned around hearing the clang of quick footsteps that suddenly slowed and stopped.. ..

I kept on, with a final effort pulling myself up the handrail, stumbling across the deck.. collapsing onto the mattress.

"Hey.. Phil!.. ..Phil!"

I stared blankly at Billy, his hands shaking my shoulders.

"Yer shouting yer f-----n' 'ead off .. Yer'll bring t' Watch t'see what's f------n' 'appening'."

"The Watch? Oh yes them. . I was dreaming.. I think yes dreaming.. awful dream.. the Bo'sun.. and ..Mitch.. all a terrible muddle.." I shook my head.

"Time we'se was goin' down.." Billy said yawning.

"Sure .. yeah.." I murmured rolling up the mattress.

Following Billy down the stairs I glanced a pale greyness covering the sky, a faint gleam on the horizon; soon it would be dawn .. a new day beginning..

CHAPTER TWENTY-EIGHT

This is how it must have been for the first explorers, I thought, the air humid and windless, the ship moving slowly down the broad waters of the estuary; how excited they must have been, not knowing what lay around the next bend, probably a little apprehensive too though .. .

I kept at the ship's side absentmindedly watching the bow-waves rippling leisurely out over the milky waters; was I still hoping for a letter from home then. . .?

The first time I had picked out the dark outline of the Australian landmass on the horizon I had a sudden, certain conviction that there wouldn't be a letter for me. Yet how little that seemed to matter at the time.. . Like the rest of the ship I was once again gripped by shore-fever.. and Billy and I spent every free moment talking over and over what a great time we would have once we were ashore again ..

But now as I gazed at the grey margins of the Swan River fading into an overcast sky, the sun glaring faintly behind the thin layer of clouds, I was gripped by a uncertainty; would it really be so wonderful.. ? And watching a shiny blue pilot launch, a whitish smudge at the bows come churning swiftly past, I had a sense of events working to some end, blindly indifferent to my expectations ...

I sighed; better get back to work I thought before the Sec. finds me.. what a hard task-master he is, I mused stepping into amidships...

Once the florescent tubes had flashed into a glaring brightness I closed the metal door to the cold-store behind me, glancing perfunctorily towards the thick plastic curtains covering the door of the freezer-room; almost forgetting that Old Pete's corpse was lying inside frozen stiff; shipboard life carrying on quite as if he had never existed.. .

Before long small flies began to buzz around me trying to settle on my face and arms.

"Go away .." I shouted irritably, vainly striking at them ; yet flies were a sure sign we were close to land. . earth .. growth and decay.. life really..

But how unfair it was of the Sec. to give me these awful jobs, I thought inwardly picking up the wire- brush to scrub the butcher's block, it's deeply scarred surface coated with dried blood, fat and bone fragments. Very quickly the wire bristles became clogged with a gooey, grey paste which I had then to dislodge with an old knife.

Surely there must be a better way.. and yet when I had said this to Billy he had shrugged indifferently. "That's 'ow we always done it.." Was his response.

A vague despair settled over me. . . Really it was unbearable hopeless.. the greasy, gummy muck, the circling buzzing flies, the smell of dried blood..

'Christmas.. soon it would be Christmas' Why had that come into my mind? Surely I was glad that I wouldn't be home for Christmas .. all that fuss about presents.. and going shopping. .. with the crowds.. the shops blasting out carols music on loudspeakers so even walking along the streets you couldn't escape the fake, synthetic, forced cheeriness…. Yes really I was glad that I wouldn't be home for Christmas.

The sound of the steel-door closing with a soft clunk made me start, I looked up to see Mitch standing inside, his puffy face a bright red, staring intently at me. Perhaps he wants to get something, I thought my heart beginning to race.

"Like showin' yer arse don't ya. ." Mitch said shuffling unsteadily towards me, his arms hanging down. "Dancin' about t' f-----g Crew Mess…"

He's been drinking, I thought absently his beery stale breath spreading through the cold air.

"Now the Sec. n' that f----n' fat lump of lard ain't in the way…." Mitch sneered lewdly amiably. "Just youse n'me ..what yer say..darlin'?"

"No.. not really…." I stammered backing away; my legs trembling.

"Does it t'yereself does ya.. Is that why yer spotty?" Mitch jeered slowly following me across the room.

Involuntarily I touched at a pimple on my cheek.

"Or maybe yer does it with them f----g carcasses."

I shook my head, my back against the plastic curtains of the Freezer Room. If only Old Pete could come back to life I thought, fantastically imagining the white frosted hulk rising up.. advancing indomitably.. ham-like arms wide .. ready to crush Mitch to a pulp...

"Gotcha yer f----n' sneaky poncy faggot.." Mitch snarled one hand grasping at my shoulder.

"Please don't.." I demanded strangely calm.

"Or what yer f-----g pansy . ?" Mitch gasped, threads of spittle drooling from the corners of his mouth.

Blindly I lunged forward with both hands sending Mitch, arms waving backwards and down onto the floor.

In amazement I stared at the pudgy body, struggling drunkenly back onto his feet; had I done that ?

"Really sorry Mitch.. . ." I said grinning nervously jerking back at the sudden blow to my jaw, hearing a faint crack.

"Bet yer sorry now." Mitch rasped, in a crouch swinging his arms fixing me with a fierce glare.

"One day you'll be sorry too Mitch.." I said with composed authority, meeting his eyes unflinchingly.

Mitch frowned and shook his head and then lowered his arms.

"Maybe that'll learn ya.." He muttered and abruptly turned away

I watched the short figure waddle over to the door, struggle to open it and then disappear out into the Companionway, leaving the door open.

So that's that, I thought with mingled relief and exhalation; going and over and carefully closing the door.

I wiped at the dribble on chin and then studied the pale pink foam on the back of my hand, putting a finger into my mouth I felt along one side of my jaw, coming to a tooth that moved back and forth.

Looks like I've lost another tooth, I thought absently returning to scrubbing the butcher's block; my own words echoing in my head: 'Someday you'll be sorry too..' What had I meant? How strange; the words coming of themselves; and how absolutely fearless I had been.. as if from something outside myself...

I glanced back at the yellowed plastic curtains shielding the freezer-room.

"Thanks old Smelly "I grinned.

Above the door hung a painted sign of a squat whitish bird a single yellow eye and red beak at the end of a short neck; above large black letters read: *THE SWAN*.

Really more duck than swan, I thought smiling, following Billy and the two Deck Boys down a passageway and into a large L-shaped bar-room reeking with stale cigarette smoke.

One after another we stomped across the rough wooden floor to one of the small round tables, the tops ringed with water marks and pulled up the flimsy bent-wood chairs; our voices sounding loudly in the empty room.

"Aussie style.." Norrie bellowed reappearing from a small door set in a partition across the room and thumping a large jug brimming with beer onto the table.

"Cheers .." We chorused grinning at each other.

Shipmates ashore, I mused taking a long draught of the warmish beer but still felt myself as one apart and took another long gulp beer... Yes ..that was the way to dissolve into the surroundings.. get rid of the self-consciousness...

I looked up absently hearing my name.

"Billy here says ya had a go at Mitch.." Norrie said a smirking grin on his round face.

"Sort of .. he went for me and well I sort of retaliated..."

I looked away across the room, recalling the scene in the cold- store the day before and yet strangely distant.. Had it changed me in some fundamental way though ? .

"Zee.. brava man..hero. "Tad squealed.

I shrugged modestly, using my tongue I touched the wonky tooth; oddly it seemed much firmer; could it be it was healing itself?

"Better watch yerself..just the same .. 'e'll f-----n' stick a knife in yer some day." Billy growled from behind a haze of cigarette smoke.

"Ezz one bad man.." Tad giggled, spattering the table top with specks of beer froth.

"Nown worst.." Norrie boomed.

"Yeah.." I grinned complacently; could it be that I had lost my fear of Mitch?

I took a long swallow of beer my mind going back to just before we docked.. under a diffuse glowering sun, the far bank of the Swan River appeared a faint margin of scrubby trees and bushes merging into the glaring grey sky.. a land stubbornly unresponsive to human influence, I had thought.. .

'I wonder what Old Pete would have said..' I had mused out loud, glancing aside at the two Cooks and Mitch staring out over the sluggishly rippling water.

'He always had some interesting facts to impart…' I had added hiding a smile.

'Don't do 'im much good now, do it..' Ronnie had whined.

'A guid maun fer all a'that…' Jock had groaned..

'When yer dead yer dead.' Mitch had growled turning to me.

I had smiled confidently back quite as if I knew more than I was willing to say.

It was then a plaintive squeaking had made us all look around. Balancing awkwardly on the sill of the Amidships doorway, unshaven and dishevelled, his pot-belly sticking out of his unbuttoned officer's jacket was the Chief Steward.

For a minute or two he had stood rubbing his eyes staring indignantly at us.

'Lazy louts..the lot of you ..get to work at once' He had shrilled pathetically before disappearing back inside.

'F----n' drink yerself t'death.' Mitch had taunted.

I had grinned gleefully; so it was true! Mitch had fallen out with his old crony during a drinking bout. But then glancing at Billy beside me scowling down at the turgid waters below I had felt uneasy. . could it happen to us? Distantly I had become aware that our movement along the river was becoming slower and slower, as if we had lost all purpose and we were merely drifting with the tidal flood. Was it inevitable we would go our different ways .. I had mused absently studying the flotsam bobbing slowly along the hull until excited voices had made me look up.

A passenger liner, had come abreast of us, a gleaming white shape against the pale grey sky.

'Suum ship thaat.. *Canberra*' one of the Deck-Crew passing by had exclaimed, telling us it was the latest *P&O* Liner shaking his head over the problems they were having with the engines.

I had surveyed the ultra-modern, stream-lined shape the covered decks in tiers, studded with rows of portholes, the narrow curving bridge close to the sharply cut bows; wisps of white smoke trailed from the low, sharply-raked funnel.

'More like a f----n' toilet boawl.' Mitch had jeered winking at me.

'Not a real ship..' I had agreed at once.

Mitch had then begun to recount the battles he had witnessed when a Steward on liners between jealous 'Queens'. "'Leave 'im alone darling or I'll scratch yer bleeding eyes out..'" He had simpered amusingly in a falsetto; going on to describe vicious fights sometimes with razor-sharp filleting knives between the brawny seamen with their exaggerated feminine mannerisms in the galley, far away from the staid world of the passengers.

How awful I had thought made conscious of my ignorance of what went on in the real world.. .

Ronnie not to be outdone had begun to boast of how when working as a Kitchen Porter on Cunard Liners he had been lured into the 1st Class cabins by rich, glamorous women who loved nothing better than a tough, rough willing sailor.

Billy too had then began speaking about his experiences as a cabin-boy on different *Castle Line* ships and how he had spurned the determined advances of rich women passengers when serving them tea in their cabins.

"Really?" I had exclaimed picturing the luxurious cabin interior the plush opulence reflected in the large mirrors; a beautifully dressed, elegantly coiffured woman smiling enticingly.

'Any old scrag 'll do fer Phil...' Billy had said and the others had roared with laughter.

Now recalling it I flushed hotly again; did Billy somehow despise me?

"Hey Phil..!"

"Ezz dreamin' of zee women...!"

"Your turn matey..!"

"Sure thing..." I said cheerily snatching up the large glass jug. Am I drunk already? I wondered walking carefully across the room glancing down at my shiny leather shoes, remembering my doubtful excitement dressed in my shore-clothes swaggering casually down the gangway after the others, marvelling at the the shock of solid land beneath my feet as we crossed the dockside.. the ship once again fixed to the land by the swooping hawsers... the rat-catchers shining in the late afternoon sunshine.. the Dock Gates.. unmanned ..wide open.. and before us Fremantle.. Australia.. . once again we were British Tars ashore.. only somehow it seemed different this time..

I shrugged off the thought and put my hand to the narrow door set in a panelled booth, it sprang open and I stumbled inside, the flimsy door banging shut behind me.

Pressing myself against the small counter I could just see through an open hatch to the front bar-room, seeing a section of the counter and the rows of bottles and glasses behind it.

As I waited patiently the low growl of men's voices and the smell of stale beer took me back to a time as a small boy when on an errand to the local public house to get beer for my grandfather, severely crippled after an accident in a wartime munitions factory, recalling how proudly I had carried the china jug covered with a square of white cloth fringed with coloured beads entrusted to me by my grandmother, the coins hot in my other hand, when reaching a side-door up several steps I had entered a cubicle enclosed by frosted glass panels and putting the jug and the money on the counter almost level with my head I had waited patiently to be served..

Now here I was waiting to be served again but now a sailor off a ocean-going ship ..on the other side of the world.. how amazing .. almost inconceivable..

"Yes . ." A low calm voice demanded; a woman's form and face presenting itself on the other side of the counter.

"Another jug please.." I muttered hastily averting my eyes from her beautifully defined features.

Silently she picked up the jug passing gracefully under the hatch to the front bar.

I pressed against the counter, feeling my heart beating heavily; how amazingly beautiful she was ..a loveliness beyond all I had ever known.. or imagined.. ..

The voices of the men at the front bar came to me ; loud brash, twangy voice; uncompromising.. unhesitating.. ..

"What yer say mateys. .."

"Same again, my girl!"

"Make it a double Elly lass.."

How sure they are of themselves, I thought with an envious sigh. So her name must be Ella.. Ella .how lovely .. perhaps though it was short for Helen. . .

Perhaps I could begin a conversation with her, I thought: 'By the way is Ella short for Helen? Do you know the line from Marlowe's Faust?" the face that launched a thousand ships. ." I frowned, that sounded as if was showing off. How about: 'Pleased to meet you Ella ..my name's Phillip.. a cabin-boy off *MV Grimethorpe*....just docked, you see, my first time in Fremantle.. more than three weeks at sea.. out of sight of land.. being so long at sea does strange things to you with just other men .it's a strange feeling to see women again especially a beautiful woman.. like you..' I shook my head angrily.. How inane... puerile ..

There was a sudden roar of laughter from the front bar and I leant eagerly forward making out some of the men along the counter.. blunt, sun-browned faces ... And then with a thrill of joy I heard a woman's voice .. low... .. even...with the slightest of Australian accents.. yes... her.. how wonderful..

Still I waited perhaps she has forgotten about me? I mused conscious of becoming ever more nervous .. .as if I was expecting something to happen; something of immense importance to me.. my life..

From behind me came a sudden loud shriek. Tad of course .. I thought irritably and then a jazzy tinkling of a piano and even more shouting and laughter. What was happening with them I wondered vaguely. But really I didn't care all I wanted was to see her again ..perhaps though I would be disappointed..

A shudder passed through me.. a sense of satisfaction .. resolution as I saw her duck beneath the hatch top her slender figure, straightening effortlessly, her grey-blue eyes calmly meeting my staring gaze; strawy golden hair piled up on her head like a crown .. yes, a queen I thought as she lowered the jug, my eyes catching at the push of her breasts through the thin wool jumper.

"Is Ella your name..?" I blurted scrabbling in my pocket for money.

"Stella actually." She responded cooly her eyes straying away from me.

"A lovely name.." I muttered my hand shaking as I held out the bank-note, my eyes fixed on the hollow at her throat.

A wry smile flitted over her exquisitely shaped lips.

"Someone plays er the piano here ..?" I stammered desperate for something to say; the tinkly piano music now louder than ever.

"Yes. Solly they call him." She said with a slight frown.

"I see…" I lifted the jug, conscious of her eyes resting on me, yet abstracted as if she was thinking of something far removed; such a supremely calm presence I marveled; more than a queen .. a goddess..

"Hey Elly!"

"Elly let's have ya! "Several men's voices called demandingly.

I frowned angrily. Her fine collar bones visible above the scoop of her jumper moved in the slightest of shrugs and then stooping gracefully she passed back to the front bar.

Dizzy with emotion I stepped out of the booth with the jug of beer.. such beauty.. 'the beauty of the bended bow..' Where had I read that? But how did such an astonishingly beautiful woman come to be working as a barmaid? Like a goddess come to earth … .a mystery. ..and yet without such a mystery I would never have been privileged to see her.. truly a most wonderful mystery…

But where were the others? I found them at the back of the room clustered around a figure seated before an upright piano; showing the back of a maroon jacket and a head of curly black hair with a round bald spot.

"Where ya been Phil?" Billy grumbled as I brought over the jug of beer. "We're all f----n' dyin' of thirst."

"Chattin' up t' Baarmaid." Norris bellowed. "A real looker ain't she Phil.. Betcha ya fancies a go with her."

I shook my head angrily.

"Phil..zee liar .." Tad squealed.

"This is Solly, Phil. "Billy said pouring out a glass of beer from the jug and handing it to a large, heavy-set, man seated in front of the piano. I nodded politely my eyes fixing on the polka-dot bow-tie under the fleshy double chin.

"Howdy..Phil" Solly drawled in a affected American accent. "Yes siree. One helluva laady our Elly. "He winked knowingly. "Too bad about the husband.. heh heh.. Well.. here's to all you bold bad sailors."

"Cheers! "I hastily echoed the others, swallowing the beer in great gulps, the sharp ache fading away; of course she was married but why had there been no wedding ring?

Or perhaps I hadn't noticed.. What difference did it make anyway?

Solly put his half-empty glass on the piano and like a conjurer performing a trick produced a large handkerchief and dabbed his thick lips and then thrusting his wrists out of long shirt cuffs, interlaced his fingers and flexed them with a series of cracks.

"What a poseur." I whispered to Billy.

"Wait n' see.." Billy answered, frowning.

"The Maple Leaf Rag!" Solly announced grandly, his heavy figure swaying in time to the music, stubby, nicotine stained fingers skipping and hopping rapidly over the keys.

I glanced at the others; all eyes were fixed on Solly's leaping, darting hands. Norrie mouth wide open, Tad biting his nails his eyes bulging, Billy hanging over the side of the piano looked down with a satisfied scowl. I too felt my eyes drawn irresistibly back to Solly's hands, scrabbling madly up and down the keys; the syncopated rhythms, shakily piling up and then falling apart in broken cascades of notes, the original tune distorted and fragmented yet still vaguely discernible beneath the crashing and pounding.

With a final mad flourish Solly lifted his hands from the keys and hung his head in mock modesty.

There was a pause and then we all began to clap and stamp; grinning and laughing in an ecstasy of admiration. Is he really such a virtuoso performer, I wondered and if so what was he doing in such an obscure place....and yet perhaps ..he was just unlucky.. life was unfair.. ..

After wiping his face and sipping more beer Solly began again this time singing in a drawly maudlin way, leering and winking at us.

"On top of Old Smokey .. All covered in snow ..I met my first love... "

I shut my eyes letting myself drift into a sentimental melancholy; how amazingly beautiful Stella was .. really a goddess come to earth ... beyond my wildest hopes..

With a dramatic scrambling crash of notes Solly brought the song to a triumphant conclusion throwing his hands into the air.

"Solly zee greatest!" Tad screeched waving his arms wildly.

"Like he's got six hands..." Norrie chortled his face flaming red.

"What's wrong with that f-----n' lot through there. "Billy exclaimed savagely motioning down the passageway to the front bar.

"Philistines!" I shouted angrily, rather surprising myself.

Solly shrugged turning to extract a cigarette from Norrie's packet and bending to get a light from Billy.

"Thanking you gracious sirs.. Live and let live is my motto.." He pouted, one hand tinkling along the piano keys while blowing out cigarette smoke.

"Zolly ezz a real artiste.." Tad shrieked.

"The greatest ! "We shouted together clinking our glasses and excitedly gulped down our beer.

"Now let's hear it from you sailor boys!" Solly chortled crashing out chords.

"*Oh when the Saints..!*

"*Oh! When the Saints...*" We all warbled enthusiastically, grinning at each other; astonished at the sound of our own voices. "*Oh! When the Saints go Marching in...*"

Is this really happening? I wondered more than once blinking at the little group clustered the piano obscured by a wreathing cloud of cigarette smoke, Solly tirelessly hammering away at the piano, his voice becoming ever more gravely; pausing briefly at the end of each song to sip beer and take a few puffs from his cigarette burning on the edge of the piano while we stamped and whistled joyfully; exchanging gloating looks at our discovery of this unique talent.

"They think we're nuts.." I laughed to Billy noticing some men appear at the passageway stared at us before shaking their heads and going away.

"They can go to 'ell." Billy grinned back.

Once Stella came by with a bucket to empty the ashtrays but I quickly looked away from her, singing all the more strenuously as if somehow defying the reality of her beauty, the others I noticed too steadfastly ignored her .. fearful like me of the wonder of her beauty, I thought.. such power she has..

And then thinking she had must have left the room and glancing around I was surprised to see her composedly watching us from the passageway; at once I looked away again, a stabbing pain in my chest.; was it my heart.. was my heart breaking?

"Need a leak!" I shouted to Billy; he stared back hardly seeming to recognize me.

"On Blueberry Hill.. Time stood still…"

The raucous singing echoed around the room as I carefully steered myself between the empty tables and chairs aiming for a door at the back of the room, I winced at the scraping noise as I pushed it open stumbling down into a small courtyard; a sour disinfectant smell rising into my nostrils.

I turned and thrust the door shut, the hoarse warbling from inside at once cut off; the only light coming from a window above the door.

My eyes slowly adjusting to the patchy light, I went over to the urinal against the back-wall; from close by water trickled persistently; a deep sadness took hold of me.. how impossible life was .. I thought .. never would I achieve anything..

Was it because of Stella or had I just drunk too much? I wondered raising my eyes, astonished to see how bright the stars were, so glittering and brilliant as if pinned by some giant hand to the velvety darkness and as I gazed in wonderment distantly I became aware of a faint yet intense ringing .. .that rose and fell..

It's the stars, I thought in awed bewilderment, the stars are singing… and Stella means star, I told myself in a moment of profound revelation.

Never.. no matter what might happen to me in my life, will I forget this moment I vowed solemnly .... .never .. never.. never..

There was a harsh scraping noise and light streamed into the courtyard; ungainly shadows leapt about the walls.

"What ya f----n' doin' Phil..?" Billy asked stepping towards me.

"Don't ask...." Solly simpered Tad and Norrie snuffled with laughter.

"Coming. ..." I replied, startled by the sound of my own voice; holding the door jamb I glanced back at the starry sky already though the moment had become remote.. not quite believable... even as my words echoed in my head: 'never, never will I forget this moment..'

CHAPTER TWENTY-NINE

'Stop it! ... Stop it please.' I begged but Solly only looked pityingly at me and carried on banging down the piano lid .. more and more aggressively... 'Bang!. . Bang!.. Bang!' I must get away, I thought distantly but I was trapped.. my legs quite absurdly twisted together so I could hardly move them..

I opened my eyes....just a dream! .. and the banging was the Sec. knocking on the cabin door for us to get up. I smiled with relief.. sitting up.. blinking at the cabin walls and the dark circle of the porthole.. Yes, morning... and so the day beginning like all the other days since I had been aboard. But what an awful dream.. already though the weird sequence of events was quickly fading.. leaving traces of fuzzy absurdities and a gloomy feeling. Where did such horrible dreams come from I wondered pressing a hand to my throbbing forehead and slipping down from my berth.

"Got a rotten hangover "I groaned slowly realizing that Billy's berth was empty. He hadn't come home with me, then? No.. that was right; recollection of the previous evening began to filter into my waking mind.

Yes.. that was me walking alone beneath the street lights and then going to a small area of wasteland and squatting down retching violently behind some bushes; recalling vividly the stones and weeds close to my face.. and a tiny beetle with a metallic sheen.

But how had I got there? Of course Solly had invited us back to his house after another evening at *The Swan*. There we were gathered around the piano drinking beer and singing.. just like the other nights.. though I had the impression our enthusiasm for Solly and his wild honky-tonk piano playing was diminishing . .. certainly mine was ..

Returning the empty beer-jug I had mentioned the invitation to the Stella, who to my amazed delight had to come to accept my silly chatter, and at once a disdain had come to her lovely face … a queenly disdain deserving nothing less than complete obedience I had thought; immediately I had decided I wouldn't go with the others to Solly's house. But then before I could tell Billy I wasn't going I had found myself outside in the warm night beneath the stars being pushed into the back seat of the taxi with Tad and Norrie; mentally reviling myself for being so weak-spirited.

Perhaps too, I mused yawning, pulling on my T-shirt, I was a little curious to see where our artist hero, Solly lived; rather expecting something unusual, reflecting his extrovert artistic personality. .

But when the taxi had stopped to let us out beneath the lurid glare of the street lights I had looked with dismayed disillusionment down the concrete path between two squares of weedy grass leading to the front door of a small, characterless bungalow, identical to all the others in the street. Perhaps I had thought the décor inside would be more "artistic"

It was true I had felt momentary exaltation stepping through the front door, acutely conscious that it was the first time since leaving Vancouver that I had entered a private house. But any excitement quickly vanished; the blank walls were grubby with dribbled stains, the ceilings a brown yellow. Doubtless Solly lived on his own and despised housework, I had concluded. And just as depressing was Solly himself now changed into a garishly patterned shirt and slacks tittering smugly: 'Welcome honoured dear sirs to my humble abode'.

Sipping the vodka and lemonade that Solly had generously dispensed to all of us I had wandered dispiritedly around the small front parlour pretending an interest in the framed prints of sentimental pictures of dogs and cats; marvelling that I had ever for a moment thought Solly was a genius.

I could even remember a time while washing the companionway floor I had begun to mentally compose a letter to a local newspaper: 'Dear Sir. As a visitor to your fair land I am appalled, nay disgusted, to see how you treat with contumely your native talent. Every night in the Public House known as *The Swan,* one of the supreme exponents of Rag-Time.' And then, wringing out the floor-cloth, dirty brown water splashing into the pail, I had been overwhelmed by the idea of a genius unrecognised, aspiring talent doomed to obscurity.. a life wasted.. tears had come to my eyes.. such a cruel..cruel fate…

Now I could only marvel that I could have been so absurdly naïve ..ignorant.. perhaps it was group hysteria.. it was blatantly obvious Solly was nothing but a mediocre hack. . no wonder then the men in the front bar had come to the doorway to stare at us with amazement ..and that such a beautiful person as Stella so pointedly showed her dislike of him.

I pressed my hand hard against my pounding forehead. How much had I drunk? I shook my head ; vaguely remembering Solly continually filling up our glasses while he became more and more giggly, smirking and leering unashamedly ; calling us his dear, darling, rough tough.. sailor boys. My only response it seemed was to gulp down yet more of the colourless glasses of vodka.. in what seemed like a desperate attempt to anaesthetize myself.. blot everything out . . deny my very existence.

But what would the Sec. say once he found out Billy was missing? I thought dragging myself down the companionway to the pantry. Fortunately a lot of the Officers had gone away on a coach trip together and wouldn't be back until later in the day.... so I should be able to manage the breakfast duties alone.. …

Perched as usual on a counter despite my nausea I forced myself to swallow the ship's bread coated with margarine and jam washing it down with sickly sweet tannic tea; the voices of the two cooks and Mitch a distant rumble.. How everything is changing I mused. Old Peter gone for good and now Billy missing from his usual place next to me. What could have happened to him I wondered, my thoughts irresistibly going back to the night before; remembering distinctly being all alone in the front parlour, vaguely conscious of the sound of the front door opening and closing and loud shouts and hoots of laughter but feeling totally aloof from it all; once someone I didn't recognise came to doorway a tall man his face gaunt, pock-marked, he had stared deliberately then left without a word. Or was that in my dream? Definitely I recalled sitting on the arm of the broken-down sofa, dizzy from the vodka and yet still painfully conscious of an inner emptiness. the alcohol somehow failing to deaden my feelings. Was this my great adventure, I had wondered despairingly.. was this why I had braved the vastness of the Pacific.. left home family and friends.. to end up alone in the shabby front parlour of a shabby suburban bungalow, slowly drinking myself into oblivion..

That must have been when Solly had abruptly re-appeared a tipsy leer on his fleshy face, lined and haggard streaming with sweat; the sudden dream-like image breaking vividly into my memory.

"Naughty boy keeping to yourself.." He had simpered his large body swaying as he went over to the cheap veneer cocktail cabinet and dragged out a bottle.

Passively I had let him top up my glass, another glass should make me unconscious I had thought wearily.

"Genuine Russian vodka.. present from my Russkie sailor pals.." Solly had smirked suggestively.

"Is that your mother?" I had idly asked pointing to a photograph in a tarnished silver-frame on the cocktail cabinet of a scrawny, unsmiling woman, a little boy at her side.

"Yeah .. me and my mam.. Died of cancer stupid woman..Never knew me dad." Solly had mewed sullenly. "Life sure is hell ain't it...."

"Yes.. but still you have such talent.. piano playing...." I had argued determinedly, quite as if on my own behalf.

"Tinkling the old ivories heh...? Shucks ain't nuttin'." Solly had jeered, his small black eyes fixed intently on me.

337

"But I.. that is we, think.. well.. that you are a real.. artist only not appreciated. "I had gone on, was I being sarcastic.. malicious perhaps, I had even distantly wondered.

"I hate it ..I'd rather wash dishes.... "Solly had whimpered ferociously; tears running down his bright red cheeks.

"Solly!."

"Hey Solly!"

Raucous shouts had come from outside the room.

"You good..sweet.. boy.." Solly had cooed tipsily then abruptly leant forward, resting his hands on my shoulders choking me with cheap deodorant smells and before I could pull back had pressed his wet lips full on my mouth. "Drink deep the cup of pleasure ..you only live once dear boy.." He had giggling whispered in my ear before staggering clumsily out of the room.

I had wiped my mouth and then tossed down the neat vodka shuddering as the fiery alcohol burnt down to my stomach; thinking that I had to get away at all costs.. and yet not wanting to desert Billy.. Yes.. Billy.. my Billy.. my shipmate.. ....whatever might happen to us ..that would never change we were shipmates ..forever.. But where was he and the others? How deathly silent the house had become; a light shone out a doorway at the end of the unlit hallway and like a sequence in a dream I had walked towards it, amusing myself by seeing if I could keep to a straight line.. then entering the small kitchen absently I had noticed the cooker-top was covered with blackened debris.., the sink beneath the window full of dirty dishes, the small table crowded with bottles and glasses a cigarette burning in an ashtray, the back-door wide open. Where were they all then? It was then Tad had appeared in the doorway blinking at the light, goggling and gesturing at me. Really he's crazy, I had thought going over and peering into the small back garden, making out a small shed with a pitched roof overhung by large trees the upper branches tinted a livid mauve-orange from the streetlights.

"Heza' doin' it.. Solly in zee shed.. all of us ..Billy sezza you comza get it.." Tad had shrilled before turning away and vanishing back into the shadows.

With one hand on the doorjamb I had stared into darkness; my heart beating heavily; the red tip of a burning cigarette glowing cynically.. suggestively…

'Go on … you only live once..' the words had come of themselves. But strangely my legs trembled so much I couldn't move and then I had turned abruptly, using my hands to guide myself down the dark hallway thrusting open the front door and so outside; my shoes striking the pavement with a clear ringing sound; in the sickly orange light, two shadows beside me; the second shadow eerily falling behind only to catch up again.. as if I was beginning to split apart I had thought intent on getting away.. walking ever faster not caring if it was the right direction .. just to get away.. and it must have been then I had turned aside to a patch of wasteland and vomited ..and felt a tremendous relief and yet now sitting on the Pantry counter-top, a new day beginning, I felt again .. the impulse to get away ..but how and from what ..from myself.. . ?

Just forget about it, I told myself, don't even think about it.. getting off the counter and letting my mind go deliberately blank, submerging myself in the physical actions of the daily tasks.

Later that morning while washing the upper-deck Companionway floor I looked up to see Billy coming toward me.

He grinned casually. "What 'appened to ya last night?"

"I didn't feel very well.. too much vodka I guess and so I came back to the ship." I answered not able to meet Billy's eyes.

"Solly says we can go back 'ome with 'im again t'night "Billy smirked . "Treat us the same again .."

"Yeah.. Really? Great." I said pretending an eagerness.

Billy stared at me doubtfully before shrugging and going off to catch up with his duties.

Suddenly restless I left the pail and cloth and went out on deck and looked across the flat, oily waters of the harbour to the warehouses, the skeletal cranes pointing into a sky dark heavy with dark clouds..

I took a deep breath of the warm air heavy with drying seaweed and mud smells; across the harbour shards of brilliant light pierced the heavy black clouds; why is life so difficult I wondered dully.

"Looks like rain's passing over eh sonny…?"

"Hello Chips.." I said managing a smile, the ship's carpenter moving to the rail beside me.

"Look..! "I pointed to a broad rainbow arching over the far shore.

"His promise to us.." Chips said nodding.

"Going away though." I commented seeing the softly coloured arch fading into the brightening sky.

"A promise is a promise.." Chips smiled knowingly.

"By the way how is "Natty ?" I asked suddenly remembering the tiny bird, Chips had saved.

"Heh.. heh I wondered when you'd ask.." Chips chuckled. "As soon as we sighted land.. Away he went.. Like an arrow from a bow.. He knew what he wanted.."

"You must miss him… "I said rather saddened.

"Aye I do that.." Chips said bending to take up his worn canvas hold-all, bulging with tools. "It's for the best though I do believe.."

"I hope he'll be all right. Strange birds are often picked on.." I observed rather pessimistically.

"He'll be alright never thee fear…." Chips pronounced confidently his eyes on me. "And what about thee sonny? Are thee alright?"

"Me? I'm fine.." I muttered unconvincingly; looking across the harbour seeing the rainbow had vanished completely.

"Maybe thee should think of getting back home.." Chips said a gentle smile on his tanned leathery face.

"I don't want to go back.. ever. "I insisted almost angrily.

340

"Well.. well.. sometimes what we want is not for our best.." Chips remarked serenely.

For a minute I watched the small figure walk off down the deck in his easy ambling gait. How content he is .. I thought wondering if his time alone on the life-raft had changed him.. How I would like to ask him about it.. and yet each time something held me back... as if I was afraid of knowing too much.. Absently I touched my tongue to the tooth Mitch had broken, thinking it really it was getting firmer; quite amazing.. the body healing itself..

But where was Billy? I knew the deck-boys had gone ashore together but after cleaning the pantry after lunch together Billy seemed to have vanished.. unable to settle I had roamed the ship..

Twice I found myself at the stern rail, nostalgically recalling the endless afternoon breaks Billy and I had spent under the sun's blaze squinting sleepily at the frothy wake trailing away across the vast gleaming waters of the Pacific. And our talks.. and the time we had thrown the chairs into the wake and watched them smash to pieces... .. and our make-believe games of British Commandoes with the deck-Boys as the Jerries.. .. How distant that all seemed now.. a sort of day-dream world.. But surely it won't be long before we're back side by side sunning ourselves again, I had told myself though without conviction....

Sauntering back along the afterdeck my eyes were drawn to a ship on the other side of the harbour; of a slender build, a number painted in white figures along the hull, in the centre of the superstructure prickling with aerials was a large dome; squat turrets fore and aft projected gun-barrels.

It must be warship, I thought quite fascinated by the implied menace of the guns.

"Why if it ain't our poh-etic cabin-boy doin's soam sight-seeing "Hobbsie boomed coming along with the day-gang.

"What ship is that .." I asked pointing across the water at the grey painted vessel lit by the afternoon sun.

"Royal Navy frigate thaat." Hobbsie bellowed knowingly.

"Hey, it's leaving!" I exclaimed as dark black smoke rose from the amidships, a line of sailors in navy blue with white flaps at their backs could be seen rapidly hauling in the mooring lines, almost immediately the frigate's bows moved away from the quay; the stern lines were now taken in with equal rapidity.

"Nouw that be seamanship loike" One of the day-gang called out admiringly as the ropes neatly coiled, the sailors stood to attention in two lines either side of the ship.

"Ain't naowthing." Hobbsie snorted dismissively. "They haas four toimes the men we does fer the job."

"I suppose so...." I murmured glancing at the powerfully built A.B, his heavy brows drawn as critically he watched the departing warship. How sure he is of himself, I thought so certain of his abilities, supremely confident that he knows better than anyone else.. yet isn't it men like him that do the world's work? Arrogant.. brutal perhaps but also resolute.. capable. . a real sailor. something I would never be.

My eyes went back to frigate now moving quickly through the shiny harbour waters, a white-crested wave leaping from the sharply raked bows... trailing of white froth, smoke bending sharply backwards the Red Ensign fluttering from the narrow stern.

"Aye sight to be proud of thaat .." One of the Deck Gang now spoke giving voice to the others.

"My grandfather was in the Royal Navy." I blurted out.

"Do hear that laads? His bloomin' granpa. So tha thinking of joining the Royal Naavy too are tha.." Hobbsie scoffed genially.

I bit my lip and shook my head yet seeing the efficient crew in action I had felt a vague longing for a such a life; ordered.. disciplined .. ..

"Hello what's this Mr Hobbs? Not wasting time are we.."

Unnoticed the 1st and 2nd Mates had come along the Amidships, both in full uniform, on their way ashore I guessed.

"No siir juust pointing out loike for the benefit of this bright young chaap here, how yonder frigaate.. Royal Navy sir letting go.. you know the way Royal Navy does.. Bristol style siir.." Hobbsie drawled in his usual obsequiously insolent manner.

"Well, Mr Hobbs I glad to see that even a sailor of your experience appreciates real seamanship when he sees it." The 2nd Mate laughed dryly.

"And is this young chap benefiting from your wisdom Mr Hobbs?"

The 1st Mate wondered his bushy black eye-brows gathered into a stern frown.

"Yes siir, a smart un..him.. topper of a caabin-boay.. ain't it so laads?" Hobbsie bellowed looking challengingly around and then suddenly clapped me on the back so I staggered forward to a roar of laughter from the others.

"Careful Mr Hobbs." The 2nd Mate said raising his eyebrows, smiling despite himself. "You'll put a premature end to a successful career at sea."

I flushed proudly. . or was he being sarcastic perhaps?

"More to the point Mr Hobbs. how about getting the No.4 Hold ready for this cargo of Australian wheat we're expecting…" The 1st Mate added impatiently.

"Righto siir. Always glaad to oblige as tha knoaws." Hobbsie drawled sanctimoniously winking at me before slouching away, followed by his men, their boots dragging down the deck.

"Right then….." The 2nd Mate said glancing fixedly at me as if about to say something.

With a curt nod from the 1st Mate the two officers walked briskly away down the deck, talking in low, engaged tones.

Yes, I mused they are in command and without them directing him Hobbsie for all his blustering manner would be lost ..confused .. and I had once thought I could be an

officer.. command men .. win their respect.. loyalty ... love..
How foolish.. just a self-indulgent fantasy.. I turned back to
look out over the harbour, the frigate still visible, a column
of smoke rising towards the streaming clouds above.

"Farewell.." I murmured feeling as if I had been left
behind.. . abandoned. Was I finally realizing that I had made
a mistake in coming to sea then? I wondered despondently
walking slowly back to the amidships.. I stubbornly shook my
head; just think what lay ahead for me; the crew were
convinced the ship would be returning to England after one
more voyage to China.. and then the Indian Ocean.. the
Persian Gulf.. the Suez Canal.. the Mediterranean ..and then
Gibraltar .. Gib my grandfather always called it.. through the
pillars of Hercules.. ..before sailing up the English Channel..
La Manche, the French called it ..past the white cliffs of
Dover.. then the Thames .. so rich in history.. Tilbury.. Queen
Elizabeth's famous speech at time of the Spanish Armada.. to
dock at Limehouse or the Pool.. with Billy beside me.... to
show me around when we got ashore.. returning to the land
of my birth.. fulfilling my manifest destiny.. I thought
breathing exultantly and yet even so a doubtfulness persisted
at the back of my mind...

'I don't think I'll go to *The Swan* tonight .. not feeling so
good... '

I looked blankly around the empty Crew Mess hearing
my own words and then Billy's faintly caustic: 'F----n'
please yerself matey.. '

Now alone on the ship for the first time since coming
aboard, unable to settle to anything I was beginning to
regret my decision. Perhaps I should go to *The Swan*
anyway, I thought pacing restlessly around the crew mess
where I had come with a book feeling suffocated in the
cabin and yet I couldn't overcome my overwhelming
repulsion at the thought of meeting Solly....

Old Paddy appeared in the doorway. What could the
miserly old fool want I wondered as he shuffled slowly
towards me.

"There's a lady want to see you, surr." He said winking a rheumy eye. "Waiting bottom of gangway..surr"

"Me?" I stared sceptically at the plate with two eggs in their shells and two rashers of fatty bacon the old Irishman was holding, his hand shaking slightly.

"Me, supper surr.." He added noticing my gaze.

"Are you sure "I demanded irritably convinced he must have made a mistake.

"Yes sorr.. cook it on the boiler in the engine room"

"No.." I snapped impatiently . "This lady..I mean ..are you sure she wants *me*?"

"So she says .. Beg yer pardon surr." He smirked gently. "A right colleen. .. A Rose of Sharon you might say.. Stella she said her name was ..."

"Stella .. ?" I gasped grabbing the greaser's bony hand and shaking it violently; turning at the doorway to call back the old Irishman smiling wanly, bemusedly: "Thanks.. Paddy.. Thanks.. you're.. .well .. a wonderful old man...." before rushing down the Companionway.

For a second or two I stood as if fixed at the top of gangway, looking down at the slender figure under the dock-side flood-lights; her arms wrapped around her body, the fawn skirt and cream-coloured jumper I knew so well, gazing across the quayside. Impulsively I hurled myself down the gangway.

"Stella.. Stella …. You..? here..?" My voice quavered becoming harsh, almost accusing as I came towards her.

"Yes.. me.. here.." She said composedly turning at my voice, with an amused smile ; without the least embarrassment or confusion.

I stared in wondering silence; quite I thought, as if it was the most the natural thing in the world to be waiting alone at the bottom of the gangway of a freighter on the open dockside in the fading evening light.. and somehow it was .. her beauty endowing her with a rightness.. a perfection. …

"I wasn't sure if that old man understood me. He seemed a bit dotty. I was just going to leave." Stella remarked breaking the silence.

"Old Paddy. Yeah.. the ship's Watchman. He's ancient.. Crew despise him ..he's such a miser.. never goes ashore…spends the whole evening reading the Bible .. . But actually he's not such a bad sort . "I bit my tongue; don't gush I warned myself.

"Can you drive?" Stella abruptly asked, beginning to move away along the dockside.

"Drive..?" I wondered blankly following her. "A car, you mean?"

"Yes a car.." She said looking at me with gentle seriousness.

"I think so.. that is ..why yes! "I said grinning at my own confusion; my mind flashing back to my first attempts with my mother as teacher; the car bucking violently as I tried to master releasing the clutch at the same time as pressing accelerator; and then the test.. so nervously clumsy .. I was sure I had failed and my relieved amazement at being told by the grim-faced examiner: 'You'll be pleased to know you have passed.'

"I want you to drive me to Perth." Stella said equably, tiny lines wrinkling her smooth forehead.

"When… ..?" I laughed dizzily, my heart thudding heavily.

"Now… "Stella smiled quickening her steps as if it was settled.

"Yes .. now ..of course.." I laughed my mind racing; thinking how fortunate that I was in my shore-clothes having decided at the last minute not to accompany Billy and the deck-boys.. yes surely it was ordained.. my fate…

Without speaking we walked on side by side, one of her arms brushed against mine and I trembled as at an electric shock; passing as in some strange day-dream through the dockyard gates and out into the deserted streets; glancing half-disbelievingly at the slim figure walking with quick even paces beside me; pressing my nails into my into my palms as hard as I could; yes this is real.. this is happening to you.. I rejoiced and yet still was unconvinced ..

A few pedestrians passed us and I noticed how man or woman their eyes instinctively sought Stella.. it isn't just me .. I thought gravely, everyone is touched .. by her beauty.

A few streets further on Stella stopped beside a battered, dark blue American saloon car thick with dust, as if it hadn't been driven for months.. she handed me a single car-key .

"By the by I don't have any money on me.." I thought to say opening the passenger door for her.

She gave an amused shake of her head and got in and I shut the car-door with a resolute thud.

'She must really like me..' I exulted moving around to the driver's side noticing the faint pink gleam in the darkening sky and touched by a solemnity; how amazing my life was..

I pulled the car-door shut with a decisive clunk; the shadowy car interior producing a sudden frightening intimacy.

"Been a long time.." I said, nervously waggling the column gear-stick; stealing a glance at the upright form beside me;

"You'll be alright "Stella replied calmly reaching forward hands to tug her tight skirt over her knees.

"Sure.. with you beside me." I dared my voice a hoarse croak.

"Yes... "Stella murmured coolly.

"Here's goes then.." I turned the key and the engine whirred feebly; sweat ran down my body; so it was all going to end in nothing just as always.. but then there was a sudden clattering roar, the car-body vibrating violently.

With grinding of gears, I let the clutch out and the car jerked violently forward only to abruptly stall.

"Sorry ..." I murmured my face hot; the plastic-coated steering wheel slippery with perspiration.

"You're doing fine.. Phillip." Stella commended in a low, even voice.

I shut my eyes; half swooning .. so she knew my name .. knew who I was.. and it wasn't all some absurd incomprehensible mistake.. .

Once again the car lurched forward, I stabbed my foot on the accelerator, the car wallowed and juddered the engine roaring fiercely as it moved slowly down the street.

"Getting the hang of it now.." I laughed excitedly, the car picking up speed as if it had a will of it's own. How easy it is, I marvelled, gaining confidence..

"Straight on..?" I asked as we approached a junction

"I think so. ... ." Stella murmured diffidently; the car shot across and a car horn blared.

"Go to hell.." I cried, a recklessness taking hold of me; the hero rescuing the beautiful Princess from evil forces, I thought fantastically grinning to myself; yes.. fantastic and yet at the same time astonishingly.. wonderfully.. real.

Soon the lighted streets disappeared, a highway presented itself, the broken white line in the middle leading me on ; I caught a blurred glimpse of road zsign : *PERTH* and smiled wonderingly to myself; the car irresistibly drawn through the mysterious onward rushing blackness; now and again headlights from oncoming cars glared at us; casting a glow on her slim upright form, then abruptly vanished, leaving the road empty.

"By the way is er.. something er.. wrong..?" I thought to ask darting a wondering sideways glance.

"No.. nothing like that.." She laughed.

It's the first time I've heard her laugh, I thought my heart swelling as at some undeserved yet wonderful gift.

"I just needed to get away.." She murmured as if to herself.

"Sure .." I sighed sympathetically; rejoicing that it had fallen to me of all the people in the world to serve her .

Twin red tail-lights gleamed out of the darkness and I hesitated momentarily, then turned the steering-wheel and pressed hard on the accelerator, the engine roaring as we swept triumphantly past ..

If only it would last forever, I thought dreamily; the soothing hum of the car engine, the musty smell of the interior, the dim glow of the instrument dials; a supremely beautiful woman sitting beside me....

Coming around a sharp bend, two fuzzy discs of light appeared at a distance.. rapidly grew brighter and brighter.. became dazzlingly bright. I half-shut my eyes against the blinding glare imagining the two vehicles colliding head-on.. in an instant mangled, smoking metal and dying bodies lay on the road..

Already the car was cresting a long slope the headlights raking the shadowy roadside; far away a sickly green glow flushed the night sky; a chill shiver ran through me ..death ..oblivion .. nothingness.. so close..

CHAPTER THIRTY

"Had this stupid dream." I muttered struggling out into the companionway, rubbing my eyes; the dim-lit cream metal walls so familiar and yet at the same time.. different.. almost as if I was still dreaming....

"I was driving this car down a hill.." I went on following Billy into the "head". "Going faster and faster ..you see and suddenly there was this great black hole in the road. .I tried to stop but the brake-pedal was like jelly.. my foot just sank further and further and .. .then I woke up.. what a relief."

"Youse always 'aving f-----n' weird dreams.. ." Billy grumbled.

"Yeah.." I murmured watching the pale yellow stream running down the stainless-steel urinal; this was real wasn't it and yet somehow the dream was just as real.. in a way even more so.. so vivid.. so terrifying.. .

"I expect it was because I was driving a car for the first time ..the other night with Stella. "I said yawning; was I boasting perhaps?

"I reckon yer on aright loser Phil. "Billy muttered. "Same as all of 'em .. right tease."

"I don't think so.." I murmured; my heart thudding forcefully.

"So when ya gonna see her next?" Billy demanded.

"Quite soon.. . . "I said casually steadying myself on the sink, a fierce shudder passing through me.

"I reckons yer betta off with yer shipmates. "Billy growled. "Solly says ....."

"I don't care what he f----g says.." I snapped.

"Ave'it yer own way.." Billy shrugged. "Can't say yer weren't warned.."

"By the way has something happened to Solly?" I asked following Billy out of the "head. "Stella said he's not playing the piano in *The Swan* anymore"

"'E's keeping' to 'is bed. "Billy laughed hoarsely heading. "Murdoch and some others came with us to 'is 'ouse t'other night n' f----n' really went fer 'im…"

"Really.." I murmured quite shocked; in my mind seeing the shed in the black garden overhung by trees stained by mauve-orange street lights; a moment of extreme tension and then a frenzy of kicks and blows and blubberings and whimperings from the shadowy heap on the ground.

"'E 'ad it f-----g comin' to im." Billy growled turning into the Pantry.

"So is he badly hurt?" I asked, wondering vaguely if that what he wanted all along.. to be abused.. humiliated.. punished..? Perhaps because of his childhood..?

"Nah..'e'll be O.K." Billy . "Ya wanna visit 'im?"

"Not really.." I muttered glancing at Billy sitting on the counter beside me; was there something different about him? I wondered watching him light up a cigarette, his slab of bread and jam untouched Or was it just me? Could it be that my mind was effected? Yes.. I thought, love is a kind of madness. But nothing had really changed.. I was still a mere Cabin-Boy on a bulk-carrier.. bullied and bossed around.. caught up in same unending, unchanging routine.. from the minute the Sec. banged on the cabin door .. and now a hurried breakfast sitting on the counter-top in the Pantry with the same heat and smells, hearing the faint crash of pots and pans from the Galley .. and the Officers noisy assembling in the dining-room .. and no doubt Mitch would be snarling at me for being slow to bring the plates to the Hatch.. and the Sec. checking up.. and yet how infinitely distant I felt from it all…utterly detached.. going about my daily routine in a daze of excited, anxious anticipation….. .

Every once in a while though I was gripped by a cold fear; what if I had imagined it? Dreamt it perhaps? But once my heart stop thumping her calm voice would come to me soothing and exciting; it was true.. as true as my exulting, swelling heart .. all I had to do was wait; surely it was my inescapable destiny.. to love her ..?

Musing dreamily I stood at the Pantry sink blinking into the glare of light through the portholes, distantly hearing the iron clangings and loud shouts coming from the foredeck, in my mind, back in the car driving boldly through the night...the speedometer needle unwavering in the lighted dial ...the engine humming steadily as the headlights pierced the darkness ahead.. the road, a shadowy ribbon unwinding from an endless spool..

And then ....? Mechanically I sluiced another dirty plate through the scummy dishwater ..strange I couldn't remember coming into Perth itself.. all I could remember was passing down a grid of almost empty streets, lined by flat-roofed buildings; randomly it seemed, turning this way and that.. until we were moving slowly along a broad drive sweeping through dense shrubbery broken by giant trees that spread darkly bristling arms into the faintly glowing night-sky.

'Anywhere will do.. 'I remembered Stella had said in a subdued voice and impulsively I had turned the steering wheel, the car mounting a grassy verge as if of it's own volition, running up a slight bank.. fierce scratchings against the metal car body ..the engine stalling ....and then an intense silence.

I had turned off the ignition, my heart beating faintly, beyond a dim blur of light visible through the leafy shadows, conscious of a musty, faintly medicinal smell.. the rustling of leaves ..branches brushing tentatively at the side windows the silence rising and falling in vast, effortless waves; a surreptitious sideways glance had shown her head, neck and shoulders in profile.. stray hairs shining in the dim light .. like an elegant head on an antique cameo, I had thought distantly even as she raised her arms as in some courtly dance.. her fingers working at her coifed hair, turning to me.. faintly smiling ..her eyes proudly bright.

'My God.. how beautiful you are..' I had moaned as her hair rippled down, a final shake of her head sending richly shining tresses swaying about her shoulders..

'You understand now, Phillip. ." She had said putting a hand lightly on my shoulder, her lips parted, her breath warm on my face.

I had nodded solemnly; my arms enclosing her slender form; boldly meeting her softly pressing lips.. our two bodies joined in a deeply swooning embrace.. the gentle drumming of raindrops on the roof of the car..

"C'mon Phill ... 'urry up or we'll never get finished .." Billy grumbled snatching a plate from my hand "And look at this.." He added irritably; scraping at dried-on egg with his fingernail.

"Sure.. say Billy Did I tell you about this crazy thing that happened that night in the car?" I began, blindly fishing in the sink-full of grey, greasy water for another plate; the words rushing from me unchecked... .

"Like I said we drove to this park somewhere .. and suddenly there was this tapping noise on the car-roof .tap tap.. like crabs or insects walking over it.. just like in a horror film.. then pow! there was this dazzling light.. blinding.. Maybe an atomic blast, I thought... Guess what it was ?"

Billy shook his head impatiently.

"The Police. .! Two of them! They'd been rapping on the car-roof trying to get our attention it seems.. so then they switched on a couple of those huge metal torches .. Finally I understood and rolled down the window.. They wanted to know what we were doing. 'Just talking about the meaning of life Officer.. 'I said politely and that seemed to satisfy them. 'By the way' says one of them in a twangy Australian accent. 'Do ya realize sport you're parked in the middle of a bloody flower-bed.. And it was true! I'd driven the car slap bang into the middle of a flower-bed! Nothing to do with them only the Park Keeper.. but then when I tried to reverse out, the ground had become soft from the rain and the rear wheels kept spinning. So I had to get out.. you should have seen me.. blundering about in the dark in the rain, ripping off branches to put under the wheels.. about the craziest, thing in my life. I started to laugh..... God knows what she thought .. there I was soaking wet and covered in mud chuckling away like a madman.....but she just smiled as if it was the most normal thing in the world. Crazy eh?"

"Yeah.." Billy muttered indifferently. "Yer c'n finish off here.. I've gotta go and see about summat.."

I shrugged and turned back to the sink, smiling to myself recalling the look on the face of the two Policemen when they had shone their torches on Stella.. stunned into silence overwhelmed.. awed.. humbled. . by her sheer beauty.

And yet it was more than simple beauty wasn't it? Something far more deeper...profound and yet perilous too.. taking me to the edge of some immensity .. What had she told me? 'Now you understand' And there tightly clasped in the shadowy confines of the car.. our lips pressed in an endless kiss.. I had understood.. everything.... completely.. magnificently.. for all time...

I stared around, slowly realizing that that I must have finished washing the companionway floors.. and was now in Officer's Smoking Room already, sniffing doubtfully at the stale air heavy with beer and cigarette smoke, and sceptically studying the stained patterned carpet marked with cigarette burn holes, the shiny red-vinyl settle ..the round tables with beaten- copper tops and wooden stools.. the small padded bar in one corner and the dart-board, the backing-board heavily pockmarked from all the missed throws in rough seas....yes, I was here.. half way through my daily tasks.. and yet everything so vague.. disconnected ..insubstantial.. as if I belonged to some other world.. another existence .. This must be was it was to be in love.. I thought letting the softly pulsing wonder subsume the doubtful.. fearful spasms.

Better not let the Sec. catch you day-dreaming though, I warned myself; forcing myself to start cleaning the room; almost immediately my mind going back to my visit to Stella's flat.. not far from where the car was parked. In the day light the two-storey stucco apartment building appearing smaller, shabbier.

My pulse quickening thinking of how I had boldly pushed open the front door and began climbing the bare stairwell, slipping past an old woman who had given me a suspicious, disapproving glance; and my relief when after what seemed an interminable wait she had opened the door to me.. a slight smile so beyond all my imagining, my eyes fixing rudely on her lovely figure so perfect in tight-fitting jeans and sleeveless blouse, her hair tied tightly back ..like my sister I had thought absently, stepping inside and gazing around the large airy room; remarking how tastefully furnished it was.

She had looked a little surprised, explaining that the flat came furnished but she had decided it was too cluttered and so had thrown away a lot and then added a few of her own things. Sitting me at the large wooden table she had brought two mugs of coffee from the small kitchen and we had sat down opposite each other; a distance between us quite as if our kissing in the darkness of the car, was something I had imagined ..or dreamt.. only managing some desultory talk.... mostly about me.. and how I had come to be in on ship in Fremantle and the life of a cabin-boy... .. and how I got on with the others on the ship.. especially those that came with me to *The Swan*..

So I had told a little about Billy and Tad and Norrie vaguely ashamed of them.. and their admiration for Solly.. A long silence had fallen on us when I had finally dared to ask her about herself. Faint lines had creased her lovely forehead and she had looked distantly away through the single large window as seeing something in the bright sky and passing clouds .. in a low voice almost as if reciting she had told me about her life.. an only child.. her father a dentist .. and very important in local politics.. always going to meetings and conferences.. her mother too very busy with different charities ... organizing fundraising events....that sort of thing.. The family lived in a large old house in one of the best residential areas of Sydney .. Stella was by nature a free-spirit, disdaining all restrictions, inhibitions; smilingly telling me how when a little of girl of three she had taken off her clothes and left the house until she was found by neighbours wandering the streets and taken home.. How my heart had gone out to that little girl-child.. alone.. naked as at the day of her birth, so vulnerable.. yet fearless …

Her parents were Roman Catholics and at first she had enjoyed going to Mass especially her first one ..dressed in a white dress with everyone whispering how lovely she looked and Confession.. naughtily inventing various sins and then confessing that much to the confusion of the doddery old priest…. but then one Sunday she had refused to go to Church preferring to stay in bed reading.. once she told me she had stayed in bed for two days reading *Gone with the Wind*.. Her parents didn't insist and she had never been back inside again .. except once for a funeral.. her best friend.. from school days a girls only private school.. dying of some awful cancer.. How she hated the service everyone so smugly sad everyone saying how happy Teresa was now in heaven when Teresa thought it was all a monstrous fraud to frighten people into behaving properly and so did Stella .. . .

A daddy's girl, her father had objected strenuously and persistently to Arnold.. that was the name of her husband.. how I had stiffened at this declaration ..wanting to leave there and then and yet incapable of doing anything but listening devotedly…

Arnold was quite a few years older than her… they'd met at her first dance with boys from another private school…despite her father's objections .. perhaps even because of them she had said with wry smile they had married . ..one weekend without telling anyone.. a civil ceremony with some strangers as witnesses..

She'd decided not to go to University ..and Arnold had left before completing his first year and then they had begun moving around the country doing different jobs.. now Arnold was now working as a clerk in a lawyer's office and studying to become a lawyer… Her eyes resting on me she had told me they had a baby but decided to have it adopted .. her parents didn't even know about it .. she had spoken without sentiment or shame.. . perhaps wondering about my reaction…All I had felt was a deep, aching sadness.. .

She too had worked in casual jobs usually as a waitress or barmaid.. like at *The Swan*.. that way if she didn't like it she could just leave.. In the summer they had both sometimes worked on the seasonal agricultural jobs or in food processing plants; she told how once in a cannery the safety-guard had been left off a machine and her hair had got caught and she was being dragged in when just in time another worker had turned the switch off…

I had groaned out loud, almost sick at the idea of her lovely body mangled and torn.. She had frowned and pursed her lips. 'They said it was my fault for not following rules and taking off my hat.' She had explained adding perhaps that's why she had never learnt to drive, she didn't like being told what to do..

In the end they though they had had enough of moving around and settled in Fremantle.. and now she was studying to go to University that's why she only worked part-time; she wanted to become a lecturer in philosophy.

'How wonderful ..' I had whispered, picturing her elegant figure on the podium of a lecture hall, a black gown falling off one shoulder, graciously dispensing her knowledge to serried ranks of rapt, attentive students ..

Her father had wanted to help her, now he and Arnold were on friendly terms at last, but she had refused. 'I want to do things by myself 'She had said pushing back a stray hair, her eyes calmly meeting mine.

'Sure.. like me' I had boasted .

'That way no one can tell me how to live my life.…' She added regarding me thoughtfully.

I had smiled blissfully back thinking what a joy it was to serve her .. to meet her every wish no matter how extravagant or fanciful…

'You should have been a princess.. a queen ..'I had stammered out finally.

She had smiled graciously, adding with a quick laugh: 'Not in Australia I couldn't .. perhaps if I'd been born in England in the Middle Ages ..'

And I had half closed my eyes in a sudden fantasy seeing her dressed in richly embroidered full-length white gown, brightly coloured ribbons floating from the tall pointed headdress as she had gracefully taken her seat in the stand reaching forward a slender hand while I reined in my pawing coal-black steed taking her glove to decorate my helm before closing the visor and galloping off to do battle in lists in honour of her beauty.

'Anyway I couldn't bear such formality..' She had mused a little sternly.

'But even nowadays. .. you're so beautiful.. surely everyone wants to help you.. like me ..to please you.. 'I had gasped out, flushing hotly; proud at last of having openly declared my feelings.

She had made a slight movement of her slim shoulders; replying thoughtfully that yes.. being beautiful had it's advantages at times but often other women were extremely jealous imagining she wanted to steal their husbands or boyfriends... ..just because she was friendly and while most men were ready to help ..like the landlord of *The Swan* who let her use his car and there were others who made nuisances of themselves.. with crass innuendos and deliberately press against her and then there were men like Solly who seemed to fear her .. hate her..

'You'd think I was danger to them. 'She had mused.

I had nodded; recalling the time in the back bar-room of *The Swan* when I had deliberately avoided looking at her; yes I had known too a fear of her...such a supreme loveliness... demanding complete, unconditional obeisance ... .

'And when all's said and done..' She had gone on, her head in her hands a wistful smile on her lips as she gazed at me across the table. 'Being beautiful doesn't mean you don't have problems in life . . just like everyone else.. '

Again I had nodded admiring her delicately modelled features . her clear gazing eyes.. suddenly noticing her softly rounded forearm was criss-crossed with dark red scratches.

'How did that happen?' I had demanded indignantly.

She had looked critically at them explaining from playing with her kitten, a stray they had taken in.

'They look sore....' I had said half-sternly wetting a finger-tip and running it down the crusted ridge of a scar. 'Bad, bad kitty ..' I had moaned dizzy with emotion.

As if on cue there had been a mewing sound from the window and she had got up quickly and gone over and thrown it up; turning around to me stroking a pure-black kitten nestled in her arms. If only I was an artist I had thought, to fix for all time this picture of loveliness ... her slim, rounded arms and slender figure lit by the sunbeams streaming through the window, illuminating her composed features, her hair a helmet of pale gold....... never I thought despairingly could I be worthy of such womanly beauty.. .

Abruptly the kitten had leapt from her arms to the floor and rushed over the floor to wrap itself around my leg purring loudly.

'He likes you ..' She had mused. 'I call him Sartre.. after the French Existentialist Philosopher '

'Hello Sartre ..' I had said, thinking how far I was from my ship-board life; reaching down and stroking the kitten so it purred even more; the small body vibrating powerfully. 'So you're not superstitious .. Black Cat I mean .. bad luck and all that?'

She had shaken her head, with an amused smile..

'How about you ..? 'She had asked after a long pause, sliding her hands forward across the table.

'Not really....' I had laughed and then excitedly began to gabble on about the ship and how superstitious most of the crew were .. how they didn't like women on the ship and things like that and then about the Officers.. the 1st such a strong commanding presence and 2nd Mate who had wanted me to become an Rating then an Officer.. Who knows .. perhaps one day I might be a 1st Mate or Captain I had smiled, modestly boastful.. ... And about the Captain.. what a useless old woman he was.. and about the some of the crew ..Hobbsie a real blow-hard.and Murdoch.. a vicious brute and yet magnificent seaman for all that.. She'd met old Paddy already.... and about the two cooks ..Jock a Scotsman what an odd character he was ..always going on about whisky.. he and Ronnie a real Cockney ..always squabbling like an old married couple.... and Mitch from Liverpool ..a Scouser.. so sharp .. and nasty too.. my tongue going to my wiggly tooth... but not mentioning the fight...And the Sec. ..such a humourless, severe taskmaster . and the two Deck Boys ..She'd seen them in *The Swan* .. Tad a crazy Pole and Norrie like a lump of lard ..but harmless.... and of course Billy the other cabin-boy .. my cabin-mate .. wasn't he handsome .. I had boasted ..a really smart dresser and what great times we had together though recently we weren't getting on so well but once we were out to sea again I knew we would get back to being best mates.. After all it was one of the greatest things in the world, I had declared, becoming a little emotional, to be shipmates.. .

There was a long pause my mind for some reason settling on Chips.. At first I had to explain that wasn't his real name just what a Ship's carpenter was always called .. How enthusiastically I had described the small, tough leathery-faced old Virgin Islander .. and the story of how many years ago he had been shipwrecked, floating alone on a raft in the middle of the Pacific for weeks and weeks before he'd been spotted by a passing ship .. really a chance in million.. and been rescued and how it must have a profound effect on his life but he never talked about it.. How he had taught me how to tie knots.. and rescued a little bird blown out to sea ..such a simple yet wise old man.. believing it was only in the vastness of the open sea could you.. well.. find.. well.. God.. Hesitatingly I had gone on to describe how my first duty of the day was cleaning the Chief Engineers Day Room on the top deck and how going out onto the balcony and seeing the light materialize out of the dawn darkness gave me such a strange feelings ..awe and joy .. impossible to describe.. something outside myself.. .

I had stopped abruptly, as if I had given away too much of myself.

There was another long pause and then looking away she had begun relating how a year or so ago she and Arnold had been driving across the outback.. miles of empty road .. bare red earth . and dried-up bushes.. and stupidly they had run out of fuel.. so Arnold had hitched a ride in a passing car to go to the nearest town ..there wasn't room for her so she had stayed.. an hour had passed .. she had become terribly restless and despite all warnings got out of the car and begun to walk about.. the sun set quickly red and fierce angry .. and then a deep darkness so different to the darkness in a city the stars had come out cold and distant.. and she had felt so alone.. quite as if she was the only person left alive.. she'd become aware of sinister whisperings all around her.. she'd panicked and begun to run ..suddenly she realized she was completely lost....on all sides dark shadowy clumps of bushes. I'm going to die. .. she had thought; no one would find her.. there were always newspaper reports of people lost in the bush never found.. or just a skeleton years later... She had laid down on the dry hot ground.. now I should pray to the God.. or the Virgin Mary she had thought but at once had felt ashamed at giving in to such childish sentimentality.. And then she had begun thinking of all the problems of life.. how to get enough money to live.... what to wear.. what to eat.. where to go.. what to do.. always having to please others.. getting up .. going to bed.. everything such an effort.. all so mechanical ..meaningless.. really death wasn't so awful.. just like going to sleep she had thought .. She had woken up to hear Arnold shouting her name.. 'For a minute or two couldn't almost be bothered' She had said wryly 'But I could tell he was desperate.. so. . '. She had shrugged and made little grimace.

'You're the first I've ever told this.. not even Arnold.. Since then I often think of death as a well a friend.. almost.' She had added, her beautifully shaped lips tightly pressed, her eyes intently on me.

I had looked away, indefinably constrained, my heart beating heavily, absently studying the kitten now curled up on a chair vigorously licking it's shiny black coat, the tiny tongue like a pink ribbon.

'Stella.. oh Stella' I had murmured, a pity tearing at me; boldly lifting her hands lying open on the table; such beautiful slender fingers, no ring, I had thought gently pressing them ..so icy cold.. blurting out. 'I want to marry you'

She had frowned severely and told me not to be so silly.

I had nodded ashamed and a little hurt; an embarrassed silence falling over us.

'Would you like to dance.. ? 'She had asked suddenly getting up and going over to a record player on a table in the corner of the room.

'Sure..' I had responded excitedly getting to my feet and at once beginning to jerk and spin to the fast beat of rock and roll music. Boldly I had danced before her, advancing and retreating approaching as in awed worship of her womanly; our two figure writhing and gyrating in an wild ecstasy of movement; her eyes bright.. unseeing, her lips pressed in a mysterious smile, her pony tail lashing about her behind her lovely head...

The music had suddenly stopped; the silence broken by a feeble scratching sound. I had gazed wonderingly at her; an exquisite flush to her lovely face; her breasts rising and falling beneath her blouse; conscious of the moments slipping away; now was my chance to take her in my arms .. master her .. free her from herself I had thought dizzily. .. but I kept still ..restrained .. fearful... a coward ..

'I think you had better go now ..' She had said finally turning to the door then one hand on the handle she had paused; her eyes resting calmly on me; speaking in matter of fact voice: 'Come here the night after tomorrow.. Arnold will be away. Not before eight though..'

I had bent my head in mute acknowledgment, a distant clamour echoing through my brain.

'Not before eight pm. though... Remember.. It's my study time..'

'No.. eight..' I had murmured obediently reeling through the doorway, crossing the landing in a daze and almost colliding with a man coming up the stairs, he had stepped back, a surprised look on his small, fine-boned face.

Absently I had noticed he was neatly dressed in a dark suit and matching tie; a bottle of milk in one hand a brief-case the other.

Unhesitatingly Stella had introduced him as her husband, Arnold, just returned from his office.. and then smilingly she had waved her hand at me; speaking airily yet earnestly: 'This is Philip ..Arnold, he's off a boat in the harbour, he joined it in Vancouver after this Australian Cabin-boy left in mysterious circumstances.. the ship's taking wheat to Red China because of the famine there. They were meant to return to Vancouver after the first trip but came to Australia instead.. ..he doesn't know when if ever he'll get back home ..a real -life Ulysses.. I really admire him.. so eager for life.. a real adventurer don't you think? '

Arnold had nodded gravely, putting down his briefcase and offering his hand.

'Pleased to meet you Phillip.' He had said, his handshake very soft, then noticing my eyes on the bottle of milk, added with a shy, nervous smile 'For Sartre.. the kitten..'

"Yes.. sure.. you bet.. Nice to meet you too.' I had mumbled and then turned and fled down the stairs, pausing halfway down to look back up seeing the two figures, cross the landing, before rushing on out into the street; pausing to hurriedly light a cigarette before running as fast as I could back to the ship; the sky overcast a warm wind blowing with spits of rain; violently pulling myself up the gangway as if desperate to find refuge in the acrid smelling gloom of the amidships.. beginning to feel faint flushing hot and cold… my pulse racing .. my legs aching terribly.. Had I become ill then.. perhaps malaria.. or something worse.. . Or was it love? Yes.. yes.. that was it ..I was lovesick… terribly.. terribly lovesick…

CHAPTER THIRTY-ONE

"Stella ..Stella.. star of my life.... .." I murmured, frowning with concentration. How about 'shining star'..? Or 'bright star'.. .. Like Keats.. What rhymed with 'life' ? 'tithe.. strife.. rife... yes. wife.. ! 'How pathetic.. just doggerel.. Give up, I thought impatiently making a despairing sweep with the cloth over the Pantry floor beneath the counter; always the strip of black slime against the wall beyond my reach. But how demeaning it was to be washing the floor on hands and knees ..really an affront to her.. .my lady of the exquisite mien.. deserving only the highest knightly courtesie .. such peerless beauty .. and now mine.. a prize.. a gift.. more than I ever could have imagined.. deserved .. I paused in mid-movement but surely I merited her more than Arnold, just like Sir Lancelot and Guinivere .. for him she was just a wife... unexceptional. . . an everyday experience.. .for me . ..for me.. my heart begin to throb heavily.. .an adventure .. a marvel.. .a a mystery.. . And tonight .. this very night I thought, a violent shudder passing through me, to be revealed to me in all it's wonder.. and such a perfect shapely figure ..and to show herself.. like a Venus rising from the waves.. naked .. I shut my eyes, suddenly helplessly weak, all manly vigour oozing away..

"It must be love.. real love.." I muttered feebly to myself.

"Wight.."

I opened my eyes and looked around seeing the Sec. standing in the Pantry doorway, watching me curiously.

"Something up Sec.?" I said jokily, not able to meet his serious look.

"Captain wants you in his cabin. Right away.." The Sec. went an edge to his usual dry monotone.

"The Captain..? Me..?" I stammered getting awkwardly to my feet; my heart beginning to pound; what had I done?

"That's right.. Where's Billy?"

I shrugged, not wanting to admit he was skiving; he had told me frowning and edgy that he had to meet someone in the crew quarters at the stern but on no account to tell anyone.

"Never mind.. I'll finish off here." The Sec. said rubbing his chin. "What are you waiting for? Go on now.."

What a grouch he is, I thought stepping out into the Companionway to find both the Cooks watching me from the Galley doorway.

"Ye'll be getting a promotion laddie I doot.." Jock chuckled.

"Got caught out 'ave ya.. naughty boy.." Ronnie sniggered.

I grinned back; pushing along the Companionway; speculating wildly; could it be something to do with Old Pete's death? Or perhaps Solly being beaten up..? But I had nothing to do with that. Once again rumours that some of the crew were going to mutiny unless the ship returned to England were going around; could it be the Captain wanted me to act as a spy? 'With all due respect Captain I could never inform on my fellow crew-members....' Yes.. that was it.. polite but resolute.. Never would I betray my fellow shipmates, I thought proudly.

"For the f-----n' High Jump are we, darlin'.." Mitch jeered gleefully putting his head out of the Officer's Dining Room as I came past.

Bet he was listening at the hatch I thought; toiling up the four flights of stairs to the top deck. Soon the whole ship will be talking about me.. but who cared..? I stopped abruptly on the first landing .. Could Jock be right? Perhaps I was going to be promoted to Assistant Steward in place of Old Pete. How amazing.. to think in just a few months my abilities had... But what about Billy? I shook my head and started up the next flight. He would never forgive me. And surely it would have been the Sec. or Chief Steward who would have spoken to me.. not the Captain. I hadn't as much as glimpsed him since I'd been on the ship. Like the rest of the crew I considered him incompetent ..corrupt .. weak...an old woman. So why was I so nervous? The same as when I was a schoolboy I thought scathingly, and ordered by the class teacher to report to the headmaster for some misdemeanour. Even now I could vividly recall the chalky dusty smells of the empty corridors gripped by anxiety and the awful feeling of being alone..

But you're not a boy now, I told myself sternly crossing the top deck landing, glancing at the brass-rimmed, roll-indicator, on the bulkhead the single brass hand motionless in the dial; reminding me of when it had oscillated so wildly during the typhoon. Yes.. I had been at sea during one of the most severe typhoons in living memory .. And what had Stella said of me? '..a real adventurer..' Fiery prickles ran over my skin; what if her husband had complained about me? No.. impossible.. anyway.. I could say nothing had happened. . .just kissing wasn't it.. I scoffingly told myself and then flushed with shame; how could I dismiss something so profound.. so important to my life..

My arm raised I stared at the brass nameplate: *CAPTAIN* swallowing hard, sweating heavily ; was this some defining moment of my life.. or was it all another in a succession of trivial events..? Nothing for it.. I thought, rapping defiantly on the door and grinning wryly, my knuckles smarting.

The door opened and I stepped forward sinking into the deep-piled carpet, my bravado failing me as the door closed behind me. Vaguely I recognised Captain Proser behind a large shiny mahogany desk, glancing around I was surprised to see how large and luxuriously furnished his cabin; two large square portholes let in the afternoon sunshine reflecting off the glass-fronted cabinet lined with books; on a massive Chinese style sideboard a silver tray with crystal decanters and glasses sparkled. I took a deep breath; conscious of an eye muscle twitching spasmodically.

"Er Wight .. this is er the Reverend Messenger. "Captain Proser said in a weak, irritable voice, making a jerky gesture to a tall figure beside the desk.

I nodded curtly at the lanky, long-faced man in a dark suit with a dog-collar; regarding me with a slightly condescending look, bringing out a reflex of resistance; another f----g clergyman was it..

"Thank you Captain Proser. "The Reverend Messenger said effusively stepping in front of me. "Er pleased to meet you young man.. Phillip ..isn't it?"

I nodded again, relishing the Reverend's obvious surprise at finding himself addressing a sun-blackened tramp in a soiled T-shirt and ragged cut-offs; bet he thinks I'm something the cat dragged in, as my mother would say, I thought with a inward smirk.

"Well.. I am here.. that is to say.." The Reverend Messenger said as if making a formal declaration..

With a sudden apprehension I watched as he took an envelope with red and blue chevron edging from his inside jacket pocket; extracting several sheets of flimsy blue paper.. a letter.. an airmail letter.. for me.. something terrible must have happened.. Oh.. God .. please God.. not that..

"This is her letter… your mother that is to say…. "The Reverend Messenger went on evenly.

I stared blankly, biting my lip; so it was *from* mother, an intense relief flooding over me; the Reverend's voice a faint buzzing.

"You may read it yourself if you so wish but very briefly she has written to me to express her fears for you in this present life as a common sailor ..and the urgent need for you to return home at once to commence your university education.."

I stood stiffly silent, slowly comprehending; a letter from my mother. .. demanding my return…. but mother, I groaned inwardly; how could you .. treat me like an errant child; even as I struggled to keep back tears .. at last a letter home from my mother ..she was .. fine.. oh my dear, dear mother and father

"So you see.. Phillip.." The Reverend Messenger said kindly. "Your own mother… ..

"Now er...look her er...Wight..." Captain Proser broke in testily. "There's a ship just along the dockside...Swedish.. Krona Line; I've already spoken to her Captain. They can do with a deck-boy it seems. They do a scheduled passage to er,, Vancouver.. she's a mail-carrier.. sailing on the tide.. just enough time for you to get aboard.."

So that meant I would get away from the slime under the pantry counter, I mused abstractly and I would be a deck-boy.. out working on deck in all weathers a real seaman.. not shut away inside.... but it would mean leaving the *Grimethorpe*.. no I couldn't .. never.. impossible..

"And I must add Phillip that your mother's letter touched me deeply, such a warm, loving mother.. indeed you are truly blessed. "The Reverend Messenger smiled suavely.

I bent my head in dazed acknowledgement.

"So what d'ya say.. Wight.." Captain Proser gruffed pettishly.

"The Reverend here has gone to a lot of er.. trouble on your behalf, you know.. .."

"Or if you preferred I could arrange for you to attend University here. I'm confident that would satisfy your mother's wishes.." Reverend Messenger interjected smoothly. "Perth University you know, has an international reputation."

I gave an impatient shake of my head, a fierce anger rising in me; who asked him to interfere in my life?

"Right then,er, Wight .." Captain Proser snapped, rapping impatiently with a pen on the desk-top. "That's er settled. Get yourself below and get your gear packed. I'll get the Chief Steward to arrange for transfer any earnings you have coming to you.. and a Discharge. You'll find your new berth next but one ship along the dockside.. Swedish Flag .. *MV Gottland*.. Captain Thorsson ...You'll have to get your finger out.."

'Say no.. say no 'A voice within me whispered urgently, despairingly yet I stood staring ..stifled.. speechless; frozen in a dream-like torpidity .

"Just found a replacement for the Assistant Steward.. Died at sea of all things… "Captain Proser muttered testily, shaking his head. "Now I need a new cabin-boy.. Who'd be a Captain eh? But don't you worry er.. Reverend. Wight will be fine.. Captain Throrson's an excellent captain.."

Numbly I felt my legs moving me towards the door.

"And Phillip think how it much it will please your dear mother. You'll be home for Christmas ..I'll write at once to let her know…" The Reverend Messenger intoned gravely holding open the door. "And God be with you.."

"So that's that. Now if I can only get this Dockers Union to agree to start loading my ship.. Not really cut out to be a er seaman ..still we try.. we try.…"

The door shut on Captain Proser's voice with a loud click and I staggered across the landing and hung onto the banister.

"Mother .. mother .. mother.. I hate you!. Yes! hate you! "I whispered fiercely. How could you interfere in my life. But how awful the thought that something might of happened to her..

I gave a deep sigh; of course ultimately it was her love for me; imagining her in her pale blue brushed-nylon nightgown wandering the house in the middle of the night, wringing her hands .. her face lined.. .dark rings about her eye… all prayers and supplications exhausted.. overwhelmed by nameless fears.. monstrous anxieties.. poor.. poor mother. But it was my life wasn't it? To do with as I liked ? And father.. why didn't you do something? But of course, he had .. tried his best to reassure her; suppressing his own fears with stoic restraint; respecting my wishes. Dear, dear father.. but how well I knew how impossible it must be for him; she wouldn't be comforted ..or denied .. she would have had to *do* something.. But why not write to me directly .. why humiliate me before that sanctimonious, dried-up stick of a clergyman and the grumpy old Captain. .. ?

Quick.. quick, I urged myself, picturing myself striding determinedly over the landing, wrenching open the cabin door, shouting in commanding tones: 'Now look here.. I'm not leaving the *Grimethorpe* .. and that's that!'

But even as the thought flicked over my mind I knew it was impossible.. 'So that's that then..' Captain Proser's words rang dully in my head.. how could I dare face him again .. no.. I had lost the chance.. ..I had consented.. voluntarily committed myself.. and I had no choice now but to carry out what I had agreed to ..

"Oh mother .. mother .." I moaned feebly holding to the banister rail and moving slowly down the stairs. But how had she done it? From so far away.. without any official position.. such an amazing power.. and yet ultimately it was my own doing wasn't it. . . . some part of me wanted to get away .. I had betrayed myself, my destiny.. such a miserable coward.. I would never forgive myself.

"Leaving us are you Wight?" The Sec. asked looking up from the bottom of the stairs; his voice a little less stern than usual, I thought.

"My mother.. a letter you see.. on the next tide.. a Swedish ship.. I have to see the Chief Steward about it." I shook my head, tears filling my eyes; how unfair it all was ..and yet all my own fault..

"Sometimes we have to accept the inevitable.." The Sec. said dryly. "Better go and get started packing… you don't have much time.."

I nodded dully and carried on down the companionway. Was it inevitable? The Captain .... ..the clergyman .. my mother.. they were mere agents.. passive mediums for some immense power that was ruthlessly sweeping me along.. utterly indifferent to my desires or feelings..

Abruptly I staggered and stopped, my hands clutching frantically at my face. Stella!.. Stella! How could I have forgotten her? Even for a second…? And I believed I loved her.. What a fraud.. a fake I was .. false .. cowardly..

I spun about, my mind raging with possibilities.. I could leave the ship and hide out on the dockside.. and then at night.. Or perhaps I could ask to stay with her and Arnold.. or rent a room hadn't I seen a *For Rent* sign somewhere on the street? But I had no money .. No entirely impossible.. But at the very least I must go and tell her what has happened... .

In my mind the gangway was swaying wildly beneath my pounding feet and there I was running like a madman until I reached the dingy old apartment building ..gasping for breath as I staggered up the stairs crossing the landing to her door...

But something was holding me back, a shadowy presence.. blocking my way.. forbidding me.. a gently commanding voice... 'No.... Phillip ..you know it's not right...'

And even if I *did* see her what could I say? 'I'm sorry but you see I have to ..' No! I would tell a lie.. 'I'm afraid my mother is seriously ill..' How despicable.. No! I would throw myself at her feet and beg forgiveness...promise to love her forever.. How hollow.. how insincere that would sound? And what if Arnold was still there.. hadn't left yet..? Her words rang in my head: 'Not before 8pm.. Remember '

No it was impossible.... .yes impossible... Oh what had I done? To fail her.. without warning.. How cruel of me.. despicable.. shameful.. beyond forgiveness..

Perhaps I could get Billy to tell her? I thought anguishedly; in any case I must tell him that I was leaving..; our dream of sailing up the Thames together finished .... . But at least we could wish each other a last goodbye.... 'Best of British me old shipmate. ..' I mouthed darting along the companionway way and leaping over the amidships sill, recalling wryly how Billy had laughed at me when I had tripped over it and barked my shins my first time aboard.

Striding quickly down the afterdeck, my mind ran with memories of the time when we had strolled side by side beneath a blazing sun, on all sides the dazzling vastness of the Pacific, to our secret place in the stern.... bronzing our bodies stripped to our shorts.. side by side . ..sharing the pure joy of relief from the daily routine.. dozing .. smoking.. chatting... and all our crazy games.. tying a rope to a chair and throwing it into the wake and gleefully watching it smash to pieces ..and then our fantasy of fishing for a shark.. and the make-believe as commandoes.. and ambushing the deck-boys how crazily funny.. and that time in Yokohama when he had helped me back to the ship and put me to bed terribly drunk.. and there crossing the quayside his arm around me.. before us the flaming red sky. I blinked back tears.. stepping through the open doorway to the Crew Accommodation Block, absently sniffing at the sweat-laden stale air; the bulkhead lights casting a dim glow in the shadowy Companionway.. Why did I always feel such an unease when I came here? I wondered moving along hearing voices.. noticing a cabin door slightly ajar.

"Billy..? Billy?" I called, my voice echoing faintly.

Through the partly open door, a tall figure, came out holding the door close behind him.. as if I might see something I shouldn't, I thought distantly.

"What yer want kid?" He grinned showing broken stained teeth; not one of the crew I thought abashed by the cold stare; the guant pock-marked face vaguely familiar

"Billy. ." I whispered hoarsely.

"He's busy see. Why don't ya come back later .." The strange man leered contemptuously stepping back and closing the door firmly in my face.

"Sure .OK…. "I muttered turning around and walking back down the afterdeck; dulled by shame and grief. But who was the strange man..? Yes ..I had seen him in Solly's house.. he had looked in the front room and stared at me and then left without saying a word.. What could Billy want with him? Oh.. Billy.. Billy.. my shipmate.. my pal.. my mate.. What is happening to you? And no chance to say goodbye. How sad.. And the same with Stella… How unbearable…. Why did life play such tricks on one? Was it all meant to be? No.. of course not! It was all random.. stupid.. meaningless .. pointless…. ..

Mechanically back in the cabin I changed into my shore-clothes and then began to stuff the rest of my clothes into the old kitbag; remembering the day I spotted it amongst other items covered with dust at the back of a 2nd Hand shop in

Vancouver and proudly dragged it out.. my great adventure.. my destiny.. before me and now here I was ..like a beaten dog with my tail between my legs.. retreating ..defeated... back home .. all so pointless..

At the bottom of the drawer I came across the red pocket-size New Testament my mother had given me on the dockside; never opened.. On an impulse I opened it, turning the flimsy pages and reading at random.. *This above all.. forgetting what is past, and straining for that which is to come....* I shook my head in angry bafflement and thrust the book viciously into my kitbag.

At the cabin doorway I gave a last quick look back into the cabin... my eyes ranging around the narrow space.. the bunk-beds . the wall long cupboard.. the glare from the porthole.. finally meeting the wistful blue eyes of the blond starlet of Billy's pin-up beside the mirror over the sink.. as if she really cared .. I thought bitterly...just a delusion.. all of it a stupid.. . meaningless.. delusion.. ...

I turned away into the Companionway and moving along to the Pantry.. empty .. remembering how in the darkness of early morning I had joined the men waiting in the harsh fluorescent glare for the start of the day ..talking in low voices. How dear those moments seemed. . . now lost forever.. .

I crossed over to the Galley.. deserted as well hearing faintly the echoing crash of pots and pans and Jock and Ronnie shouting at each other.. Presumably everyone had gone ashore I thought so no chance to say goodbye.. .. perhaps it was for the best, I sighed. How Mitch would have jeered.. 'Goin' 'ome to mummy are we..' but how little I would have cared.. sunk in despairing misery ..impervious to all abuse. ..

"There you are .." The Sec. appeared around the corner of the Companionway "The Chief Stewards in the Crew Mess with your papers"

How fast it was all happening .. like some stupid dream.. I thought events.. sweeping me helplessly on ..like a scrap of flotsam swept past the ship's hull..

"Here we are.. our dear cabin boy.." The Chief Steward squeaked amiably as I came in. He's being sarcastic, I thought, noticing his face had lost it's plumpness, the skin loose and sallow… maybe he's been ill..

"Your passport.. and discharge papers.. all sealed and signed. "He smirked lamely, pushing my passport and some other papers across the table towards me.." Now.. this is what I worked out you have coming to you.. less of course your subs and the *Bond*. "

I nodded; of course, the *Bond*; remembering once how excited I had been about it. … another delusion . .

"Mostly on cigarettes.. What will your mother say about your smoking I wonder?" The Chief Steward tittered winking absurdly.

I shrugged frowning irritably; how he had guessed at my mother's disapproval; what business was it of his anyway?

"Now.. The Chief Steward's went on explaining his calculation; his pudgy finger tracing down a column of figures on the ledger laid out on the table; my eyes wandered around the cream painted metal walls and the empty grey formica-topped tables and black steel chairs with red vinyl padding.. recalling the evenings playing cribbage with Billy.. the regular thud of the engines.. outside the vast dark of the Pacific night. . the air thick with sweat and diesel and cabbagey cooking smells.. hazy with blue cigarette smoke .. Old Paddy his pure white skin streaked with oil earnestly studying his Bible at one end ..and the sailors striped to the waist playing cards.. their thin faces lined and weatherworn .. How little those in the comfort of their homes round the world appreciated them ..day in day out.

"So that's what I'm transferring to your new ship .." The Chief Steward concluded. "Sign here .. dear boy.. Something wrong with your eye?"

"A twitch suddenly started.." I explained frowning pretending to examine the figures; noticing the total; so this is what all those days of toil resulted in I thought distantly, vaguely surprised it was so much more than I would have guessed.

I picked up the pen, hesitating, intently conscious that once I signed it would be the end of my time as cabin-boy on the *Grimethorpe*.

"Something not correct ?" The Chief Steward queried impatiently dabbing his face with a handkerchief.

"No.. no.." I murmured plunging down and scrawling a signature.. 'It's over .. all over now..' rang dully in my head..

"We'll be sorry to lose you.. . The Chief Steward puffed with unctuous geniality . "Eh Sec.?"

The Sec. gave a curt nod.

"Thanks.. .." I muttered grudgingly having to admit his cleverness with figures was for my benefit. "For everything.."

"My pleasure.. entirely my pleasure.. I only wish all the crew were as easy to please, my young sir.." The Chief Steward gasped waving a hand dismissively.

Yes.. he is a vital part of the ship's organization, I thought glumly, putting my kitbag on my shoulder; compared to him I'm utterly superfluous .. disposable.. without real significance.

Stepping out into the Companionway I sniffed the sour, stale air; surely that smell will always be with me for the rest of my life I thought, passing along narrow cream-painted metal walls.

"Well Phillip.." The Sec. stopped at the amidships doorway.

"Yes.. I guess.. Sec," I said rather unnerved by the his use of my first name.

"Adam, Adam Green "The Sec. said with a faint smile. "I hope you don't think I've been too hard on you.. but it was for your own good...." .

"But Sec. er Adam.." I objected petulantly. "It was really hard... I mean no regular hot water or detergent ..not even a mop to wash the floor.... really impossible.."

Adam frowned severely. "Perhaps you didn't realize it Phillip but you had it pretty easy actually. Billy did all the toilets.. the Crew Mess.. a lot more than you in fact .."

"I see.. Billy? Did he? He never said. "I murmured abashed.

"Perhaps this can be a lesson for you.. Phillip.." Adam went on evenly. "To work harder and complain less .."

"Yes.. Sec.. Adam. "I muttered shamefaced. "Can you say goodbye to Billy for me.. I tried but.. I hope he's not in trouble...some strange man with him.." I looked away down the dockside.

"Don't you worry about Billy, he can look after himself .." Adam said brusquely.

"Sure.." I said swallowing hard.

"Well a few weeks and you'll be home." Adam held out his hand.

I winced at the powerful grasp; recollecting a framed photograph in his cabin of a woman with two little boys by her side.

"I expect you wish you were going home Adam; see your family again"

Adam nodded stiffly, a spasm passing through his finely muscled body. How much he suffers being away from them I thought.. Such a good, disciplined man .. How badly I had misjudged him..

"Go on now ..you'll miss your berth if you don't look smart.." Adam said frowning.

I nodded looking down the gangway; so this what it was to leave alone.. as if escaping..

"By the way Sec.. Adam, I mean.." I said half turning "What actually happened to the Australian Cabin boy .. the one I replaced.."

Adam hesitated absently thumping the edge of his hand against the doorjamb. "A bad business .. it was his choice.. what he wanted.. I'd have to lock him in the brig else."

I nodded absently straining to catch the low monotone voice; not fully comprehending ..as if I didn't want to understand.. .. something about the Bo'sun was it? I swallowed hard; conscious of a sickening feeling.. .

"Just couldn't take it any more I suppose. He just wasn't there one morning... I felt sorry for the lad but what could

376

I do?" Adam shook his head one hand suspended in mid-air.

"No.. nothing "I muttered absently sympathizing; hopeless, yes hopeless..

"Go on now you'll miss your ship.. Best for you anyway.." Adam concluded turning abruptly back inside.

O.K.. sure .. Cheerio Adam.. and thanks .." I threw over my shoulder, the gangway swaying uneasily beneath me; walking along the dockside past the ship's stern high above the water, showing crusted barnacles, the hawsers drooping to the iron bollards; steadfastly refusing to look back; looking towards the line of ship's moored further along the quayside..

How hateful life is, I thought bitterly.. Billy .. Stella... the other cabin-boy. everything ..and me So this is how my great adventure is ending I mused despondently.. in failure.. yes ..utter ..complete.. unredeemable failure....

CHAPTER THIRTY-TWO

Who is this then..? I wondered wearily; looking up I had seen a small, familiar figure approaching me along the dockside.

Yes.. it was Chips.. but somehow quite unlike him in a suit and tie; conscious of an antipathy I looked around for a way of escape.. but already it was too late.. . ..

"Aye sonnie. Thee be on thy way" The ship's carpenter said slowing as he came up to me.

I nodded mutely, what could this simple old man know about . love.. despair .. suffering ..life..

"Thee did well "Chips added cheerfully.

"I don't think so.." I said sullenly not able to overcome my resentment.

"It all has some purpose ..." Chips suggested calmly with a smile.

I nodded indifferently looking away over the flat glittering harbour water; how .. stupid.. hateful it all was...

"Been visiting an old mate .. greaser ..on yon tanker." Chips remarked after a long pause, nodding back towards the ship next in line along the dockside.

I looked up; absently studying the ship, a long foredeck the Bridge at the stern, a broad yellow band around the thin black funnel.

"Always on tankers.. Ulsterman.. blown up once.. survived though.. First death by fire and then by water ..Heh heh.. Says he must either be too good or too bad. Brave chap says I. "Chips ran a hand through his silvery hair and smiled.

I nodded; scuffing the ground with a shoe; what did any of this have to do with me?

"Well sonnie.. better be off .. to the Chandlers for supplies. . So all the best.."

"Sure Chips.... same to you.." I responded mechanically, moving away down the dockside; he knows exactly what he's doing I thought gloomily; surveying the oil-tanker as I passed alongside; making out *M/V POLESTAR* in rusty white lettering on the bows; the foredeck crossed with gratings, pipes and valves; beneath the Bridge in large red letters was written *NO SMOKING*.

Two officers in uniform stood with a third man in a dirty orange boiler suit, their attention directed to a large valve wheel; one of them glancing up, stared incuriously at me before looking back down.

Had I really thought I could be an officer like them, I thought sadly; they knew exactly what was required of them; an integral part of a world-wide organization ..bringing vital oil supplies without which daily life would become impossible...... . while I was a mere adjunct ..dispensable.. insignificant; the Captain,.. Chips and the rest more than happy to see me go; mere flotsam drifting in the current; my bold adventuring now shown to be an absurdity ..utterly pointless..

Passing the stern I looked up and a scrawny old man in a oil-stained singlet, just like Old Paddy I thought, his arms resting on the ship's side, looking meditatively down at the darkly glinting harbour waters, perhaps the greaser Chips was visiting I thought, what was he thinking.. dreaming of home or past dangers.... or perhaps rejoicing in the simple fact of being alive..

He looked up and seeing me nodded in friendly way, seeing me as a fellow seaman, I thought, little guessing what a failure I am.

I gave a perfunctory nod back without pausing; picturing myself a solitary figure, kit-bag on shoulder, walking alone along the empty quayside in the bright sunshine, the harbour waters glinting pitilessly beside me.. . .

Perhaps I should kill myself, I concluded and yet even that was infinitely beyond me; death.. life.. all of it pointless.. walking a mere reflex of muscles. . thinking. . a random electrical flickering... everything empty .. meaningless..

I raised my head a dark blue stern rising out of the blackish green harbour water; a yellow and blue coloured flag drooping from the flagstaff .. This must be my new ship I thought remembering my gleeful, anxious excitement when I had first seen the *Grimethorpe*.. never again would I have such feelings, I mused.. Now I understood what life really was … the inevitable disappointment .. disillusionment.. failure .. all my best efforts nullified. Wasn't that why my father came home and collapsed into an armchair, immersing himself in his newspaper.. letting the miseries of others blot out dissatisfaction and frustration of his day.. .. ? And I thought my life at sea would be so different.. real.. active.. vital..

Even so I was conscious of a stir of interest as I stared down at the raised black letters:

MV Gottland
STOCKHOLM

Stockholm.. . Sweden.. so far away… like the Vikings of old.. boldly crossing the world's oceans..

Glancing up at the white superstructure immaculate in the sunlight, I noticed the hazy line of grey smoke drifting up from the funnel.. .so the engines had been started.. the ship ready to brave the trackless immensity of the Pacific …

But what was that to me? I sighed; really I should never have come to sea.. just stayed at home.. spared myself this disillusionment .. humiliation.. shame..

"Phillip.. Yaw? New Dekksgutt Yaw?"

I nodded finding myself facing a tall, well-built man a few years older than myself, long sun-bleached hair reaching to broad shoulders.

He grinned at me holding out a large hand; blue eyes smiling from a tanned face.

"Me.. Lars.. also Dekksgutt.."

"Pleased to meet you.. Lars.." I said involuntarily smiling back; conscious of the firm pressure of a calloused palm.

"Need to hurry yaw. Ship waiting.." Lars said sweeping the kitbag from my shoulder and striding away down the dockside and then bounding athletically up the gangway ahead of me.

"Kapitan not like to wait yaw.." Lars grinned reaching out a hand to pull me onto the deck, the gangway already lifting under my feet

"We got to stop again down river.. can't lose the tide.."

"Really .." I murmured looking back along the dockside picking out amongst the derricks and roofs of the warehouses, the mass of the *Grimthorpe,* the outline of her funnel breaking into the clear blue sky; so it was goodbye to everything familiar and known .. all my hopes .. desires.. all gone.. forever..

I shook my head and sighed.

"You some problem yaw?. "Lars asked smiling broadly.

"No .. not really "I said looking down over the ship's side, the gangway already pulled up alongside the hull; below a slowly widening strip of water danced and sparkled in the sunlight;, the ship vibrating fiercely; from above the ship's hooter sounded a loud blast.

I groaned inwardly, why had I ever agreed to leave the *Grimethorpe* and my chance of a night of exquisite love? I shuddered; surely it would haunt me for the rest of my life.. poisoning my life with bitter regret.. ..

"Komm Phillip.. ..you bunk with me.. I show you .." Lars said giving me a friendly pat on the back.

I followed Lars carrying my kitbag along the Afterdeck to the Crew Accommodation Block at the stern; the steel of the deck painted a dark green, the bulwarks freshly white with hardly a spot of rust… how very different to the *Grimethorpe.*

Just pretend it's all an illusion.. not real.. like a dream.. I told myself; merely to be followed through . not lived .. really my life was over ..just the dregs remaining.. .. .

"What's that smell. ." I wondered as we entered the bright-lit Companionway; instead of the stale bilge tinged with diesel smells of the *Grimethorpe* there was a strange spicy, earthy smell.

"Yaw.." Lars laughed "We have Chinese Crew except for Deck.. . they don't like Swedish food so they cook in their cabins.. brings the cockroaches. .real big ones…"

Lars opened the door into the large square cabin lit by two portholes, panelled in a pale wood.

I went over and examined a model Chinese junk complete with slatted bamboo sails suspended by a cord from the ceiling and swinging slowly with the roll of the ship.

"Amazing detail.. hasn't it.." I commented admiring the intricate carving on the bows and stern.

"Yaw .. she nice thing. Top bunk O.K. with you?" Lars asked amiably.

"Sure .." I said throwing my kitbag onto the top bunk; noting how the berths were athwart the ship instead of in line as in the *Grimethorpe*.

"So you don't pushed about when you sleep." Lars explained.

I nodded remembering how I had to endure being endlessly stretched and compressed on the *Grimethorpe*; really everything seems to be better here, I thought bitterly.

"You hungry I bet." Lars said leading me back down the Afterdeck to the Amidships and into a small Crew Mess, fitted out in a yellow pine, shining from the light coming through the large portholes; the bulkhead ; blue and white checked plastic table- cloths covered the four tables with benches; the engines steady throb barely audible.

I sat down at one of the benches while Lars went to a small fridge and got out a plate of cold meats; half a lobster in a scarlet case, assorted cream cheeses in triangles and pickles. Putting them on in front of me he added some dark rye-bread then sliced some fresh red tomatoes.

"Not that hungry. "I said listlessly; mentally comparing the attractive display before me with the stolid gristly meals on the *Grimethorpe* but surely that meant nothing compared to what I had so foolishly lost .. .?

"Ice tea yaw? Lars asked bringing out a large jug of amber-coloured liquid dripping with condensation and filling a large tumbler.

I took a long swallow of the ice-cold lemon flavoured tea.

"Really refreshing.." I admitted.

While I ate Jacob explained that the ship was going to stop again further down river to take on a deck cargo of sheep for Manila; all the crew thought it a stupid idea, absolutely crazy; the animals would all surely die from the heat or from thirst.... the Captain too had been against it but the owners had insisted.

"They real stupid.. the bosses.. only think of money.." Lars laughed good-naturedly pouring me another glass of ice-tea.

"Sure.. always the same isn't it.." I agreed. "Didn't realize I was so thirsty.."

I started at a loud metallic crashing followed by violent high-pitched shouting.

"Chinese cooks.." Lars grinned. "Get mad each other ..throw things around the Galley. Chinese crew do all cooking and cleaning for us.. ."

So no more washing dishes in cold greasy water or fretting about the black slime under the counter I thought, all those things that I had loathed so much and longed to get away from ..but ironically how little I cared now ..

"So this is our new Deck-Boy, eh Lars ?"

"Yaw.. this Phillip .. this 2nd Mate.."

I stood up to meet the slender fair-haired Officer, with a neatly clipped beard and moustache who had stepped into the Mess and now held out his hand to me with a gentle smile; the fine lines around his blue eyes crinkling.

"Hello Phillip … Axel Neilson .. 2nd Mate ..Welcome aboard.." He said with only a trace of an accent.

"Thanks. …" I murmured uneasy despite his friendly grasp.

"So you need to get back to Vancouver.." Axel remarked flushing faintly beneath his tan.

I nodded, self-conscious.. constrained; my temples throbbing.

"A bit different to your last berth .. I should think.. out on deck… "He went on thoughtfully smoothing his short beard. "But don't worry we won't be too hard on you..eh Lars?"

"No...! "I protested vehemently . "I want .. the same as everyone .. I like.. to work hard." I added more calmly my words rather surprising me.

"Good.. excellent .. just what I like to hear.." Axel said with an amused smile. "I'll be sure to tell the Bo'sun.. You'll be on duty once we've loaded these sheep.... A stupid business if there ever was one.. eh Lars..?"

"Yaw.. all die at sea.. I think. "Lars grinned cheerfully.

Axel nodded. "Still ours is not to reason why. Is that not the English?"

"Yes... that's right .. .." I muttered."

" *Ours is not to reason why ..*

Ours is but to do and die"

Tennyson : *The Charge of the Light Brigade;* about this stupid military blunder in the Crimean War . almost all the men and horses killed... utterly pointless really.." I frowned and looked away; what inane babble. ....

"Yes.. Quite.... still a fine poem just the same.." Axel said looking at me curiously. "Good to have someone aboard who likes poetry. Heine is my favourite..."

"A bit gloomy isn't he..?" I countered having a vague memory of reading something by him in an anthology.

"A little.... sometimes life too.." Axel said frowning slightly.

"Well ..we can talk more later.. You'll keep him right eh Lars.."

"Sure.. I show him. ..everything .." Lars laughed winking at me.

"I know best places in Manila. .for women and drinking. "He added grinning broadly once the 2nd Mate had left.

"The 2nd seems a decent sort.." I commented endeavouring to be fair.

"Yaw .. officers same as us.." Lars said seriously. "No need to show who boss ..it Swedish way.. only Bo'sun shout at you.... but he Dutchman..yaw ."

"Really .. our last Bo'sun... "I began then shook my head; better not to think about it.

"You like women.. I bet.." Lars said slapping me on the back moving to the doorway.

"I guess…. "I conceded manfully as we went out on deck together.

"Me too.. I go with lotsa women…pretty women usually. "Lars grinned going over to the ship's side.

How did I get to be here ? I wondered dully looking around at the flat land far down the estuary, the greenish grey scrub shimmering dully in the rays of the low sun.

I pulled out a packet of cigarettes and lit up; staring down; large clumps of foam and big brownish bubbles drifted about the swirling estuary water.

"You smoke eh?" Lars as I blew out cigarette smoke.

"Sort of necessity somehow.." I explained gloomily. "Don't you..?"

Lars shook his head. "Kapitan not like smoking. Only Bo'sun smoke ..cheap cigars. terrible stink.." Lars added with a laugh.

My life was changing before my eyes I thought absently; watching the ship pull itself ever so slowly towards a single wooden jetty projecting out of the low mud banks, thick with reeds.

"It reminds me my first docking "I thought to say. "I was sure the ship was going to smash into the pier.." how long ago that seemed now.. how much had happened to me since then..

"Yaw.. it seem like that.." Lars laughed. "After first time you learn yaw .. ."

"I guess so.." I murmured doubtfully squinting at the sprawl of rickety old wooden sheds, lost in the flat grey scrubland. What a godforsaken spot, I murmured with a sigh;

"You miss your old ship.. yaw.." Lars said with a sympathetic glance.

"Yes though there was a lot bad feeling too you never knew what was going to happen next.. and so always rumours going about… there was even talk of mutiny. One A.B .. Hobbsie was his name meant to be a Communist was always stirring things up .. the food was awful too "I paused conscious of a betrayal.

"Yaw.. good food is important." Lars observed solemnly.

"Even so .." I went on musingly, gazing away into the bright sky." My mind going back to time in the Crew Mess, the seamen stripped to the waist lined and weathered silently smoking or playing cards Old Paddy studying his Bible .." Hard to explain for all their grumbling. .there was something really fine about them.. fine men .seamen "I declared defiantly.

"Yaw. Sure .. sure "Lars murmured.

"Some real characters too.." I went on with a smile. "Jock the 2nd Cook.. a Scot.. he went around his chest stuck out chanting I'm Willie McClucky frae Auchtermuchty.. so funny .. and he loved whisky. He and 1st Cook.. a real Cockney were always squabbling .. like an old married couple.. And then there was this really huge Canadian Assistant Steward.. chest like a barrel.. he had the most awful smell.. we nicknamed him Old Smelly .. a bit cruel really. He died suddenly of a heart attack out at sea.... they put his body in the Cold Store until we reached port and then one time when I was cleaning the butcher block and ... . "I shook my head, studying the eddying water, the surface marked with intricate circular patterns. How surreal it all seemed now, how could anybody believe it?

"The other Assistant Steward was a Scouser.. from Liverpool.. very sarcastic quite cruel sometimes yet so funny you couldn't help but smile.." Automatically I touched the tip of my tongue to the broken tooth, registering a slight wiggle; would I ever understand what it all meant?

"And the Sec. the Second Steward I mean though we always called him "The Sec." he was stern and strict but fair actually. I found out just as I left his real name was Adam.. a bit of a shock that was. to find out he had a name I mean.. somehow he was just ..well "The Sec"... "I smiled nostalgically "Then there was old Chips.. been at sea since a boy ..he taught me how to knot a Turk's Head.. and a lot of other things.. He rescued this little bird out at sea and cared for it.. but then when we came near land it flew away.."

I gazed wonderingly out across the palely glimmering land.... Was Nat out there fluttering happily about..? I wondered More likely dead.. a tiny bundle of feathers with the eyes pecked out .. slowly mouldering away.. I shook my head and sighed.

"But some Crew .. same age as you I guess.." Lars said encouragingly.

"Yeah.. that's right ! The Deck Boys Tad he was a Pole bony and thin a bit crazy and Norrie short and fat. Like a comedy duo... They were always fighting with me and Billy.. he was my cabin-mate Cabin-Boys.. .." I explained gasping a little "You wouldn't believe some of the things we got up .. crazy sometimes I thought I die from laughing so hard... Yeah Mates .. Ship-mates... .."

"Yaw.. Ship-mates is best. "Lars said smiling broadly.

"I wanted to say goodbye to him.." I went my voice wavering. "But when I went to cabin where he was.. there was this strange man .. really nasty-looking.. face all pock-marked.. a friend I think of Solly..maybe you know him he plays the piano the *Swan* pub.."

"Yaw.. I know about him.... "Lars growled. "He dirty man ..not real man.. someday he choke to death I think..good thing too I say"

"Yeah .." I giggled. "Anyway it's all in the past now .. .."

"I think you and me good ship-mates.. yaw?" Lars said with a deep laugh.

"I hope so.." I laughed back.

"We have good time ashore before Vancouver." Lars smiled.

"Yes ..of course Vancouver.." I mused struck by the thought that I was going home. "By the way where did you get the Chinese Junk I saw in the cabin? I need a present for my father ."

"I give it you! "Lars exclaimed slapping me on the back.

"Really ? No .. I couldn't ...Gosh Thanks Lars..".

I gazed up at two fluffy cloud puffs floating serenely over the blue sky; how easily the old life was passing. But Stella.. Stella .. I moaned inwardly.. surely the loss of her would always haunt me. I trembled with anxiety trying to remember her face ..but all was shadowy ..indistinct.. But my love for her would never fade. I vowed .

"Here they come.." Lars shouted excitedly ; above the roaring of the engines a hoarse baaing was distinctly audible and then between a channel of rough wooden poles, a stream of yellowish fleeces marked with blue numbers flooded down, some leaping ..and bounding as if in wild delight.

What a bizarre scene, I thought as the close-pressed sheep, baaing unceasingly, overhung with swarms of flies, churned restlessly about the wire-mesh pen; clouds of thick dust drifted over the grey bush-land reaching in all directions. And how is it I am here seeing this? I mused abstractedly; was it really meant to be..?

Before long the grim-faced stockmen began driving the sheep their hooves clattering, up a cleated ramp onto the ship's Foredeck, there to be channelled down runways into slatted wooden pens erected on either side of the Hatch blocks; rank wool smells tinged with ammonia reached my nostrils. A few of the sheep slipped and fell, almost buried by the press of bodies behind before getting to their feet and scrambling desperately on again.

"Sheep to the slaughter .." I commented. "Don't have a clue what's in store for them do they.…"

"Yaw it true.." Lars agreed genially.

"Not so different to us humans I guess though.." I mused out-loud. "Except we don't need to be driven…. we do it to ourselves…" I gripped the rail tightly, closing my eyes, a fierce stab of pain in my chest.. Yes it would never leave me ; the pain of losing such an exquisitely lovely woman; and I had done it willingly ..it had been my own choice.. How could I have been so stupid… so weak .. so cowardly..

"Heat gonna kill em.. you bet "Lars observed shaking his head as the sheep jostling and pushing formed a solid stream of dirty white fleece; their hooves scraping and hammering on the wooden gangway; an acrid stench rising into the air, filling my nostrils.

"We gonna rig up some canvas for shade. But lots gonna die I guess.. Have to be thrown over side.. stupid business that for sure.." Lars said raising his voice over the incessant baaing.

"Yes stupid! So stupid !" I sighed anguishedly; never would I forgive myself.

"Something ..wrong with you.. Phillip?. "Lars asked frowning sympathetically. "You tell me .. shipmate.. yaw."

I hesitated .. surely to tell was to cheapen it.. sully it .. and yet inside me it was churning and swelling .. as if I was going to burst and suddenly without meaning it in gasps and sighs it came out in a great rush of emotion. Her beauty.. how I had admired her.. a goddess ..and then how beyond all expectation she had come to the ship.. our car ride to Perth .. her flat ... how I was to go and spend the night her husband away and then .. the summons to the captains cabin.. the letter from my mother.. and my consent .. my cowardice .. my stupidity .. never would I forgive myself..

"Oh Stella.. Stella.." I moaned, looking away half-blinded by tears streaming down my face.

"She work in *The Swan* pub sometime. I tink.... "Lars said thoughtfully.

"Yes.. yes...that's right "I sighed. "One of the most beautiful woman ever.. but more than just beautiful.. . "I shook my head.

"2nd Mate..you met him.. he too very much like her too.. Last time we in Fremantle . .." Lars reminisced staring down at the gangway now empty of sheep.

"Did he.. ? I breathed; a dull pounding in my ears.

"Sure..." Lars said amiably. "He sometime drive her around in old car. We see them...."

"Really.." I laughed hoarsely; pierced by a jealous hatred.

"But.. she finish it.." Lars shrugged. "She need time to study.. he say ... Maybe she not really want him."

"No .. yes .. study .... philosophy.." I wheezed faintly, steel-like bands around my chest contracting ever tighter.

"It happen to other men I hear.." Lars said musingly.

I looked up gazing down the estuary; the sun now setting; the flat expanse of water flickering with golden sparks; high above pink and grey wisps of cloud shaded deep black; how bitter my life was .. yes. bitter ..bitter ..unbearably bitter..

"Oi! Lars! Dekksgutts! "A squat muscular-looking man, an unlit stub of a cigar clenched between his teeth, came bustling along the deck towards us.

"That Jan.. Bo'sun...." Lars grinned. "Come now. We start to work.."

Oh .. Stella.. Stella.. is it true? Is it possible? I whimpered slowly following Lars along the amidships and out onto the foredeck passing between the slatted sheep-pens towards the ship's bows; the sheep bleating pitifully; endlessly jostling each other.

Yes.. of course it was true; Lars.. wouldn't lie.. why would he? And the 2nd Mate.. yes.. she would like him.. such a handsome intelligent man .. an officer and of course her beauty inevitably attracted men.. like moths to a flame.... And other men too.. a anguish gripped me with an unbearable torment...

"Yes . unbearable.." I gasped meeting the mute gaze of some of the sheep their heads thrust through the slats, their liquid black eyes.. full of sadness .. suffering.. Yes.. they do know what is going to happen ..they know .. I thought in rush of sympathy. Just like me.. doomed ..

I stopped suddenly my mind reeling back to that time leaving Stella I had looked back up the stairwell and seen Stella and Arnold together on the landing and his selfless love for her.. complete all-forgiving.. married love.. an unbreakable compact.. like my parents ...rich or poor ...in sickness or health .. until death...

And I had utterly suppressed it.. denied it .. until now..

"Bless him.. bless both of them...." I breathed out; the tightness loosing from my chest. Was it meant to be then? Had I been saved.. .. saved from more heart-break.. saved from myself...

What had Chips told me once.' Who knows what is good or bad for us.. or which is which...' What a wise old man he was.. ..

"Oi! Decksgutt.. ya.!. You on ship to work.. not make love to sheeps !" The Bo'sun bellowed from the fo'cosle rail.

"Sure thing Bo'sun . "I said eagerly bounding forward and up the stairs.

"Over there. "The Bo'sun shouted impatiently as I hesitated at the top step, pointing to two other seamen both tall, heavy-set men with blonde beards and hair standing on one side. "Hey Bo'sun.. we not deaf.." One of them yelled back cheerfully.

"Maybe .. if he keep shouting we be .." The other seaman bantered mildly, stepping aside to make room for me.

"Velkomm *Gottsland* !" He added with a grin.

Like the happy, noisy Nordic giants I had seen in the Duke of Wellington in Singapore I thought remembering too that Billy had told me that Mitch had viciously attacked one of them with a broken bottle, my tongue instinctively going to the broken tooth; strange that I didn't hate or fear him anymore......

"Now we work yaw!" One of Swedish seamen shouted cheerfully.

What are we to do I wondered as one of the mooring hawsers was passed around a huge black capstan almost as big as myself. The Bo'sun shouted something and the capstan slowly began to turn, slowly pulling aboard the coarse hairy hawser, dripping wet; as it came off the capstan it was passed hand over hand from man to man; a large coil of rope began to build up in the middle of the fo'c'sle deck.

"O.K..?" The seaman next to me shouted with a friendly grin.

"You bet..! "I shouted gaily back; my hands unthinkingly taking and giving the heavy wet rope; all around me shadowy bodies moving rhythmically as in some archaic ritual dance; glancing around and seeing the coil growing steadily higher in the fading light; like some monstrous beehive-like construction ... a watch-tower ..or shrine I mused distantly, rejoicing that I was one with the band of men united in purpose to build them .. ..

Soon though my arm muscles began to ache and still the lengths of hawser kept coming...wetter and colder and heavier now; the deck beginning to lift and fall in a slow, sickening rhythm; a cold despair rose within me.. I wasn't strong like them ..so unfair I wasn't used to this kind of work .. 'Give up .. give up' .. I mouthed silently ..dulled and dizzy with the unceasing effort; needle-sharp pains running up and down my legs and back.

Then abruptly I felt the end of the rope pass through my hand and all movement ceased, .. the men falling back ..

It was over .. I had done it!' I sighed shuddering with sheer relief; rubbing my hands raw from the coarse rope fibres.. Yes .. I thought elatedly, breathing in the cool salty air, looking up at the darkening sky .. I'd showed myself equal to the others.. a seaman .. a man.. Never would I doubt myself again ..

"Oi Deksgutt .!. Deksgutt ! Here!. Take! Take!"

I started dismayed to see another hawser had been wrapped around the capstan; a length of heavy rope was thrust into my hands. 'No .. this can't be ..' I wailed silently passing it to the next man; my arm and leg muscles ached unbearably. I glanced around ; the evening light now gone entirely; flood lights mounted on the masthead glared down on the deck; making shadowy giants of the men who lumbered slowly around, shouting at each other in guttural voices over the whine of the capstan motor. How weird ..

surreal .. and I was part of it... or was I? My arms and hands moving of their own volition .. automatically grasping and releasing. . grasping and releasing.. feeling my mind become free from my aching body.... floating away .. back .. back to when I had left the *Grimethorpe*. ...

What had the 'Sec' .. Adam .. told me? 'Well so the Bo'sun took him to live in his cabin...... . and then some others got in the act.. poor lad .'

So finally I understood what had happened to the cabin-boy I had replaced.. so this was the mystery that no one wanted to talk about.. the Bo'sun must have worked on him. .. yes how well I could understand that.. given him sweets.. cigarettes ... shown him girlie magazines.. He would have been vulnerable.. seeking a father's affection ..submitted to being fondled .. touched .. a mixture of pleasure and shame that I had known that night on the life-boat deck.. and then he been offered to some of the others probably Hobbsie .. ..No wonder he ran away.. no one seemed to know what had come of him .. who knows he might even have drowned himself in Seattle harbour. And that could have been .. me .. yes

"Hey Phillip.. man.... we finish now.." Lars's voice broke into my dazed trance-like state.

I nodded my arms hanging down by my side; my palms stinging .. I had survived, I thought blearily.

"We eat some supper .. then turn in.... .up early tomorrow.." Lars said yawning.

"Yeah.. sure thing "I laughed strangely excited .. yes survived. I followed the dark forms of the seamen down the stairs and along the foredeck, their loud cheerful voices and laughter ringing out; how pleased they are with themselves I thought. A salty breeze blew against my face bringing the scent of a cigar, mingled with the sheep urine and wool smells. The Bo'sun must have lit up his cigar I thought, smiling as at some secret joke. Above me the navigation lights showed a red and green blur, the Bridge showing a narrow streak of faint light; the rest of the superstructure lost in a wreathing mist.

Patches of fog drifted past the ship's side; from out of the darkness came the dull groan of a distant foghorn. I sighed thinking of what had happened to the Australian cabin-boy.. Yes I was blessed.... Isn't that what Reverend Messenger had said. Even now far away on the other side of Pacific Ocean my parents were eagerly expecting me; into my mind came the family car waiting on the quayside and as I came down the gangway; relief and joy etched on my mother's face.. and beside her my father with a boyish smile. And once again I would be back in the life I had tried so hard to escape; yes .. I had failed. What had Stella said of me? 'He's so eager for life .. a real adventurer' ..Surely it was still true; life would always be an adventure ..

Yes.. now .. this present moment.. now.. *forgetting what is past, and straining for that which is to come*.... Yes, yes.. oh yes.. I whispered to myself; catching at the sound of seething water, then a sudden rattle of hooves; a faint bleating rose into the night; a few stars gleaming dimly....

THE END

Lightning Source UK Ltd.
Milton Keynes UK
172096UK00001B/3/P